Newcastle
City Council

Newcastle Libraries and Information Service

☎ 0845 002 0336

Due for return	Due for return	Due for return
– 1 JUL 2008		
– 7 AUG 2009		

Please return this item to any of Newcastle's Libraries by the last
date shown above. If not requested by another customer the loan
can be renewed, you can do this by phone, post or in person.
Charges may be made for late returns.

Five interesting things about Whitney Gaskell:

1. At the age of twelve I was convinced I was destined to be an Olympic competitor in the equestrian Three Day Event, just like Sarah in *International Velvet*.

2. I have a pug named Tallulah Bankhead. We call her Lulu for short.

3. I used to be a lawyer, but I've never been to court.

4. I bake when I'm stressed out. My brownies and strawberry-rhubarb pies are to die for.

5. I live in Florida, even though hot weather makes me cranky.

Also by Whitney Gaskell

Testing Kate
Pushing 30
She, Myself and I

True Love
(and Other Lies)

Whitney Gaskell

little
black
dress

First published in the USA in 2004 by BANTAM DELL
A division of RANDOM HOUSE, INC.

First published in Great Britain in 2007
by LITTLE BLACK DRESS
An imprint of HEADLINE PUBLISHING GROUP

First published in paperback in Great Britain in 2007
by LITTLE BLACK DRESS
An imprint of HEADLINE PUBLISHING GROUP

A LITTLE BLACK DRESS paperback

1

ISBN 978 0 7553 4110 8

Typeset in Transit511BT by Avon DataSet Ltd,
Bidford-on-Avon, Warwickshire

Printed and bound in Great Britain by Clays Ltd, St Ives plc

Headline's policy is to use papers that are natural, renewable and recyclable
products and made from wood grown in sustainable forests. The logging and
manufacturing processes are expected to conform to the environmental
regulations of the country of origin.

HEADLINE PUBLISHING GROUP
An Hachette Livre UK Company
338 Euston Road
London NW1 3BH

www.littleblackdressbooks.co.uk

In loving memory of my son, George Henry Gaskell

When you look up at the sky at night,
since I'll be living in one of them,
since I'll be laughing in one of them,
for you it'll be as if all the stars are laughing.

– Antoine de Saint-Exupéry,
The Little Prince

Acknowledgments

I'd like to thank the following people, all of whom were instrumental in the creation of this book: My wonderful editors, Danielle Perez and Anne Bohner, who helped me guide Claire through her journey, and whose suggestions, insights, and encouragement helped me write a better book than I could ever have done on my own. The amazing team at Bantam Dell, who have done such an incredible job of turning my manuscripts into actual books. My agent, Ethan Ellenberg, for his wise advice. My parents, Jerry Kelly and Meredith Kelly, for their enthusiastic support, and for forcing everyone they know into buying multiple copies of my books. My husband, George, who has never stopped believing in me, and who proofread the manuscript nearly as many times as I did. And finally, Sam, for keeping me company while I wrote, and for returning the smile to my face.

At the advanced age of thirty-two, I've learned enough about the world to have developed a well-established set of personal rules by which I live my life. Here is the first one: The whole concept of a One True Love Who Completes Your Soul is total bullshit.

I don't mean love in general, of course – I love my parents, my sister, a few assorted friends, and Churchill, the English bulldog I had when I was growing up. I'm talking about the fairy-tale, Prince Charming, marriage-as-a-happy-ending, love-at-first-sight kind of thing. As far as I'm concerned, that's a brand of snake oil concocted by the online dating and wedding industries for the sole purpose of bilking millions of unsuspecting women out of their hard-earned money. Maybe it's because I don't have any role models to look to who've actually sustained long-term love, much less successful marriages. My parents, and most of my friends' parents, were of the generation who believed strongly in the power of divorce and remarriage as an alternative to buying a sports car when in the midst of a midlife crisis.

You could call me cynical, or jaded, or even a little bitter, and I wouldn't argue with you. It's not as though I arrived at my philosophy on love when I was thirteen and still thought I was going to marry the lead singer of Duran Duran. No, it took years and years of bad dates, horrible setups, and one real bastard of an ex-boyfriend for me to come to my senses.

Which is why I never imagined I would meet someone on an airplane. I mean, how random would that be? After all, in real life, lovers are not brought together by a quirk of fate, or by some random act that realigns the universe; most people who get together meet through friends, or work, or something equally mundane. Those syrupy tales of two halves of one heart reuniting are just Hollywood fairy tales, usually starring Meg Ryan, and marketed to women in my age, gender, and marital-status demographic. But I have always refused to buy into the hype, just as I refuse to transform my pin-straight hair into Meg's adorably scruffy, Sally Hershberger–designed coif.

So when I boarded the American Airlines flight from New York to London, my battered old knapsack slung over my shoulder (I never can pull off that glamorous world-traveler look – really, I'm only one small, scary step from completely throwing away my dignity and embracing the butt pack), the last thing I was expecting was romance. In fact, I was fully prepared for a boring, six-hour trip full of bad food and uncomfortable seats, and – if experience was any guide – a small child sitting behind me, screaming the whole way.

I snagged a window seat, and was glad that I only had to share one armrest. I had desperately hoped to get upgraded to business class – that Shangri-la for travelers, with its cushy seats, free drinks, and plentiful armrests – but the same grouchy airline employee who wouldn't give me a seat in the emergency-exit row certainly had no interest whatsoever in upgrading me (he'd been far more accommodating to the Ricky Martin lookalike who'd been ahead of me in line, I'd noted). I was relieved when a middle-aged woman wearing a pashmina shawl and carrying a thick paperback sat in the empty seat next to me.

I usually get seated next to obese men who have personal odor problems and who snore so loudly they actually drown out the roar of the jet engines. This woman tended in the other direction – as thin as a greyhound and marinated in Obsession perfume – but still, a definite improvement. Or so I thought.

Shortly after takeoff, the woman began twisting around to whine to her husband, who was sitting directly behind her, about how her back was hurting her and why couldn't the airlines provide orthopedic pillows, and how could he not have remembered to pack his blue jacket, and why hadn't the airline honored her request to sit next to an empty seat so she could stretch out during the flight, and had she known they were going to stick someone next to her, she would have rather sat with her husband. Considering her tone, her husband's weary answers, and the fact that every time the woman turned around she knocked me in the side with her pointy little elbow, I was starting to suspect that the husband had lucked out by not having to sit next to her. It was probably the first peace and quiet he'd had since marrying her (not that she showed any intention of leaving him alone to enjoy it). On her third go-round, this time lodging a complaint on the too-cold temperature of the airplane, I heard the man sitting behind me offer to trade places with her so that she and her husband could sit together.

'Oh, *thank you*. We would have booked our seats together, but I was supposed to have an empty seat next to me. But then they sat *this woman* here,' she said, her voice laced with self-righteous indignation, as she shot me a dirty look.

I returned her dirty look – a skill I could win a gold medal in – and Mrs Pointy Elbow was properly chastened … or scared, I actually couldn't tell which, as I've been told that my signature dirty look is quite intimidating. I base it on a combination of Jack Nicholson in A *Few Good Men* ('You can't handle the truth!') and Hillary Clinton when she thinks no one is watching her, with just a hint of Clint Eastwood as Dirty Harry thrown in for some color. In any event, Mrs Pointy Elbow averted her eyes and stopped complaining – for the moment – and turned her attention to collecting her things. It took her a while, a laborious process of gathering her book and newspaper and purse and pillow and blanket together, all while this guy was standing in the aisle, waiting patiently for her to finally clear out of what was now his seat.

To my surprise, the guy was cute, in a scruffy sort of way. I hadn't noticed him in the airport lounge when we were waiting to board, but then he wasn't exactly a head-turner. He was tall and lanky, although not skinny, thank God (I can't deal with men who have thinner thighs than I do). He had a long, angular face, shaggy dark blond hair in need of a trim, and his too-long nose was slightly crooked, as if it had never been properly set after being broken. From the barely noticeable lines fanning out from the corners of his eyes, I guessed his age to be about thirty-six or -seven – definitely on my side of forty. It wasn't until he smiled at the woman as she thanked him for changing seats with her that I was struck by how appealing he was – his smile lit up his whole face, his grin open and genuine, his eyes crinkling pleasantly. And I don't normally go for blond men – there's something too California-ish, too frat-rat about them, too much like Jeff Spicoli in *Fast Times at Ridgemont High*. But this guy was more Owen Wilson than Sean Penn.

And his considerable height was a definite plus. Men who are shorter than I am face automatic elimination under the rules set forth in the Official Claire Spencer Dating Handbook. It's not that I'm prejudiced against petite men – it's just that the last time I went out with one of them, my date spent the evening saying things like 'Wow, you're a lot of woman, aren't you,' and then challenged me to an arm-wrestling competition over dinner. Around the time I turned twenty-five – about the same point I stopped slouching in a misguided attempt to appear dainty – I decided that I would no longer date short men, and this policy has saved me an enormous amount of humiliation. Now I only have to deal with my good friend Max Levy, who doesn't reach five foot six in his cowboy boots, and who is always trying to get me to dance with him so that he can act out the scene in *Sixteen Candles* where Long Duck Dong rests his head on the massive bosom of his 'sexy American girlfriend.' Needless to say, I don't find this nearly as funny as he does.

My new seatmate folded his long frame into the seat next to mine, slouching down like a teenager, and, to my complete humiliation, caught me checking him out.

'Looks like we're stuck together,' he said while smiling pleasantly at me.

'Hmmm,' I said, and to cover for my previous ogling, gave him a polite, dismissive smile, before hiding behind my copy of *Elle Decor*.

But he wasn't put off. 'I'm Jack,' he said, holding his hand out sideways.

'Claire,' I replied, taking his hand.

It was awkward to shake hands in the narrow space, but actually I was secretly pleased at the attention. Even though I don't believe in the One True Love thing, I'm not against a little harmless flirting now and then – it's all a matter of controlling your expectations. I did wish that I'd dressed in something a little more glamorous than my favorite jeans and a black turtleneck sweater, and that I'd worn my contact lenses instead of my horn-rimmed glasses, but I'd been hoping to catch a little sleep on the plane, and so had dressed for comfort, not for a date. At least my hair was clean, and freshly blown out, and I was reasonably sure that my makeup was still intact.

Oh God, what am I doing? Don't even think about it, I told myself. *I'm sure I'm not his type. He's all preppy and outdoorsy looking, and he probably goes for skinny women who like to run marathons and go camping. Certainly not someone like me.*

Because the thing is, I'm big. *Big*. I'm very tall for a woman, five feet ten inches from head to toe, and hardly fall into the current beauty ideal of being Gwyneth Paltrow thin. I'm big all over – big arms, big hands, big feet, big boobs, big hips, and one of my thighs is probably about the same size as Gwynnie's entire body. It's not that I'm fat, really – in fact, through rigorous gym sessions, I'm at a healthy weight, even if I'm not about to go parading around in public in a bikini. And although I've definitely grown to be comfortable with my body – well, more comfortable, anyway – it's still hard to live in a culture where the last two full-figured women to achieve prominence were Monica Lewinsky and Anna Nicole Smith. There are guys out there who have a thing for fuller-figured women, but since there are also fetishists of toe licking and underwear sniffing, this was not necessarily a reassuring thought.

I pretended to go back to reading my magazine, while Jack turned his attention to what looked like paperwork he'd retrieved from his briefcase. It wasn't until the dinner service arrived, and we were offered our choice between a seafood dish of some sort and chicken with pasta, that Jack packed up his files and stuck them in the storage pocket in front of him.

'I think I'll have to go with the chicken. How about you?' he asked.

'Yes, definitely the chicken. Having the salmon would be just asking for food poisoning,' I said.

The flight attendant, who'd been all charm and smiles while handing Jack his dinner tray, shot me a dirty look and plunked my tray down with quite a bit less grace.

'I think she's a little sensitive about her salmon,' Jack said in a mock whisper once the flight attendant had moved on.

'I don't know why. It's not like she cooked it,' I said.

'Well, you never know. They might give us the pre-packaged crap back here, but the food in first class is pretty damn good. I wouldn't be surprised if there were a tiny chef up there, slaving away in a tiny kitchen,' he said.

'Do you normally fly first class?' I asked.

'Yeah, usually. I mostly travel for business, so my company foots the bill.'

'Well, then, why on earth are you back here in steerage?'

'Steerage,' he repeated, and smiled at my joke. He had a disarmingly cheerful grin, warm and open. 'Actually, I was planning to stay in New York for another couple of days, but I have some things I need to take care of in London, so I caught the first flight back. The only seat they had open was back here. How about you? You come here often?' Jack asked, his tone irreverent to keep the obvious line from being cheesy.

'To London, you mean?'

'No, I meant the steerage cabin. Are you such a fan of their . . . what is this?' he asked, poking at the mound of red gelatinous goop on his plate. 'SpaghettiOs with imitation chicken on top?'

'No, don't be silly. You only get real SpaghettiOs in first class. This is some kind of a cut-rate pasta product,' I said. Jack laughed. It was a nice laugh, deep and endearingly goofy.

'So when you're not dining on imitation pasta, what are you doing? Do you live in London?' Jack said.

'No, New York. I'm going to London for work. I'm a travel writer for a magazine,' I explained, and then hesitated, as I was enjoying the interest registering on his face. My job – or at least, my job title – always has this effect on people. They assume that I get to jet around to exotic locales and eat out at swishy restaurants for free, and then have a forum in which to spout off my opinions. Ah, were it only so.

'Really? Would I have read any of your work?' Jack asked.

And this is the part where it always gets tricky. Because, in reality, my job is a teensy less glamorous than it initially sounds. I don't write for *Vogue* or *Gourmet* or even the American Airlines in-flight magazine.

'I doubt it. I, um, work for a magazine called . . .' I began, then paused. After three years on the job, I still had a hard time saying it. '*Sassy Seniors*.'

Jack's forehead wrinkled with confusion, and I knew that he had never heard of the magazine. No one ever did.

'It's aimed at retirees,' I explained.

'So you write articles on how to travel with an oxygen tank, and the best places to eat dinner at three in the afternoon?'

I giggled. I'm not much of a giggler – it's not an especially attractive habit for an Amazon-sized woman to have – but I couldn't help myself.

'Yeah, pretty much. Let's put it this way – in every piece I write, I have to include information about whether the hotels, restaurants, and attractions have handicap access or senior discounts or early-bird specials,' I said.

'Still. I'm an attorney, so I spend all day locked in a high-rise, putting out fires. Getting paid to travel sounds fantastic,' he said.

'Well, I suppose it would be, if I ever got to go anywhere interesting. But I don't get to pick the destinations, and the magazine only sends me to budget-oriented domestic locales, you know, places that seniors can travel to cheaply. San Antonio, Orlando, Minneapolis, cities like that.'

'And London?'

'I don't know how I talked my editor into it, but I did. I told him that the dollar was strong overseas, but honestly,

I'm not even sure what that means,' I admitted. 'What about you? Are you going to London on business?'

'No, I live there. I've been an expat for a few years,' Jack replied.

'Really? My best friend lives there, too. She loves it, although she said that the British aren't always all that friendly to Americans,' I said.

'Yeah, I get a lot of that. Every time politics is brought up, I'm supposed to defend the actions of the American government, not just in the present day, but at every historical turn for the last two hundred years,' Jack said. 'And somehow, no matter what I say, I come off sounding like Kevin Kline in *A Fish Called Wanda*, you know, where he says that without the U.S., England would be the smallest province in the German empire?'

I laughed, and paused for a minute as the flight attendants passed by and picked up our dinner trays. 'How did you end up in London? Do you work for an American law firm there?' I asked.

'No. I used to practice in Manhattan – I was an associate at Clifford Chance – but once the big-firm machine ground me up and spat me out, I moved to an in-house position at British Pharmaceuticals, about eighteen months ago.'

I was suitably impressed. I'd considered going to law school, but got cold feet when I realized that the whole Socratic torture method John Houseman had employed in *The Paper Chase* wasn't just fiction.

'What do you do there?' I asked.

'I head up their legal department,' he said modestly – and contradicting his previous claim that he hadn't done well at his law firm. Clearly, he was highly successful, and just self-effacing about his accomplishments. It was an odd trait to find in an attorney. Most of the lawyers I know, especially the ones who've put in time at the big firms, are usually so impressed with their own credentials and how important they are, they do everything in their power to make you aware of it.

'Wow,' I said. 'You must be really good to have gotten so far, I mean for a guy your age.'

'Oh, well, I'm really sixty-two. The Botox injections take years off,' he said, flashing another grin. 'So, do you like what you do? Being a writer? I've always envied people who have creative jobs.'

'I don't know how creative it is. Let's put it this way – my editor and I have very different visions of what my column should be, and it's a fight that I rarely win,' I said.

That was an understatement. When my editor, Robert Wolcik, went over my column, he was so heavy-handed with his red marker that it sometimes looked like the pages of copy were bleeding to death by the time he was done with them. True, my writing style is a little edgy and quirky (although Robert would describe it as 'strident' and 'sarcastic'), but I honestly don't understand what his problem is. I include all of the pertinent information about early-bird specials and hotel package deals. I just also like to poke a little fun at the destination I'm writing about. Robert doesn't tolerate my color commentary; he wants the column to be a bare-bones listing of hotels, restaurants, and attractions. Boring, boring, boring.

'Let me put it this way – as part of my job, I actually had to visit a museum devoted entirely to Dr Pepper, and I couldn't even point out the absurdity of it all,' I explained. 'Not even in a good-natured, campy way.'

'There's a museum devoted to Dr Pepper?' Jack asked in disbelief.

I nodded. 'In Waco, Texas. And strangely enough, touring it is more fun than you might think,' I said.

'So, if this isn't your dream job, what is?' Jack asked, managing not to sound like an interviewer at a college admissions office.

I thought about it for a minute. 'I'd still be a writer, but I'd have a column at an edgier magazine with a younger, hipper readership, I guess. And I'd have complete control over my content,' I said. 'What about you? Or do you already have your dream job?'

'I don't know how many kids daydream about one day growing up and being a corporate attorney. No, when I was younger, I wanted to be an artist,' Jack said. 'In fact, I took a year off before going to law school, and spent it in Florence, pretending to be an artist.'

'Really?' I asked. As petty as it might make me, I hate hearing stories like this – people striving for their dreams, taking risks, grabbing for the brass ring. It made me acutely aware of just how many hours I wasted while in my twenties, vegging out on the couch, watching oddly compelling crap shows like *Melrose Place* and *Beverly Hills 90210*. 'That's . . . amazing. You must be really good.'

'Nope,' Jack said cheerfully. 'I mostly just did it to pick up girls. It's shocking how many women actually go in for the scruffy starving artist. The only thing I got around to painting was my impression of the Palazzo Vecchio, and it was pretty pathetic.'

'Still, I can't paint at all, well, except for those paint-by-number kits,' I said.

'Are those the ones where you paint the happy tree and the happy sky?' Jack asked.

I laughed. 'No, that was Bob Ross. You know, the guy with the enormous Afro who had that painting show on public television. He was way, way out of my league. All I can paint are depressed trees in need of Prozac,' I said.

We both had our seats reclined back, and were twisted to the side, so that we were facing each other as we talked, discussing everything from the best place to get a hamburger in New York to which Charles Dickens novels we'd suffered through in our college English lit courses. It was strangely intimate for being in such a public place. Every one around us was sleeping, or watching the in-flight movie, and the cabin was dark and quiet except for the white-noise drone of the engine. The more we talked, the more it felt like we were on an amazing, albeit completely bizarre, first date.

Around the time that the plane was over Scotland and turning south, Jack said, 'In the interest of full disclosure, I should tell you something.'

My heart sank. *Here it comes*, I thought. He's going to tell me he has a wife and three kids, or that he's gay but thinking of going straight and wants me to be the guinea pig. Nothing I hadn't suffered through before, of course. I'd gone through my whole life being disappointed by men, having my hopes raised only to have them come crashing back down under the weight of reality, and as a result I was pretty careful not to invest in anyone until I got to know him better (and, let's face it, once I did get to know any of them better, I usually wished I hadn't). I didn't even think I was capable of being smitten with a man on first meeting anymore . . . but Jack had definitely piqued my interest. I liked the way his hair flopped down over his forehead, despite his repeated efforts to push it back, I liked that he smelled of soap and freshly laundered clothes (I can't *stand* the overpowering stench of cologne, and consider it grounds for automatic rejection), and I liked that he didn't take himself too seriously. And I really liked the way he looked at me when I talked, as though he was paying careful attention to everything I said, no matter how banal, and wasn't just waiting for his own turn to speak. So I braced myself for his declaration.

'It's the reason I'm going back to London early. When I said I had something to take care of . . . well, it's personal. There's someone I've been seeing, and . . . I'm going back to break things off with her.'

Argh! I knew it! What were the chances that a thirty-something, attractive, smart, straight, successful guy like Jack would be single? And what was I thinking that someone like me, someone for whom a size six is as much a fantasy as getting together with Russell Crowe (even before he was married), would just happen to stumble across the most eligible bachelor of the year on board an airplane? I just knew the 'girlfriend' Jack was speaking of in such a cavalier way was most likely a 'wife' or a 'live-in,' and when he said he was going to break up with her, that was just code for 'I want to string you along with the fantasy that I'll leave her for you just long enough to get you into bed.'

'Ah,' I said, turning away from Jack for the first time that night to stare into the vast darkness that lay outside my tiny window.

I was surprised when his hand reached out and caught mine. The hard-edged city girl in me should have ripped her hand back and muttered 'Get a life' under her breath. But instead I turned back to look at him, and something in his face stopped me.

'I'm not lying to you. I know it sounds convenient, but it's true. I have a girlfriend, someone I've been seeing for a while, someone I thought that maybe I could . . . but I can't force myself to feel something for her that I don't. I think I've known for a while, but it seemed easier not to face it. I like her, and I figured I wasn't hurting anyone. But then I was talking to her on the phone yesterday, and she started hinting about wanting us to move in together, and I realized that if things keep going as they are, that, well, someone would get hurt. But now that I know I have to end things, I didn't want to wait, so I booked the first flight back to London. I'm going to meet her at her apartment when she gets home from work and tell her then.'

He looked so earnest as he talked, still holding my hand, and running his free hand through his shaggy blond hair.

The moment had a surreal feel – the odd hour, the strange location, holding hands with a relative stranger who seemed oddly familiar. I like to think of myself as having a hard, cynical shell that protects me from false hopes and insincere men, but somehow I believed him. Maybe it was his tone, or the obvious anxiety he was having about breaking things off with this woman.

'If it makes you feel any better, you're doing the right thing. I don't know anyone who would want to stay involved with someone who didn't return her feelings,' I said. This was an outright lie – I knew many people, men and women alike, who'd gladly delude themselves into believing that their significant other was committed for life, rather than be confronted with the unpleasant truth that he or she was no longer loved. But since Jack was trying to do the right thing, I didn't see any reason to make it more difficult for him.

'I know, I know. Even if I don't love her, she's still a great person, and I hate to hurt her. Is it appropriate to bring flowers to someone when you're breaking up?' Jack asked.

'No! When you're breaking someone's heart, you never bring a consolation prize! In fact, you should make a good-faith effort to remove your things from her apartment as soon as possible,' I said. 'And don't ever break up in public, just to avoid a scene. It's a chickenshit way to handle it.'

'I wasn't going to do that,' Jack said, offended. 'I would never do that.'

I felt vulnerable suddenly, as though I were the one he was about to break up with. I knew it was ridiculous (we had just met, after all), but I could easily imagine what this woman was thinking – looking forward to her boyfriend coming home, planning a romantic reunion. She had no idea that her heart was about to be broken. Here was this great guy whom she cared about, but she wasn't going to be able to keep him. I felt for her. After all, I was well acquainted with what it felt like to have your heart shredded.

'Claire . . . I'd really like to see you again. I know this is a little weird, meeting on a plane and all, but . . .' he trailed off, and actually looked a little embarrassed.

'But what?' I asked.

'I was going to say I thought there was a connection here, but then you'd just think I was a big dork who sits around watching *Oprah* all the time,' Jack said.

I laughed. 'Are you an *Oprah* fan?'

'You're avoiding the question.'

He was right – I was. I just didn't know if I wanted to take a chance on a guy that (a) I met on a plane, and (b) had already admitted that he had a girlfriend. So I stalled. 'I'm only going to be in London for a few days,' I said. 'And . . . there's the girlfriend thing.'

'Almost ex-girlfriend,' he reminded me. 'What if I break up with her before I ask you out? As I said, I'm going to tell her tonight. I'll call you afterward, and maybe we can get together before you go back to New York.'

'Well . . . ask me again afterward,' I said, not believing for a minute that he would. But really, really wanting him to.

'I will. I promise you, I will,' Jack said.

I know this sounds pessimistic, but I honestly never expected to hear from Jack again, even though he had carefully written down the name of my hotel on a crumpled drink napkin, which he had then folded neatly and deposited into his shirt pocket. And as the plane suddenly lurched down, beginning its heart-stopping, overly steep descent, he had reached for my hand again, and said, 'I meant what I said. I'm definitely going to call you.'

Part of me believed him when he said he'd call, and the other part wanted to believe him. But a nagging little voice in my head kept piping in, reminding me that in the romance department, I didn't have the best track record. It was hard enough to trust someone I'd gotten to know over time, had seen in a variety of situations, and who had actually called me the day after we slept together. It was harder to believe in a friendly, interesting, handsome guy I'd just met, who had already admitted that he had a girlfriend.

In any event, that day I paid for my brief in-flight romance. My plan had been to pop a sleeping pill shortly after takeoff, squeeze in six hours of sleep on the plane, and then spend Thursday visiting four of the hotels I'd researched ahead of time, each of which either offered a discount to seniors or was rumored to be a generally good value. That way, other than checking out restaurants, I'd have all day Friday and Saturday open. But by the time I'd checked into my hotel – a clean if somewhat impersonal establishment that advertised a package deal for retirees – I was almost dizzy with exhaustion from having stayed up all night. I looked longingly at the bed in my room, and for a moment was overcome with desire to throw myself on it, facedown in a prone position, and sleep for the next ten to twenty years. Instead, I forced myself into a lukewarm shower and change of clothes. I only had three days to spend in London; I wasn't going to waste time sleeping during the daylight hours.

Before I left my room, I called Maddy to let her know that I'd arrived. Madeline Reilly was one of my oldest friends, and the main reason that I'd finagled my way into a free trip to London. We'd been roommates in college, and then moved to New York at the same time, even sharing an apartment for a brief period back when we were barely surviving in entry-level office positions. Maddy is gorgeous, sweet, and lucky beyond all sense. She really has it all – a great boyfriend, Harrison (the latest subject of her rambling e-mails that usually run along the lines of 'Isn't my boyfriend *dreamy*?'), and the very best job in the world. Maddy works for Nike as a trend spotter, meaning her job consists of reporting on what the hip city kids are wearing.

When she first told me what she'd been hired to do, I couldn't believe that such a position actually existed, but leave it to Maddy to find it. We'd been roommates at the time, sharing a studio apartment in the East Village that was barely big enough for both of us to stand up in at the same time. It was our first postcollege home, and in lieu of a couch, chairs, or a table, the entire space was filled with our twin beds, which is where we slept, ate, and hung out. I'd just begun a stint as an editorial assistant at *Cat Crazy*, the only magazine in town I could coax into paying me (although an alarmingly large number of glossies had responded to my carefully typed cover letter and résumé with offers of unpaid internships). Maddy was still slogging away at a nightly waitressing gig while she searched for a job in marketing during the day. One night, she came bursting into the apartment, smelling of kitchen grease and cigarettes, her cheeks pink from the cold.

'I have a new job!' she announced.

I looked at her, perplexed. 'Waitressing?'

'No! With Nike! In their marketing department!'

'Oh my God, that's fantastic! I didn't even know you interviewed there.'

'I didn't,' Maddy said, dancing a little jig in the two square feet of open floor space. The entire apartment – all four hundred square feet of it – was floored with dirty linoleum. We couldn't afford to replace it (the landlord had laughed when we suggested that it was his responsibility to do so), or even the cost of a throw rug, so we handled it by covering the floor with balled-up clothing and dog-eared magazines. Or at least, I did. Maddy played the neurotically neat Felix to my slovenly Oscar.

'Tell me, tell me, tell me,' I begged.

Maddy stopped dancing and threw herself belly-first onto her bed and propped herself up on her elbows. 'Sunny – you know, one of the other waitresses – has a niece who's turning twelve, and she wants to know what to get her. Well, I start to run down what's hot among teens right now – thank God I read so many magazines – and this guy sitting at one of my tables overhears us talking. So he sort of jumps into our conversation, and one thing leads to another, and somehow I end up telling him that I was a marketing major and looking for a job in my field, and as it turns out he's an executive with Nike! In the Trend Development Department! And he's been looking for an assistant! He told me to come in on Monday and he'd give me a trial. Can you freaking believe it?'

I couldn't. Such a thing would never happen to me. And I was a little suspicious of the guy's motives – I don't know if I've mentioned this before, but Maddy is *gorgeous*. I mean Kate Moss, Kate Hudson, Cate Blanchett gorgeous. But I wasn't about to raise this concern with Maddy – who was now chortling about how she was going to score free sneakers for us – and ruin the moment for her. When *Cat Crazy* had extended me a job offer, Maddy was thrilled for me, and even attempted to bake me a celebratory cake in our tiny, crap oven. Granted, the cake came out so burnt and lopsided that in the end we just licked the insulin-shock-inducing frosting off it, but I appreciated the effort. So to celebrate Maddy's momentous career change, we splurged on a bottle of corked wine – a true luxury in those days – and toasted her success, and then stayed up all night talking, long after the buzz from the wine had faded, dreaming of the day when we'd be able to afford an apartment big enough to accommodate a sofa.

And even if the guy who hired her did have suspicious motives – there ended up being one drunken office-Christmas-party proposition, but it was oblique enough that Maddy easily sidestepped it – Maddy was so talented and hardworking at her new job that she quickly made herself indispensable to the Nike marketing team. She'd been transferred to London from the New York office three years earlier, which came with a big promotion and a hike in pay. I cheered her success, but missed her terribly. Although we e-mailed each other frequently and talked on the phone at least every other week or so, we now only got together on those rare occasions when she returned to Manhattan – the last time was when she surprised me by flying in for my birthday and hosted a surprise party for me at Calle Ocho on the Upper West Side – and so I couldn't wait to see her.

I don't exactly run around with an enormous posse of friends. After Maddy, my closest friend is Max, my manic next-door neighbor. Max is one of my favorite people – his collection of vintage eighties T-shirts is reason enough to adore him – but I missed having someone to do girly things with, like shoe shopping and manicures and browsing at the M.A.C. counter. The only place like that I can drag Max to is the Kiehl's store (which has a respectable selection of masculine skin products). He says he has a hard enough time living down the misperception that he's gay, and can't risk being seen in public helping me pick out sling-backs.

Maddy didn't answer her phone, but it was already ten-thirty, so she was probably at the office. Rather than bother her there, I left her a message to call me when she got home, and then headed out into the busy streets of London.

The rest of the day passed in a fog of sleep deprivation and jet lag. I wasn't just tired – every last inch of my body was demanding sleep, and it took all of my effort to keep my legs moving forward. I was achy and bleary-eyed and so disoriented I felt like I was wandering around inside a Stanley Kubrick film. Stopping at every Starbucks I passed for a venti latte didn't seem to help, either. The influx of caffeine just made me jittery.

Also, I kept forgetting that the traffic in London flows in the wrong direction, which meant that I had to look right instead of left while crossing the street, and I was nearly mowed down by unsympathetic motorists on three separate occasions. It was the third incident – a close call with an enormous black taxicab that I swear was gunning for me – that prompted me to call it quits. It was already six o'clock, and after grabbing an early lunch at a cheap but good café, I'd seen three of the four hotels on my list (two of which I could recommend without reservation; the third was in a sketchy area of the city, and probably not a great place for seniors, anyway). I'd have to squeeze in seeing the fourth hotel at some point on Friday, but with most of my work completed I was now basically free.

On my way back to my hotel, I stopped at a sandwich shop and picked up an inedible-looking egg sandwich to have for dinner (despite their many contributions throughout history to the arts, sciences, and literature, the Brits have yet to master the simple sandwich), and wolfed it down as soon as I got to my room. I shucked off my grimy clothing, pulled on a comfy pair of cotton plaid flannel pajamas (noting for my column that even with the heater set on high, the room still had a draft), and was happily ensconced in bed by seven. I've struggled with insomnia before, and have spent many a night lying tensely in bed, my body exhausted but my brain wired and wide awake, but this was one night I didn't have to worry. A heavy, dreamless sleep claimed me almost immediately, and it seemed like only a minute after I'd drifted off that the insistent ringing of the hotel telephone was jarring me awake.

I fumbled for my glasses, and peered at my travel clock: it read ten-thirty, but thanks to the very effective blackout drapes, I had no idea if it was morning or night.

'Hello,' I said, my voice thick with sleep.

'Did I wake you?' I didn't recognize the voice. It was male, but too deep to be Max, too young to be my editor.

'Who is this?'

'Please tell me you remember me . . . I'm the devilishly handsome, witty, brilliant man you sat next to on the plane this morning?' a teasing voice said.

I sat up in bed, suddenly wide awake. 'Oh . . . hi. I didn't . . .' I was going to say 'expect you to call,' but that would sound churlish. '. . . recognize your voice on the phone . . . not, you know, in person,' I finished, trying without success not to mumble incoherently.

'What are you doing? Were you sleeping?' Jack asked.

'Mmmm . . . I'm exhausted. I was up all night talking to you, remember?' I practically purred into the phone, before cringing with embarrassment at how eager I sounded. What was wrong with me? Why was it that whenever I talked to this guy, I ended up flirting shamelessly? I was thirty-two years old – hardly at an age where I should be acting like a giggly teenager with a crush on the cute boy in homeroom. Although from what I could remember, Jack *was* pretty cute. I was still so exhausted from the jet lag and from staying up all night, my memory of him was a little fuzzy around the edges.

'Yeah, I'm pretty ragged today, too. I'm going to hit the sack in a minute, but I wanted to find out if you had plans for tomorrow,' Jack said.

'What did you have in mind?' I asked. What I really wanted to say – but didn't – was, 'What about your girlfriend?' Could I really go out with someone who'd already admitted he was attached, even if the girlfriend at issue might be on her way out? After all of the years spent carefully honing my dating criteria, of which practically the first bullet point after 'Don't date serial killers' was 'Don't get involved with unavailable men'?

'I thought maybe I could take tomorrow off, show you the city. That is, if you don't have other plans,' Jack said.

My heart somersaulted and did a few handstands. 'You can take the time off?'

Jack laughed easily. 'I'm the boss. I can take as much time as I want. Besides, I was working around the clock the entire time I was in New York. I think I have some free time coming to me,' he said. 'I'll pick you up at your hotel tomorrow morning, and we'll get some breakfast before we start. How does ten sound?'

I hesitated again. I didn't want to say it, but my conscience was prodding me. 'What about, you know, what we talked about on the plane?' I said.

Jack sighed, and the playful note disappeared from his voice. 'I told her. It was pretty awful. She cried. A lot. And, well . . . it had to be done, let's just leave it at that,' he said. He sounded weary.

'Are you sure you want to get together? Is it too early?' I asked, praying that he would say no.

'No,' Jack said. 'It may not be the best timing, but I'd like to see you again. So tomorrow, then? Ten o'clock?'

'That sounds great,' I said.

After we hung up, it took me a while to fall back asleep. I realized that for the first time in a long time, I was actually looking forward to a date. And the idea that I was letting my guard down worried me.

Despite having slept for twelve solid hours, I was still conked out when my wake-up call jostled me out of sleep the next morning. I stumbled into the bathroom, and then shrieked when I saw my reflection in the mirror. In my half-awake stupor the night before, I'd forgotten to wash off my makeup. I recently read a magazine article that advised applying eyeliner before you go to bed as a fail-safe way to wake up the next morning with a cool, gothic-rocker-chick look. I looked like a rock star all right – Alice Cooper after a week of wild partying. Black eyeliner and mascara bled outward from my eyes, and – *oh God* – an enormous pimple was sprouting on my chin.

'No, no, no!' I said, scrubbing the makeup off with a rough, hotel-issue facecloth.

I hustled into the shower, making sure to wash my hair and shave my legs (I had no intention of letting Jack find out whether my legs were smooth or as prickly as a cactus, but it's always better to be safe than sorry in these situations). Luckily, the zit on my chin felt worse than it looked – it was still mainly under the skin – and I managed to cover it with some concealer, while praying that it didn't erupt in the middle of the day. After blowing out my shoulder-length dark blonde hair, which cooperated for once by flipping out at the ends a little (just like Sarah Jessica Parker's had in the picture I showed my stylist the last time I went in for a trim), I then turned my attention to fretting over what to wear. My chunky high-heeled boots were by far the best choice to go with my black trousers, but I wouldn't last through a day of sightseeing in them. I finally settled on a navy V-neck sweater, dark stretch jeans that flattered my behind, and my super-hip black laceless Nikes, which Maddy had sent me a month earlier with a note saying they were the newest, hottest thing and sold out of every store the minute they hit the shelves. True to her word, Maddy had been shamelessly pilfering company merchandise for me since practically her first day of work.

The sneakers reminded me that I hadn't heard back from Maddy. I was dying to fill her in on my new romantic prospect, and also to make sure that someone knew I was going off with Jack in case he did turn out to be a serial killer. I tried calling her again, at both home and work, but she wasn't answering either phone. Maddy had said work was insanely busy lately, but I still thought it was strange I hadn't heard from her. She'd been so excited when I told her I was going to be in London, and couldn't wait to introduce me to her new boyfriend, Harrison, a Brit whom she assured me was The One. I hated to remind her she'd been convinced she was meant to marry three out of her last four boyfriends. But Maddy was Maddy, and part of her charm was the ease with which she routinely fell in and out of love, although she was so softhearted – sometimes annoyingly so – that she couldn't bear to break up with anyone. As a result, her relationships tended to drag on forever while she mustered up the nerve to end them. Men never left her; at least, I couldn't think of a single time she'd been jilted.

'Just tell him the truth – you like him as a person, but don't have romantic feelings for him,' I'd advise her whenever her current romance had soured, and yet the man in question was happily ensconced in the Saturday night routine of dinner-and-a-video-rental, with no apparent intent of pushing off on his own.

'I don't want to hurt his feelings,' Maddy would wail in response.

And even after she would pluck up the nerve to confront him, she'd feel guilty about it for days. More than once, when we were still in college and too young, stupid, and usually tipsy to know better, I'd done the deed for her. I'd call up the unsuspecting guy, disguise my voice in a fairly good imitation of Maddy's, and briskly tell him that the relationship was over. But when I did the heart–squashing for her, Maddy felt even worse.

'He's such a great guy, he deserves better,' she'd insist.

'Maddy. Look, whenever he gets drunk – which, I shouldn't have to remind you, is nearly every day – he strips naked and runs around his fraternity house, snapping towels at other drunken, naked men. I'm not even sure he's heterosexual. Clearly, you can do better,' I'd reply. '*You* deserve better.'

'I think he may have hidden depths,' she'd say, a sentiment at which I'd just snort derisively.

Maddy and I couldn't be more different in our love philosophies – she's an incurable romantic, while I am an incurable realist. A lot of my dating psyche was forever traumatized by the abrupt exit from my life of my ex-boyfriend, Sawyer Clarke. Sawyer was an investment banker at Goldman Sachs, and although on the bony side, he was sort of sexy, like a good-looking version of Ichabod Crane. I always had this secret terror that when people looked at us they thought, 'Jack Sprat could eat no fat, his wife could eat no lean,' but at least he was taller than me. We went out for about a year when I was twenty-seven, and I thought it was true love. But, as it turned out, I was an idiot.

We saw each other frequently, went out to dinner, had the occasional weekend out of town, and what I'd consider better-than-average sex, despite Sawyer's preference for oral over regular (receiving, not giving, of course). But all relationships have their quirks, I reasoned, and I was willing to overlook the fact that every time we were in bed, he'd start pushing my head down while simultaneously arching his hips upward, since he was otherwise the ideal boyfriend. He was smart, had a decent sense of humor, and whenever we did sleep together, he would always spend the night, wrapping his long arms around me and holding me tight, which made me feel precious to him.

After we'd been together for just over a year, Sawyer told me that he had some important news to celebrate and that he'd made reservations for us at Tavern on the Green. I was half expecting an engagement ring. Okay, I was *convinced* of it – in fact, I'd played the whole scene out in my head. As soon as the dinner plates were cleared, Sawyer would pull out a robin's-egg-blue box from Tiffany's wrapped with a white ribbon, and with a sly smile would push it across the table toward me. He wouldn't get down on one knee – not his style – but he might murmur, 'Marry me,' in a sexy growl. Then a waiter would appear with a prearranged bottle of champagne, while I admired the ring on my hand and maybe even cried a little.

Needless to say, when Sawyer instead cleared his throat and announced over the endive salads that he had requested, and received, a transfer to his company's Tokyo office, I was more than a little taken aback.

'You *requested* the transfer?' I repeated dumbly.

'Yes, of course. This is a big promotion for me. And I've always wanted to live abroad, you know that,' Sawyer said, spearing some lettuce on his fork. Unlike me, this change in plans did not seem to be affecting his appetite.

The sugarplum visions of a wedding on Nantucket and

the china department at Saks had not yet dissipated from my mind, and I asked, with real confusion, 'But what about me? Do you want me to come with you, or did you think we'd try and make the long-distance thing work? I mean . . . how long are you going for? A few months? A year?'

But as the words were spilling from my mouth, completely beyond my ability to stop them, I saw that Sawyer wouldn't meet my eyes. Nor was he producing a beribboned blue box . . . or even asking me to visit him.

'Come on, Claire. You knew this wasn't that serious,' Sawyer said, keeping his voice low so that the middle-aged couple sitting only inches away at the next table wouldn't be able to eavesdrop.

And then it hit me: not only was Sawyer *not* proposing, he was breaking up with me in the most clichéd way possible – in a crowded restaurant to ensure there wouldn't be a scene. And not only was he breaking up with me, he was planning to then *leave the country* in order to get as far away from me as possible.

Why is it that in moments like these, I can never pull myself together? If I were not me, but instead Sandra Bullock playing me in the movie of my life, she'd throw down her napkin and have a snappy comeback, like 'Oh yeah? Well, I'm glad you're leaving. Because you don't deserve me,' before flouncing out of the restaurant with her head held high, and generally coming across as adorable and spunky in the face of adversity – and not like the pathetic and unwanted loser I was at that moment. The real crowning moment of my humiliation came when I dissolved into incoherent tearful babbling and fled the restaurant, knocking over a pitcher of water in the process.

Sawyer was really the last time I'd let myself seriously fall for someone, and a large part of the reason that I always expected the worst when it came to men. My abrupt breakup with him wasn't the first time my heart had been broken, but rather the last in a long line of disappointments – and I was determined not to let it happen again. I would no longer allow myself to be lulled into thinking I had a special connection with another man until I was positive he felt the same way. If this made me overly cautious, so be it. At least I'd never be humiliated that way again.

So, considering my track record, it was understandable that as I closed the door to my hotel room and headed for the elevator, I was a little nervous. I knew it was entirely possible that when I got down to the lobby, the only people waiting there would be a few bellhops and tourists milling about. It's not as though I go through life getting stood up all the time; it's just that I'm not all that confident in my ability to close the deal. Maybe, I thought, that's how we should approach dating in our thirties, like it's a business deal. Mercenary? Perhaps. But it would probably be a lot less emotionally messy. And all of those cheesy motivational sales books could be put to new use by eager singles.

I was so busy contemplating the ramifications of this brilliant idea that when the elevator doors opened with a ding, and Jack was standing directly across from the elevator bank, looking a little uncomfortable as he perched on the edge of a modern purple upholstered chair, it took me a minute to register that not only was he there . . . he was there waiting for me. I was dismayed to discover just how glad I was to see him.

Jack hopped up when he saw me approaching, and looked as nervous as I felt. He was wearing a cream fisherman's sweater, brown corduroys, and brown suede hiking boots – not at all the image of the successful young lawyer (although perhaps I was overly influenced by the ascot-wearing model in the magazine ads for Chivas Regal), and – *oh my God* – he was actually more attractive than I remembered, all broad-shouldered and long-limbed. He looked like he'd climbed out of an L.L. Bean catalogue. For a horrible moment I was seized with panic that Jack hadn't gotten a good look at me on the airplane, and now that he saw me on the ground and in daylight, he would have buyer's remorse.

'Hi,' I said, not sure whether to hold my hand out or hug him, so I just stood there awkwardly, my arms hanging down by my side, and then, at the last minute, took a step toward him. Jack leaned in to hug me at the same time that I was moving in, and we ended up bumping into each other, his nose hitting my cheek.

'Oh, I'm sorry,' I began, at the same time that Jack said, 'Sorry about that.'

And then we each took a step back and grinned at each other.

'You want to try that again?' I asked.

'Couldn't do a worse job,' Jack said, and this time he stepped forward, pulled me into his arms, and kissed me lightly on the lips. It was a nice kiss, a perfect first kiss. Warm and sweet, and it lingered just long enough to make it clear that it meant more than just hello. I hadn't expected such a greeting, and was stunned into momentary speechlessness.

'So, what are we doing? I haven't been to London in years, and I want to see as much as I can,' I gabbled nervously to fill the silence as I stepped away. I liked the kiss – okay, I *loved* the kiss – but I didn't want to just stand there swooning like a lovesick groupie, even if I was starting to feel like one.

'We'll do it all. But first, breakfast,' Jack said. 'What's your breakfast speed – a big spread, or are you more of a coffee-and-pastry kind of a woman?'

Yeah, right, like I was going to pig out in front of him, especially first thing in the morning. It's not as though I have an eating disorder, and I've more or less resigned myself to my size, but still – it's considered charming when women the size of toothpicks wolf down copious amounts of greasy, fried food, but somewhat less appealing when done by women with Rubenesque proportions.

'Oh, just a bagel or something would be fine,' I said, and we went across the street to the same Starbucks I'd hit on my way out the day before. I'd always thought of England as a kingdom of tea drinkers, but Starbucks seemed as popular here as it was back home, which was fine by me. Even though I'd slept forever, I still felt a little worn at the edges from the jet lag, as though I had a nonalcoholic hangover, and I needed a good strong shot of caffeine. We ordered two cappuccinos and lemon scones, and then sat at one of the tiny tables in the back to consume them.

'So, where are we going to go? The Tower of London? The British Museum? Parliament?' I asked as we munched on the scones, which were surprisingly good.

'Absolutely. All of it. I have a surprise first, and then we'll start hitting all of the places you most want to see,' he said.

'What surprise?' I asked. I couldn't keep the suspicion out of my voice. I hate surprises, which is entirely understandable given that my parents decided that Christmas morning was a good time to spring it on my sister and me that they were divorcing. I'd thought when they said they had something to tell us, that the punch line was going to be the revelation of a fabulous present – the kind that's so over-the-top, it doesn't even fit under a tree, like a Mediterranean cruise or a pair of new cars. In the midst of such high hopes, there was instead the perfunctory announcement that our family was being dissolved.

'Don't worry. You'll love it, I promise,' Jack said, popping the last of his scone into his mouth. He checked his watch. 'In fact, we should get going, or we're going to be late.'

'Late? Come on, just tell me where we're going,' I said.

'You'll just have to trust me,' Jack said, and although his tone was light and teasing, I felt a stab of fear.

Jack seemed to read my thoughts, since he placed a reassuring hand on my arm. 'Don't worry, it'll be fun,' he promised.

I nodded, suddenly excited at the prospect of the day before me. It was that birthday morning feeling, full of anticipation of the cake and presents and balloons and fun ahead. I decided that for once, I wasn't going to spend the day worrying about what could go wrong.

'Okay, let's do it,' I said, surprising myself by feeling almost as enthusiastic as I sounded.

'It' turned out to be the biggest damned Ferris wheel I'd ever seen in my life. Called the British Airways London Eye, it stretched four hundred and fifty feet into the sky. Groups of passengers soared over the London skyline in glass-encased pods that somehow stayed upright, even as the Eye rotated slowly around.

'There's no way in hell I'm getting on that thing,' I said, shaking my head and backing away.

Jack placed his hand on my lower back, preventing an escape. 'It's perfectly safe, and it gives you the most amazing view of the city,' he said. 'Besides, I already have the tickets, so you can't back out now.'

'Nope, uh-uh, not gonna happen. I have a fear of heights and of small spaces, so putting me in a coffin that dangles from the sky is pretty much a worst-case scenario for me,' I said, shaking my head, although despite my protestations, Jack continued to lead me to the entrance line.

'I think each capsule fits about twenty-five people, so it's hardly coffinlike. Come on, I promise I'll hold your hand the entire time,' Jack murmured in my ear.

'Fat lot of good that will do us as we plunge to our deaths,' I retorted, but finally I allowed myself to be coaxed onto the pod.

For the first ten minutes of the ride, I was terrified. We stood at the far end of the capsule, opposite the door, my hand clutching Jack's, as we looked out at the spectacular sight of Big Ben nestled next to Parliament on the bank of the river Thames. It was a gloriously bright day, and the sun danced over the water. Despite the fact that the ride continued to climb slowly upward, I started to relax. The pod felt safe and secure, and I was so entranced by the view of London, vast and wide, that I forgot to be afraid. I even loosened up my grip on Jack's hand in order to lean forward and point excitedly at Tower Bridge as it came into view.

Jack laughed, and shook his hand with comedic exaggeration. 'I thought you were going to break it, you were holding on so tightly,' he said.

I flushed and turned away, completely mortified and ruing my large, clunky, manlike hands. Why couldn't I have dainty little hands that no one would ever accuse of being able to break anything? I wasn't aware that Jack had stepped behind me until he spoke, his breath so warm and ticklish against my ear, it caused me to shiver.

'Where're you going? You're not still afraid, are you?' he asked, and then he lightly held the sides of my waist, and leaned me back toward him, so that my back was resting against his chest. My embarrassment disappeared, replaced by a strangely contradictory combination of out-and-out lust and tranquility. Jack's close presence calmed and reassured me, but at the same time, I was so aware of his physicality, of the muscles in his chest, the strength of his arms, the gentle touch of his fingers, that I had a strong urge to wrestle him down onto the bench and have my way with him. That would certainly shock the throng of German tourists riding in the pod with us, I thought, and laughed out loud at the idea.

'What's so funny?' Jack asked, turning me around toward him.

'Nothing. I'm just having a really good time,' I said, smiling up at him.

'Well, the day's just begun. We have a lot to see,' he replied.

Next on our sightseeing tour was the Tower of London, where we spent the remainder of our morning. Jack and I took a tour of the complex led by a rosy-cheeked Beefeater who related the bloody history of the Tower with a dramatic flare and was particularly fond of detailing the ghoulish executions. I'd brought my camera, and despite my laughing protest, Jack made me stand between two of the Beefeaters, both wearing the traditional costume – just like the drawing on the gin bottle – and took a corny picture of us. We dutifully trooped through the display of the crown jewels and through the armament, but to me the most incredible building was the little chapel where Anne Boleyn's beheaded body was interred. The chapel was small and lovely, but had a melancholy ambiance to it, heightened by the knowledge of all of the people who were put to their grisly deaths only a few yards away.

After we left the Tower, we stopped for lunch at one of the restaurants on my list – a pizzeria chain not too far away from the Tower. We shared a thin-crusted pizza topped with pesto, goat cheese, and tomato slices and then studded with walnut halves. It was gooey and decadent and absolutely delicious. Walking around in the cold weather always perks up my appetite, and I scarfed down my food, while Jack derided one of my favorite guilty pleasures – musicals.

'I hate musicals,' Jack insisted, and then puffed out his chest in mock machismo. 'That's girly entertainment.'

I rolled my eyes. 'Oh, please. Everyone pretends to hate musicals, but secretly loves them. It's like watching *The Brady Bunch* on Nick at Night – everyone does it, but no one actually admits to it.'

'I don't think we get Nick at Night here,' Jack interrupted.

'You know what I mean. Tell me you haven't seen *The Lion King*? *Phantom*? *Les Mis*?'

'No, no, and God no. I did see an incredibly annoying one, where all of the actors – are the stars of those things called actors? – were dressed up like cats and pranced around the stage like idiots,' he said. 'I can't remember the name.'

'You mean *Cats*?' I asked.

'Mmmm, sounds about right.' Jack smiled. 'That was more than enough for me.'

'Okay, well then, you probably wouldn't like *The Lion King*,' I agreed. 'But you should really give *Les Mis* a try. I know, it's touristy and dorky, but I swear, it's surprisingly good.'

'I just let you take my picture next to one of those crows at the Tower,' Jack began.

'Ravens,' I corrected.

'Whatever. I think it proves that I'm not above looking like a dorky tourist,' he pointed out. 'In fact, if you're done, we should probably get going. Where do you want to go next? St Paul's Cathedral? Westminster Abbey?'

We went to both, and then finished up the afternoon with a tour of the underground headquarters from which Winston Churchill ran the British forces during World War II.

'I can't believe Churchill's bunker is just right there, smack in the middle of Westminster, but completely underground. You'd never know it was there,' I remarked as we walked from the Tube stop back to my hotel.

'I think that was sort of the point. Can you imagine how foul it must have smelled, what with everyone living in such close quarters?'

'You think?'

'Dozens of men, packed together in those tiny rooms, probably eating disgustingly large amounts of cabbage,' Jack said, comically wrinkling his nose.

I laughed, despite myself. Jack was refreshingly complete, and seemed to have emerged into manhood without the scars that most men my age carry. I'd only known him for a short time, but I just didn't get the sense that he was damaged in any way, and I'm a fairly good judge of character (okay, okay, besides Sawyer, I mean). But even this stellar example of modern manhood couldn't resist making fart jokes.

We arrived at my hotel, a squat white building in South Kensington with a colorful set of flags flying out in front and a uniformed doorman standing in front of the revolving door. It was already dark, and the city was drawing itself up, quieting for the night. I paused, not knowing what to do. It had been an extraordinary day – really, the best first date I'd ever had in my life. And although I was tired and my feet were aching from hours of walking, I didn't want to say good-bye to Jack. It was just my luck. I'd finally met a guy who had everything I'd ever wanted – sex appeal, intelligence, a great sense of humor – and he lived on a different continent. And, I had to remind myself, he'd just gotten out of a semi-serious relationship with another woman, even though he hadn't once mentioned her or their too-recent-for-comfort breakup.

'So,' I said.

'So,' Jack agreed.

'Here we are,' I said, not knowing what else to say.

What I wanted to do was invite him up to my room. In fact, ever since the kiss we'd shared that morning, the promise of something more had not been far from my mind. Jack was a sort of slacker yuppie, with his shaggy hair and relaxed style, but there was a distinct, sinewy heat to him – the flicker in his eyes, the set to his mouth, the soft yet insistent pressure when he held my hand. But other than one unmemorable fling while on vacation at a Club Med in Cancún, I just don't do the one-night-stand thing. Maybe that sounds a little prudish, but once sex has entered the picture, it's hard for me to stay detached. When I sleep with someone, I tend to imprint on them, sort of like those orphaned baby birds who become attached to a nanny-minded dog (not the most flattering comparison, I know), and I certainly wouldn't want to imprint on someone who only saw sleeping with me as a one-time deal. Jack didn't seem like that kind of a guy, but then again, what did I really know about him, other than that he was funny and smart and was a good sightseeing companion, and that he had no qualms whatsoever about going on a seven-hour date the day after breaking up with his girlfriend? Those qualities alone do not recommend someone as a person to hand your heart over to.

Jack smiled his amazing smile and reached out to brush a hair from the side of my face. 'I'm not ready to say good night,' he said softly, and took my hand in his.

Kiss me, I silently willed him. No way, no how could I

make the first move. *Could I?* No, I absolutely could not. It would be just my luck to swan in, lips puckered, and have him dive to one side to avoid making contact. And then I'd have to die of embarrassment.

But as Jack looked down at me, his greenish brown eyes intent on my face, I was suddenly sure he was going to save me the trouble by asking if he could come up to my room. This just cleared the way for a new and even fiercer debate between the part of me that wanted to drag him off like a hormonally charged cavewoman and the part that was sounding an alarm, warning me not to risk it. But before one of the two sides could claim victory, Jack smiled and glanced down at his watch.

'Are you up for getting some dinner, or are you too tired?' he asked.

'That sounds like fun,' I said, relieved, although I did feel a twinge of guilt over abandoning Maddy, even though we didn't have firm plans to get together that evening, since she hadn't returned my calls.

I debated for a minute whether I should check with her before accepting, or at least ask Jack if he'd mind if I brought a friend along with us (which would have the added benefit of getting a second opinion on Jack). But then – and I'm not proud of this – a small, mean, insecure little voice in my head said, *Do you really want to introduce your beyond gorgeous friend to this amazing guy? One look at her, and he'll lose all interest in you.*

And just like that, my decision to ditch Maddy for the night was made.

'Give me a chance to freshen up,' I said, rationalizing wildly that Maddy would want me to make this date. And besides, she and I still had a whole day left to spend together before I returned home.

'What time should I pick you up? Let's say we meet back here in the lobby at seven?' he asked.

'Perfect,' I said.

Jack kissed me on the cheek before he left, his lips lingering, feeling hot against my windblown skin. I smiled all the way up to my room, and after I let myself in – it took me four attempts, I absolutely *hate* those stupid card key things, and made a quick mental note to mention this in my next column – I checked my messages. There were none. I was glad that Robert wasn't hounding me with last-minute directives to review the Ye Olde Tacky Tourist Trap, but where the hell was Maddy? This truly wasn't like her, and I was starting to worry. I called her apartment, got her machine again, and so left another message to please call me *as soon as possible*.

After hanging up, I had just enough time to take a hot shower, curl my deflated hair into hot rollers, and figure out what I was going to wear. I don't normally bring formal clothes with me on these business trips – one does not need to dress for dinner to go to the Shoney's in Tempe, Arizona, after all – but since Maddy has a habit of dragging me to cocktail parties where everyone's clad in black Prada, this trip I'd thought to throw the standard LBD (little black dress) into my suitcase. I'd hung it in the bathroom while I showered to steam out the wrinkles, and now, curlers still in my hair and makeup freshly reapplied, I held it out at arm's length to scrutinize it.

The truth is, I have a hard time dressing. I always have. It's one thing to pull on sexy little slips of clothing when you have no boobs, and everything looks as good on you as it does on the mannequin. But when you have large breasts and the hips to match, it's harder to pull off the casually sexy thing without putting a lot of thought into it, as well as procuring the kind of undergarments that hold everything in place. My fear of a wayward breast popping out has always kept me from wearing strapless dresses. Plus it's hard enough to get any respect at work by virtue of the fact that I'm the youngest person on staff by about twenty-five years and most of my male colleagues come from a generation where it's perfectly acceptable to call women 'gals,' so at the office I normally lean toward heavily tailored clothing, and nothing low-cut or stretchy.

My new LBD was one of the few risks I'd taken in my wardrobe. It was made of a knit material and was a knockoff of a Diane von Furstenberg belted wrap dress. It wasn't that the dress showed off a particularly large amount of skin, with its long sleeves and knee-length hem, but it draped on my body without leaving much to the imagination. It emphasized my waist, while hugging every other curve, as well as exposing enough cleavage to make me uncomfortable. I would only consider wearing the dress if supported by a heavy-duty bra and a pair of those gut-cinching girdle panties, but once everything was sucked in and pushed up, it was pretty sexy.

'Va-va-va-voom,' Max had said approvingly when I tried it on for him, anxious for approval before wearing it in public. 'Very Marilyn Monroe meets Jackie O.'

Still, I felt a wave of anxiety as I tried it on, and examined my reflection in the full-length mirror the hotel had thoughtfully provided. Would it look as if I was trying too hard? Would it be too dressy for wherever we were going to dinner? And, most important, did it make me look *fat*? I checked my watch and saw that I was running late, so I didn't have time to second-guess it. I pulled the rollers out of my hair, shook out the curls so that I didn't look like a French poodle, pulled on my long winter coat, and headed out the door.

The swarm of butterflies in my stomach began to take off, flapping their wings and roaring around, and for the second time that day, I felt slightly nauseated as the elevator descended to the lobby. This time I wasn't worried that Jack wouldn't show up ... I was worried that he would. The carefree attitude that had buoyed me earlier in the day vanished, and I was now terrified that I might lose myself in something that was quickly growing beyond my ability to control.

Of course, that could only happen if I believed in love at first sight, I reminded myself.

Which I don't.

When the elevator doors opened, Jack was again waiting there, this time standing, and again looking anxious. When he saw me, his face relaxed into its brilliant smile, and he came forward to take my hand.

'For some reason, I'm always a little nervous that you're not going to show up,' he said, gently squeezing my hand as we walked out of the hotel. The cold November air swirled up around me, nipping at my stocking-covered legs. Despite all the walking we'd done, I felt wide awake, revived by both the frigid wind and my nervous anticipation of what the night before us held.

'Why?' I asked, genuinely confused.

Jack shrugged. 'I just get that feeling,' he said, and then nodded at a black car waiting at the side of the curb. 'Here we go.'

He opened the back door for me, and I climbed in and sat on the leather seat. The interior had that great new-car smell, and there was a minibar and phone built into the back of the driver's seat. The last time I'd ridden in a car that had a minibar, it had been a limo that I'd shared with eleven other high school seniors on our way to the prom. This was decidedly less tacky.

'Wow, your taxis here are amazing,' I said, admiring how clean and luxurious the cab was. And the driver was so discreet; he didn't even have a visible meter or radio.

'It's not a cab. It's a private car service that my company uses,' Jack said, as if this were no big thing, and that all Londoners have luxury cars complete with drivers given to them as a job perk. I tried – and failed – to imagine *Sassy Seniors* springing for a car service for its employees. Hell, on what the magazine paid me, even taxis were a luxury.

'Do you like Indian food?' Jack asked.

'Love it.'

'Good, because I know a great place,' he said, and again took my hand in his.

The restaurant was not at all like any other Indian place I'd been to. For one thing, the interior was not dark and dreary, but hip and youthful. The walls were a bright, lipstick red, with funky, chrome wall sculptures hanging on them, and the tables and chairs looked like they came straight from a spaceship. But despite the bright colors and modern furnishings, the soft glow of candlelight and the jazz music coming from the speakers gave the restaurant an ambiance of quiet glamour.

When we entered, the hostess asked if she could take my coat, which Jack helped me out of. I handed it to her, and then felt self-conscious as I realized that Jack was staring at me.

'Wow,' he said.

'What?' I asked.

'You look amazing,' he said. 'That dress is just . . . wow.' His voice trailed off, and he just stood there gazing at me, with a look of frank admiration on his face. I know that I'm not a troll, and it's not like I feel the need to cover my head with a sack when I venture forth into the world. But I'm also not used to getting ogled, and under this close scrutiny, I could feel myself blush. Jack seemed oblivious to my discomfort, as well as to the fact that the hostess, who was thin, blonde, and about a thousand times prettier than me, had returned from depositing my coat and was waiting to escort us to our table.

I'm genetically incapable of accepting a compliment, and

had to fight back a nearly irrepressible urge to snort, and say, 'Yeah, right.' But I managed to swallow hard and say 'Thanks' with a tight-lipped smile, and was glad when we were finally seated.

It had just been such an unexpected day, and dinner was the perfect conclusion. I've always enjoyed Indian food, but this was a gourmet feast. We wolfed down potato turnovers, Tandoori chicken, lamb in a cream sauce, saag paneer, and naan, all washed down with a crisp, cold white wine. It was so good, I forgot to be concerned about pigging out in front of my date, and even sopped up every last bit of the delicious cream sauce with a piece of the bread. Jack and I didn't talk about anything important – no in-depth discussions about life choices or lost loves – but we couldn't seem to stop laughing. I don't know if it was the wine or the exhaustion after a day of sightseeing, but everything the other said struck us both as hysterically funny.

It wasn't until we'd polished off the meal and the plates had been cleared that we grew quiet. The flickering candlelight caused shadows to dance over Jack's face, and before I could stop myself, my hand reached out, as if acting on its own accord, and my fingers brushed softly over his cheek and then lightly touched the end of his crooked nose.

'How did you break it?' I asked.

'Do you want the official story or the truth?' Jack asked.

I started to withdraw my hand, embarrassed to find myself petting him, but Jack was too fast for me, and he reached up and lightly gripped my hand in his.

'Officially, I always tell people that it was broken in a bar fight, and that the other guy didn't get off so well,' Jack said. He spoke slowly, a laid-back cadence that had sounded a little strange to me at first, especially since I talk so quickly that the words sometimes trip over one another in their haste to leave my mouth. But now that I'd gotten used to his easygoing drawl, I liked it. It matched his personality.

'What really happened?'

'A car accident. A truck hit some black ice, spun out of control and into me, and this happened' – he pointed to his nose – 'when the air bags went off. I know it isn't pretty.'

'No, I like it,' I said simply, and then turned crimson. This was starting to get ridiculous – holding hands, incessant blushing, a searing new crush. I was thirty-two going on fourteen.

The car was waiting for us when we came out of the restaurant, and Jack held the back door open for me. I was a little tipsy – the food had been very spicy and the wine was the only cold drink on the table – but mostly I felt warm and relaxed, not out-of-control drunk. Apparently the British treat ice as though it were a commodity as precious as gold, and I'd already learned during the few meals I'd had here that no matter how many times I asked for ice water, the most I could hope for would be a lukewarm glass with one tiny ice chip floating in it.

'Did you like dinner?' Jack asked as he settled comfortably into his seat, his long legs sprawling out before him.

'It was wonderful. Thank you so much,' I said, annoyed at how prim I sounded. I've seen those reality television shows where groups of single, gold-digging women are set up to compete for the heart of a wealthy bachelor, and it always amazes me how at ease these women are with just throwing themselves at the guy in question. They purr and flirt and stroke his ego, and all without the least bit of shame. Was I somehow born without the minx gene? Because here I was on a romantic date with a sexy man, and I was channeling Miss Manners.

'Are you in a rush to get back? Because I thought we could take a turn around the city, so you can see London when it's all lit up,' Jack said.

'I'd love to,' I said, delighted at the charming idea, and

wondered, not for the first time, how it was that this guy was single. He was funny, and obviously very smart and thoughtful (and not in a smarmy, ingratiating way). Jack asked the driver to take us past Westminster, Big Ben, Buckingham Palace, Hyde Park, South Kensington, Mayfair – everything was lit up, giving it a dreamy, unreal quality.

I'd often heard Paris being described as the world's most romantic city, but seeing London as I did that night, sitting comfortably next to Jack, I doubted it could get any better than this, particularly when Jack pulled me toward him, cuddling me against his chest. His camel hair overcoat felt soft against my cheek, and as I breathed in his now-familiar clean scent, I felt ridiculously happy. The interest that had been percolating within me all day, particularly when Jack smiled down at me or when our hands touched, had now erupted into full-blown lust. I wanted Jack, and if it meant swatting away the little voice of concern echoing in my head, then so be it.

Still, it was strange – through a few of his comments, and particularly his anxiety that I might stand him up, I gleaned that Jack seemed to have the completely moronic idea that I was less interested in him than he was in me. Ha! Yes, it happens all the time that Amazon-sized single women in their thirties see a single, successful, attractive, and – most important – non-freakish man, and think, *Oh, no, not another night of being wined and dined!* Either Jack had criminally low self-esteem – and that didn't seem to be the case – or he was completely ignorant of the power shift that occurs between men and women in their thirties. I knew this guy had just broken up with his girlfriend and all, but . . .

And then it hit me.

I was so shocked that I actually audibly gulped and sat straight up, pulling away from Jack's embrace. He gave me a strange look, but now that I knew what was going on, why

Jack was paying so much attention to me, I was too startled to care. There was only one possible explanation for what was going on. Jack was a Chaser . . . the kind of guy who's only interested in a woman when he's pursuing her. I'd met his type before. They're engaging, romantic, seemingly without flaws . . . but only as long as you appear to be unavailable. As soon as you relax even slightly into the relationship, as soon as you call them out of the blue, or suggest that you get together, then away they run like gazelles fleeing a lioness on the hunt. I couldn't believe I'd allowed myself to miss it. The signs were all there – out of nowhere a guy who has just gotten out of a relationship suddenly starts showing interest in me, keeps asking me out, actively pursues me. Clearly this was not normal behavior. There was just no way a guy this great – well, apparently this great – would appear out of nowhere and start romancing me. Not unless he had a twisted agenda of his own.

Of course, Jack would never admit it if I confronted him. What Chaser would? They have nothing to gain through honesty. And just running away would probably encourage him even more – playing hard-to-get was the ploy advocated in those stupid books on how to attract men (but ensured that all you'd ever get would be the immature, moronic ones who'd bolt the minute you showed the least bit of interest in them). In fact, there was only one way that I could think of to prove what Jack was up to, one way to find out for certain if he was just pursuing me for the sake of the hunt.

As the car pulled up in front of my hotel, I looked over at Jack. The streetlights softly illuminated his face, and he seemed to be unsure of what to say, his expression a question mark. His unruly blond hair had flopped down over his forehead again, his face pale and vulnerable, and for a minute I wavered. One-night stands might not be my thing, but for my own sanity I needed to know once and for all what Jack was really after, and there was only one way to do that – I'd let him catch me.

Before I could lose my nerve, I inhaled a deep, shaky breath and bluntly said:

'Would you like to come up?'

I woke up with no idea where I was or what time it was. It wasn't that I was hungover – I hadn't had very much to drink the night before – but between the strange hotel room and my jet lag, it took me a few long moments to remember where I was, and . . .

Oh my God.

Jack.

Where was he?

For a long, dreadful moment, I thought that he had sneaked out of my room in the middle of the night, but . . . no, I definitely heard splashing sounds in the bathroom. I grabbed for my watch and saw that it was seven in the morning. And – *Oh God* – I was naked. I shouldn't have been surprised, not after . . . well, not after the rather spectacular night Jack and I had just spent together. But I never sleep in the nude. I'm not comfortable with anyone seeing me naked, including myself. I wondered if I had time to hop out of bed and throw on some pajamas before Jack emerged from the bathroom, but then I heard the door opening, so I just pushed my hair out of my face and sank back under the covers, hoping that I could find a modest way of emerging from the bed without letting him catch sight of my bottom.

'You're awake,' Jack said, smiling, and leaning over to kiss me. He was wearing the hotel-issued terry cloth bathrobe, and had the minty breath of someone who had recently brushed his teeth. He must have used my toothbrush (an image I found oddly charming), and I prayed that my morning breath didn't smell too foul. Just to make sure, I pulled the sheet up to my nose. Jack perched on the edge of my bed, smiling down at me, and I couldn't help but beam back up at him from under the sheet. If he was a Chaser – and I still couldn't be sure that he wasn't – then he at least had some manners, and didn't abandon me in the middle of the night.

'So are you,' I said. 'Why are you up so early? I think it's about two a.m. New York time.'

'I know – you must be exhausted. What are your plans for the day?' he asked.

I hesitated. I knew I should try to spend some time with Maddy . . . or at least make sure that she was alive. I looked over at the phone, but the message light was off. I didn't know whether to be annoyed that she hadn't called me back or frightened that something might have happened to her.

'I have one more hotel and a few more restaurants to check out while I'm here,' I said cautiously.

'Are you busy later on? I have an errand to run today, something I have to do, but I could come get you after. You were talking about going to the British Museum yesterday. We could go this afternoon? And maybe get dinner tonight?'

Jack looked so earnest, his hair rising in untidy blond tufts around his head, the white terry robe a little skimpy on his long frame. On impulse, I reached out and gently touched his rough, unshaven cheek.

'Okay,' I said happily, although even as I said it, I felt a twinge of anxiety at how endearing I found Jack in his sleep-rumpled state. Despite my best intentions to stay detached, the whole postcoital imprinting process had been activated. It was incredibly stupid, because even if Jack did have the best motives possible, even if we were somehow destined to be soul mates – if I believed in destiny or in soul mates, which I *don't* – then there was still a large, rather obvious obstacle to any kind of a relationship developing between us: I lived in New York, he lived in London. End of story. This was a vacation fling, that's all, and there was no room to get attached. I withdrew my hand.

But Jack grabbed my hand and held it back up against his cheek for a minute, and then smiled with a wicked glint in his eye. 'So, about last night . . .' he said.

And then he dove back into the bed, leaving the robe behind.

It wasn't until two hours later, not long after Jack had left, and as I was just getting out of the shower, humming happily, that I realized I'd failed to obtain a fairly important piece of information: I didn't know Jack's last name. *Oh. My. God.* How could I not have asked him? My mind raced over the previous two days – when he introduced himself to me on the plane, when we arrived at the restaurant, when I saw a credit card . . . but no. The hostess had known him on sight at the Indian restaurant, and I think he paid for everything in cash. I tried – and failed – not to feel like a complete slut. What's more trashy than sleeping with a man with whom you're only on a first-name basis? It was one step away from picking someone up in a bar, or being featured on a Jerry Springer show about women impregnated by their boyfriend's father.

Had he done it on purpose? I wondered. Was he a Chaser after all? Was he just after a quickie, planning to extricate himself from the situation with as little fuss and leaving as few tracks as possible? No, I couldn't believe that. There are easier ways to pick up women than taking an entire day off of work to go sightseeing with them. And the night before, when we were in bed afterward, lying close together, Jack had suddenly turned onto his side, so that he was propped up on one elbow, looking down at me, and said, 'You know I'm not playing you, right?'

'No,' I said, and laughed. We'd been joking all night, and I thought he was still kidding around.

But Jack hadn't laughed. Instead, he looked at me with somber interest, and said simply, 'I don't normally do this. And I don't think you do either. I just want you to know that.'

And not long after that, I'd fallen asleep, feeling strangely safe for one sleeping naked so close to a man she barely knows. It wasn't until now that I remembered those words, and thought – no, *knew* – that he meant them, even if only at the moment he said them. And so what if I didn't know his last name? I'd just ask him today, when he called me at three o'clock before picking me up, as we'd planned. Surely it was just an oversight on his part that he didn't tell me. Surely.

The phone rang, sparing me from further obsession.

I reached for the phone. 'Hello,' I said.

'Claire?' The voice was muffled, but unmistakable.

'Maddy? God, where have you been? I've been calling you for two days, haven't you gotten my messages? You're never going to believe what happened, and . . . what's wrong?' I asked, puzzled by the sniffling at the other end of the line. 'Are you sick?'

And then Maddy burst into tears.

Normally when Maddy and I haven't seen each other in a while, our greeting is punctuated with hugs and squeals and we begin the ancient female bonding ritual of exchanging compliments along the lines of 'I *love* your hair!' or 'Where did you get those shoes?' But not this time. When Maddy opened the door, she looked horrible. She's never been much of a crier; unlike me, she's one of those eternally cheerful people. But now her eyes were dull, her nose red, and her skin blotchy . . . it was the worst I'd ever seen her look, at least since the night in college when she went a little nuts on tequila shooters and ended up hunched over the industrial dormitory toilet, puking uncontrollably.

Maddy let me into her apartment, although she referred to it as her 'flat,' and as I entered I tripped over a white fluffy throw rug that looked like a skinned white sheepdog lying in the center of the hallway. When I recovered and had a chance to look around, I wasn't surprised to see that Maddy's apartment looked like it belonged in a magazine spread. It was very modern and very white, and furnished with an immaculate white sofa, black leather and chrome side chairs, groovy lamps, and carefully placed orange-popsicle-colored vases and pillows. An entire wall of floor-to-ceiling windows on the far side of the apartment flooded the space with light, filtered through frothy white curtains. It was the kind of place that made me feel entirely inadequate and underdressed to even be there.

'Come on in,' Maddy said. 'Let's go to the kitchen. Do you want a glass of wine? I know I need one.'

'Wow,' I said, looking around. 'This is . . . incredible.'

Maddy, wan and upset, looked around and shrugged. 'I think the white thing is over. I'm thinking about changing everything, maybe doing a retro-eighties design.'

'Isn't it too soon for the eighties to be retro?' I asked, and Maddy, despite her obvious distress, managed to muster up a pitying look for me.

Maddy's terribly hip and stylish, and always has the hottest new thing, whatever it is, and in whatever category – clothing, shoes, home decor. It was no wonder that she was employed as a trend watcher, and she excelled at it. In fact, she was so effortlessly cool, it would be easy to hate her. I certainly tried when we first met during our freshman year at Boston College. The last thing that I needed was a petite, flawlessly beautiful sidekick, whose very presence only served to highlight my every flaw. Maddy had done some catalogue modeling as a teenager, and was even one of the runner-ups in the *Seventeen* magazine cover-model contest. When she told me this, it made it even harder for me to be friends with her, since I hate all fashion models on general principle. I can't stand the way they pout and toss their hair around and announce in thick South American accents that they just adore french fries, preferably smeared with mayonnaise, and then titter that their only exercise is daily bouts of sex with their French photographer boyfriends. Not that Maddy's anything like that, but still.

The only thing that kept Maddy out of professional modeling was her height – she's only five feet two inches tall – because other than that, it was hard to find a blemish on her. Her mother was of Japanese descent, and her father a redheaded Irish-American, and Maddy had inherited the best of both worlds: she has cream-colored skin, long glossy black hair, her mother's perfectly proportioned dainty features and her father's wide blue eyes. Perhaps her most offensive trait is her ability to eat anything and everything she wants and yet remain waifishly thin. She has the body of a professionally trained dancer, which is completely unfair, since I happen to know for a fact that she's a complete klutz and her idea of working out is running for a cab. But despite these loathsome qualities, Maddy has an enormous heart, is compulsively generous, and although she isn't book smart, she does possess a sharp insight into human nature. Frankly, she's pretty hard to hate . . . she's too damn nice.

But Maddy has been so much more to me – she's more like a sister than just a friend. When my parents finally put an end to their decaying marriage during my sophomore year in college, Maddy stayed up with me during the long late nights, chain-smoking Marlboro Lights and plotting revenge on the latest of my father's extramarital girlfriends.

When her father, a stockbroker, died of a heart attack at the young age of fifty-one, I sat next to her at the funeral, holding her hand and keeping her supplied with tissues. But it was more than just support during sad times – we'd vacationed together, socialized together, and were roommates for the first year we lived in Manhattan. Maddy had always been there for me . . . and if she had a tendency to be a little scatterbrained at times, she certainly made up for it with her loyalty and compassion.

'What happened?' I asked.

Maddy gave me a glass of chilled white wine, and then sat down next to me at her Scandinavian stripped-pine table. She smelled so familiar – her signature scent was Joy perfume, she'd worn it for years – and she looked distressingly thin. I had forgotten this was another one of her offensive traits – unlike most of the female population, who turn to chocolate for solace, Maddy actually loses weight in the midst of a crisis.

'I've just never felt so alone . . . so unloved,' Maddy said, starting off slowly, but then her voice caught in her throat, and pretty soon her words were punctuated with small sobs. 'He said he didn't love me, and that he never has. Said we weren't right for each other. I can't believe it . . . I thought he was the one. You know, *the one*. I can't believe that he doesn't want me, that this is happening to me. How could he not love me?' she asked, looking at me with her wide, confused bottle-blue eyes. 'I've never had anyone break up with me before. Never. I don't know how I'm supposed to act.'

It occurred to me again, perhaps uncharitably, that Maddy's ego might be more bruised than her heart, that she was more shocked by the fact that Harrison had broken up with her, rather than truly mourning the fact that he was no longer in her life. But then I quickly dismissed the thought – yes, Maddy was blessed in all things, and yes, sometimes it was hard to watch everything come so easily to her when my life always felt like an uphill battle through the mud on a rainy night. But she was human after all, and just as capable as the next person of being hurt and disappointed.

'I owe you an apology, Claire,' Maddy continued. She cupped her wineglass in her delicate hands. They were tiny and birdlike, with long, elegant fingers. I coveted those hands, and folded my own – large, capable, clunky – under the table.

'I never really understood how you felt when Sawyer dumped you. I didn't tell you at the time, but I thought you overreacted a little. No offense,' she continued, looking at me quickly. 'But he wasn't exactly a prize.'

'Uh . . . no,' I agreed hesitatingly, not sure if it was Sawyer or I who was being insulted.

'I just didn't know how you *felt* . . . how awful it *feels*. To have someone you love stand there and tell you that he doesn't love you, that he *never* loved you.' Her voice broke with a little sob. 'But now I know, and I understand why you just kept going on and on *and on* about it for so long after you guys broke up.'

I was eager to get off the subject of how pathetic I'd been after the Sawyer incident.

'Did this all just happen today?' I asked.

'No, a few days ago.' Maddy sniffed. 'I'm sorry I didn't call you back. But between everything that's happened with Harrison, and the presentation I have to give on Monday, I've been swamped. Not that the presentation is going to take that long . . . it's on the latest trends of urban girls, aged thirteen to seventeen, which can be summed up in two words: Jailbait Sluts.'

I snorted. 'Is that the new look? I suppose they're all inspired by Britney.'

'And a dozen other celebs who are far worse. Seriously, all I see are young girls with their stomachs bared and thongs sticking out the back of their jeans. Or, at the other end of the spectrum, there are the little comradettes, who all seem determined to find and wear the least flattering shade of olive drab possible. Can you imagine what my mother would have said if I came home dressed like that when I was fourteen?' I could not. Her mother was a tiny, frail-looking Japanese woman, but I happened to know for a fact that she ruled her household with an iron fist. Especially where Maddy was concerned. 'Anyway, I had to work late last night getting my PowerPoint presentation together, so that's why I didn't get back to you. I'm so sorry, I know we had plans.'

'It's okay,' I said vaguely. It didn't seem the time to launch into an excited recital of my whirlwind romance with Jack. It would smack of saying, *Oh, I'm sorry your life is shit, but let's get back to me and how well I'm doing*. Which would be a little ironic, considering Maddy is Maddy, while I'm . . . well, me.

Besides, I was already starting to feel guilty because my best friend in the whole world was suffering her first true heartbreak, and for the first time in three years, I wasn't a million miles away, separated by an ocean, and it was my job – no, it was my duty – to sit there with her for hours, drinking white wine and eating salty, fatty things that would make me break out, retain water, and gain weight, handing her tissues and listening to her rail on about what a son of a bitch Harrison was and how much she missed him . . . and yet I had a date that I wanted to keep. Sure, I had a few free hours, and would be happy to indulge in a tear and junk food fest for a while, but then I really wanted to see Jack.

Jack. Just the thought of him made my insides go a little woozy, a happy nervous tremor that started in my heart and then ricocheted through my limbs. I knew that even contemplating deserting Maddy in her hour of need made me the worst friend in the world, and even worse, I knew if it were the other way around, she'd immediately ditch her date for me.

The night that Sawyer left me, I showed up on Maddy's doorstep (at the time she still lived in Manhattan, but we were no longer roommates) with a tearstained face and deflated heart. She had her current boyfriend over (I think that his name was Jonathan, but really, who could keep them all straight?). She immediately expelled him from her apartment, and then took me out for chili cheese fries, after which she marched me back to my apartment to help me destroy all of Sawyer's pictures, as well as his favorite shirt, his CD of 'The White Album,' and the electric shaver he just had to have after he saw it being used in a James Bond movie (I figured if he was going overseas, he had no need for any of these things, so I was doing him a favor by crushing them into little pieces with the hammer I borrowed from my super). And she taped reminders to my phone, fridge, bathroom mirror, and nightstand lamp not to call Sawyer under any circumstance.

'For God's sake, you'll only feel worse if you do. Call me instead, and I'll talk you down from it,' Maddy advised.

Besides, I had just met Jack, and it wasn't like the relationship was going anywhere. As I kept reminding myself, I was returning to New York, he was staying in London. And I still wasn't 100 percent sure that he wasn't a Chaser . . . just because he'd asked me out again after we slept together didn't necessarily mean anything. He knew I was leaving the next day anyway, so maybe he was just being nice. Or . . . *oh God* . . . maybe he wasn't even going to call me today. It wasn't like I could call him, since I had neither his phone number nor his last name. The only way I could possibly track him down would be to call his company and ask them if they had anyone named Jack working there, which I could just imagine.

'Oh, I don't know his last name,' I'd giggle nervously,

before pausing to listen to the annoyingly clipped British tones of the receptionist asking for more information, and then snap, 'Why don't you just give me the extensions of all American lawyers named Jack between the ages of thirty and forty who work there, and I'll call each of them up myself.'

There was no way I'd ever lower myself to those humiliating depths.

Maddy was still talking. Great friend that I am, I'd been tuning her out, until something she said caught my attention.

'And then after I left work last night, I was stuck going to a dinner party at my boss's house. It was a nightmare – all couples, and I didn't even have a date. I'd been planning to bring Harrison, and it was too late to get anyone else. Well, anyone I'd want to be seen with, anyway. And then tonight there's a restaurant launch party that I have to go to, so I can't seem to get a break,' she continued. 'I'd ask you to come, but it's an invite-only kind of a thing.' And then she sighed heavily, as though someone was forcing her to attend this whirlwind of glamorous events, when all she wanted to do was stay at home in her pajamas and eat her way through a tub of butter pecan ice cream.

What? Was she really saying that she'd made plans for tonight? After not seeing me for the past two days I'd been in London, now she wasn't even planning to get together with me on my last night there? All right, maybe I was being a bit fickle, since I too had made plans for the night, and had just been wondering how I would get out of spending it with her. But at least I'd made the effort. She'd just gone and made other plans, with no thought or consideration of me.

'God, I'm surprised you had time to see me at all,' I said tartly.

'Oh, please don't be mad,' Maddy said, smiling suddenly. She reached out and grabbed one of my hands. 'It's a work thing. I want to spend the evening with you, really I do, but my boss couldn't go to this thing tonight, so he's sending me in his place. I'd get out of it if I could, but I can't . . .'

She looked at me beseechingly, and I softened, feeling the anger leak out of me. Maddy could sometimes be a little clueless, but she did it with absolutely no malice, so it was impossible to stay mad at her. Besides, I'd just noticed that she had a picture of the two of us from our Mexican vacation posted on her refrigerator with a magnet, the same photo that I kept at my office. In it, we're both laughing and tan, and holding up massive margarita glasses in a toast. I tried without success to remember just what it was we were toasting, or who was taking the picture. Suddenly I realized how stupid and hypocritical it was to get annoyed at Maddy for being otherwise engaged that night.

'Don't worry. I'm just glad I got a chance to see you,' I said, squeezing her hand.

'Me too. Although I also had an ulterior motive in asking you to come over,' she said, looking bleak again. 'Harrison is coming by today to pick up some of his things. There's not much here, really – a few CDs that I borrowed, a DVD, a sweater. Nothing I thought he would even want, but he seemed eager to get them back. I didn't want to be alone when he got here. Will you stay and be my moral support?'

'Of course,' I said patting her hand. Then I raised my glass in a mock toast. 'To Harrison. Good riddance.'

Maddy did not toast with me. She just looked a little more miserable. Wow, she really does have it bad, I thought. She's not even up to joking about who needs men, and the whole fish-and-bicycle thing.

'No, it's not good at all,' Maddy said sadly. 'He's really wonderful. I just wish he loved me as much as I love him. In fact . . . when he said he had to talk to me the other night, I thought he was going to propose. Just like what happened with you and Sawyer!'

Her eyes filled with tears, and she collapsed against the table, resting her head on folded arms, her silky black hair pooling around her shoulders. I quickly stood and scooted around the table, so I could pat her back sympathetically while she sobbed quietly. Maddy usually has such an effervescent spirit, and it was strange to witness her falling apart. I hadn't seen her so upset since she lost her father, and even then she'd been so composed in her grief. Before I could think of something to say to cheer her up – knowing that there was nothing I could do to make her feel better – there was a sharp rap at the door.

'Oh God, it's Harrison. He's here early,' Maddy said, her head popping up so quickly, she hit it against my chin. The impact was hard, and my eyes stung as they filled with tears.

'Ow,' Maddy cried out, reaching for the top of her head, which, if the pain in my chin was any indication, probably hurt like hell.

'Oh . . . ouch,' I agreed, holding my chin in my hand, waiting for the radiating pain to subside. There was a second knock at the door.

'Oh . . . Claire, will you get it? I look horrible. Christ. I need to put some lip gloss on,' Maddy said, and she ran out of the room, leaving me little choice but to walk back through the frigid elegance of the flat to the front door and swing it open.

'Look, Maddy will be just a minute,' I said, before I was able to register who was standing there. When I did take him in, I gasped, and felt as though I'd been punched in the stomach, rather than the chin.

Standing there on the other side of the doorway was Jack. He looked as surprised to see me as I was to see him.

5

'What are you doing here?' I asked, gaping at Jack. My mind was racing as I considered the possibilities, which ran from the flattering (I was being stalked) to the scary (I was being stalked). How had he known to find me here? I suppose he would have had to follow me from the hotel, which was . . . well, actually, that would fall under the scary-stalking category. But Jack didn't look like a stalker . . . in fact he looked confused, squinting at me as if I were completely out of place.

'I might ask you the same thing. Is this supposed to be some kind of a joke?' Jack asked. He looked so grave, so serious, and there was no pleasure in his face as he considered me with bright, sharp eyes. Something about this careful appraisal made me uncomfortable, and I got the feeling that he was on edge, like a patient waiting to hear an unwanted diagnosis.

'Joke? What do you mean? You didn't know I'd be here?' I asked, now completely bewildered.

'Of course not. How would I?' Jack replied.

'Why are you here then?' I asked.

'To see Maddy.'

'What? How do you know Maddy?'

Jack sighed. 'Up until two days ago we were seeing each other,' he said. Suddenly the sharpness vanished from his voice and face, leaving him hollow-eyed and haggard.

I stared at him, not comprehending what he was saying. It was a lot like the sensation you must feel when you open your door and find Ed McMahon and the Publishers Clearing House Prize Patrol on the other side, holding a bunch of balloons and an enormous cardboard check made out in your name for ten million dollars . . . only the exact opposite, more like a reverse lottery, where winning means that you've lost and your tribe is about to stone you to death.

'You told me your name was Jack,' I whispered, wrapping my arms around my body. I felt cold and empty, as though someone had pricked me with a pin and all of the happiness and smug postcoital self-satisfaction I'd been feeling earlier had leaked out of me.

He nodded. 'It is. Jack Harrison,' he said.

Before I could interrogate him further, Maddy appeared at my elbow. I glanced down at her, wondering if she'd overheard any part of our conversation, but I didn't think she had. Instead, her face – now perfect again with the minor addition of mascara and lipstick – was hurt and brave and sad as she looked up at Jack. He towered over her, making Maddy appear even more delicate and petite. She was every bit the plucky heroine, ready to stand up and fight for her man.

'Harrison,' she said in a dignified voice. 'This is my friend Claire.'

Jack looked from Maddy to me, and despite my bewilderment at this bizarre turn of events, I couldn't help but cringe at knowing that when we stood there, side by side, it was all too easy to make the usual comparisons between us. Maddy – thin, beautiful, glamorous, dainty. Me – big, big, big. I wouldn't be surprised if pimples were popping out all over my face at just that moment, along with the scary braces and thick ugly glasses I'd worn as a teenager suddenly materializing.

Jack was Harrison. Harrison was Jack. And why the hell

did Maddy call him by his last name? Jack Harrison. What were the chances? One in a million? One in a billion? How could the great guy I randomly met on an airplane just happen to be my best friend's newly ex-boyfriend? There was only one answer, only one thing that made sense: I'd been wrong when I thought that there was no such thing as fate. Because fate did exist after all . . . and it was intent on screwing me over.

I wanted to scream, to kick someone, to hit something (expressing anger has never been an issue for me). Why did this always happen to me? Over and over and over again. This was what my life had come down to, these were the kinds of men I meet. Men who are witty and smart, but would never consider dating anything less than four women at the same time. Men who are accomplished, but are obsessed with their careers. Men who seem emotionally available, but turn out to be married.

I'd known for a while that my love life was not destined to be the subject of syrupy wedding toasts. The best I could hope for was to turn my hideous run-ins with the opposite sex into amusing anecdotes to be recounted at cocktail parties. This was the very reason I had stopped dating . . . or at least I had until I met Jack. But a single lapse, one toe barely dipped in the water, my hopes slightly raised that I'd met someone who was witty, smart, accomplished, and emotionally available, without any other obvious baggage to go along with it, and look what happened. He'd just broken up with my best friend.

But then, looking at Maddy, and seeing the pain radiating from her sad eyes and bravely set chin, I realized that as confused and angry and upset as I was, this wasn't something she could find out about. Having Harrison . . . I mean, Jack . . . break up with her had crushed her, had broken her heart. I'd never seen her so upset over a man – normally she was the one doing the breaking up, so even if she did worry about hurting a guy's feelings, she herself wasn't the one being rejected. How much worse would she feel if she found out that her best friend of nearly fifteen years had, less than six hours ago, been in bed with her ex? I shoved aside my frustration and disappointment, and made a rather rash decision.

'Claire Spencer,' I said, holding my hand out to Jack in a rather formal way.

He stared at me for a minute – I suppose considering what that very hand had been doing only a few hours earlier made a handshake seem farcical – but I widened my eyes, silently imploring him to play along. He hesitated for a long minute, looking back at me with inscrutable green-flecked eyes, not saying a word.

He's not going to play along, I thought unhappily.

'Nice to meet you, Claire,' he said, and shook my hand.

After that unpleasant episode, I escaped. I ran from the apartment, from them, like the coward I apparently was. I didn't even have to feel guilty about abandoning Maddy (which was fortunate, as I was already overcome with guilt at having slept with the man who'd just broken her heart). Shortly after Jack had entered her flat, Maddy had asked him if they could talk privately. He'd agreed, and she nodded at me, letting me know that she was not only okay to be on her own with him, but that she'd prefer it if I left. And so I made my getaway, barely throwing a good-bye over my shoulder as I hurried out.

I'd be lying if I said that the thought of perfect Maddy and perfect Jack sitting alone in Maddy's perfect apartment discussing their previously perfect relationship didn't make me a little jealous. It did. In fact, I was so overcome with jealousy, that I was – at the same time – hot, cold, nauseated, lightheaded, nerved up, depressed, not to mention hyperventilating, and so incredibly unhappy at the thought of the two of them alone together that I'm surprised I didn't literally turn an unflattering shade of pea green. Jack was supposed to be with me. *Me!* Not Maddy. For once, not Maddy.

Maddy's my friend, my *best* friend, and it wasn't her fault that she was achingly beautiful. It wasn't her fault that my clothes size runs to the double digits. It wasn't her fault that one time when we were out having drinks, a man actually shoved me into a garbage can in order to get closer to her (and to Maddy's credit, she was the one who pulled me out, before turning on the guy and assailing him with a tirade of salty four-letter invectives).

But at that moment I hated her. I hated her glossy black hair, her snub little nose, her charming laugh, and – most of all – how tiny she was. I hated her for how easily everything came to her, I hated her for her ridiculously glamorous job, for her effortlessly chic apartment, for her thriving social life.

And as for Jack . . . I knew he was too good to be true. I *knew* it. Only Jack wasn't a Chaser – oh no, I'd gotten that part totally wrong. Instead, this guy who had seemed so perfect for me, such an incredible fit in every way – so much so that I had actually (although I'm mortified to admit this) thought for a minute that maybe I was wrong about the whole love-at-first-sight thing being bullshit – turned out to be the love of my best friend's life.

Of course something like this would happen. This was me after all, cursed Claire, ungainly Claire, poor, loveless, miserable, never-an-instant-winner Claire. I'm not the girl that stars in the romantic comedy opposite Hugh Grant – I'm the one they get to play her plump, homely sidekick. And now the pretty star of the film was about to win back the handsome man of her dreams, and look where that left me. I was alone, walking the streets of London (and completely lost at that, as I had no idea where I was going, nor where I had just come from). And then, to make matters just that much worse, it started to rain. And not a little sprinkle to give a good atmospheric feel to my present mood. Instead, huge, fat raindrops, the size of golf balls, started pouring down like the world was gearing up for some kind of biblical flood.

'That's just perfect,' I said out loud, which garnered some strange looks from passersby – all of whom were, I noticed, equipped with umbrellas (or brollies, or whatever the hell they call the damned things over here). Unlike me. 'Just perfect.'

When I got back to my hotel, my hair was plastered to either side of my head, my wool coat was heavy and dripping a trail across the floor, and my über-hip Nikes made sloshy squishing sounds as I walked across the room. I caught sight of myself in the mirror – I looked like a drowned rat. I stripped out of everything, took a steaming hot shower, donned my favorite, ugly flannel pajamas, and – after raiding the minibar for a Toblerone and the world's smallest (and most expensive) bottle of white wine – nestled into bed, propping myself up against a couple of uncomfortable pillows. I only had a few more hours to get through, and then I would be on a plane back home, leaving this whole miserable mess behind.

I turned on the television and flipped through the channels. My choices were a political panel, a game show, and an old rerun of *The Simpsons*. I turned it off and just lay on the bed, staring up at the ceiling, which, I noticed for the first time, was badly in need of a coat of paint. A hairline crack cut a pattern across the yellowing plaster, although I looked at it for a long time before I realized what I was seeing. I wasn't really thinking about Jack and Maddy and me, although I wasn't really thinking of anything else. I was just feeling . . . miserable.

I tried to reason my way through it, hoping that a rational dissection of the situation would make everything seem less horrible. As for Maddy, unless Jack told her, there was no reason for her to know that he and I had slept together. And why would he tell her? Either they were going to stay broken up, in which case he wouldn't be talking to her anyway, or they would get back together. If they did end up together, he certainly wouldn't want to share our short, sordid history with her.

And as far as Jack and I went . . . well, that was as over as it could be. It was only meant to be a vacation fling after all, even if I had been perilously close to forgetting that, and surely there was no way that Jack would be able to refuse Maddy's pleas to give it another try.

But, then again . . . although Jack had dated Maddy, and was now talking to her about that relationship, he had also broken up with her. And then pursued me.

Of course, at the time he was choosing to do this, he hadn't seen me naked, or Maddy and I side by side. It wasn't too hard to imagine he was regretting his earlier choice. If I were him, I'd choose her over me, too. We lived on different continents, for one thing, and for another he was seriously out of my league. No, he wasn't classically handsome, but he was sexy and very successful. Guys like that don't have to be soap opera hunks to get the Maddys of the world.

The message light on the phone was blinking, which I'd been trying to ignore without much success. I doubted that it was Jack – surely if he was having a big talk with Maddy, he hadn't yet had time to call me, that is if he ever planned to call me again. And even if it was Jack, I wasn't yet ready to talk to him. I hadn't had time to compose what I was going to say, and I still needed some space and perspective, which would hopefully give me the strength to forget him.

When I couldn't stand the insistent blinking any longer,

I grabbed the receiver and punched the lit button. A well-honed BBC-type voice told me I had two messages. The first was from my boss, Robert. Double shit. And I'd thought he'd be too cheap to call me over here.

'Claire. Robert. I need to get a status check on the London story. We had an editorial meeting on Friday, and we're laying out a special issue on dream vacation destinations, and want to fit your London piece into it. Try to get a lot of material, because we'll want to draw this one out. Oh, and I wasn't happy with your piece on San Antonio. Let's meet early Monday to go over the changes.'

Oh God, I thought. I was screwed. I'd been so busy mooning over Jack and consoling Maddy that I hadn't finished looking at my original list of hotels and restaurants, and now, at the last minute, my creep of a boss was expanding the assignment! He hadn't even bothered to call and tell me about it on Friday, when he'd obviously known. I knew Robert hated me and had been itching to fire me – apparently he didn't think my sardonic, incisive prose fit in with a magazine whose focus was pepping up the country's seniors (and, to give him his due, he was probably right) – but to expect me to completely change the scope of the story at the last minute was too much, even for Robert. I'd be lucky if I could finish the original shorter travel piece – and to do so, I was going to have to get myself out of bed and back out into the London rain immediately, no matter how unpleasant the prospect seemed. But even if I did manage to see as much as I could over the next few hours, there was no way I was going to have time to expand my original list to include additional hotels and restaurants. I figured I could write up the sights I'd taken in on Friday with Jack, but it still wouldn't be enough to carry a full-length feature piece.

I was so busy panicking over the work crisis that I wasn't really paying attention to the second message when it started to play, and so was taken aback when I heard Jack's warm, slow voice in my ear.

'Claire, hi, it's me. Jack. Just wanted to see if we're still on for this afternoon. I have to go take care of something, so I'll call you when I'm back.' He paused, and I thought that was the end of the message, but then he continued on, sounding a little shy. 'I had a great time yesterday, and I'm really looking forward to tonight. Bye.'

The message service clocked the time of the message at one p.m. – he'd probably called just before he'd left for Maddy's apartment. Just before we'd had our unfortunate – and bizarre – run-in.

To my dismay, my stomach lurched at the sound of his voice.

'Forget about him,' I reminded myself. As if saying it aloud would make it happen.

I replaced the receiver on the phone, and it instantly started to ring. Knowing it was probably Robert again, calling to torture me, I picked up immediately.

'Hello,' I said, between chews of the Toblerone bar.

'Hi.'

I froze, the chocolate bar an inch away from my lips. It wasn't Robert after all . . . it was Jack. And I had absolutely no idea what to say to him. My insides, which only seconds earlier had been writhing with jealousy at the thought of him and Maddy together, had again turned to marshmallow fluff at the sound of his voice.

'Oh . . . hi. I just got your message,' I said stupidly, lowering my hand.

'I didn't know if you'd call back, so I thought I'd try you again,' he said.

'I couldn't call back. I don't have your phone number,' I pointed out.

'Didn't I leave it? I meant to,' he said, and then hesitated, perhaps waiting for me to respond. When I didn't, he continued. 'Why did you pretend like you and I had never met?'

Well, he's getting right to the point, I thought.

'For starters, Maddy has been my best friend forever. How do you think it would make her feel to know we . . .' I groped for the right word, 'um, slept together?'

'I think she's a grown-up and could handle the truth,' Jack said, thus demonstrating he lacked any insight whatsoever into the female heart.

'Oh, please. It would have devastated her. She thought you were going to propose to her the other night,' I said, and then immediately felt flooded with guilt. Maddy had told me that in confidence, and I didn't know if he was aware of her expectations.

This is why you don't sleep with your friend's ex, I thought grimly. It wasn't just the idea of your friend and your ex sleeping together that hurt, it was also that you knew they'd be sharing intimacies, and more to the point, talking about you. 'Oh, she's completely frigid, was never able to have an orgasm,' the ex might say, while the friend might agree, 'Mmm-hmm, she told me about that. I recommended that she try a vibrator. But, you know, she's always been uptight over that kind of thing.' It was the stuff that real mortification was made of.

Jack sighed. 'I'm very sorry that I hurt Maddy, and I do care about her. But I *never* said or did anything to make her think I wanted to marry her, and frankly, I'm amazed that she would think that, in light of . . . well, whatever. We only dated for six months, and even then, I've been traveling so much for work, that we rarely saw each other more than once a week.'

I considered this. 'Six months is a long time to continue dating someone you know you're not in love with,' I said.

'Haven't you ever done that? Continued to see someone you knew wasn't right for you, because he was a nice person, a decent person, and you were sick of going on bad dates?'

I bit my lip and examined my Toblerone. I knew exactly what Jack was talking about. I was a single, thirty-two-year-old woman after all – up until my recent moratorium I'd been dating for sixteen years (I was a late bloomer – it wasn't until the glasses were replaced by contacts, and the boys I'd been towering over finally had their growth spurts, that I saw any action). During that time, I'd been on my share of painfully bad dates, wondering all along, *Do my friends who set me up with these guys really think that a man who bathes in Polo cologne, wears a chunky gold bracelet, and neglects his nose hair is a good match for me?* So, yes, if I occasionally went out with a man who was able to chew with his mouth closed and hold an intelligent conversation, I might continue to see him even if he didn't get my insides humming.

'Please believe me, Claire. I wasn't using Maddy. I did like her – she's a great person in a lot of ways. But there was just never that spark between us,' Jack continued.

Aha! This was one of those Mars-Venus approaches to dating. Yes, I might have dinner again with someone I didn't click with, if he was nice enough and I'd enjoyed spending time with him. But unlike Jack and most men in the same position, I wouldn't sleep with someone I wasn't interested in. Dinner, yes. Sex, no.

Well, okay, there was that one time. His name was Peter something . . . damn, I totally blanked on his last name. There hadn't been that many guys in my past, shouldn't I be able to remember all of their names? In any event, Peter was an ungainly man with a weak chin, narrow shoulders, and a potbelly, and I didn't find him remotely attractive. But I was still licking my wounds after being dumped by the odious Sawyer, and Peter was sweet. Spending time with him was like a salve for my bruised ego. He was bright and witty and took me to interesting places – the symphony, the Museum of Modern Art, a weekend at his parents' picturesque weekend house in the Hudson Valley. We dated casually for a few months, and did sleep together during that time, although in order to get through the encounters, I tried not to think about the way his paunch rubbed against me, and instead closed my eyes and pretended he was Matt Damon. And when I started to get the feeling that he was eyeing me for something a bit more permanent (I think his taking me to meet his parents was the clue), I ended things with him as gently as I could. I felt like a shit for doing it, and for feeling relieved that I didn't have to sleep with him again.

It was completely different for men. In fact, it was probably the promise of a steady diet of sex with a supple beauty like Maddy that kept Jack around for as long as six months, even if he truly wasn't interested in her. A vivid picture of Maddy and Jack together suddenly began rolling in the cinema of my mind – her lithe, compact body straddling his long, lanky one, her head tossed back and breasts thrust forward, silky hair cascading down over creamily perfect skin, Jack's eyes wide with admiration and lust. I squeezed my eyes shut and gritted my teeth, trying to banish the unwanted imagery from my thoughts. Knowing that the two of them had been together made my mouth taste bitter, and I mentally catalogued all of my flabby bits and what they must have looked like to someone who was used to Maddy's sleek, nymphlike body.

'She thought there was,' I said, my tone more glacial than I meant it to be. After all, I could hardly be angry that a man I didn't even have an established relationship with now had slept with someone before he met me. Could I?

'I know. And as soon as I figured that out, I ended things with her. I never lied to her,' Jack said. He paused. 'Or to you.'

'It's just . . . this is just so . . . awkward. Maddy is an old, old friend, and she's already upset by your breakup. I don't want to add to that. And I don't like drama,' I said.

'I know it's all weird as hell. But I would like to see you again. We . . . you and I, I mean . . . I think that there's something there,' he said.

The rabid swarm of butterflies that had taken up residence in my stomach since meeting Jack began careening around again. Damn . . . I didn't know a man could still do that to me. I thought that when you got to a certain age you were immune to those nervous emotional flutterings. And this wasn't just any guy. It was Jack, also known as Maddy's dreamy, to-die-for Harrison (Why did she call him by his last name? Why?). For her sake, for the sake of girlfriendhood everywhere, the next words out of my mouth should have been, *I'm sorry, but I can't see you anymore*. Or maybe I should go into more detail and say, *You seem like a very nice man, and under different circumstances I might like to get to know you better, but if I continued to see you it would hurt someone who is very important to me, and I'm just not willing to do that*. Yes, that sounded good, particularly if I said it with a crisp finality that would put an end to any further discussion, and would leave Jack admiring me for my strong moral code. And when I started to speak, that's what I truly meant to say.

But this is what actually came out of mouth:

'Are you doing anything now?'

G uilt. Guilt. Guilt.

It blared like an out-of-control car alarm in my head, and as I huddled miserably in my pitifully small airline seat, I looked around furtively to see if any of my fellow travelers on the New York-bound flight could sense the sins that I'd committed. If they could, I was sure they would all be glaring at me and pelting me with the remains of their pitiful box lunches (and how is it possible that the airlines could make a ham-and-Swiss on rye taste like something that doesn't even remotely resemble ham, Swiss cheese, or rye bread?).

I am a bad person, I thought. *A horrible, terrible, bad person who deserves every awful thing that will ever happen to me in the future.*

Jack had indeed come over the night before, and had taken me out to dinner again – this time to a swank French restaurant. Over dinner we talked quietly, uncovering a little more of our lives for the other to peek at. I talked about my parents' divorce, and how they'd conducted it in the manner of a Mafia-style blood vendetta, bickering over every last measly possession they'd acquired over the course of their twenty-five-year marriage, right down to the worn, otherwise worthless table linens. It was a battle their attorneys happily suited up for, considering each charged three hundred dollars per hour.

'So those crap place mats, which cost all of ten dollars in 1984, and which no one ever really liked in the first place, ended up costing about twelve hundred dollars in legal fees,' I said, shaking my head, still amazed by this a decade later. 'No offense, but your profession is the pits.'

Jack smiled. 'So who won?'

'What?'

'Who got the place mats?'

'Dad. And the napkins. Mom got the pots and pans, and the everyday dishes. She turned around and sold all of it at a garage sale,' I replied.

'You're still angry about it?' Jack asked.

I shrugged and then shook my head. 'No. I was, but you know, I got over it. I was in college at the time, and wasn't around for the worst of the fighting. My little sister didn't get off so easily – she was still at home, in high school.'

'Are you close? You and your sister, I mean.'

I shook my head again. 'Not really. She ended up going to UCLA for college, just to put as much distance between her and our parents as possible. And I think – although she'd never admit it to me – that she's anorexic or bulimic or both. She started to get really weird about food at about the same time our parents separated. How about you? Any brothers or sisters?'

'A half sister on my mom's side, and a half brother and two half sisters on my dad's, all younger,' Jack said. 'My parents cashed in their chips when I was a baby, so I don't have any memory of them being together.'

'Was it a bad split?'

'I'm not really sure. It might have been at first, but they both moved on, and both remarried. Still, it isn't the same,' he said, looking wistful. 'Even though we all get along, we don't see one another all that frequently. My dad and I keep in touch, and my mom occasionally, but everyone has pretty much gone their own separate ways. It hasn't been a real family for a long time.'

We didn't speak of Maddy or of Jack's relationship with her, or any of the women Jack had dated. He implied that there hadn't been anyone all that serious, which did raise a flag of caution, since most guys in their late thirties who seem to have everything going for them usually have at least one ex-wife or live-in girlfriend or fiancée in their past. But I couldn't press him too much without being forced to cough up the same information on myself, and I didn't want to do that. I was afraid that if he heard about my bleak romantic history, it would cause him to rear up and gallop away, like a horse running from a burning stable.

After dinner, I fully intended to break out my speech about how I couldn't see him again – I was sure it wouldn't come as too much of a shock, since I was leaving the country the next day. But I couldn't seem to find a good time to broach the subject – not as he placed his hand on my lower back as we walked out of the restaurant, nor as I fell against him when I tripped over the last step on the way out and he caught me against him, nor as he held my hand to help me into the car. And then, on the ride back to the hotel, Jack lightly touched the back of my neck, an entirely innocent caress that had the not-so-innocent effect of melting my entire body. The next thing I knew, we were kissing, and pulling at each other's clothing, all the while generally oblivious to the driver sitting two feet away. When we arrived at the hotel, we tumbled out of the car, my makeup smeared and Jack's shirt untucked from his pants, and sprinted for the elevator. As soon as the doors closed – we were, thankfully, alone – Jack pulled me to him again, his thumb grazing my nipple through the thin cotton of my sweater, and had I known how to stop the elevator, we would have had sex right then and there, just like Michael Douglas and Glenn Close in *Fatal Attraction* (minus the psychotic bunny boiling, obviously). We finally got back to the blessed privacy of my room and fell on each other like a couple of horny teenagers.

Jack spent the night, cuddling me in his arms while I slept. It had never been that way, not that I could remember. Everyone always talks about how crappy monogamy is, and that it goes against human nature to expect anyone to be with just one person for the rest of her life. But in my experience, quality trumps quantity, and developing a routine with one partner, who knows without being told just where to touch, and how much pressure to use, is vastly more pleasurable than the novelty of a new, and usually fumbling, partner. But not so with Jack. He apparently came preprogrammed with the knowledge of all of my erogenous zones, and intuitively knew how and where to touch me so that my insides would rise and explode and rise again.

My reverie was broken by a sharp hacking noise, followed by a throat-clearing slurp and then some more hacking. In karmic retribution for my sins, instead of sitting next to another Jack on the flight back, this time I was stuck next to a repulsive man who smelled as though he hadn't taken a shower in the past calendar year. His hair was greasy, his ears were waxy, and he kept coughing something up into his handkerchief. I prayed that it was just a disgusting habit, and that he wasn't infecting me with the Norwalk virus.

Since it was impossible to daydream about making love while being interrupted by this disgusting display of phlegm removal, I allowed my guilt over Maddy to seep back in. She had called me shortly before Jack arrived to pick me up for dinner, and with fresh tears, had told me that it was truly over between them. He'd made it clear to her that he didn't want to get back together, and – being a complete shit of a would-be friend – I actually breathed a sigh of relief when I heard about how final he'd been on the subject. Despite what Jack had told me, I'd been harboring a worry that they might have reconciled, and sealed their reunion by copulating on her fuzzy white sheepdog rug.

'I tried everything. I tried talking things out with him, I tried asking for a second chance. But he was very firm, and just kept saying that this was for the best,' Maddy said fretfully, her voice jagged with sorrow.

'Was he rude about it?' I asked.

'No, not at all. He was very nice . . . he is very nice, nicer than any man I've ever been out with. So why does he have to be such an asshole?' Maddy sobbed. 'Why can't he feel about me the way I do about him?'

We went through a few more versions of this, during which I did my best to soothe Maddy and tell her all of the usual crap you feed friends in these situations: that it was Jack's loss, that there were plenty more men out there, better men, nicer men, and (once again) good riddance to him.

But as I comforted her, I felt like a fraud. No, it was worse than that. I was duplicitous, dishonest, and selfish, the lowest of the low. Because even though I'm sure I sounded like the same old reliable, loyal Claire to Maddy, that mean little part of me – the same ugly voice that had warned me about inviting Maddy to join Jack and me for dinner – was now whispering with vindictive glee over Jack having chosen me.

There was one thing about this mess that was certainly clear – I was going straight to hell.

And if it wasn't bad enough that I had betrayed my best friend (and therefore the entire institution of girlfriend-hood), I'd been so caught up in all of the goings on, I'd completely forgotten to finish my restaurant and hotel investigations. I'd spent three days in London, and during that time I'd managed to find only three hotels, a sandwich shop, and a pizzeria to recommend to my readers. I had no choice – I was going to have to include the pricey Indian and French restaurants where Jack and I had eaten, but doing so was just asking for the wrath of my editor. Even if I flat-out lied about the prices of the entrées, they were the entirely wrong sort of restaurant – too voguish and swank and ethnic, not traditional places that served staid favorites like roast beef and potatoes. I didn't even have a good fish-and-chips shop to recommend. Robert was going to kill me, and unless I found a travel guide to do some major cribbing out of, he'd probably fire me, too.

The thought of losing my job, and the devastating free fall that would result – humiliation, bankruptcy, ruination – caused my anxiety to spike. Panic seized me – my heart began pounding, my chest tightened, my breath came in shallow uneven puffs. I gripped the two hand rests, unintentionally knocking Phlegm Man's arm off of the one we shared.

'Sorry,' I muttered, trying not to hyperventilate.

'A nervous flyer, are you? Don't worry, we're as safe as can be. Except for that Pan Am explosion over Lockerbie a few years back, there's been very few mishaps on the London-to-New York flight,' he said unhelpfully, and then hocked up another hunk of spit.

Ugh! I hadn't even been thinking about plane crashes or terrorist attacks, but now, thanks to Mr Disgusting, that too was playing on my nerves.

I tried to focus back on Jack again, as he seemed to be the only subject I could think about without falling into a shame spiral or having a panic attack. Although that wasn't quite true . . . there was something about Jack that was bothering me, too.

In the short time I'd spent with Jack, it hadn't occurred to me that he and Harrison were the same person. But then, I really didn't know much about Maddy's Harrison. She had told me that he was an attorney, but there are zillions of lawyers in London. Besides, I'd never seen a photo of him, and for some reason, Maddy hadn't told me that he was American – so I'd just assumed he was British (he lived in London, after all) – or that his first name was Jack. I knew she had a tendency to be a flibbertigibbet, and that she had a habit of glossing over the details, but *come on*. If you really want to keep your friends from falling into bed with your boyfriend – *ex*-boyfriend – then you shouldn't omit such crucial details.

But – and here was the part that worried me – how did Jack not recognize *me*? Surely Maddy had talked about me, told him about her old friend Claire who worked as a travel writer for a senior citizens' magazine. My job was just unusual enough that someone who'd been told about it was certain to remember. And on top of that, Maddy had a photo of us posted on her stainless-steel refrigerator door. It was the only thing on the fridge, so if Jack had spent any time at her place at all, he must have seen it.

The night before, while we were lying in bed, both of us propped up on our sides so that we were facing each other, I couldn't help but bring it up. Well, actually, that's not true. Jack had been tracing his finger first down and then up the side of my body, and although his movements were slow and lazy, it was having much the opposite effect on my body. It was taking all of my willpower not to throw myself at him, like a quarterback tackling a goalie (or whatever it is that happens in football – it's not like I ever watch the stupid game), much less find a tactful yet direct way to ask Jack if he'd been lying about not knowing that Maddy and I were friends. I had no reason to think that he was lying, but I still found it strange that he hadn't heard of me. I forced myself to ignore (for the moment) the way his fingertips were meandering over the mound of my hip, into the hollow of my waist, and then – oh God – over the soft, tender flesh of the side of my breast. I could feel my self-control slipping –

if I didn't speak now, in about ten seconds it would be too late.

'I need to ask you something,' I said, my voice sounding hoarser than usual.

'Okay,' Jack said, smiling.

I grabbed his hand, which had tired of the side of my breast and was heading downward again. 'I can't talk to you when you're doing that,' I said.

'Oh, no?' The grin grew wider, lazier.

'Come on,' I said.

Jack lifted his hand off of my side and used it to brush a stray piece of hair out of my face, and said, 'Talk.'

'I was wondering . . . I mean, I just wanted to know,' I said, and then took a deep breath. Was there a way to ask this without sounding like I was accusing him of lying? He was still smiling, still looking at me as though he couldn't *wait* to hear what I was about to say.

'Just say it,' Jack said. And then a wicked glint appeared in his eyes. 'Or, if you'd rather, we could get back to what we were doing.'

I swear, I was turning into Pavlov's dog. Only instead of a bell, at the smallest hint of a suggestion from Jack, and *bing*, every last millimeter of my skin was on high alert waiting for his touch. I've never even been all that interested in sex. Sure, it can be okay, but when all was said and done, I'd just as soon spend the time taking a hot bath while drinking a glass of red wine and reading a magazine. Plus, I've never been all that big a fan of the sweaty, sticky, soreness-afterward part of it. But after the past two nights I'd spent with Jack, I was starting to figure out what all of the fuss was about. Bad sex is horrible, okay sex is usually not worth the effort of undressing before and showering after . . . but great sex, the kind Jack and I were having, was an entirely different story. I wanted to completely immerse myself in touching and exploring and tasting him, never to reemerge. To discover every spot on his body that caused him to . . .

Stop that. You need to focus, I told myself sternly.

'How did you not know who I am?' I blurted out.

Jack looked puzzled, his eyebrows knit. 'What do you mean? Are you famous?'

'No,' I said, laughing, and smacked him lightly on the arm. 'I mean, didn't Maddy ever talk about me?'

'Sure. She mentioned your name a few times, and may have even told me that you were a writer. But there must be a lot of writers out there named Claire, so it wouldn't have occurred to me that you were one and the same,' he said, sounding very plausible.

'She didn't tell you I was a travel writer?' I asked, surprised when he shook his head. After all, I often mentioned Maddy in the everyday course of my life. I told people where she was living and what she did (mainly because no one can ever believe that anyone could make a living by writing reports on the favored footwear of high school girls), and I'd assumed she'd also tell the people in her life about me.

'But you must have seen my picture. Maddy had one on her refrigerator, one of the two of us in Cancún,' I protested.

Jack was shaking his head again. 'She never had anything up on her refrigerator, not that I saw. In fact, I don't think I ever saw any pictures in her apartment – she has that cold, sterile, minimalist thing going,' he said.

I stared at him. He was right – Maddy didn't have *anything* in her apartment that wasn't part of the decor plan. She'd always been like that, had always hated knickknackery of any kind. She was the only girl at college who didn't have unframed posters tacked to her walls, and two dozen photos of high school friends and boyfriends in cheap plastic frames scattered about. It was one of the reasons we were a near-disaster as roommates – I was a pack rat, and my habit of keeping my living space more like a bird's nest, with all of my favorite bits out around me, had driven her crazy. Part of why I'd been so touched to see the photo of us up on her fridge was because it was so unlike her, her one small homage to sentimentality in an otherwise style-smoothed world, thus proving how truly fond of me she still was. So if Jack was telling the truth – and really, why wouldn't he be? – then Maddy must have put that picture up only because she knew I was coming over, probably to humor me. What was she afraid of, that if she didn't placate me like a small child, offering tangible proof that we were still friends, I'd stamp my feet and cry? The thought irritated me beyond all reason.

'Why are you scowling like that?' Jack asked, laughing as he touched my pouting lips.

'Nothing,' I muttered. Despite my annoyance with Maddy, I couldn't very well start complaining about her to Jack. Although, I thought with another twinge of guilt, perhaps it was just a wee bit hypocritical of me to worry about bitching behind my friend's back to her ex while I was lying naked next to him in bed.

But then Jack replaced the finger with his lips, and we were kissing again, and pretty soon I wasn't thinking of anything at all.

'Hack, hack, hack,' coughed the Phlegm Man, again interrupting me from my reverie.

I twisted miserably in my seat and looked out at the blue nothingness of the sky. I had come to London hoping for some fun sightseeing and quality time with my oldest friend. I left with my job and friendship in jeopardy, and a painfully unreasonable crush.

This isn't going to end well, I thought, and felt a shiver of unease.

7

Going into work the next day was a nightmare. The start of the workweek always fills me with dread, but today it was made worse by the knowledge that I was going to have to face the Inquisition completely unprepared and with maybe half of the research completed for my London column. I was planning to supplement my research with a London tourist guide (and yes, I was aware that this wasn't a strictly ethical thing to do, but it wasn't like I was going to plagiarize, just crib some basic information). However, my feeble attempt at tracking a guide down had failed – the book kiosk at LaGuardia didn't have one in stock, and by the time I got home from the airport it was too late to trek out to my local Barnes & Noble. I prayed that in the meantime Robert wouldn't ask me to go into the details of my research at our meeting that morning.

It also didn't help my mood that I really wasn't up to facing my co-workers. They're mostly much older than I – the magazine, after all, is a senior-interest rag – but the differences seem greater than just years. I'm a Gen Xer, part of a generation known for our apathy, sarcasm, and devotion to the pop culture of the eighties. My aging-boomer-or-older office mates veer to the opposite extreme, oozing with the kind of over-the-top optimism that makes me wonder where they've been for the past thirty years. It's oddly disconcerting. I'm never quite sure how to react when they sing out 'Happy Monday' to anyone who risks eye contact or insist on sharing the daily joke from their knock-knock-joke-a-day calendar.

I don't dislike everyone, of course. Helen, a peppy sixty-two-year-old, could be hysterically funny. She writes adventure articles, and for research is always off doing something cool, like kayaking, hang gliding, or attending grandparent-grandkid camp in the Cascade Mountains. I also got along pretty well with Olivia, the food editor, who has ageless skin the color of milky coffee, and if it weren't for her wiry gray curls, it would be impossible to tell if she was forty-five or sixty-five. But as both are grandmothers, with seemingly dozens of children and grandchildren apiece, they're not exactly women I can take long gossipy lunches with. Besides, I hate eating with Olivia – her specialty is transforming high-fat, high-calorie entrées into lighter versions, and she knows, and frequently announces, the nutritional content of every bite you put in your mouth. She also has an annoying habit of lecturing anyone who tries to butter a slice of bread or order a soft drink.

I dumped my purse and coat in my gray-walled cubicle – which, after the payroll tax, may be the corporate world's most depressing invention – and made my way to Robert's office, telling myself that no matter what he said, I would not lose my temper. Between my botched research in London and whatever it was that Robert didn't like about my San Antonio piece, I was on thin enough ice as it was.

I liked to think that Robert hated me because of my youth, beauty, and talent (and not necessarily in that order), but I think it had more to do with the fact that he doesn't think I respect his authority (and on that point, and that point alone, he was absolutely correct – I also don't respect his editorial vision, his tightfisted approach to the year-end bonuses, or his tendency to wear the same pair of pants day after day). Lately he'd been particularly irritated at me, because while he was out of town for his summer vacation, I sneaked one of my rants (one on New Orleans, and the apparent disaster-level shortages of antiperspirant available to the populace) past the associate editor, assuring her that Robert had already approved the text. This was, of course, a bald-faced lie, and as a result, I'd dropped even further from his good graces. I don't know why he would object – there were already a ton of articles and books out there listing the usual places to hear jazz in the French Quarter, or revealing the restaurants that are obvious tourist traps, but who else was going to warn you about the unpleasant smell? No one, that's who. So at least I was original, and if the tone of my prose was a bit tart, a bit snarky, I say it made it all the more interesting. And it was futile to point out the pile of fan mail I'd gotten from the piece – it turns out that some of our readers have wickedly keen senses of humor and appreciated my sharp wit. Myopic Robert would just fix me with a dour stare and produce letters of his own – all from prissy old biddies lecturing me on my lack of manners.

I knocked tentatively on the glass pane of his door.

'Come!' he called out imperiously. I rolled my eyes and pushed open the door.

'You wanted to see me?' I said with as much crisp efficiency as I could muster up so early on a Monday morning.

Robert grunted, and turned his back on me to start shuffling through a stack of papers sitting on his battered old credenza. Knowing I wasn't likely to be extended an invitation, I plopped down into one of the visitor chairs, and peered disdainfully around at his sad collection of macramé plant holders and cheap ceramics. Robert had graduated a few years before the hippie movement took over the college campuses, and apparently he so deeply regretted missing out on participating in the counterculture that he was eager to recapture those lost days. His hair was too long, his politics were leftist and reactionary, and he was still carrying a grudge against Richard Nixon thirty years after the man had resigned the presidency. When I really wanted to annoy him, I'd chirp, 'Well, only Nixon could go to China' – and not necessarily in the context of what we were talking about, either. It never failed to cause Robert to turn purple and start ranting about the evils of the Nixon administration, which then led to a tirade on how unjust he thought the Vietnam War was, and how he marched in three – *three*, he would proudly bellow, holding up his three middle fingers, thumb and pinkie folded back against his palm as though he were about to take a scouting oath – protests against the war. It was fun to provoke him.

He'd found what he was looking for – the draft of my San Antonio column that I'd handed in the previous week. He wheeled around to face me, holding the paper out between two of his fingers as though it pained him to touch it. True to form, it was dripping with red ink, every other word slashed out. I looked at the murdered article with dismay, trying to fight my growing irritation.

'I'm afraid what you turned in just wasn't acceptable,' Robert said, pulling a face that was supposed to communicate his stern disapproval, but which actually came off as a supercilious smirk.

'What exactly was the problem with it?' I asked patiently, crossing my legs and folding my hands on top of them. I knew getting argumentative with him wouldn't work – I'd tried it many times before without success.

'Well, let me see,' Robert said, grabbing the pages back, eager to point out my deficiencies. He put on his bifocals and rustled the papers. 'Well, here. Was it necessary to go into how your taxicab driver erupted into road rage when the woman in front of him stopped at a crosswalk?'

'Why not? It was the most exciting thing that happened to me while I was there. And don't you think seniors would be interested in the behavior of the local cab drivers?'

Robert ignored me for a minute. He'd found something else he didn't like in the column and was slashing through it anew with a fat red marker. I noticed that he was wearing a large peace symbol dangling from a ratty leather cord tied around his neck.

'I doubt it,' he finally said. 'I also doubt they'd be interested in your suggestion that "all drivers in the state of Texas be issued Prozac with their driver's license." And here, where you said the chili you had for dinner "made you gassier than a helium-filled balloon" – that's just crass.'

'I think our readership would appreciate a warning to steer clear of that restaurant. If it gave me gas, what do you think it would do to a seventy-year-old man?' I asked.

'And this entire section on how the boat ride down the Riverwalk is, and I quote, "the single lamest farce of an attraction ever to be perpetrated on tourists anywhere. The artificial canal looks and smells as though it were filled with recycled brine, and the only thing to see from your uncomfortable plastic seat is an array of overpriced, unexceptional chain restaurants."'

'That's all true,' I exclaimed. 'Have you ever been there? I can't believe they try to pass it off as a tourist attraction. I did say nice things about the Alamo, and a few of the restaurants I reviewed were decent,' I said.

'If I published this, the San Antonio tourist council would sue us the next day for libel,' he said. And before I could protest how ridiculous this assertion was – *libel*, give me a break – he raised his voice, apparently so I would know he meant business. 'Rewrite that, and then get to work on the London piece. I hope you found more to recommend there than you did in this,' he said, flicking his finger at my San Antonio column with distaste.

I scowled, and felt crabbier than ever as I shuffled out of his office. Maybe he wasn't entirely wrong – the piece had been peppered with sarcasm – but wasn't that more interesting than just another puff piece that sounded like it had been written by the city's Chamber of Commerce?

It had always been my dream to have my own column. But in that dream I'd seen myself at someplace . . . well, someplace with a pulse. Someplace where a little more attention was paid to art exhibits and new restaurants helmed by celebrity chefs, and a little less to which brand of meal-replacement shake tasted the best. Maybe my attitude sounds ageist, but I'm really not an age bigot. I'm just not all that passionate about issues facing today's seniors, which may have something to do with the fact that I'm thirty-two, single, and childless, and so don't really want to spend the majority of my waking hours focusing on menopause, long-term care facilities for married couples, or how to talk to your grandchildren.

I looked up from my overedited column to see an alarming apparition of gray hair, powdered skin, and stretch polyester blocking my way.

'Hello, Claire. Why are you looking so glum? Don't tell me – you have a case of the Mondays,' she cackled. It was Barbara Downs, Robert's busybody of a secretary. I looked around, hoping there was a large plant I could hide behind, but before I could escape she'd clamped down on my wrist with a surprisingly firm grip.

'I'm glad I found you, dear. We're planning Doris's birthday party this Friday, and everyone's bringing something in. You're the only one who isn't signed up,' she said, dragging me to her desk, parked right outside Robert's door, from which she could monitor all of the comings and goings of the office.

'Um, okay,' I said, although I positively *hate* office parties. As if it weren't bad enough that I had to work with these people, the dreary little birthday celebrations meant I had to socialize with them, too. I glanced down at the list and noticed that the only open slot on her sign-up form was for the sheet cake.

'I don't understand – you want me to buy the whole cake?' I asked incredulously.

'Well, as you can see, you're the last one to sign up, dear,' Barbara said slyly.

'Wait . . . there are three, no, *four* people splitting the duty of bringing in paper napkins, and I'm solely responsible for a forty-dollar sheet cake?' I said.

Barbara was still smiling. She seemed to think that she'd pulled one over on me, but between my jet lag, my run-in with Robert, and the whole Jack-Maddy situation, I lacked my usual patience (which, to be honest, wasn't normally all that high to begin with).

'No,' I said calmly, handing the paper back to her.

She gaped at me as though I had refused to accept the Congressional Medal of Honor.

'What do you mean, "no"? Everyone's bringing something.'

'Everyone else is bringing in a bag of chips or a bottle of soda, and I'm supposed to front the entire cost of the cake? That's ridiculous. I won't do it,' I said.

'It's only fair. It was first-come, first-served on signing up, after all. And if you're not going to chip in, I'm afraid you can't attend the party,' she concluded sadly, as if this would be some great loss for me.

'I totally understand. And actually, it all works out for the best. I'm so overloaded right now, I really can't afford to take the time off for the party anyway,' I said, turning on my heel, feeling victorious at the lemon-sucking expression on Babs's face I'd caught before I strode away.

Of course, I knew Barbara the Mouth would be spreading our tiff around the office in no time – doubtlessly editing out the part where she'd tried to manipulate me into bearing the largest cost of the party supplies. Not that anyone would find this unfair – I'm sure they would all welcome the attempt to foist the cake-buying on me. I already took enough crap from my co-workers about the amount of money I spend on shoes and haircuts, as if it's any business of theirs (and as though going down to Supercuts and paying ten dollars for a hairstyle that looks like the wig Vicki Lawrence wore in *Mama's Family* is something to be proud of). But for once, I didn't care . . . I'd managed to wriggle my way out of the obnoxious party, and pissed Barbara off in the process. Happy day.

I've worked in places where everyone is young and full of energy, the kind of offices that have open floor plans and funky office furniture from Herman Miller, and on any given day there are a half dozen people eager to go out to lunch, or grab a drink after work, and the place practically shimmers with the energy and enthusiasm of youthful vigor. The office intrigue usually swirls around who slept with whom, and whether or not the guy in accounting was still coked up when he came into work that day. Yes, sometimes the constant drama could get old, but at least it made the day interesting.

At *Sassy Seniors* the only excitement that was ever stirred up was when someone put a dirty coffee cup in the office kitchen sink instead of immediately rinsing it out and placing it in the dishwasher, thus disobeying the hand-written note taped up over the sink: *Your Mother Doesn't Work Here! If You Use a Dish, Wash It!* I'm not kidding – people go ballistic over one slightly used mug sitting in the sink for ten minutes. Peggy, the office manager, and quite possibly the most condescending person who has ever lived – she talks in the fakey-sweet tone of an elementary school principal and has the supercilious habit of peering down at people over her bifocals – had been known to take the offending coffee cup and traipse up and down the hall with it, interrupting everyone hard at work to interrogate them on whether they were the culprit. And even though I was usually the guilty party, I only did it because I figured it would just be easier to rinse out my dishes at the end of the day (although to be honest, I rarely remembered), but now I just did it to piss Peggy off, as she was the worst of the office group – officious, bossy, and a complete tattletale. And on top of that, with her ultra-blue eyes, pale skin, and thin lips, she had a Germanic appearance that became faintly sinister when you pictured her as a matron of the Third Reich, as I frequently did.

As I dragged myself home from work, I was fantasizing about a hot bath and twelve hours of sleep, but when I got to my apartment, Max, my next-door neighbor, was playing his favorite Elvis CD at a wall-shaking, earsplitting volume. Still wearing my pea coat, with my work tote slung over my shoulder, I banged on his door until he answered.

When the door opened, and his impish, smiling face appeared, I said, 'Don't tell me. Elvis is actually in your apartment, putting on a live concert.'

'I wish,' Max said, hugging me.

We had met the day I moved in two years earlier – I found Max in the hall, shamelessly rifling through the box containing my DVD collection – and we had been friends ever since. A lot of people think Max is gay, probably because he's a fashion photographer, and he's small and thin and tends to be manic, and he uses an ill-advised amount of gel in his short, dark hair to keep it spiked up all over his head. But he's actually as straight as an arrow, and completely unapologetic for his rather flamboyant personality. His long-suffering girlfriend, Daphne – an ethereal massage therapist whose pale, milky skin and red Raphael curls make her look like she should be headlining Lilith Fair – worships him. She's one of those New Agey, vegan types, but not in an aggressive, in-your-face way; in fact, she's remarkably down-to-earth, and I looked for her as Max let me into his apartment.

'Is Daphne here?' I asked.

'No. She had a late booking, and then was going to have her tarot cards read,' he said, rolling his eyes. 'I'm sure they'll tell her she's destined to marry a sex machine whose name begins with an M. I don't know how much longer I can put her off. Yesterday she left the Tiffany's catalogue on my table, after circling all of the engagement rings with a Sharpie marker.'

'Tiffany's? Really? I'd have thought they were too corporate for her. I see her as the vintage, estate-jewelry type,' I said.

I tried very hard not to think about the Tiffany-ring-box fantasies I'd indulged in while dating Sawyer. Nothing feels quite as foolish as being a marriage-obsessed single woman – it evokes memories of the chicken that stalked Foghorn Leghorn while screeching 'Ah need a ma-an!'

'Apparently, when it comes to diamonds, Daphne's a corporate gal,' Max replied.

Max's apartment is literally four times the size of my little hovel, which was the only reason Max has stayed at our scruffy building, since, unlike me, he could certainly afford a more stylish address. It's stuffed to capacity with midcentury modern furniture, including a Saarinen 'tulip' table, a Knoll credenza, and his prize possession: a vintage leather Eames lounge chair and ottoman. I settled in on his armless sofa as he turned Elvis off.

'So?' I asked.

'So what?'

'When are you going to pop the question?' I teased him.

Max rolled his eyes heavenward and shook his head. This was a running joke between us. Max claimed to be a commitment-phobe, but I knew he loved Daphne. If she ever put her foot down and issued the clichéd ultimatum, he'd come groveling, Tiffany box in hand.

'So, tell, tell, how was London?'

'Complicated,' I said. Max – bless his heart – fetched a glass of red wine for me. 'Mmmm, this is just what I wanted. It's freezing out tonight.'

'Is it still raining?'

'No, was it earlier? I wouldn't know, it's not like my cubicle has any windows,' I said, pulling a face. This was not an uncommon pattern for us. We'd have a glass of wine together, sometimes just the two of us, sometimes with Daphne, during which I'd complain about my job, and Max would entertain me with funny stories about how bitchy the fashion models are. I never tire of hearing that the genetically blessed human clothes hangers are drug addicts or kleptomaniacs or that they can't talk without using the word 'like' as a noun, verb, and adjective in every sentence: 'Yeah, like his new collection, like, is like totally, like you know, like hot.'

'So, I'm intrigued. How was your trip complicated? Did you meet a tall, dark Brit who wanted you to dress up in a riding habit and hit him with a crop?' Max asked, leering comically.

Max has a rather blunt sense of humor that a lot of people take offense at, but which I find hilarious. He's very fond of saying 'What? I just say what everyone else is thinking.'

'No, not even close. Well, you're close on the man part, but not the riding paraphernalia,' I admitted.

I told him about meeting Jack and our incredible dates and then finding out he was Maddy's ex-boyfriend. I didn't go into the details of our lovemaking – I don't believe in kissing and telling, particularly to Max, who would immediately start making vulgar jokes at my expense.

Max whistled. 'Sounds like a good time was had by all. So why the long face?'

'What do you mean? What I did was horrible! Maddy's my friend, and I went out with the guy who had just broken her heart,' I protested.

Max made a face. He hadn't liked Maddy the one time he'd met her, at the birthday party Maddy had organized for me at Calle Ocho. Max can be a bit of a prima donna, and he was put off by what he saw as Maddy swanning in and taking over. Maddy was perplexed by Max – she didn't really get his sense of humor, and thought he was laughing at her, which he was, just not in a mean way. It was actually his attempt to be friendly. And Maddy didn't help matters by constantly referring to Max as 'your gay friend who isn't really gay.'

'So, no harm done. She'll never know. And it's not like she wouldn't do it to you if it was the other way around,' Max said.

'No, she wouldn't,' I protested, but he just rolled his eyes.

'You're prejudiced, you've never liked Maddy,' I said.

'You're right. At your birthday party, she insisted on being the center of attention. As soon as the conversation stopped being about her, she'd pout. And I can't stand that Daddy's Little Girl routine. I get enough of that at work,' he said.

'You're completely exaggerating. Maddy just likes to be in the middle of things, she always has. I don't know why the two of you can't get along – you're worse than my parents,' I said, but Max just snorted.

'Okay, so she's a peach, but I still don't see what you're worried about. It's not like she's going to find out what you were up to, unless Mr Sexy Brit Man tells her,' Max said.

'He's not British, he's American. And I don't think he would tell her,' I said, and then bit my lip. Because the only other way Maddy would ever find out was if Jack and I continued to see each other. This was implausible at best.

And yet . . . there was a tiny flower of hope blooming in my cynical heart. Jack had asked for my phone number, as well as my work number, fax number, and my e-mail address, and he'd carefully written all of his contact numbers down for me. He promised up and down that he'd call me – and not in a disingenuous way, but with real enthusiasm. It was . . . convincing. Max saw through me immediately.

'Oh, I can't believe you,' he said, shaking his head with disgust. 'No wonder you can't find a boyfriend. You have a thousand little nitpicky rules about who you will and will not date, and end up disqualifying 99.9 percent of all men everywhere, and then you go and fall for some guy that you're never going to see again. It's pathological.'

'I didn't fall for him,' I protested weakly.

'Yeah, right. You went and found yourself the world's Most Unavailable Man – he lives in a foreign country *and* used to date your best friend, and so there's no chance that the relationship will ever go anywhere, and that's who you fall in love with,' he ranted. He drained the rest of his wine, refilled his glass, and then offered the bottle to me. I waved him off – one glass of wine was my limit on weeknights.

'God, who said anything about love? And I know I'm not going to see him again, I'm not an idiot,' I said, but then completely undermined my credibility by blushing bright red.

Max grabbed my hand and squeezed it affectionately. He was very physical, the kind of person who was forever rubbing your shoulder or hugging you.

'I never said you were an idiot,' he said. 'Quite the opposite. I just wish you wouldn't set yourself up to be unhappy. You hungry? How 'bout Chinese? Grab the phone and call it in. I think the delivery man has a crush on you, because he always gives us extra crispy noodles whenever you place the order.'

*

After we ate, I begged off of watching *Lord of the Rings: The Fellowship of the Ring* on DVD for the twentieth time. It was Max's favorite movie, after *The Empire Strikes Back*, and he has an annoying habit of reciting the dialogue along with the actors. The very fact that Daphne loves that stupid movie as much as he does should be reason enough for him to marry her. Instead, I hauled my bag and coat back to my apartment. Once in, I dropped my things on the middle of the floor (something you can do when you live alone) and drew in a deep breath. It was a relief to be home.

My apartment has none of the sleek style of Maddy's or Max's, and I hauled most of the furniture home from the wallet-friendly IKEA, but it's comfortable and suits me. The furniture is all of the overstuffed, cozy variety, the kind that you can sink into for hours while you cuddle up with a good book. A few select pieces were ordered from my much beloved Pottery Barn catalogue (which Max, a self-proclaimed expert on mid-century design, sneeringly refers to as 'yuppie porn').

I've always been an addict of those high-end home-interior magazines, even if it hasn't exactly rubbed off on my own decorating skills. Really, it's more of an escapist fantasy. I spend hours paging through them, devouring the profiles of homeowners. It's not just that I want their homes . . . I want their lives. I want to be one of those women, the kind who rinse baby arugula leaves in the sink of a gourmet kitchen with slate green walls, stainless steel appliances, and marble countertops while wearing high heels with pointy toes. The kind who furnish their houses with a casual mix of priceless antiques and little gems they've picked up while shopping at French flea markets. The type who have exquisite paintings given to them by their artist friends hanging on their walls. Women like that don't work for a pittance at a fourth-rate magazine that goes unread in the waiting room of a doctor's office while everyone fights over the three-month-old, tattered issue of *People*.

I settled onto my tan slip-covered couch, putting my feet up on the coffee table, and felt the overwhelming relief to be home that I always had at the end of a hard workday. I'd spent the rest of my afternoon reworking the San Antonio piece, grudgingly taking out all of my favorite bits, making it as colorless and dull as the Holiday Inn guest room I'd stayed in while there. It was demoralizing watching all of the spark being bleached from it. Was I ever going to reach a point in my career when I could write what I wanted to write, without it being edited and reedited, without all of the personality being wrung from it? There was always the choice of freelancing, I knew, but there was a lot of competition and no guarantee that I'd be given any artistic license, plus I'd lose the perks of steady pay and health insurance. No, the only real choice was jumping to yet another magazine . . . but who would take me? Robert wasn't about to give me a good recommendation (unless, of course, he saw it as a good opportunity to get rid of me), and it wasn't as if any of my best writing made it into print, so I knew no one would come knocking on my door, ready to lure me away with a lucrative signing bonus.

So I was stuck, which was a depressing reality to be faced with. When you're young and full of pie-in-the-sky ideas about adulthood – *No parents telling you what to do! Your own place! Your own money! No more school!* – it never occurs to you that you might end up in a soul-sucking job. Okay, maybe my job wasn't exactly soul-sucking, but it also wasn't a barrel of laughs.

I slumped against the back of the sofa and debated whether I should check out whatever ridiculous reality show was on television or take another stab at editing my column. Before I could decide, the phone rang. I reached over to pick up the receiver, assuming it was Max, intent on reciting the opening dialogue of *LOTR* to me. Why he continued to watch that movie over and over and over, when he'd clearly memorized it, was beyond me. Personally, I think he had a thing for Liv Tyler wearing her elf ears.

'Hey, you. I guess this means you got home all right,' a familiar, slow drawl said. My heart did a cartwheel . . . it wasn't Max after all. Instead, the now-familiar, slow-cadenced voice speaking in my ear, his words pinging on the slight delay of the international line, belonged to Jack Harrison.

'Hi,' I said excitedly, and then without thinking, blurted out, 'I didn't think you'd call.'

'Why not? I said I would. I would have called you last night, but I figured you'd be too tired after your flight,' Jack said.

Yeah, right, I thought incredulously. Like it or not, I had a monster crush on this guy. I'd have welcomed his call even if it had come at three a.m. But, deciding to play it cool, I instead said, 'What are you doing?'

'Well, it's midnight here, so I'm in bed,' Jack said. There was no missing the flirtatious tone in his voice. 'I stayed up late so I could get a chance to talk to you. I didn't know if it was okay for me to call you earlier at work,' he continued.

I felt a warm rush go through me. All of my lingering stress drained away, and I felt wide-awake, sparked with fresh energy.

'No, you could. But I work in a cubicle, so everyone around me would be listening to our conversation,' I said. 'I'm glad you waited up.'

'Me too.' He paused. 'It's too bad you were here for such a short time.'

'I know. We still had loads of sightseeing to do,' I sighed. 'I didn't get to the National Portrait Gallery, or the V & A, or even Hyde Park.'

'Well, I guess that just means that you'll have to come back,' Jack said. His tone was light but sincere.

'I guess so,' I agreed.

'When do you think you could?' Jack asked.

'Oh God, I don't know. I mean, I have to work, and I couldn't really afford it,' I said, my voice trailing off.

'I'll arrange for your ticket,' Jack immediately offered.

Which was embarrassing – I didn't want him to think I was asking for money, of course – but nice. *Nice*. I'd never really gone for nice guys in the past. Not that I was ever into girlfriend-beating or leather-mask-wearing sadists, but I think I've always been too swayed by charm and magnetism, thinking that men like that are somehow more attractive, even though experience has borne out the opposite. Usually the more charming a man is, the more he's just trying to overcompensate for his shallowness and insecurity. But nice was something different, something new. Maybe something I could get used to.

'Um. Wow. I mean, that's an incredible offer,' I hedged. 'But I couldn't accept.'

'Of course you could. I have an entirely selfish motive . . . I want to see you again,' Jack said, as if it were the most simple thing in the world.

The idea of seeing him again was tempting. But then again, it raised all kinds of problems. As Max had said, if I never saw him again, I could (eventually) forget about him, and forget that our brief affair was a complete betrayal of my best friend. And if I continued to see him, I'd have to do it behind Maddy's back. Could I do that? Could I really go to London to see Jack and *not* tell Maddy? And what if I did and ended up running into her? I knew it wasn't likely, but it was possible, particularly if Jack took me anywhere that he and Maddy used to frequent, somewhere that she might continue to go to also. But then, on the other hand, I really did want to see Jack again, in fact I wanted it with such an intensity it surprised me. God, this was entirely too complicated, and I knew I should just stop it now. I just wish I didn't like him so damn much. But therein lay the problem.

'I'll think about it,' I hedged.

'Good,' Jack said. 'Now tell me all about your day. Anything interesting happen?'

From: Jack Harrison <jharrison@britpharm.com>
To: Claire Spencer <claire.spencer@ssmagazine.com>
Subject: testing . . .
Date: Tuesday, November 12

You asked last night if there's anything I miss about home, so I set aside some time during a crushingly boring meeting today to map out my response.

Top Five Things I Miss About the U.S.:

5. One-dollar bills
4. Ice cold drinks
3. Baseball
2. Not being constantly referred to as a 'Yank' (they never say it in a nice way, either)
1. Peanut butter

Do I have the right e-mail address for you? If not, and this is going into some general, *Sassy Seniors* in-box, then I want you to know that I'm seventy-eight, an avid reader, and desperately seeking more information on which assisted-living centers have the hottest chicks.

From: Claire Spencer <claire.spencer@ssmagazine.com>
To: Jack Harrison <jharrison@britpharm.com>
Subject: Re: testing . . .
Date: Tuesday, November 12

Yes, it's me, and I'm glad to see your work hours are well spent. Don't forget, there is a downside to living here. On my way to work this morning, a man on the subway actually started stroking my hair . . . and I don't even want to know where his fingers have been. I just sprayed myself with Lysol, but I don't think I'm going to feel clean again until I have the chance to submerge myself into a vat of boiling hot water and scrub with antibacterial soap.

From: Jack Harrison <jharrison@britpharm.com>
To: Claire Spencer <claire.spencer@ssmagazine.com>
Subject: Re: Re: testing . . .
Date: Tuesday, November 12

Are you going to be around tonight, or do you have plans with your hair-stroking freak?

From: Claire Spencer <claire.spencer@ssmagazine.com>
To: Jack Harrison <jharrison@britpharm.com>
Subject: Re: Re: Re: testing . . .
Date: Tuesday, November 12

Don't talk about my fiancé that way.

But, yes, I should be around. Why?

From: Jack Harrison <jharrison@britpharm.com>
To: Claire Spencer <claire.spencer@ssmagazine.com>
Subject: Re: Re: Re: Re: testing . . .
Date: Tuesday, November 12

I thought we could pick up our conversation where it left off last night. As I remember, the last thing you were saying was something about how you're pining away for me, can't live without me . . . something like that, right?

From: Claire Spencer <claire.spencer@ssmagazine.com>
To: Jack Harrison <jharrison@britpharm.com>
Subject: dreams
Date: Tuesday, November 12

Since I said nothing of the kind, I can only surmise that you must have been dreaming about me.

From: Jack Harrison <jharrison@britpharm.com>
To: Claire Spencer <claire.spencer@ssmagazine.com>
Subject: Re: dreams
Date: Tuesday, November 12

Mmmm . . . yes, I believe I was.

Okay, I'd better get back to work. I have empires to topple, people to fire, lives to ruin . . . I'll talk to you tonight.

From: Madeline Reilly <mreilly@nike.co.uk>
To: Claire Spencer <claire.spencer@ssmagazine.com>
Subject: life sucks
Date: Wednesday, November 13

Hey, sweetie. Sorry I didn't get a chance to spend more time with you while you were here, and thanks for coming by and holding my hand when H came over. I still can't believe that it's really over. I knew he was angry at me, but I thought it would all blow over. Maybe it still will . . . I just can't accept that I was the only one falling in love, know what I mean? Do you think I should call him, and see if he wants to talk again, or wait and see if he comes to me?

From: Claire Spencer <claire.spencer@ssmagazine.com>
To: Madeline Reilly <mreilly@nike.co.uk>
Subject: Re: life sucks

Date: Wednesday, November 13

Why was he angry with you?

From: Madeline Reilly <mreilly@nike.co.uk>
To: Claire Spencer <claire.spencer@ssmagazine.com>
Subject: Re: Re: life sucks
Date: Wednesday, November 13

Didn't I tell you? Well, I don't want to go into it now via
e-mail. I'll tell you the next time we talk.

So do you think I should call him? He seemed so final about
everything on Saturday, but I just have to think that he'll
come around. What do you think? You know what, never
mind . . . I'm going to call him. I know if we can just talk it
out, he'll see there's no reason to be upset, and that this
entire thing has been just a big blowup about nothing. I'll let
you know how it goes.

From: Claire Spencer <claire.spencer@ssmagazine.com>
To: Madeline Reilly <mreilly@nike.co.uk>
Subject: Re: Re: Re: life sucks
Date: Wednesday, November 13

Do you really think that's a good idea?

From: Claire Spencer <claire.spencer@ssmagazine.com>
To: Madeline Reilly <mreilly@nike.co.uk>
Subject: Re: Re: Re: life sucks
Date: Wednesday, November 13

Are you still there, or have you gone home for the day? You
didn't reply to my last e-mail.

From: Norfolk, Peggy
To: All staff list
Subject: Birthday Celebrations
Date: Thursday, November 14

It has come to my attention that not all of our Team Members are interested in participating in our office birthday parties. These informal celebrations are a wonderful way of raising morale, as well as giving the *Sassy Seniors* family a chance to socialize. The gatherings are not compulsory, of course, but in the future if you know you will not be attending a gathering, please let us know *before* food assignments are made, to ensure that all of the items we enjoy at these events are available to us.

Thank you for your attention.

P.S. In light of a recent non-contribution to Doris's birthday party, we are collecting an extra $2 from everyone who is attending to pay for the cake. Naturally, Doris is exempted from this collection.

From: Spencer, Claire
To: Norfolk, Peggy
Subject: Re: Birthday Celebrations
Date: Thursday, November 14

Peggy,

Due to my strenuous workload, I will not be attending any birthday parties in the foreseeable future. I will, of course, let you know if this status changes.

Cordially yours,
Claire

From: Claire Spencer <claire.spencer@ssmagazine.com>
To: Madeline Reilly <mreilly@nike.co.uk>
Subject: ?????
Date: Thursday, November 14

You never got back to me ... did you call Jack? What
happened?

From: Jack Harrison <jharrison@britpharm.com>
To: Claire Spencer <claire.spencer@ssmagazine.com>
Subject: sorry ...
Date: Thursday, November 14

Sorry I didn't get a chance to call you last night. Got tied up
at a work thing. Was famished when I got home. Are you
going to be around tonight?

From: Claire Spencer <claire.spencer@ssmagazine.com>
To: Madeline Reilly <mreilly@nike.co.uk>
Subject: Are you there?
Date: Thursday, November 14
Where are you?????????????????

'Oh, good, you're there,' Jack said, when I picked up the
phone.

It was the third time he'd called that week. I was used to
men who said they were going to call either not calling at
all, or waiting two weeks to pick up the phone and then
pretend that this was an acceptable way for a mature adult
to act. Almost daily phone calls, from across the Atlantic,
were unprecedented.

'I can't imagine what your phone bill must look like,' I
said, but then worried that I sounded shrewish, and quickly
added, 'Not that I'm not glad to hear from you.'

Actually, what I wanted to do was interrogate him on

whether Maddy had called him, and if so, what she had said, and how he'd responded. And since Maddy's e-mail announcing she was going to call Jack the night before coincided with the first night that he hadn't called me since I'd returned home, I was a little freaked out about what might have happened. I didn't know what was worse – the idea that Jack might disclose our ongoing flirtation, or that Maddy might tempt him back. Either way, I was screwed. But since I couldn't figure out a tactful way to bring it up, I resigned myself to stewing in my own anxiety.

'How was your day?' Jack said. It was always the first thing he asked, and unlike anyone else who asks this question, he actually seemed interested in my answer.

'Hmm, let's see. I turned in the revisions on my San Antonio column, after editing out all of the humor, interest, and color, so my editor should love it. And I'm apparently on the outs with everyone at the office since I took a stand and am no longer attending any of the staff birthday parties.'

'Like Elaine on *Seinfeld*,' Jack said.

'What?'

'Elaine did that, when she was working for J. Peterman. Remember? She refused to attend the daily office party, but then she needed to find a way to get her late afternoon sugar fix, so she ate that fifty-year-old piece of wedding cake,' he said.

Why are men able to retain this kind of information? Every man I meet, no matter how intelligent he is, or how demanding his job may be, is able to recite every episode of *Seinfeld* and *The Simpsons* line for line. I wondered if the President did this, if while reviewing his State of the Union address, he chuckled to himself, reminded of some wisdom Homer Simpson once put forth.

'Oh, yeah,' I said, hoping that Jack wasn't going to start thinking of me as Elaine, who I'd always thought was kind of mean. 'So . . . that was my day. How about you?'

'Boring stuff, mostly. We've been talking about acquiring a German pharmaceutical company, but there are all kinds of roadblocks in the way, so I've been knee-deep in it, trying to sort it out, see if it's at all feasible,' Jack said. 'Thrilling stuff, really.'

'It sounds like it. I always fantasized about having an important job like that, being a whiz at finance and corporate lingo, but I'd be fired for incompetence my first day out. I can never even understand what language people are speaking when they start talking about takeovers and things like that,' I said.

'I'm sure you'd be great at anything you tried, but why would you want it? You have the world's greatest job, traveling and eating out for free,' Jack said.

I snorted. 'Ah, yes, the glamorous life of working for *Sassy Seniors*,' I said.

'Maybe you should change magazines,' Jack suggested.

'Easier said than done,' I sighed. 'It's not exactly like there are just dozens of glossies out there with empty column space throwing money at me. The truth is, I'm lucky to have my current job, although I can never seem to remember that when I'm antagonizing my boss.'

'What's he like?' Jack asked.

'He's your typical hippie wannabe. Far out, man, and all of that. He's terrible. And he hates me,' I said.

'Why?'

'Because he hates my writing style, and actually, to be fair, I guess I can't really blame him. I don't write for our readership, I write the kind of articles I would want to read,' I said. 'I know I should be more compliant.'

'Why should you? You should be able to write what you want to write. You just need to find a place that will embrace your style,' Jack said, as if it were the easiest thing in the world.

'Well, now that you mention it, I have been besieged

with phone calls from all of the magazine publishers who read my thrilling piece on "Disney World's Best Bets for the Senior Set," who are now dying to lure me away so that I can write similar cutting-edge stories for them,' I said.

'Is Disney World a big vacation destination for seniors?' Jack asked. 'I could see kids digging it, but I thought that was the kind of place that adults without young children avoided.'

I sighed. 'How should I know? I just write about these things. I don't claim to have any actual knowledge of them.'

'Well, you never know. Maybe something will shake loose soon. I wasn't looking for a job when I ended up switching over to Brit Pharm. A headhunter contacted me, and I just spontaneously decided to go on the interview, and look how that turned out,' Jack said.

'Um, I hate to tell you this, but I'm not a hotshot attorney at a top law firm, so headhunters are not exactly banging down my door,' I said.

'You never know,' Jack said again.

'Please don't tell me you're one of those insanely cheerful glass-is-half-full people. I just couldn't bear it,' I said, although I made sure to keep my voice light so that just in case he was that kind of a person, he wouldn't take offense.

'So I suppose you don't want me to tell you to "seize the day"?'

'I'd rather you didn't.'

'How about if I just recite some bleak and fatalistic Irish poetry instead,' Jack suggested.

'Okay, go ahead,' I said.

'Um . . . okay, I don't actually know any bleak, fatalistic Irish poetry,' he admitted. 'Not off the top of my head. I do know a few off-color limericks, though. The Brits love limericks; in fact, they use them as a form of torture here. They force you to drink warm beer, and then make you memorize crass rhymes.'

I laughed, and snuggled back into the corner of the

couch, resting my head against the soft cotton fabric. 'Okay, tell me a limerick,' I said, and despite myself, I felt the grouchiness that always followed me home from work dissipate yet again, as it so often seemed to do when I talked to Jack.

From: Max Levy <bobafett5473@hotmail.com>
To: Claire Spencer <claire.spencer@ssmagazine.com>
Subject: Shaken, Not Stirred
Date: Tuesday, November 19

Three words: You, Me. New Bond Movie Tonight. (ok, 6 words).

Levy. Max Levy.

P.S. Please come. Daphne refuses to go to the movies with me . . . something about the evil corporations behind them, blah, blah, blah.

From: Claire Spencer <claire.spencer@ssmagazine.com>
To: Max Levy <bobafett5473@hotmail.com>
Subject: Re: Shaken, Not Stirred
Date: Tuesday, November 19

Can't tonight. Maybe Friday?

From: Max Levy <bobafett5473@hotmail.com>
To: Claire Spencer <claire.spencer@ssmagazine.com>
Subject: lame ass friends
Date: Tuesday, November 19

Sigh . . . whatever. Just tell me you're not ditching me just to talk on the phone to Mr Smoothie.

From: Claire Spencer <claire.spencer@ssmagazine.com>
To: Max Levy <bobafett5473@hotmail.com>
Subject: Re: lame ass friends
Date: Tuesday, November 19

XXXOOO

From: Claire Spencer <claire.spencer@ssmagazine.com>
To: Madeline Reilly <mreilly@nike.co.uk>
Subject: Are you still alive?
Date: Wednesday, November 20

Okay, I'm starting to worry. You haven't returned my e-mails or my phone calls. Please call me ASAP. Really, I'm worried.

'Hey, it's me.'

'Maddy! God, where have you been? I've been trying to get a hold of you for a week,' I said.

Okay, I wasn't really all that worried about her – we frequently went that long without speaking – but my anxiety over the Jack situation had been steadily rising until I felt like I was a steam engine ready to blow at any moment.

'I know, I'm sorry. Work's been a nightmare, and I've been trying to get out at night so I won't just sit around and sulk,' she said, sighing.

'How are you doing?'

'Terrible. God, Claire, I had no idea it would hurt this much. I've been through dozens of breakups – literally *dozens* – and I've never felt like this before. It's like I'm going through some kind of drug withdrawal. I can't sleep, I'm shaky, I can hardly concentrate at work,' Maddy said.

She sounded awful. I could hear the exhaustion in her voice, and she was missing her characteristic sparkle. My heart squeezed with sympathy and guilt.

'I'm sorry you're having such a hard time,' I said, feeling

like the world's biggest hypocrite as the words left my mouth.

'I know, thanks, sweetie,' Maddy said, and she sighed again.

'Um . . . so what was it you were talking about in your e-mail last week? You said something about Ja . . . Harrison being angry at you?'

'God, I don't think I can bear going into it right now. Mind if we talk about it later? It's just a long, sordid story, and, well,' Maddy said with a little laugh, sounding tired, but more like her old self, 'I don't come off all that well in it, and I don't think I could bear your disapproval right now.'

'I wouldn't be disapproving,' I said.

'Oh, I just don't feel like talking about it now. I promise, I'll tell you later, 'kay? Anyway, I called Harrison last week – I know, you said not to, I should have listened – and he really didn't sound angry. Just . . .' She paused. 'Final. As far as he was concerned, everything was over, and that was that.'

'Gosh,' I said, having nothing better to contribute than this insightful comment. I was still intrigued over this apparent point of contention between Jack and Maddy, but I knew not to push her. She'd tell me in her own time, when she was ready, but until then she'd remain slippery on the subject.

'Yeah. I'm still not giving up, though. I think all he needs is time. Isn't that what they say about men? They may leave, but they always come back,' she said.

Actually, I've never heard that philosophy before, unless it was being applied to married men leaving their wives and kids for another, younger, firmer woman, and then later having buyer's regret and missing their family. And I'm not even sure how common those reunions are.

'Um, well, I suppose that could happen,' I hedged. 'I've been meaning to ask you, why do you call him Harrison?'

'It started as a joke. We were playing tennis, and he

started to call me Reilly – you know, in a jokey way, the way guys always call one another by their last names when they're playing sports – so I called him Harrison, and after that, it just sort of stuck. It was our thing, our couple thing, you know?'

I did. It may have been a while since I'd been in a relationship, but I did remember the couple thing. Sawyer and I used to read the luxury home section of the Sunday *New York Times* and fantasize together about being able to buy an estate in Sag Harbor or Southampton. That was our 'thing.'

'So what was it you wanted to tell me?' Maddy asked.

'What?' I had no idea what she was talking about.

'In your message, you said you had something you needed to tell me. Don't you remember?' she asked.

'Oh . . .' I said, trying desperately to think of what to say.

I had, in a fit of guilt, decided to confess all to Maddy, figuring that honesty was the best policy, and that I owed it to her to tell her the truth. But now I couldn't remember why I'd ever thought that was such a good idea. After all, once I did tell her, two things were sure to happen – (a) she would get really pissed at me, and (b) I'd have to promise not to talk to Jack anymore, and neither consequence was all that appealing. Besides, I couldn't wait to talk to Jack that night and tell him about my latest offensive maneuver at work. I'd set the radio at my desk to the local conservative talk radio station, and when Robert had walked by and heard what I was listening to, he'd developed a facial tick and started muttering under his breath about right-wing fascists. It was truly a stroke of brilliance on my part.

'I can't remember what I was talking about, so I guess it was nothing important,' I said. I was going to tell her eventually. Of course I was.

Just not quite yet.

A few days later, I had lunch with my friend Jane Swann. Jane had been a student intern at *Sassy Seniors* the first year I worked there, but had since graduated from NYU and landed a job at *Runway*, a newish fashion-and-celebrity-voyeurism magazine that was quickly becoming one of the hottest titles in the industry. I tried not to hate her for this. She only held the lowly position of Assistant to the Assistant Beauty Editor, but I knew how talented she was, so it was only a matter of time before she started to climb up the ranks. Since that hadn't happened yet and she was still stuck in a job that was slightly worse than my own, I could still bear to see her, especially since she was as miserable slaving under the tyranny of her boss as I was under mine.

'Bavmorda the Evil One made me give her a *pedicure* last week,' Jane said. Bavmorda – who was the malevolent queen in the movie, *Willow* – was her not-so-flattering nickname for her boss, who had a notorious reputation for being a hard-to-deal-with diva. 'She was going on the *Today* show to plug a new article about beauty bargains, and was determined to wear her new open-toed Manolos on the air, but didn't have time to get to the salon. So she made me *sit on her office floor* while she waved her stinky feet around, and I had to file and paint her toenails while she made phone calls to her friends. Not even business calls . . . she was inviting people to a cocktail party at her apartment. And she didn't even invite me. Can you believe that?'

I shook my head. 'That's disgusting. You would have been well within your rights to say no.'

Jane snorted, and mutinously stabbed at her coleslaw. 'Yeah, right. Do you know how many people would kill for my job, who would happily scrape the corns off her feet if it meant having an in at the magazine?'

'Please, don't talk about feet, I'm eating,' I begged.

I have a thing about feet . . . they revolt me. I know it's a little strange to have a phobia over a body part, but I can't help it, and the very thought of stinky, calloused feet was a little more than I could handle over lunch.

We were eating at a deli on Broadway that was equidistant between our two offices. As I'm on a permanent diet, I was making do with a rather bland turkey-and-yellow-mustard-on-whole-wheat, with a soggy pickle on the side. Jane, on the other hand, is one of those high-metabolism people and remains elegantly slim no matter what she eats. She was tucking into an enormous Reuben sandwich dripping with melted cheese and Thousand Island dressing, along with a mountain of french fries, a tub of coleslaw, and a giant full-sugar Coke. There are United States Marines who eat fewer calories per meal than Jane. I'd spent my entire life believing in the calories-in, calories-out approach to weight control, so I found this phenomenon – a woman who eats three times the amount of her caloric requirements on a daily basis yet stays as thin as a reed – to be fascinating. Where did all of the calories go? Did she have some kind of a superhero power not to absorb them? Did she make a pact with the devil?

'How can you eat all of that?' I asked, amazed. I asked Jane this every time I had lunch with her, and she had yet to give me a satisfactory response.

'Dunno.' Jane shrugged, so unconcerned about her

ability to pack it away like a defensive lineman that I couldn't help but say a little prayer that she would suffer a reversal of fortune, and all of a sudden – overnight, if possible – she'd wake up as fleshy and rotund as a sumo wrestler. It would be as gratifying as the time when the beauty queen of my high school washed peroxide through her hair once too often and it all turned green, like oxidized copper, and began falling out in clumps.

'So have you ever had to do something like that to keep a job? Something disgusting and degrading and horrible? Like sleeping with your boss, or something like that?' Jane asked hopefully.

The idea of sleeping with Robert was even more nauseating to me than the subject of icky feet. I shuddered at the thought.

'No, nothing like that. Although while I was in college, and doing a summer internship at *Good Housekeeping*, I did end up spending more hours babysitting my supervisor's kids than working on the magazine,' I said. 'Their favorite game was Throw Things at Claire, preferably hard, sharp-edged objects. Apparently, whoever was able to draw the most blood won.'

I could tell from Jane's defeated expression that she didn't rate babysitting – even if it involved watching demon spawn – to be nearly as humiliating as giving pedicures under duress.

'Don't worry,' I said. 'You won't be in this position forever, and you're making great contacts at the magazine. When I first got out of college, I spent two years as an editorial assistant at *Cat Crazy*. That's probably why I'm working at *Sassy Seniors* and not *Vogue*. At least you're starting out somewhere a little higher on the food chain.'

This seemed to brighten Jane.

'Yeah, I guess you're right. I'd die if I had to work for one of those dorky magazines. I'd rather give Bavmorda pedicures. No offense,' she added quickly. 'So, what are you doing for Thanksgiving?'

I actually blanked for a minute, before remembering that the holiday was only a week away. 'Oh God, I don't know. I'd forgotten all about it.'

'It's next week,' Jane reminded me. She rolled her eyes. 'I'm going home to Boise. Unfortunately. I couldn't find an excuse not to go, and my parents wore me down.'

I tried to remember if I'd talked about Thanksgiving plans with either of my parents. This is what happens when your nuclear family goes through a hellish divorce – holidays are something that everyone tries hard to avoid. And it looked like we'd succeed this year. My mom now lived in Florida with my stepfather, while my dad and stepmom lived near where I grew up, in Maryland. Since I hadn't made travel plans to visit either set, it was doubtful I was going to be leaving town. Although actually, the idea of four whole days to myself, with nothing planned and nothing to do, sounded wonderful. I could take lots of bubble baths, read through the stack of paperback books I'd been compulsively buying and not yet had time to read, and catch up on my sleep. It would be a little mini-break from life.

'I guess I'm going to stay in the city,' I said, warming to the idea. Maybe I'd finally get around to taking down the hideous floral wallpaper border the previous occupant of my apartment had put up around the kitchenette, apparently using superglue to attach it. I'd been tearing down scraps, but really needed to rent some kind of an industrial steam remover to get it all off.

'Lucky you. So what else is going on? Are you seeing anyone?' Jane asked. She was only twenty-five, and thus too naive to know that this wasn't a question you should pose to a woman in her thirties, so I decided to forgive her.

'Sort of,' I hedged, a battle rising between the side of me that was desperate to talk to someone about my new romance with Jack and the side that knew how horrible it sounded to admit that he had just broken up with my now-heartbroken best friend. 'I met a guy while I was in London two weeks ago, and we've been e-mailing and talking on the phone a lot.'

'*Really* . . . so, tell me everything,' Jane said, sounding a lot more interested than I would have thought she'd be. I knew for a fact that she was something of a wild child, while I could just barely remember what it was like to have enough energy to go out clubbing all night after working all day. I would have thought that a staid, overseas corre-spondence between two thirty-somethings would bore her to pieces.

'There's not much to tell,' I lied. 'I met him on the plane ride over, and we went out a few times while I was there, and since I've come back we've kept in touch.'

'You are the only person I know who could make a torrid affair with a hot foreigner sound so boring,' Jane complained. 'I was hoping for some juicy details.'

'Well, I'm not going to tell you the juicy stuff, but he is pretty great,' I admitted. 'But he's not a foreigner – he's American.'

'Oh, that's no fun. I'm sick of American guys,' Jane said, with a jaded wave of her hand. 'They're all the same. I want to go out and find a sexy Italian or Frenchman. Someone who's dark and complicated and talks with a thick accent. Do you think Gérard Depardieu is sexy?'

'Um, no,' I said.

'I guess I don't really either, except for his accent, which is yum,' she said.

I stirred my iced tea and poked at the bloated lemon bobbing around next to the melting ice cubes with my spoon. 'I don't know. I've never had a thing for European men. I think it's their lax attitudes toward monogamy. And I tend to think of French men as being fussy.'

Jane was looking at me like I had two heads. 'Monogamy,' she snorted. 'Who cares about monogamy? The whole concept is sexist and outdated.'

Now I remembered why Jane and I didn't get together that often – she was fun, but she always made me feel so old. Of course monogamy would sound boring to her. When your breasts and ass are in roughly the same places as they were when you were sixteen, you tend to focus more on momentary fun than long-lasting commitment.

'I don't agree. I think infidelity is toxic to a relationship,' I said, thinking of my father's affairs and what they had done to my parents' marriage.

Dad had never fully grasped the concept that exchanging wedding vows was meant to put an end to his dating. I was five years old the first time my mother kicked him out of the house, and I remember huddling in bed, desperately hoping that the warm cocoon of blankets and pillows would protect me, as I overheard their screaming fight on the night he left. The next day the house felt ominously empty, and I came upon my mother sitting on the ground, their white satin wedding album on her lap, calmly cutting up every photograph with a pair of pinking shears. Mom eventually let him back in, only to bounce him out again two years later after his then-current girlfriend had called and announced to my mother that she'd accompanied my father on a business trip to San Diego. And back and forth they went, a circle of screaming fights and changed locks, and then a tearful reunion, followed by a period of indifferent antagonism, trailed by the discovery of yet another infidelity, until they finally – mercifully – decided to stop torturing one another and divorced. As I said, they were hardly marital role models.

'Well, what about this new guy? Do you think it's serious with your new boyfriend?' Jane asked.

Boyfriend. I rolled the word around in my mouth, liking the sound of it.

'I don't know,' I said. 'I mean, probably not. He lives in England, after all. But I'm trying not to think about it too much,' I said, wondering when I had become so adept at lying. I had hardly thought of anything else since I'd returned from London.

'Oh, I know what I wanted to tell you! Did you hear that *Retreat* is hiring a writer? A headhunter sent around an e-mail to everyone at *Runway*, to see if anyone was interested in applying for it,' Jane said.

Great. Jane was only a few years out of college, and already headhunters were scouting her out. But a job opening . . . the idea was intriguing. I knew there was no chance I would get it, of course – *Retreat* was out of my league. It was a high-end travel magazine that targeted the same readership as *Town & Country* and *Vogue*. Its features revolved around exclusive Caribbean resorts and hotels in Sydney or Stockholm renowned for their four-star chefs and cutting-edge architecture. On the rarified pages of *Retreat*, the articles were nestled in between advertisements for Louis Vuitton luggage and Patek Philippe watches, and the word 'budget' was only used in an ironic sense, if at all. So the odds that they were in the market for a writer who was well versed on the best of the low-end national hotel chains and how to dine out at a discount (eat early, skip the cocktails, ask for a doggie bag) were low. But I could always try for it. What was the worst thing that could happen – that they would reject me? Besides, this was just what I needed to get my mind off of Jack. A job search.

'Are you going to apply for it?' I asked, hoping that she'd say no. After all, Jane was a friend, so I couldn't go after a job that she was interested in, although the irony of this wasn't lost on me. I had no problem poaching my best friend's ex-boyfriend, and yet had moral qualms about going after the same job as an old work colleague. Apparently I did have some standards after all, as twisted as those might be.

'God, no,' Jane snorted. 'They don't have an office here, and there's no way I'm moving to the Midwest. I'm not cut out to be the wife of a corn farmer.'

'Midwest? Jane, the *Retreat* offices are in Chicago. I don't think you have to break out the overalls and pitchfork in order to work there,' I said.

'As far as I'm concerned, if it's not Manhattan, it's not civilization,' Jane said, sounding final on the subject.

Actually, I was quite pleased. If she wasn't going to go for it, then I could pursue the job with a clear conscience. And who knows, other writers might have the same reservations about moving out of the city, so maybe the competition for the position wouldn't be as fierce as I'd originally expected. As for me, I would happily live on a corn farm – for that matter, in the pigsty of the corn farm – if it meant being free of Robert and *Sassy Seniors*.

I spent the rest of the afternoon furtively working on my résumé, hoping that Peggy or Robert wouldn't suddenly materialize and catch me in the act. I was trying to figure out if there was any way to make my stints at *Good Housekeeping*, *Cat Crazy*, *The Great Outdoors* (the magazine I had worked at just before coming to *Sassy Seniors* – during the time I was there Maddy had teased me mercilessly about how ridiculous it was that someone who thought that a picnic in Central Park was roughing it was writing for a magazine that focused on camping and hiking), or *Sassy Seniors* sound remotely modish enough for *Retreat*, before coming to the conclusion that there was simply no way. I was tempted to just start making things up – substituting an internship at *Elle* for the one at *Good Housekeeping*, swapping out *Cat Crazy* for *Allure*. But I didn't dare do it. The magazine industry is only so large, and there was always a chance that if I insisted I once worked at *W* magazine, I'd end up being interviewed by someone who had actually worked there.

By midafternoon I remembered my conversation with Jane about Thanksgiving and decided I'd better ring the folks and find out what their plans were for next week. I knew they'd each be upset that I wasn't going to spend the holiday with them, so I figured I needed to do some damage control. It would just be a matter of letting them down easy, of promising visits in the near future and all of that, but still. It was important to keep the lines of communication open. I called my mom first.

'Hello,' my mother said, answering the phone on the first ring.

'Hi, Mom,' I said.

'Who's this?'

Sigh. The woman only had two children . . . was it really too much to ask for her to recognize us each by voice? And how was it possible that even after all of these years, she still had the ability to make me feel less important than her weekly manicure appointment?

'It's your *daughter*. Claire,' I said.

'Oh, hi, honey. I've been meaning to call you. Did you hear that Pammy and Hector Thompson are getting divorced?'

She sounded vaguely excited at the prospect. Ever since her own divorce, my mother has greedily lapped up the news of marital discord in other couples. It was a rather disturbing habit, one that reminded me of those old people who sit at home listening to the news of car accidents and drug busts on their police scanners. It was a particularly incongruous image, though, if you knew my mother, who is one of the most unfailingly elegant women I've ever met. Unlike my sister, Alice, I inherited neither my mother's grace nor her poise nor her slim figure, and instead took after my tall, broad father. I don't think my mother has ever really forgiven me for this lapse of judgment.

'No, but then I don't really keep in touch with anyone

back home. Other than Dad, I mean. Anyway, I called about Thanksgiving,' I said.

'What about it, dear?'

'Well . . . I didn't know what your plans were . . .' I said, bracing for the onslaught of maternal disapproval when I announced I wasn't going to Florida.

'Oh, didn't I tell you? Howard and I are going on a cruise! Doesn't that sound like fun? We're sailing out of Fort Lauderdale on Wednesday, and then going to Key West, and Cozumel, and then someplace else in Mexico – I can't remember the name – Howard!' My mother didn't bother to move the phone receiver away from her mouth as she yelled for my stepfather. I held the receiver away from my ear, wondering if the damage to my hearing would be permanent. 'Howard! What's the other place the cruise is stopping at? Georgetown? No, I don't think that sounds right. I think it was a Mexican name.'

'That's okay, Mom. I really don't need to know,' I said, my ears ringing.

'Well, anyway, doesn't that sound exciting? There's going to be dancing every night, and they're going to have a big Thanksgiving buffet, and the Andersons are going – you know the Andersons, don't you?'

'No,' I said.

'Yes, you do. They live down the street from us,' my mother continued.

I rolled my eyes. No, I didn't know the Andersons, and I can't believe she went and made plans for Thanksgiving without even talking to me about it. She was supposed to be my mother, for God's sake. Didn't she care that I was going to be all alone for the holiday?

'But what about me?' I asked. 'You're just abandoning me?'

My mother laughed. 'Sweetheart, you're a grown woman. I just assumed that you had made plans to go see your father and that woman.'

My mother never refers to my stepmother by name. I suppose you can't blame her, since my Dad did begin dating Mitzi while he was still married to my mother.

'No. I don't know what they're doing,' I said.

'Well, I'd invite you to go with us, but I happen to know for a fact that the cruise has completely sold out. The Gubmans – you know the Gubmans, don't you?'

'No,' I said.

My mother continued talking as if she hadn't heard me. Which she probably hadn't.

'The Gubmans tried to book the same cruise last week, and there was nothing available. They're on a waiting list, but it doesn't look as if they'll get on, which is a shame, because I don't think they have any other plans for the holiday. Although I'm sure they can always go over to the Donaldsons',' she trilled on.

Great. Not only was my mother blowing me off for Thanksgiving, but she was far more concerned with whether the Gubmans were going to be alone (although, since there were presumably two of them, they'd at least have each other) than she was about me. I eventually got off the phone with her, but first I had to hear about how the Donaldsons' daughter, whom I've never met, had just graduated from law school, and wasn't that just fabulous, and how my mother wished I'd gone on to get an advanced degree in something. I finally managed to wriggle away from the conversation, and dialed my father's office number.

'Hi, Dad,' I said.

'Hi, pumpkin,' he said. 'Aren't you supposed to be at work?'

'I am at work. I was just calling to find out what you and, and, um, Mitzi' – I always stumble over my stepmother's stupid nickname, since it sounds like something someone would call their pet schnauzer – 'were planning to do for Thanksgiving.'

'Didn't we tell you? We're flying out to San Francisco to

see your sister, and then we're going to go on a winery tour,' he said.

I suppose this is what I get for not having a closer relationship with my sister, Alice. I had no one to help me keep tabs on my parents.

'Oh. No. I didn't know that,' I said.

'We're flying out on Tuesday, spending a few days with Alice, and then we're going to rent a car and drive north through the Sonoma Valley,' my dad said. 'What are your plans?'

'I don't have any,' I said pointedly.

'I'd invite you to come with us, but I don't think you'd be able to get a flight at this late date,' my father said.

Now I know how Macaulay Culkin must have felt in those 'Home Alone' movies when his family deserted him over the holidays. Maybe that's what I'd do for Thanksgiving. I'd rent *Home Alone 1, 2,* and *3* (was there a *Home Alone 3*?) and watch them while eating a frozen turkey dinner, the really awful kind that comes on an aluminum tray and has cardboardlike turkey, the super-whipped mashed potatoes, and the apple compote that for some reason comes out of the oven four times hotter than anything else and ends up scalding your entire mouth if you eat it too quickly.

I mean, I know that I'm a grown-up, and I understand that when my parents decided to dissolve their marriage, it pretty much put an end to those cozy, picturesque family holidays. Not that my family ever had celebrations like that in the first place. In fact, most of my memories about holidays past are pretty vague. All I can remember is a lot of anxiety, strained voices, and snippy conversations about where my dad's mother could go jump if she didn't like the idea of having a pork roast for Christmas dinner. But was it too much to ask that at least one of my two parents could make an effort to try to include me in their plans with their new spouses? In fact, I thought that when your parents divorced, they were supposed to try to buy your affection, with promises of pet ponies and such – not dump you on major holidays.

Hanging up with my dad was always much easier than it was with my mother. I think it makes him vaguely uncomfortable to talk to me directly, now that he doesn't have my mother around to translate what my sister and I are saying. In fact, all I had to do was make an oblique reference to menstrual cramps, and he quickly said, 'Oh, well, I'll let you go then.' As soon as I set the receiver down, Helen appeared at the opening of my cubicle.

'I couldn't help but hear what you were talking about on the phone. About not having any plans for Thanksgiving,' Helen said sympathetically.

Since Helen was one of the only co-workers I could stand, I tried not to get annoyed at her for eavesdropping. Besides, it sort of went along with the cubicle territory – you could always hear everything that everyone around you was doing, whether you wanted to or not. I dreamed of someday having an office with a door . . . it didn't even have to have a window. Just a nice converted broom closet, or maybe even a desk nestled in next to a leaky hot-water heater would suit me fine.

'Oh, it's okay,' I said. 'My parents just made other plans, but I hadn't really counted on traveling to see them anyway.'

'Well, you're certainly welcome to spend the holiday with my family,' Helen said.

I was so touched. And people say that New Yorkers are cold and heartless. I could just imagine what Helen's family was like – large and warm and boisterous. They probably even had a tradition of everyone going around the table and saying what they were thankful for, and of drying out the wishbone for the kids to snap between them later. Thanksgiving dinner would be something out of a Hallmark

Hall of Fame television movie – succulent golden turkeys and piles of mashed potatoes and homemade pumpkin pies, all served on Grandmother's china alongside the good linens. Just the thought of being part of something so warm, so familial made my eyes tear up, and I was just about to accept in a fit of nostalgia, when Helen continued.

'It's a tradition in my family that every year someone brings a lost lamb to Thanksgiving dinner – that's what we call people who don't have anywhere else to spend the holiday. It makes the holiday so much more special for us. It usually works out . . . well, except for one year, when my son Joe brought home what he thought was a homeless vet but the man turned out to be a schizophrenic who'd just escaped from a mental institution. He tried to hold my sister-in-law hostage with a turkey baster, so we had to call the police to come and take him away, poor fellow,' Helen said thoughtfully. 'But other than that, it's usually worked out well. And everyone would be so glad to have you. We were worried that no one had found a lost lamb to join us this year.'

The idea of being Helen's family's pet 'lost lamb' was so humiliating that all thoughts of the Norman Rockwell dinner scene immediately vanished. Was this how pathetic my life had become, that I was now getting the same pity invitations as turkey-baster-wielding lunatics?

'Um, actually, that sounds very nice, but I think my next-door neighbor is having people over for dinner, and he did ask me first,' I lied.

'Oh,' Helen said, clearly disappointed that she wasn't going to be able to fulfill her lost-lamb quota with me. 'Well, if you change your mind, the invitation is always open.'

'Thanks,' I said.

I was still stewing over my parents' apparent indifference that evening when Jack called. We'd fallen into a pattern where he called me nearly every night at seven p.m., my time. If either of us couldn't make this phone 'date,' we'd let the other know by e-mail earlier in the day. It was remarkable how quickly we'd managed to stumble into a routine, almost like a real couple. Not that we were a couple, of course . . . I knew it was ridiculous to even think of whatever this was in those terms.

I told Jack about my parents not including me in their plans, only I was careful to sound lighthearted and not at all like I was sulking over it. I didn't want him to think that my family was actively avoiding me, thus tipping him off that there was something seriously wrong with me.

'So at thirty-two, I've been turned into an orphan. Practically, anyway. Although I guess I shouldn't complain to you, since you don't even get to have the holiday off,' I said.

'Yes, England isn't so big on celebrating American holidays,' Jack said. 'But I'm going to be out of town on business that weekend, anyway.'

Hmph. That wasn't what I'd wanted to hear. I'd half hoped that once Jack heard I didn't have any plans for Thanksgiving week, he'd repeat his offer to have me come visit him in London. When he didn't extend the invite, I couldn't help but feel a little disappointed. It seemed that no one wanted to spend the holiday with me, other than Helen's do-gooder family. Somehow the idea of spending a four-day weekend immersed in a bubble bath surrounded by a stack of books didn't sound nearly as fun when it was my only option.

'Oh? Are you going somewhere fun?' I asked, hoping I didn't sound dejected.

'If you consider talking to French businessmen about a potential merger to be fun,' Jack said. 'So you're going to stay in Manhattan next week, Little Orphan Annie?'

'Oh, sure, laugh at me,' I sighed.

Robert sent around an e-mail Wednesday after lunch notifying everyone that in light of the Thanksgiving holiday, the *Sassy Seniors* offices would be closing down at four p.m.

Oh, gee, a whole hour earlier. What a prince, I thought. I knew the only reason Robert was letting us go even a little early was because he had to catch a train out of the city (I just happened to overhear him telling this to Barbara while I was hiding behind a ficus tree eavesdropping on them in the hopes of gleaning some information about the year-end bonuses).

I couldn't help but feel a little lonely as everyone else was hustling around, gathering their coats and bags, eager to get home to their turkeys and families. I was going home to an empty apartment. At least Max and Daphne would be around for most of the weekend, although they were going to spend Thanksgiving Day at Max's grandmother's house in Connecticut. I made plans to hang out with them when they returned to the city.

'I'd invite you to go with us, but I like you far too much to subject you to my family,' Max had told me. 'Besides, it's going to be bad enough as it is. My grandmother isn't going to let us leave until we've nailed down a date for the wedding.'

'Wedding? Did you propose to Daphne and neglect to tell me about it?' I'd asked.

'Funny you should mention it, but no,' Max said gloomily. 'But the lack of a proposal isn't about to stop the women in my family from planning the wedding anyway. They view my opposition to it as just another detail to be ironed out, along with selecting the caterer and whether roses should be used in the centerpieces.'

I left the office and rode the subway home to my Morningside Heights apartment. My address was not glamorous, but it was one of the only places in New York where I could afford to live without a roommate. The downside to this affordable real estate was that my block was also home to a wide variety of miscreants, lunatics, and perverts (pretty much my parents' worst nightmare when I first announced I was moving to New York right out of college). I'd often wondered if there was some kind of a Twilight Zone-like beacon planted in the middle of my street that draws all of the crazies to it, because day or night the place was teeming with everything from the batty-but-harmless souls who shuffled around in their bedroom slippers mumbling to themselves, to the wing nuts who were convinced that the mother ship was going to land any day, making it incumbent on them to convert as many people to the cause as possible. Particularly with the latter, I normally try not to make eye contact as I walk by, fearing that it will just antagonize them. Tonight I wasn't so lucky.

'Hey, pretty lady,' a male voice called out. I ignored my admirer – past experience taught me that if I did glance at him, I'd be rewarded with the sight of a dirty, smelly pervert masturbating into a Styrofoam coffee cup – and instead I got out my keys, so I could both let myself into my building quickly and, if needed, use them as a weapon to poke a potential assailant's eye out.

'Hey,' he called out again.

I hustled up the short flight of stairs leading to the front door of my building, and fumbled with my keys as I unlocked the door. But that brief instant where I couldn't seem to get my key in the door was just enough time for the man to come up behind me and grab my arm.

I'd never really thought much about getting mugged – up until now, I'd lived a remarkably crime-free life in New York. I guess it's the one benefit of being Amazon-sized; the rapists and thieves would prefer to pick on someone smaller and weaker than themselves, rather than risk tangling with someone they couldn't be sure wasn't a man in drag. So now that I was finally facing real danger, on my very own doorstep with its hand on my arm, I was amazed at how quickly my fight-or-flight impulse geared up. My heart was racing, and I could feel the heat of my blood pumping through my body. With a burst of adrenaline, I quickly reached into my purse and pulled out the stun gun my father had given me for Christmas the previous year.

'Don't touch me!' I shrieked, and I wheeled around, ready to confront my attacker. As I turned, I held out the stun gun and pressed it against the arm gripping mine. Then, holding my breath and praying that the weapon would actually work, I squeezed the button, sending 100,000 volts of electricity into his woman-molester body.

'Oof,' the man said, and promptly fell over.

It was actually quite thrilling. I'd never gotten into a real physical fight with anyone before – unless you count the time my sister bit me when we were children – and the fact that I'd not only survived but emerged victorious was terribly exciting. I wouldn't mind getting mugged more often if I could lay them all on the ground like this one. Maybe I'd even take a course in judo, so that I could learn to do battle with my bare hands. It would be a good stress reliever, even better than yoga. I was just about ready to run into my building, when I glanced down to make sure that my attacker was too debilitated to follow me.

'Oh shit,' I whispered, the blood draining from my face.

I'd been so busy concentrating on zapping the man that I hadn't bothered to look at his face before I pressed the button on my stun gun . . . which was a big, big mistake. For the person who was lying crumpled on the filthy stairway, his body twitching as he struggled to get up, wasn't a dirty, slimy sex pervert, after all. It was Jack.

'I am so, so sorry,' I said, for about the hundredth time. I'd managed to get Jack up to my apartment, slowly helping him up the four flights of stairs, and once inside, I'd propped him up on my sofa. Once I made sure he was comfortable (well, as comfortable as one can be after suffering through such an assault), I hovered over him, a glass of water and bottle of aspirin in hand, which is about the sum total of my nursing skills. I'd already tried to talk Jack into going to the hospital to make sure I hadn't done any permanent damage, but he insisted that once he got a chance to rest up for a bit, he'd be fine.

'I thought you'd be happy to see me,' Jack said hoarsely. I couldn't tell if he was joking, since he was still shaken from the electric shock I'd given him.

'What are you doing here?' I asked desperately. 'Why didn't you call me? If I'd known you were going to be waiting for me, I wouldn't have zapped you.'

'I wanted to surprise you. Which I obviously succeeded in doing,' Jack said wryly.

'I'm so sorry,' I repeated. 'I can't believe I did that to you.'

'Yeah, it wasn't the reaction I was hoping for. But really, Claire, don't worry. I'll be fine. My muscles are already starting to unclench.'

'But what are you doing here? You're supposed to be in France,' I wailed.

'I didn't want to leave you alone over the holiday.' Jack

pointed toward a crumpled white paper bag that he'd been holding when I zapped him. 'I brought turkey sandwiches and pumpkin cookies,' he said.

'Oh,' I said miserably. It was such a sweet gesture, and look what he'd gotten for his troubles.

I sat down next to him on the couch and held out my feeble first-aid supplies. Jack refused the aspirin, but he did take the water. Once he'd taken a long sip and handed me the glass back with an unsteady hand, he finally managed a feeble smile.

'Can I at least have a kiss hello?' he asked.

I leaned over and kissed him, and then sat back, putting one hand on the side of his cheek. Jack didn't look like someone who had just gotten off of an international flight. His cheeks were clean-shaven, and his clothes looked freshly pressed. But I wouldn't have cared if he showed up raggedy and rumpled and in desperate need of a shower. In fact, I was absurdly glad to see him.

'I'm going to throw out that damned stun gun,' I said. 'I didn't want it in the first place, but my father insisted, and look what happened. Clearly, I'm not to be trusted with weapons.'

'No, no, don't do that. What if I had been an attacker? I'm glad you have it, glad you have a way of keeping yourself safe,' he said.

Which was actually kind of nice to hear. Because of my size and general demeanor, I'm not the kind of woman that men tend to worry about. No one ever rushes to put jackets over my shoulder lest I catch a chill, or insists on opening doors for me. Everyone always assumes that I can take care of myself. Which, of course, I can. But I think that every woman has at least a teeny, tiny part of her that likes being protected and worried about, whether or not we're willing to admit it.

*

Jack made a quick recovery from his electroshock – although it was a full hour before his hands stopped twitching – and the rest of the weekend went without a hitch. Well, it was better than that . . . it was incredible. Having in the past only spent the holidays with my tense, jaw-clenched family, in part or in whole, it was the first completely relaxing, enjoyable, stress-free Thanksgiving I'd ever had. It turned out that the turkey sandwiches were just a snack; for Thanksgiving dinner, Jack had made reservations for us at Daniel's (I just love a man who doesn't expect me to cook for him – lacking a Y chromosome does not automatically make one Betty Crocker), where we had a delicious and romantic meal in the quiet elegance of the dining room.

For the rest of the weekend, Jack and I did a lot of cheesy touristy stuff, which I probably should have been embarrassed about if I hadn't been enjoying myself so much. We went shopping in Chinatown, where I bought a ruffled red umbrella and a pair of silver mesh beaded slides. We strolled through the Museum of Natural History and looked at dinosaur bones. We went for a long walk through Central Park, our hands linked together in a comfortably familiar way. We ate hot dogs at Gray's Papaya, and lasagna in Little Italy. We even went ice skating in Rockefeller Center – I couldn't resist – although, actually, it sounds more romantic than it really is, particularly if, like me, you have a tendency to wipe out every two minutes. Since I was clutching Jack's arm in order to stay upright, every time I fell down I managed to take him with me, falling down onto the cold, hard ice in a tangle of arms and legs.

Jack and I seemed to fit together with remarkable ease, just as we had in London. We made each other laugh, and stayed up late every night talking about everything and nothing, from the serious to the ridiculous. We made love frequently – sometimes slowly and decadently, other times at a more frenzied pitch. Jack had made reservations to stay at the Essex House Hotel – it was where he'd freshened up on his first afternoon in the city, right before I zapped him – but after that he spent every night at my apartment, saying he preferred it to the sterility of yet another hotel. In fact, he was a little wistful as he said it, and I got the feeling that there was something he was brooding about, although I didn't push at it. If I had to guess, I'd have said he was homesick for the U.S.

Besides, I liked having him in my apartment. My favorite part of the weekend was when we spent Sunday morning just lounging around, wearing sweats, munching on bagels smeared with honey-walnut cream cheese and reading the paper. In fact, the whole weekend was so perfect, it weirded me out. I kept waiting for something to go wrong, for Jack to reveal that he was a bigamist or that he had a foot fetish. But he just kept on being great and wonderful and, other than accidentally knocking my *Philosophy Coloring Book* into the toilet, absolutely perfect.

The only hitch came when Max and Daphne popped over on Friday afternoon. They'd just taken the train back from Connecticut, and when I opened my door, they came bursting into my apartment, laughing and chattering.

'Two whole days, and my father only made fun of my job once,' Max said. His father was one of those starched-collar, manly-man types, and didn't consider fashion photography to be an appropriate career for his male heir. 'My mom stayed reasonably sober, my grandmother managed to keep her tongue in check, and my sister and her brat kids were a no-show. All in all, it went as well as could be expected.'

Daphne rolled her eyes and shook her red curls out of a brimmed corduroy cap. 'Don't listen to him. His family is awesome. They actually hang out together, playing board games and talking and stuff. Like those perfect families on TV sitcoms.'

'Yeah, well, they try to keep their satanic sacrifices under wraps when guests are over,' Max said. 'Come on, Claire, we've come to rescue you. Come to dinner with us.'

'Yes, come with us,' Daphne chimed in.

Max threw himself on the couch and started to page through my recent issue of *Elle*. 'Did you know that black is the new black?' he asked, lazily flipping through the pages.

'I look terrible in black. I'm too pale, and it makes me look like a witch. Or, I guess I should say "Wiccan,"' Daphne said, sitting down next to him and leaning over to look at the magazine with him. She glanced up at me. 'Are you hungry?'

'Well . . . maybe. But there's someone I want you to meet first,' I said. Max looked around, perplexed. Jack was in the bedroom – we'd been napping (well, napping among other things) when they'd knocked, so Max was probably wondering if, in a fit of loneliness from spending the holiday alone, I'd begun making up imaginary friends.

Daphne caught on faster, and she elbowed Max. 'I think she means a guy,' she whispered, excitedly. Couples, or at least the female half, are always so eager for their single friends to hook up. It's like they can't fathom a world where everyone isn't marching around two-by-two, like the animals boarding Noah's ark.

'Where is he?' Daphne asked me.

I tipped my head toward the bedroom. 'Hold on, I'll get him.'

'A guy?' I heard Max asking Daphne. He still sounded confused, and insultingly so. Granted, before Jack came along, I hadn't dated anyone in a while. But still. The idea that I could be involved with someone wasn't that far-fetched, for God's sake.

I poked my head through the bedroom door and saw that Jack was beginning to stir from his nap.

'Hey, you. There're some people here I want you to

meet,' I said softly. Jack opened one eye and peered at me. His hair was mussed, and his smile was sleepy.

'Okay,' he said, and yawned, before stretching and standing up.

'Don't forget to put some clothes on,' I teased him, before closing the door.

'Who is it?' Max asked.

'Jack came to visit for the weekend,' I said with smug pride.

'Jack who?'

I gave Max a look. 'You know. Jack. From London,' I said.

'Here I am. Jack from London,' Jack said, appearing before us. He'd pulled on his Levi's and a charcoal gray sweater, and despite being a little rumpled, he looked sexy as hell.

Max stood to shake Jack's hand. 'I'm Max from New York,' he said.

Max's voice sounded strange – a little sharp, a tad artificial – and when I looked at him, I could see that although he was smiling, his eyes were wary and not very friendly.

'Hi, I'm Daphne,' Daphne said, grinning like the Cheshire cat. 'You don't sound British.'

'I'm not, I just live there,' Jack explained.

'Wow, that's amazing. I've always wanted to live overseas. Hey, Claire, don't you have a friend that lives in London? Maddy, right?' Daphne turned her attention back to Jack. 'Do you know Maddy?'

There was an uncomfortable, leaden pause that lasted several beats too long. I jumped in to fill the silence.

'Max and Daphne were talking about getting a bite to eat,' I told Jack. 'How does that sound to you?'

'Actually, I think we'd better make it another night,' Max interjected quickly. 'I forgot I have to go over some proofs from Monday's shoot.'

Although I'd flopped back onto the sofa, thinking we'd all hang out together, Jack and Max were still standing on either side of my cocktail table – Max looking a little hostile, Jack vaguely amused. I suddenly felt like a referee in a boxing match. Daphne was staring at Max, a little frown on her face.

'What are you talking about? You don't have to do it tonight, surely. Can't it wait?' Daphne asked Max.

'No, it can't,' Max said sharply.

Daphne opened her mouth, looking like she had more to say, but then she seemed to change her mind, and closed it again. She shrugged a silent apology to me.

'We'll do it another time,' Max said. He leaned over and kissed me on the cheek. His lips still felt cold from the brisk November wind that had been wailing outside all day. 'I've gotta run. Jack, nice to meet you.'

'You too,' Jack said.

'You just got here,' I protested, getting up and following Max to the door. As Daphne said good-bye to Jack, I grabbed Max's sleeve and hissed into his ear, 'What's wrong?'

'Nothing. No worries. I've just got to take care of some business. TCB, as Elvis would say.'

'Max, what's going on?'

'Nothing. I'll talk to you later, 'kay?'

'Bye, Claire,' Daphne said. She hugged me and then followed Max out.

I stared at the door as it closed behind them, confused at Max's behavior and embarrassed for how he'd acted in front of Jack. I know that friends and romantic interests don't always get along, but you hope for at least a semblance of accord between them. And I honestly couldn't understand what it was about Jack that had ruffled Max's feathers. All Jack had done was say hello, and shake his hand . . . had he done so in some kind of obnoxious, poser, superficial way that I was too blinded by my infatuation to see? No, that couldn't be it. Jack was anything but obnoxious, poser-ish, or superficial.

'I don't know what got into him,' I said, turning back to Jack.

'Don't you? I think I might have some competition,' Jack said mildly.

'What do you mean?' I asked, and then, realizing what he was implying, I shook my head vehemently. 'Oh, no. There's nothing going on between Max and me. He and Daphne are practically engaged, and I know he doesn't think of me that way.'

'How can you be so sure?'

'Well, you can tell when someone has a crush on you, can't you? Max has never made googly eyes at me, or ever done anything to suggest that he had feelings for me,' I protested.

'Other than being hostile to someone you're dating, you mean,' Jack said. He didn't seem too put out; if anything, Max's behavior seemed to amuse him.

'He wasn't being hostile, just a little . . . pointy,' I said. 'He's like that sometimes. But really, he's like a brother to me, and I know for a fact that he feels the same way about me.'

'If you say so,' Jack said, and then he pulled me close and began nuzzling my neck.

And we didn't see Max and Daphne again for the rest of the weekend, even though I left a couple of messages on Max's machine and knocked on his door a few times. But he never answered, even when I could have sworn he was home.

Sunday, after we'd spent the morning lounging around, and then fooling around, and then lounging around some more, we were lying together on the couch, our heads on opposite ends, our legs tangled together. I was feeling happy and content, if a little insecure since while perusing the *New York Times* Sunday Magazine, Jack had suddenly announced, 'Oh my God, I know her! We went out a few times,' and then proceeded to show me an advertisement for a pair of panty hose. The model featured in the advertisement was sitting seductively, her endless legs bent provocatively in front of her to hide her bare breasts. She had perfectly chiseled features that suggested Swedish ancestry, long icy-blonde hair that curled around her milky white shoulders, and her glossy red lips were pouting with a come-hither look.

'The naked woman?' I croaked, praying that he was really talking about the somewhat dumpy looking architect who was the subject of the article on the opposite page, although since she looked to be about sixty years old, I somehow doubted it.

'Yeah. Her name's Katrinka,' Jack said, looking thoughtful.

'Katrinka?' I repeated, not able to keep the scorn out of my voice. Why is it that models always have bullshit names like *Katrinka*, for Christ's sake? How come you never hear of a model named Denise or Susan, or something normal? No, they always have names like Lexie or Gigi or *Katrinka*. Gag.

However, since Jack obviously didn't share my hatred for all things model-centered, I tried to curb the acid in my tongue. 'When did you date, um, Katrinka?'

'Hmmmm?' Jack seemed distracted by the picture of his flawlessly beautiful, naked ex. Since he had just seen me naked only minutes earlier and comparisons were inevitable, I wanted to put a sack over my head and withdraw from the human race. I nudged him with my foot, and he glanced up at me. 'What did you say? Katrinka? Oh, we went out a few years ago. When I was living here in the city. But it wasn't anything serious, really.'

Okay, now I wanted to know – no, *needed* to know – everything.

'Oh?' I said, hoping that such a noncommittal show of interest would persuade him to continue talking without catching on to the fact that I was practically writhing with jealousy.

Jack smiled lazily, as if the whole dating-a-model thing was no big deal. 'We dated for a few months, but I was pretty caught up in my job at the time. Law firm associates have to bill out twenty-five hundred hours a year, so I didn't have time for a serious girlfriend,' he explained.

'Oh, so . . . she wanted something more serious, and you . . . didn't,' I said, trying to fathom a world in which any man would turn down a Katrinka. Suddenly I had a hopeful thought. 'Was she not very smart? I mean, you must not have had much in common with her, since your careers are so, erm, different.'

'No, she was actually very bright. More so than most of the models I've dated. In fact, as I remember, she was taking classes at NYU – a master's in art history, I think,' he said.

Ugh. Smart women never want to hear that the beautiful women, the Katrinkas of the world, are even capable of sounding out three-syllable words, much less to learn that they're actual scholars. It's not fair. That's our expertise, being sharp and witty and interesting to be around. They're just supposed to lounge against cars and sofas and carpets in advertisements, decorating whatever it was with their unnaturally shiny hair and gleaming lips. We don't infringe on their world, so it's not fair when they horn in on ours. And then suddenly the rest of what he'd said hit me.

'Did you say that you've dated other models?' I asked.

Jack laughed. 'Why are you looking at me like that?'

'Like what?'

'Like I just announced that I spend my weekends cruising the malls to pick up underage girls,' Jack said.

'I wasn't, I just . . . I didn't know that you were the kind of guy who's into models, that's all,' I muttered, suddenly wishing that I'd insisted on a lights-off policy while we were making love. Although I had no proof of the matter, I highly suspected that models did not have traces of cellulite bubbling along the back of their thighs. Unlike me.

'I don't anymore. Katrinka was nice. A little clingy and insecure, but nice. But most of the models I've met are not known for their scintillating conversation,' Jack said, and he sat up and snuggled me closer to him. He smelled wonderfully clean and fresh, a combination of soap and freshly laundered clothes.

'Then why did you go out with them?' I asked. For some unfathomable reason, I was intent on holding my hand over this flame.

'Because I was young and stupid, and I wanted to impress the other guys at my law firm by having a pretty woman on my arm. Sounds pretty dumb, huh?' Jack said, and he smiled at me wryly, amused by the impetus of his youth. 'I got over that a long time ago.'

'Obviously,' I said more tartly than I meant to.

'Oh God, no, I didn't mean . . . Claire, you're gorgeous and stunning and sexy. I just meant that I don't choose the women I date only to impress the assholes I work with. Now I date people I want to spend time with,' he said, and looked down at me with such a warm, wide smile that I couldn't help but thaw out a little. And then he pulled me toward him, and kissed me, and Katrinka fell to the ground, crumpled up next to the rest of the discarded newspaper.

After some time passed, I could feel Jack start to stir, and as he did, my heart sank. He was flying back to London that afternoon, and I knew that if he was going to take a shower before his flight, he'd have to get moving. But I didn't want him to leave. I wanted him to stay, with such an intensity it frightened me. I was overcome with a sudden desire to do whatever it took to keep him there – even if that meant sitting on him or locking him in my apartment. And I'm normally not even that comfortable being around another person for so long – I was the kind of kid who liked going over to a friend's house to play, but then wanted to come home afterward and read quietly by myself. I hated those sleepovers that little girls are so fond of, the ones that last all weekend, until everyone is exhausted and over-sugared and generally sick of one another. But Jack was different. Having him here was different. *Everything* was different. I shut my eyes, squeezing them tightly together, in the childish hope that this would somehow prevent him from leaving.

'Hey, you,' Jack said, nudging me gently with his sock-covered foot. 'I can tell you're awake from the way you're breathing.'

I opened one eye and looked at him. 'You know my sleeping sounds?'

'Well, I do have some experience with them. You also make this cute little snoring sound when you sleep,' he teased me.

This time I opened both eyes, and stared at him, absolutely horrified. 'I *snore*? No, I don't. Do I? No one has ever told me that before,' I protested, having a sudden and vivid picture of myself snorting and grunting like a wild boar.

Jack laughed. 'It's hardly a snore, more like a sigh. It's actually very sweet, and very feminine,' he said as he struggled up to a sitting position. He rested his hand on my leg. 'I have to get going if I'm going to make my flight.'

'I know,' I said sadly.

'I wish I could stay longer. This weekend has been . . .' His voice trailed off, and he looked at me, to see if I understood.

I certainly did. 'I know, for me too,' I said, nodding.

We'd spent four days together, talking about everything from American foreign policy to whether Madonna was completely overrated (Jack voted a definite yes, I thought no, if only because of her better, earlier work), but we'd somehow managed to avoid the conversation about us. I hate that conversation. It always comes at the point in a relationship where I'm just starting to feel comfortable, and thus completely vulnerable to the inevitable sucker punch when the guy announces that he's not ready for a 'serious' relationship, or that he needs to focus on his career. Or, in the case of Sawyer, that he's fleeing the country. So I didn't really want to have the 'us' talk with Jack. I wanted to freeze everything where it was right now, so we could remain forever stuck at the lazy, contented, Sunday-postcoital-nap moment.

'Have you told Maddy yet that we're seeing each other?' Jack asked.

'Um, no,' I said.

'Don't you think you should?' Jack asked.

I shrugged, and closed my eyes. When all else fails, try passive-aggression.

'Claire, I think we should talk about this,' Jack said.

God, why was he such an adult? I thought women were supposed to chase men down for these talks, not the other way around. Couldn't we forget the heavy-duty, where-are-we-going, what-does-it-all-mean part of the conversation and just spend the few remaining minutes we had making out?

'Claire,' Jack insisted, and he jostled my leg.

I opened my eyes and looked at him.

'I think you should tell her,' he said. 'I want us to be open about what we're doing.'

'What are we doing?' I asked, before I could stop myself. *Damn*, I thought. He'd reeled me in, and like it or not, we were now having The Talk.

Jack looked at me for a long minute. 'I think that we're involved. Which is what I want,' he said. 'Don't you?'

I nodded, feeling a burst of happiness that this wasn't building up to the 'I like you, *but . . .*' speech I'd been fearing.

'But there are a lot of other . . . considerations,' I said cautiously.

'Like Maddy,' Jack said.

I nodded again.

'Well, you can tell her about us, or if you'd rather, I can. But I think it would be better coming from you,' Jack said. He hesitated for a minute. 'I didn't know if I should tell you this, but she's been calling me. A lot. I'm trying to be kind but firm with her, but still . . . I think if I called her to talk about this, about us, it might give her the wrong idea.'

I shivered. I really, *really* didn't want to tell Maddy about Jack and me. What I wanted was not to feel how I was feeling about Jack. Or actually, what I wanted was to have his entire history with Maddy somehow erased, so that there wouldn't be any obstacles to our dating. And, as long as I was having unrealistic fantasies, I also wanted a new, better job, to be ten pounds thinner, and to have a lot more money.

'Claire,' Jack persisted, making it clear he was not going to let me off the hook on this one.

'Okay, okay, I'll tell her,' I sighed. 'But I don't think it's going to go over very well.'

'Maybe she'll surprise you,' Jack said.

'Maybe she will. Or, maybe she'll send me a letter bomb,' I said doubtfully.

'She's just one issue. There's also the long-distance problem,' he said.

'Yes, there's that.'

'I guess for now we'll just keep trying to get together on weekends? And see where it goes?' Jack asked.

This startled me. I hadn't really thought beyond this weekend. I guess I'd fantasized a little – or maybe a lot – about the two of us in a house in Connecticut, the very picture of domestic bliss, with a couple of Baby Gap-outfitted kids and a Volvo in the garage. But the logistics of a long-distance relationship, of schlepping back and forth on long and costly international flights, of not seeing each other for weeks at a time . . . that was going to be hard. But the alternative – *not* seeing Jack anymore, *not* having his nightly phone calls to look forward to, *not* feeling the way I felt when I was with him – was a far worse prospect.

And as I gazed at him – his eyes, kind and gentle as they met mine, the sharp yet handsome angles of his face, the shock of blond hair that was always falling down over his forehead – it hit me. This wasn't just a flirtation. It wasn't just a passing interest. It had reached the point where I couldn't just forget about him if I tried hard enough, couldn't brush our relationship off as a vacation fling. The baby-duck-imprinting process was complete – I was involved.

'What do you think about that plan?' he asked.

All I could do was nod. Because I was afraid that if I opened my mouth, the panic that was gripping me, the anxiety that was starting to spin out of control, would come spewing out, and I had no idea what form it would take. The one thing I didn't want to ever happen again, that I swore I couldn't live through again, was happening. I was falling in love with Jack. The thought scared the hell out of me.

By the time Jack left for the airport, leaving me behind with a kiss and his pleasantly clean masculine scent lingering in my apartment, I was in full-out panic mode. Jack had sensed something was a little off, and as he hustled around to shower, dress, and get his things together, he kept stopping to ask me if everything was all right. My response was always to chirp 'No, I'm fine, really' in an overly bright, plastic tone of voice that probably made him think I was losing my mind.

The truth was, I was spooked. What exactly had we just agreed to during our 'us' talk? That we were going to continue to see each other? Well, fine, but what did that mean? It was only the second weekend we'd spent together, so surely we didn't just agree to an exclusive relationship. Men don't do that after only two weekends, at least not in my experience. So we were going to continue to talk on the phone, and perhaps see each other occasionally, which sounded reasonable, except for one small detail: I was falling for this guy. Which meant that when things inevitably burned out, or when I found out that he was, of course, continuing to see other people, or when his phone calls went from being nightly, to a few times a week, to once a week, to never, where would that leave me? I knew all too well. I'd been there before, and it was a place I'd promised myself I wouldn't end up at again.

And had I really promised to tell Maddy everything? Because I wasn't at all sure I wanted to do that. I knew that I owed it to her, and that coming clean was probably the morally correct thing to do, but frankly, it wasn't an appealing prospect. Every time I talked to her, she sounded even more down about her breakup with Jack. Wouldn't it just rub salt in the gaping, oozing wound in her heart to tell her that I was seeing her ex? Could I really do that to her? And what would the point be, since it was only a matter of time before Jack left me with a broken heart, too? Should I really destroy one of my oldest friendships over a man that I had absolutely no hope of having the ever-elusive happily-ever-after with?

I needed to do some damage control, and quickly. I could hear Max next door – he had, yet again, put Frankie Goes to Hollywood's 'Relax' on the repeat setting of his stereo at full volume, and the bass was reverberating through my apartment – so I knocked on his door.

He didn't answer until I finally called out, 'I know you're in there, you asshole. Let me in.'

The door opened a crack, and Max peered out at me. 'Sorry, I didn't hear you,' he said shiftily. He opened the door a little wider and peered behind me into the hall. 'Are you alone?'

'Yes, why? Are you hatching plots to take over the world in there? Where have you been? I haven't seen you for days.'

'I just haven't felt all that social,' Max said, stepping aside to allow me entrance to his apartment.

'Since when? Why didn't you want to hang out with Jack and me?'

He just shrugged. 'I had stuff to do.'

'Uh huh,' I said, standing in front of him, my arms crossed. I wasn't going to let him off that easily. 'So, what was it that you didn't like about him?'

'Nothing. I mean, I hardly talked to the guy. He seemed

normal,' Max said. He wasn't even making an effort to sound sincere. Usually Max revels in gossiping about anyone I go out with, gleefully pointing out their personal failings, such as weak chins, bad shoes, annoying laughs, or general pomposity. There was no one Max was above making fun of, including his closest friends. Calling Jack 'normal' was more of a stinging indictment than if he'd made fun of Jack's hair, or the way he talked or dressed.

'Okay, whatever, don't tell me,' I sighed, and sat down on his couch, folding my legs up underneath me. On the stereo, Frankie and crew were gearing up to sing 'Relax' for the four hundredth time in a row. I picked up the stereo remote and silenced them.

'Make yourself at home,' Max said, sitting next to me.

'I need to talk,' I said.

'About what?'

'Is your friend Tucker still single?'

Max looked puzzled. 'Why?'

'I want you to set me up with him. On a date, I mean,' I said.

Max shook his head, now completely confused. 'What about that Jack guy? Didn't he just leave like ten minutes ago?'

So Max had been keeping tabs on us. And if I wasn't so caught up in my own neurosis at the moment, maybe I'd be able to get to the bottom of whatever Max's problem was and why he was acting so dodgy. But I was on emotional overload, so Max, and whatever it was that was simmering in the murky recesses of his twisted little mind, would have to wait.

'Yeah, he took a cab to the airport,' I said.

'And . . . it's over between you two?' Max asked.

I tried to ignore the hopeful note in his voice. 'No, I don't think so.'

'So, what then? Are you not really into him anymore?'

I sighed. 'I wish, but it's just the opposite. In fact, I'm

getting a little . . . overwhelmed. So that's why I want you to set me up with Tucker,' I explained, thinking this made perfect sense. It did to me. Going out with another guy, particularly one that was every bit as nice, charming, and handsome as Jack, was exactly what I needed. That way I'd see that there were other guys out there – with many fewer complications attached to them – and my infatuation for Jack would be exposed as being only that. A crush. A fling. A momentary lapse of judgment. Not love. Certainly not that.

And Tucker Fitzpatrick was the perfect candidate. I'd met him back when he was still dating his girlfriend, Dina. They were one of those oddball couples – Tucker's handsome in a crinkly-eyed, ruffled-round-the-edges, Hugh Grant kind of way, and he's very kind and quite smart. The last time I saw him at one of Max's many cocktail parties, we had a vigorous debate about whether Woody Allen movies were culturally significant or overrated, self-indulgent crap. He'd argued for the former position, citing *Annie Hall* and *Crimes and Misdemeanors* as his evidence. I insisted that Allen is a narcissist and that all of his movies are just the puffed-up sexual fantasies of a nebbish with Walter Mitty daydreams of scoring with women who are out of his league, and pointed to *Everyone Says I Love You*, *Mighty Aphrodite*, and *Manhattan Murder Mystery*. Tucker tried to counter with *Bullets Over Broadway*, but I scored the victorious blow by reminding him how horrible *Scenes from a Mall* was, at which point Tucker had to admit defeat.

Dina, on the other hand, was – not to mince words – a frump. She wasn't ugly – although it didn't help matters that she was short and dumpy, and her hair always seemed on the greasy side – but she never really made an effort with herself. A new haircut or a touch of blush or a good eyebrow tweezing might have made a huge difference in her overall appearance. But despite her looks, Dina was brilliant and hilarious, and Tucker seemed to truly adore her. When they broke up – she dumped him, and ended up marrying a colleague she'd been having an affair with on the side – Tucker was inconsolable, and I knew he'd been after Max to fix him up with someone (actually, if I remember correctly, he wanted to be set up with a model, but since I knew he just wanted to make Dina jealous, I didn't hold it against him). I already liked Tucker as a person, and I'd always admired him for falling in love with a woman who, like myself, fell short of the beauty ideal. He seemed like a perfect first candidate for my new Dating to Forget Jack Program.

'So let me get this straight. You're really into Mr Brit Guy,' Max began.

'He's American. You know that,' I interrupted.

'Whatever. You're really into Mr American-Brit Guy, and that's freaking you out. So you want me to set you up with my good friend under false pretenses?'

'False pretenses? No, I really like Tucker. *I* want to go out with him,' I said.

'So that you can get your mind off of the guy that you really like. I don't think so, Claire,' Max said with a tone of pious disapproval that was really quite unlike him. 'And even if I was willing to do that to Tucker, which I'm not, he's seeing someone.'

'Oh,' I said, disappointed. I collapsed back against the sofa, feeling defeated.

'However, if you really want me to set you up with someone,' Max said thoughtfully, 'I do know another guy who might be up for it.'

'Oh yeah?' I perked up. 'Do I know him? What's his name? What's he like?'

'No, you've never met Cooksey – that's his name, Gary Cooksey. He's a photographer, although he mainly does sports stuff. And he's . . . entertaining,' Max said thoughtfully.

The use of the word 'entertaining' made me suspicious. This was not the best possible description for a blind date.

It was even worse than using the adjective 'nice,' which everyone knows is just code for 'hideously ugly.'

'And why are you willing to inflict me on him, when you view me as such a threat to Tucker?' I asked.

'Because Cooksey isn't as sensitive as Tucker. And he's not as good a friend, so if you end up torturing him with your endless list of dating dos and don'ts, I won't feel responsible,' Max explained.

The glint in Max's eye as he said this made me a little nervous, but what choice did I have? I was a desperate woman – so desperate I was willing to break the dating rule I had about never going out on another blind date, ever again. But this time I wasn't dating for the purpose of meeting that special someone . . . I was dating to forget him. And I was willing to do whatever it took to do that, even if it meant coercing every person I knew into setting me up with every one of their eligible male friends.

The date with Entertaining Gary was duly arranged for the following Friday. I didn't mention it to Jack, of course, although when we talked on Thursday, I did tell him that I wouldn't be around the next night at the time he normally called me because I was going out with some friends. I felt vaguely guilty for the fib – although I have to admit, lying does get easier with practice – which was only made worse when he suggested that I call him if I didn't get in too late.

'Or if you get in really, really late, and it's already morning my time,' Jack said.

'I don't want to wake you up,' I protested.

'I don't care. I don't want to go a whole day without talking to you,' Jack said.

If I'd heard anyone else express this syrupy sentiment, it would have made my teeth ache. But coming from Jack it was endearingly sweet. And romantic. And it made me smile and begin twirling the phone cord around my finger while we talked. Is this what falling in love was? Cooing without shame? I tried to reassure myself with the knowledge that at least we hadn't reached the point where we were calling each other 'baby doll,' or blowing kisses over the phone. I've always wished for the immediate extinction of those people, along with tailgaters and the assholes who talk during movies.

I also started to wonder if during our conversation the previous weekend we had established that we were having a more exclusive relationship than I'd previously thought. If so, it would mean that my going out with this Gary person would be cheating . . . something I had never done to a boyfriend, because I'd always thought that sneaking around behind someone's back was a dishonest, shitty thing to do. Not quite as bad as adultery, but not so far off, either. But what did people say nowadays to establish that you were in a monogamous relationship? In my early dating years, I'd made the mistake of thinking that sex was a clincher. Not one-night stands, of course, but sex after the fourth or fifth date. Then I learned, through trial and humiliating error, that men don't think that way. They tend to view monogamy as something that involves the exchange of rings – and even then they liked to keep their options open. I'd always thought that men in their thirties were just older, more sophisticated versions of their twenty-something counter-parts, but after my time with Jack, now I wasn't so sure. Maybe men do mature, after all.

Gary picked me up at seven on Friday evening. We'd talked on the phone just long enough to establish a meeting time and that we'd do something casual. I was dressed in what is my typical weekend uniform – black V-neck sweater, dark-rinse jeans, and black boots (with a low heel, because Max hadn't told me how tall Gary was, and it would be Max's idea of a practical joke to fix me up with a Napoleon clone).

He arrived on time, buzzed up to my apartment, and after a garbled conversation through my low-tech intercom, I told him I'd be right down.

'Gary?' I asked the only man standing on the stairs of my building.

I tried not to visibly cringe when he nodded. Gary was . . . *rotund*. He was just shy of obese, soft all over, from his round cheeks to his jiggling stomach. I wouldn't be at all surprised to learn that his two closest relationships were with his couch and the local pizza deliveryman.

Don't be so judgmental, I chastised myself. He could be a really wonderful guy, and besides, I'm always railing against a society that has set out an impossible standard for women, expecting us all to look like the Victoria's Secret models. It would be hypocritical of me to discriminate against Gary for not having abs of steel. Besides, he was sort of jolly looking, like a young, beardless Santa Claus.

I mustered up a smile, held my hand out, and said, 'Hi, I'm Claire.'

'Claire? "That's a fat girl's name," ' Gary said. He grabbed my hand – his palms were unpleasantly sweaty – and shook it vigorously. 'Ha! You get it? It's that line from *The Breakfast Club*. You know, Judd Nelson says it to Molly Ringwald.'

'Ha,' I said, my smile withering. *The Breakfast Club* had been the most popular teen movie out when I was in the eighth grade, and the 'fat girl's name' line had been repeated to me, oh, only about four hundred thousand times. Since I was still padded with baby fat at the time the movie debuted, the teasing had stung so much I even considered changing my name in a fit of teenage histrionics. And it was even less enchanting hearing it now, nineteen years later, coming from a sweaty dork with an annoyingly cherubic face. Any empathy I might have had for Gary and his less-than-perfect physique instantly drained out of me. I knew it would be breaking an all-time record if I aborted our plans at the doorstep, but I had a sinking feeling that the date wasn't going to get any better.

And it didn't. A short time later, I was kicking myself for not following my instincts to cut and run, not to mention for breaking my rule about no blind dates ever. My perfect first date is dinner at a nice restaurant, somewhere quiet enough so that you can carry on a conversation, but casual enough so that you can relax, since it's important to have the time and space to find out if there's a possible connection without any unnecessary pressure to pose and preen. Gary's idea of a fun first date was to take me (I kid you not) to Hooters, so he could simultaneously ogle the waitresses' breasts and watch a Knicks game. Since I'm into neither boobs nor basketball, this was pretty much as bad as it could get.

'We'll have a pitcher of beer and a basket of wings,' Gary ordered from the waitress, without first consulting me on either selection. We were perched on high stools next to a tall, round table, and I had to hook my boots over the bottom rung of the stool in order to stay balanced.

'No, wait,' I stopped her, and ordered a glass of water with a lemon and a salad.

'Come on, you gotta live a little,' Gary said, his eyes never leaving the television screen, even during the commercials. 'Wow, did you see that shot? GO, GO, GO! Aw, shit.'

I didn't bother to respond. I figured that once I ate my salad, I would announce that I had a migraine and hurry back to the safety of my apartment. I could even call Jack, a thought that cheered me enormously. Okay, Jack and I might not have the perfect situation, but at least he paid attention to me, which was more than I could say for Gary, who was oblivious to everything other than the stupid basketball game. When our waitress returned to deliver Gary's wings and my salad, Gary did tear his eyes away from the television for a minute to stare at her admittedly quite large and scantily clad chest. I tried to give her a look of sympathy over her being objectified in such a manner, but she ignored me and just smiled and winked at Gary, which caused his ears to turn bright red. Apparently, the waitress was more interested in her tip than she was in the sisterly bonds of feminism.

I wolfed down my salad as fast as I could, although I nearly choked on a cherry tomato after jumping off of my stool when Gary suddenly screamed, 'REF, YOU SUCK!' shaking his fists and booing loudly in concert with the other Hooters patrons, while I coughed and sputtered until the tomato dislodged from my throat. Not that Gary, or anyone else, noticed – I could have turned blue, gone unconscious, and slipped from the plastic leather upholstered stool, and the earliest I could have hoped for medical intervention would have been at the half-time break, and only then if they weren't playing entertaining commercials starring a singing dog. It was the last straw.

'Gary, I think I'm going to take off, I'm not feeling too well,' I began, before realizing that he wasn't listening to me. I stood up, and stood in front of him, blocking his view of the television. Naturally, his eyes fixed on my chest, which I'm sure was a disappointment when compared to the waitress's cropped-T-shirt-covered implants.

'I'm going to go,' I repeated.

'What? Why? It's only the second quarter,' Gary protested.

'Um, I'm not feeling too well,' I said, not caring that my excuse sounded feeble.

'Okay, I'll take you home,' Gary said.

I was a little moved at his chivalry. It was the first redeeming trait he'd revealed. Not that I had any intention of taking him up on it, of course, but it was nice to know that he wasn't a complete asshole.

'No, no, no,' I said hastily. 'I'd feel terrible if I made you miss any of your game. I'll just get a cab.'

Gary looked at me and then looked longingly at the television set. It was previewing some kind of a half-time show, and I could tell he was torn.

'Really,' I said firmly.

'Well, okay, if you're sure,' he said. Gary hopped off of his stool and suddenly lunged at me. I shied away from him – I have well-honed survival skills and can block unwanted advances with the skill of a kung fu champion – but then I realized he was just trying to hug me good-bye, an idea I wasn't too keen on, but probably didn't merit my kneeing him in the groin. Gary wrapped two meaty arms around me, and I patted his back, trying not to wince when I realized it was soaked through with sweat.

Does this guy have some kind of a glandular problem? I wondered as I withdrew my now sticky hands.

'How about a rain check when you're feeling better?' Gary asked, so hopefully that I couldn't bring myself to swat him down. True he had about as much sex appeal as a chunk of Velveeta cheese, and I had absolutely no intention of ever going out with him again, but he seemed relatively harmless.

'Sure, maybe,' I said, hoping I sounded just nice enough not to hurt his feelings, while not giving him any encouragement.

'Great,' he said enthusiastically – and loudly – right in my ear.

And then I felt something wet and icky and . . . Oh. My. God. Did he really just stick his tongue in my ear? I wondered as I flinched away from him. It was the most repulsive sensation – it felt like someone was trying to bore into my brain with a flaccid wet pickle.

'What was that?' I asked him, so outraged that all thoughts of sparing his feelings were lost. I rubbed at my ear, which felt disgustingly wet and saturated with his spit.

'Just a special good-bye for you,' he said, winking. He then made a gun with his fingers and shot me with it while making a clicking sound with his tongue.

'What? I cannot believe you just ... how could you possibly think that's ... what the hell is wrong with you?' I said, so furious I was spitting my words out. Gary looked stricken, and started to reach out toward me – for what reason, I don't know, and I wasn't about to find out.

'Don't touch me! Just stay away, and don't *ever* call me again,' I said. And with that, I turned on my heel and marched out of Hooters with as much dignity as one can have leaving such an establishment. I stormed over to the curb and immediately started looking for a cab, when all of a sudden I felt an unmistakably sweaty hand on my arm.

'Why are you so angry?' Gary asked.

Argh! What was this guy's problem? Did he not understand that I was brushing him off? If he went around sticking his tongue in relative strangers' ears, it could hardly be the first time he'd been shrieked at. He was just lucky that I hadn't also slapped him across the face, like an outraged starlet in an old black-and-white movie.

'Are you kidding me?' I asked. 'You take me to *Hooters* to watch a freaking *basketball game*, and then when it's obvious that I'm leaving early because I could not be having a worse time, you decide to say good-bye by sticking your *tongue* in my *ear*? Are you *insane*? Or is this really your idea of how to treat someone you're on a date with?'

As I spoke, my voice rumbled from an angry bark to a furious shriek, and Gary flinched, apparently afraid that I might just hit him after all. His round face creased in confusion, and he shrugged, spreading his meaty hands in front of him.

'But Max said that you're a huge Knicks fan, and that Hooters is your favorite restaurant. I don't normally go there to watch the game, but he said you'd want to,' Gary stuttered.

'*Max* told you that?' I asked, and alarms began blaring in my head. I should have known. Max had engineered this date from hell; it was just another one of his sick practical jokes. Max was, after all, the same man who had once filled out an Army recruitment card with my name and address, and I'd only just recently convinced the recruiters who had been stalking me ever since that I truly was not interested in a career change. I could have kicked myself for not seeing this coming, although I would have vastly preferred to strangle Max. And then another thought occurred to me.

'And the ear thing? Was that Max's idea, too?' I demanded. Gary just nodded, looking miserable and embarrassed.

I smiled, and patted him on the arm, poor guy. Things had now become clear. Max had decided to play a little joke on me, and for that he must die. But I believed that Gary was completely innocent in all of it. He was not at all my type, of course, and there was no chance I would ever go out with him again (and it was beyond me how he could have possibly believed that any woman would want to have a tongue stuck in her ear, no matter what Max had told him), but we did part on friendly terms, even if Gary did still seem a little frightened of me. He hailed me a cab, and I collapsed in the back of the taxi, squeezing my eyes shut and pressing my fingertips to my temples. The date had been horrible (although, sadly, not the worst blind date in my history), and rather than break me from my Jack addiction, all it had done was make me miss him that much more. In fact, I couldn't wait to get home and call him. It was just too bad I couldn't go into detail about my evening out. Under different circumstances, Jack probably would have gotten a big kick out of it.

12

The phone began to ring almost as soon as I walked into my apartment, and before I had a chance to call Jack. I'd just kicked off one of my boots and was in the process of nudging the second one off, so I had to hop across the apartment in order to grab the phone before my answering machine picked up.

'Hello,' I gasped into the receiver.

'I think he's seeing someone,' Maddy said.

I was struggling to get out of my pea coat with one hand while simultaneously prying my other foot out of my boot, which had gotten stuck on my right ankle. I braced my boot against the edge of my couch and gave it a good tug, but in the process of freeing my foot, I lost my balance and took what probably would look like, to someone watching me, an exaggerated pratfall, tumbling to the floor in a graceless pile.

'Ack!' I cried out as the cordless phone went sailing in one direction while my body flew in another. I recovered the phone, rubbing my ankle, which had twisted in an unnatural and painful angle from my body. 'Shit! Ow! Maddy?'

'Yes, it's me,' Maddy said irritably. God, I was glad she didn't get dumped very often. It made her really cranky.

'I just got home from the date from hell,' I began. I limped over to my sofa and flopped down, peering at my ankle to see if it was swelling or turning black.

'Claire! Didn't you hear me? I think Harrison is *seeing* someone,' she said.

This time, she had my full attention. My first thought was, *She's found out I've been seeing Jack.* My second was, *She couldn't possibly have found out . . . so who in the hell, other than me, is he dating?* I wasn't prepared for the swell of jealousy I felt. I mean, I had wondered if he might be dating others, and used it as a justification for going out with Gary. But I had only gone out with Gary in order to forget about Jack – I'd never considered dating for romance.

'Claire, are you there?'

'Oh, yeah, I'm here. Sorry, I just . . .' I said, trying to think of how to finish that thought. I just had my heart torn out? I just thought that your ex-boyfriend was falling in love with me, and it turns out he wasn't? 'Had to turn off the television. Um, what were you saying? About Jack?'

'Jack? Why are you calling him that?' Maddy demanded.

I froze. 'Um . . . I, um . . . well, isn't that his name?' I gabbled stupidly, feeling ridiculously like a man whose wife has discovered lipstick on his collar.

'Yes, but . . . well, never mind, it doesn't matter. But listen, I think he's seeing someone! In fact, I *know* it. I was out last night, and I ran into someone who works with Harrison, and she said she'd heard that he went out of town to visit some woman last weekend,' Maddy said. 'How do you think he met her? Do you think she's someone he works with, or just some whore he picked up somewhere?'

Despite being called a whore (and after all, Maddy didn't know she was talking about me), relief flooded through me. Jack *wasn't* seeing anyone else! Were it not for my injured ankle, I'd have felt like dancing around my apartment, flipping my hair from side to side like the little girls on the old Charlie Brown cartoons.

'Where did he go?' I asked, wanting to be supportive and yet feeling like complete crap for the joy bubbling up inside me. Especially since the news that Jack had moved on was so devastating to Maddy. If she only knew the whole story, I thought grimly, and then winced when I remembered that I'd promised Jack I'd tell her. Clearly this was not the moment to do so.

'Huh? I don't know. Do you think it matters? Oh my God,' Maddy said, and stopped abruptly.

'What?'

'Do you think it was someone he was seeing while we were still together?' she whispered.

'Oh, no. I'm sure he wasn't cheating on you,' I said, finally on comfortable ground.

'How do you know?'

'Oh . . . I don't. But, I just don't . . . think there's any reason to assume that,' I stuttered. *Could I sound any more guilty?* I wondered. A covert-ops position in the CIA was clearly not in my future.

'I know, you're probably right. Still,' Maddy said thoughtfully, 'I do want to know who it is. And I know just how I'm going to find out. You're never going to believe this, but,' she said, and then paused for dramatic effect.

'What?'

'I'm going to hire a private detective,' she announced triumphantly.

'What?' I repeated, hoping against hope that I had somehow misunderstood her.

'You know, someone to follow Harrison around, and who can give me a dossier on everyone he sees. That way, if he is dating someone, I'll find out who my competition is,' Maddy said gleefully.

'Maddy, you can't do that,' I said.

'Why not?'

'Because it's a complete violation of his privacy.'

'Oh, give me a break. Ex-boyfriends don't have any rights. That's what you've always said,' she retorted.

She had a point. I had said that, back in college when we were making prank phone calls to Craig, a creep that I didn't even like who'd kept pestering me to go out with him until I finally agreed, only to have him stand me up (this was back before the advent of Caller I.D., of course – that little technological advance, while useful for screening out stalkers and parents, has made it difficult for dumpees everywhere to strike back at their dumpors). But a few, harmless crank calls to a frat rat are a far cry from the extreme measure of hiring someone to conduct surveillance on your ex.

'I think it's a really, *really* bad idea,' I warned. I hesitated before my next comment, because although on the one hand it was entirely self-serving, I actually did believe it was good advice. 'This kind of obsessing, of wanting to know everyone he sees . . . it's not healthy, Mads. And it's not conducive to getting over him.'

'I don't want to get over him. And I am going to hire the detective,' Maddy said. Her voice was a little shrill.

'But what if he finds out?'

'Well, then he'll know how much I love him, and maybe it will make him come back to me,' she said. 'What do you think?'

What I thought was that she was starting to sound a little loony-tunes, but I couldn't think of a nice, supportive way to tell her that, so instead I said, 'I think you should try to move on. There are, what, about a thousand guys beating down your door? Why don't you at least start dating some other men?' I asked.

Going out with someone else hadn't exactly gotten my mind off of Jack, but Maddy has more discriminating taste than I do, and she would never have let herself be fixed up on a blind date with the likes of Gary the Tongue. Maddy would only date London's most eligible bachelors, and, knowing her, she'd meet some gorgeous, wealthy aristocrat and would end up becoming the next Duchess of Whatever. I could easily picture her courtside at Wimbledon, decked out in an outrageous hat and sitting next to Prince William in the royal box.

'I don't know,' she said, sounding gloomy. 'I thought you'd think the detective was a good idea.'

'I don't,' I said firmly. And hoped that would be the end of it. But knowing Maddy and her stubborn streak as I do, I doubted it.

From: Max Levy <bobafett5473@hotmail.com>
To: Claire Spencer <claire.spencer@ssmagazine.com>
Subject: Hot Date
Date: Monday, December 9

Where have you been? How did your big date go?

From: Max Levy <bobafett5473@hotmail.com>
To: Claire Spencer <claire.spencer@ssmagazine.com>
Subject: Where are you?
Date: Monday, December 9

What's going on? Why won't you respond to my e-mails? Or return my phone calls?

From: Max Levy <bobafett5473@hotmail.com>
To: Claire Spencer <claire.spencer@ssmagazine.com>
Subject: Come on . . .
Date: Monday, December 9

Okay, I just talked to Cooksey, I guess I've been found out. It was a joke. JOKE. You can't possibly still be mad about it???

From: Max Levy <bobafett5473@hotmail.com>
To: Claire Spencer <claire.spencer@ssmagazine.com>
Subject: Hello?
Date: Monday, December 9

Please talk to me ...

From: Claire Spencer <claire.spencer@ssmagazine.com>
To: Max Levy <bobafett5473@hotmail.com>
Subject: Re: Hello?
Date: Monday, December 9

No. Go away.

'Is this Claire Spencer?'

'Yes, it is,' I said absentmindedly. The phone call was interrupting my daily hour of computer solitaire, which I play every workday from four to five p.m. I know this might not be considered by some to be a valid use of company time, but I considered it crucial to my mental health. One can focus on the needs and plights of the elderly for only so many hours per day before getting burned out.

'This is Kit Holiday from *Retreat* magazine. We received your résumé, and our hiring committee would like to meet with you,' the woman said.

I was so surprised, I nearly fell out of my nonergonomical chair. *Retreat* actually wanted to interview me? How was that possible?

'Great. That's ... great. When would you like me to come?' I asked, grabbing for my calendar.

'This week, if possible. I know it's short notice, but if you're free, we could fly you out on Thursday evening, have the interview Friday morning, and then you could fly back that night. If that's okay with you, I'll go ahead and make your reservations,' Kit said.

Under the Friday, December 13, spot on my calendar (which meant my interview would be on Friday the thirteenth . . . would that be bad luck?) there were already two entries – 'Staff Meeting' and 'London Article Due.'

'No, Friday is fine,' I said brightly. As far as Robert would know, I'd have a raging case of measles and be safely quarantined at home lest I infect everyone at the office.

'Great. I'll call you back later this afternoon to confirm your itinerary,' Kit Holiday said. Wow, what a great name, I thought, if a little ironic considering she worked at a travel magazine. Her name sounded like the moniker of a clever girl detective, or maybe a female adventurer or aviator from the thirties.

I wrote down the interview in my date book in bright red ink and added three exclamation points to it. Not only did I have an interview, they were *flying* me in! That must mean that they were interested, right?

'Guess what?' I said when Jack called me that night.

'You're coming to visit me over Christmas?' Jack said.

This announcement caught me a little off guard.

'What?' I said.

'Don't you have some time off for the holidays? You could come and spend a week – or longer, if you can,' Jack said eagerly.

'Well. Um. Actually, yeah, I will be off. The office closes down from December 24 until January 2.'

'Just say the word, and I'll make all of the arrangements,' Jack said.

'I didn't know men were capable of making travel arrangements,' I said, hedging. I was still a little freaked out. Why was it that every other guy I had ever met was terrified of making plans for the next weekend, and yet Jack seemed perfectly comfortable making plans to spend *Christmas* together? Was he some kind of a freak, a laboratory experiment concocted by mad women scientists intent on creating a man incapable of playing mind games?

'We're not. When I said, "I'll make them," I actually meant I was going to call my travel agent and have her make them, as she always seems delighted to do,' he said.

I'll just bet she does, I thought darkly, immediately imagining the travel agent to look like one of the British invasion go-go dancers from the sixties – blonde hair teased up into a sexy, Austin Powers-style shag, nonexistent skirt, long legs encased in tall, white patent leather boots. This was the problem with a long-distance relationship – all I knew about Jack's life was what he told me. It wasn't like I'd met his co-workers, or neighbors, or had seen any of the dark places that opportunistic women lurked.

'Do you have other plans to go see your family or something?' Jack asked.

I pondered this, and had to admit that the prospect of spending the holidays with Jack sounded vastly preferable to my other alternatives – dinner out with my dad and stepmom (who I could tell really didn't like me, even though she bared her teeth in a fake smile whenever we saw each other), or flying down to Florida to spend it with my mom and her new husband, who I swore was an alcoholic, although Mom insists that just because he and 'the boys' enjoy a few beers while they're golfing does not mean he has a drinking problem. I didn't disagree, but when you add on the two cocktail-hour vodkas on the rocks, the half bottle of wine with dinner, and a couple of 'dessert' beers, it's a different story.

'No, I don't, really. Don't you?'

'Nope. My dad always spends Christmas in Aspen, with family number two. And my mom likes to spend the holidays with my little sister and her family,' Jack said.

'Oh. Well. Can I think about it?' I asked.

'Yes, and while you think about it, I'll have Jenny make the reservations,' Jack said.

'Jenny?'

'My travel agent,' he said easily.

Grrr, I thought. *Curses on Jenny and her slutty miniskirts.*

'When do I have to let you know by?' I asked.

'I don't know, how about a few days?' Jack said. 'So anyway, what did you want to tell me?'

'Oh, I got a job interview! With *Retreat*, which is a really great magazine. Can you believe it?' I enthused.

'You see, someone did read your exposé on the masses of seniors invading Disney World. When's your interview?'

'On Friday, in Chicago. They're flying me in,' I said.

'Chicago?' Jack sounded puzzled. 'Would you have to move there?'

'If I get the job, then yes.'

'I didn't know you were thinking about moving,' Jack said.

I shrugged, and then remembered he couldn't see me. 'I would for the right job,' I said.

'Well, if you're willing to consider London, I know a few editor types here. Just say the word and I'll see if they're hiring,' Jack said.

I was startled. Was he really suggesting I consider moving to London? And was he just being nice, or was he implying that if I moved to London, he and I would . . . be together? That wasn't possible, was it? Men are supposed to run from commitment like rats fleeing a leaky ship, not invite it to snuggle up closer. If Jack was going to keep breaking every known rule of how men and women are supposed to behave in the initial stages of romance, then how the hell was I supposed to get a grip on whatever it was that was happening between us?

'Claire?'

'I'm still here.'

'Are you okay?'

'Yes, yes. Fine.'

I could tell Jack was waiting for me to respond to his rather generous offer to help me find a better job, but what was I supposed to say? That sure, I'd consider moving to a foreign country to be with a man whom I'd known for less than a month? It was crazy. Okay, it didn't *feel* crazy – in fact the very idea made me want to whoop with joy and start packing my bags – but intellectually, I knew that it was ridiculous. Of course, falling in love is an insanity unto itself, and therefore colors all perceptions and reactions. One should never make major decisions while either in the initial or final phases of it, such as moving out of the country or cutting all of one's hair off.

'Um. That's really nice. I guess it wouldn't hurt for me to talk to your contacts,' I said, wincing at how ungracious I sounded.

'I'll see what I can do,' Jack said. He paused. 'By the way, have you talked to Maddy yet?'

Ugh. I'd hoped we could avoid that topic for the time being, or at least until I found a way to turn into Harry Potter, so I could wave my magic wand and make Maddy forget she'd ever met Jack.

'No, not yet,' I said. 'But I will. I promise.'

'I just want to make sure she hears about it from you, especially if you're coming here,' he said. 'I think she'd be hurt if she found out from a third person.'

If you only knew that third person could be the private investigator Maddy was threatening to hire, I thought. But her hiring the detective also meant that I was out of time. I had to tell her the truth. I just hoped that Maddy would be in a charitable mood. Maybe she'd be somehow infused with the spirit of Christmas, and more willing to forgive treacherous friends.

'I know, I know,' I said, resigned. 'I'll tell her.'

From: Max Levy <bobafett5473@hotmail.com>
To: Claire Spencer <claire.spencer@ssmagazine.com>
Subject: absolution
Date: Tuesday, December 10

Okay, I'm sorry. Please stop ignoring me. What can I do to make it up to you?

From: Claire Spencer <claire.spencer@ssmagazine.com>
To: Max Levy <bobafett5473@hotmail.com>
Subject: Re: absolution
Date: Tuesday, December 10

I might have been able to forgive you for telling Gary I liked basketball. And Hooters could have possibly been funny. But the tongue in the ear? That was unforgivable. You know how I feel about ears. And tongues.

From: Max Levy <bobafett5473@hotmail.com>
To: Claire Spencer <claire.spencer@ssmagazine.com>
Subject: Re: Re: absolution
Date: Tuesday, December 10

I didn't know you had a thing about ears. I thought it was feet that you hated.

Okay, what if I let you stick *your* tongue in *my* ear? Would that make us even?

From: Claire Spencer <claire.spencer@ssmagazine.com>
To: Max Levy <bobafett5473@hotmail.com>
Subject: Re: Re: Re: absolution
Date: Tuesday, December 10

Well, now I'm disgusted by feet AND ears.

The only thing that would make us even is if Gary sticks his tongue in your ear. AND you have to take me out to dinner tomorrow night . . . I have a big interview on Friday, and I want to obsess about it. Ack, I hope no one in management is reading my e-mails. You never know when the watcher's eyes are watching . . .

From: Jack Harrison <jharrison@britpharm.com>
To: Claire Spencer <claire.spencer@ssmagazine.com>
Subject: The Top Five Reasons Why You Should Spend Christmas in London
Date: Tuesday, December 10

5. The day after Christmas is also a national holiday (they call it Boxing Day, for some reason).
4. The Queen broadcasts a really boring speech that we can make fun of.
3. You get to open Christmas crackers, and wear the silly hats that come within.
2. Father Christmas
1. I'll make it worth your while . . .

From: Claire Spencer <claire.spencer@ssmagazine.com>
To: Jack Harrison <jharrison@britpharm.com>
Subject: Re: The Top Five Reasons Why You Should Spend Christmas in London
Date: Tuesday, December 10

You really miss David Letterman, don't you?

From: Norfolk, Peggy
To: All staff list
Subject: Name change
Date: Tuesday, December 10

We have some exciting news to share. As of January 1, the name of our magazine will be changed from *Sassy Seniors* to *Sassy Seniors!* We feel that this new name will better express our passion for exploring the issues facing today's seniors.

From: Spencer, Claire
To: Norfolk, Peggy
Subject: Re: Name change
Date: Tuesday, December 10

I think there was a typo in your e-mail. You said that the name of the magazine was being changed from *Sassy Seniors* to *Sassy Seniors*.

Cordially, Claire

From: Norfolk, Peggy
To: All staff list
Subject: Name change
Date: Tuesday, December 10

There seems to be some confusion about the e-mail I sent out earlier regarding the change in the name of the magazine. The name of the magazine is still *Sassy Seniors*, but we have added an exclamation point to the end. The new name of the magazine is: *Sassy Seniors!*

Also, it has come to my attention that some members of the *Sassy Seniors!* team have been using their company e-mail accounts for personal correspondence. We ask that you please not use the company e-mail for this type of correspondence, and also that you restrict your socializing to off-duty hours.

Thank you.

From: Max Levy <bobafett5473@hotmail.com>
To: Claire Spencer <claire.spencer@ssmagazine.com>
Subject: Re: Re: Re: Re: absolution
Date: Tuesday, December 10

Okay, I just called Cooksey and he said there's no way in hell he's sticking his tongue in my ear ... so I'm going over to his place tonight and sticking my tongue in his ear instead. Will that be a sufficient amount of personal humiliation for you (especially considering he'll almost certainly become violent after I do this)?

From: Claire Spencer <claire.spencer@ssmagazine.com>
To: Max Levy <bobafett5473@hotmail.com>
Subject: Okay ...
Date: Tuesday, December 10

That will work. But I still want the dinner, too.

From: Jenny James <jjames@travelworld.uk.com>
To: Claire Spencer <claire.spencer@ssmagazine.com>
Subject: reservations
Date: Wednesday, December 11

Dear Ms. Spencer:

Pursuant to Mr Harrison's instructions, I have arranged a booking for a return business class ticket from New York to London, traveling on December 23 and returning January 1. Please find attached a copy of your itinerary, and confirm your travel plans at your earliest convenience.

Should you require any further assistance with this booking, please do not hesitate to contact me.

With kind regards,
Yours sincerely,
Jenny James
Travel World

'So are you coming?' Jack asked when I picked up the phone.

'What?' I asked, taken aback, wondering if this was his somewhat abrupt way of initiating phone sex.

'To London. For Christmas. To see me. Remember?' he said.

'Yes, but . . . I mean I haven't had a chance to think about it yet,' I said. 'Although I have to admit I was tempted when I read the top-five list you sent me.'

'What else can I do to tempt you?' Jack asked, and this time there was no mistaking the lascivious tone in his voice.

Hmmm, maybe the possibility of phone sex wasn't so remote after all. Wasn't that what couples in long-distance relationships did? Suddenly I wasn't sure, and didn't want to make a misstep. What if we did attempt it, and I couldn't talk dirty enough, or if he talked way too dirty, and we ended up feeling weird around each other afterward? And how long was phone sex supposed to last? Hours? A few minutes? About as long as a sitcom? And was I actually supposed to involve myself, erm, *personally*? Or was that just an act, a bit of cheap theatrics you throw in to keep things interesting? These were all questions that I could intuitively answer if we were in the same room, but had no idea how to handle now that we were separated by 3,500 miles and talking via satellite.

'It isn't that I don't want to see you,' I hedged. 'Because of course I do.'

'Then what is it?'

'I'm just not sure . . . I mean, I just don't know . . .'

'I see,' Jack said, and I laughed, since I was being so oblique there was no way he possibly could.

'I promise, I'll let you know as soon as I can. I got an e-mail from your travel agent today, and I wrote back to tell her that I'd confirm as soon as possible,' I said. 'Okay?'

'Okay,' Jack said, and although he sounded casual enough, he paused, and then cleared his throat. 'Claire?'

'Yes?' I said.

Here it comes, I thought, both nervous and excited. He's going to ask if we can try the phone sex thing, and I'm going to feel like a complete idiot when I don't do it right. Am I supposed to use crass terms like 'cock' and 'pussy' once we start? Because those just aren't words that roll off my tongue with casual abandon. And was there any way I could get through it without dissolving into giggles?

'Is there something wrong? I mean, is there something bothering you about . . . us, or about me?' Jack asked.

Oh great, I thought. He must have sensed that I'm feeling a little awkward about doing it. Should I tell him that I'm willing to try? I mean, I am, aren't I? Of course I am. I'm a mature woman in my thirties, and hardly a virgin. I can handle a little dirty talk, some throaty growls, a few racy suggestions. Although maybe I should put him off for a day or two so that I can draw up a crib sheet, and write down titillating things to say to him in case my mind goes blank once we start.

'No, nothing,' I said brightly. 'Everything's great.'

'It's just . . . I know you're hesitating about coming here for Christmas, and I just hoped that I haven't done or said anything that would make you feel uncomfortable about it. I had such a great time when I visited you in New York, and I thought you did too, so I just assumed . . .' His voice, tentative and unsure, trailed off.

It was a good thing Jack couldn't see me, because I blushed bright red and rolled my eyes skyward, mortified at what an idiot I was being. Not only was he not interested in having phone sex, he was yet again trying to drag me into a relationship talk. Maybe Jack and I had suffered some kind of a *Freaky Friday* gender role reversal, where all he could think about was the emotional aspects of the relationship, while my mind was in the gutter.

'No, nothing's wrong. And it's not you at all, I was just . . . well, I just want to make sure that we're not rushing anything. And I haven't had a chance to talk to Maddy yet, about us I mean, and I feel like I should do that before we see each other again. Just so that we're not hiding anything. But I promise, I'll think it over, and let you know as soon as possible. Okay?' I asked.

'You're right,' Jack agreed. 'You should tell Maddy first. Why don't you call her tonight and get it over with?'

The last time I had talked to Maddy, she'd been threatening to hire a private detective to track Jack's whereabouts. Somehow the idea of blithely announcing that not only was I dating her ex-boyfriend but was contemplating spending the holidays with him didn't strike me as a fun way of spending the remainder of my evening. Still. I knew it had to be done.

'Okay. I'll call her,' I said. And then said a little prayer that in the few days since we'd talked Maddy had met some gorgeous British rock star icon who'd swept her off her feet, planted a five-carat diamond ring on her finger, and promised to buy her an island in the Caribbean as a wedding gift. Because short of that, I had a feeling she wasn't going to take this news very well at all.

'Hi, this is Maddy. Leave a message after the tone, and I might just call you back.'

Beep.

'Maddy, it's Claire. Are you there? [pause] Okay, well . . . please give me a call when you get this. I wanted to check on you, and see how you're feeling, and I . . . well, I have something I need to tell you. So call me. Although, wait . . . I'm going out of town tomorrow, so call me over the weekend. Okay?'

13

W *ow*. The *Retreat* offices were incredible. I suppose I should have expected as much from a magazine devoted to high-end travel – after all, the break room at *Sassy Seniors!* was stocked with cholesterol-lowering margarine, Aspercreme, and Centrum Silver (all advertising sponsors, naturally). But this place looked more like a really cool hotel bar than an office building – the floors and tables were a warm, russet-hued wood, all of the upholstered furniture in the waiting area was slipcovered in flannel gray men's suiting material, and artsy black-and-white close-up photographs of pine needles and flower petals hung on the walls. Steel lamps that looked like expensive artwork graced gently curved tables. Even the receptionist was color-coordinated – she was a gorgeous redhead with a glossy bee-stung pout (what Max crassly refers to as 'blow-job lips'), and was dressed in a dove gray skirt suit with a plunging neckline, and no blouse on underneath.

'Claire Spencer to see Kit Holiday,' I said, trying to sound professional, although I instantly felt like a slob. Why is it that flawlessly groomed women always make me feel like I'm dragging a square of toilet paper around on the heel of my shoe?

The redhead was a true professional, however, and didn't even smirk at my decidedly less-than-hip outfit. It's always so hard to know what to wear on interviews, since some magazines have switched to a casual dress code where staffers drag themselves around in wrinkled chinos and scuffed loafers, while others resemble extras from the MTV Spring Break special with their thong underwear peeking out of hip-slung jeans. Then there were the fashion rags, where showing up in anything that wasn't stylist approved would earn you derisive sneers and a pay cut. *Sassy Seniors!* didn't have an official dress code, although every few weeks during the warmer months Peggy would send around an e-mail reminding everyone of the no-bare-legs policy (warnings that I ignored, since who in their right mind is going to wear panty hose when the temperature is hovering near 100 degrees?). So not wanting to be either wildly under- or overdressed, I'd gone the boring yet safe route and wore my black wool pantsuit over a crisply ironed white cotton shirt.

'I'll let her know you're here,' the redhead said in such a sexy, husky voice I wondered if she moonlighted as a porn star. Actually, she sounded like someone who'd delight in indulging in a little phone sex – exactly the kind of woman I needed some advice from on the topic – although I figured it would come across as unprofessional if I inquired into her experience in such matters.

While waiting for Kit Holiday to appear, I wandered over to the wall of glass windows that overlooked the main floor of the magazine. Just as I'd suspected, hipness abounded. No ugly, industrial cubicles for the *Retreat* staff. Instead, glass-fronted offices lined every wall, while the support staff worked at groovy steel metal desks in the open-floor-plan center. Tall plants and redbrick columns were artfully arranged so that everyone had a modicum of privacy.

I felt a shiver of nervousness. I couldn't believe I was here, that I was really being considered for a job at this kind of a magazine! A place like this wouldn't have travel features on Phoenix or Denver . . . instead, they'd do stories on Morocco, Amsterdam, Sydney. And their travel writers don't weasel out the cheapest motel in town, but instead uncover the hippest hotels, the chicest attractions, the hottest new restaurant. No more budgets! No more chain hotel rooms featuring stained bedspreads and mass-produced forest landscapes hanging on the walls! No more eating at establishments that offer cellulite-inducing all-you-can-eat buffet lunches!

Wow, I'm going to need an entire new wardrobe if I work here, I thought. I'm actually going to have to start paying attention to those articles in *Lucky* and *Marie Claire* about how to pull together five versatile pieces of clothing into an easy-to-pack and glamorous weekend wardrobe.

'Claire?'

I turned, and was greeted by a petite woman.

'I'm Kit,' she said, with a wide, open smile.

I was a little taken aback. Because of her rather glamorous name and workplace, I'd pictured Kit as a Veronica Lake lookalike with a penchant for Donna Karan. The real Kit Holiday was barely five feet tall with a boyishly slim figure and a close crop of sandy brown curls. She didn't seem to have on even a trace of makeup, and was wearing a black turtleneck over brown corduroy pants that sat jauntily on her slim hips.

'Hi, it's nice to meet you,' I said, and found that I didn't have to fake my smile. Kit was adorable, the kind of person I could definitely see myself being friends with, and was a stark contrast from the blue-haired brigade that staffed *Sassy Seniors!* In fact, between the beautiful surroundings and more age-appropriate staff, this place was making *SS* look more and more like the Gulag, and even less like the kind of place that any writer with even a modicum of talent would be caught dead in. I was immediately seized with panic . . . there was just no way anyone who worked here would have the slightest bit of interest in hiring someone from a schlumpy rag that existed merely to pander dubious products to the unsuspecting seniors of America. I was completely and totally outclassed, and it was only a matter of time before the *Retreat* people would sniff out that I was a complete fraud.

'Thank you for coming in on such short notice. We were just so impressed with your résumé that we wanted to make sure we got a chance to meet with you before the interview period closed,' Kit said as she led me from the reception area, down a flight of stairs, through a double set of steel doors and into the main room that I had just been admiring from my perch above.

Impressed with my résumé, I thought, and wondered if I might have, in a moment of insanity, actually followed through on my plan to overhaul it with a few not-so-truthful additions. I was feeling proud of myself for not making the obvious and moronic joke of 'Gee, how funny is it that your last name is Holiday and you work at a travel magazine' – a joke I'm sure she'd heard even more frequently than the 'Claire, that's a fat girl's name' line, and which if I had made it, would likely have lost me the job before the interview even began.

Kit led me into a conference room, where three rather intimidating-looking people sat on one side of a long, oval table. Kit made the introductions, and in my nervousness I promptly forgot two of the three names. The one I did remember – Sabrina Taft – belonged to an elegant African-American woman dressed in a gorgeous cream pantsuit that made me feel instantly better about opting for the buttoned-up look. She had dramatically sculpted cheekbones and wore her hair up in a twist, which showed off her long, graceful neck. Her two companions were both startlingly handsome men, and strangely similar in appearance. They were both tall and slim, with chiseled jaws, strong features, and perfectly tousled hair. The only way I could distinguish them was that one wore a light purple shirt with a matching lilac silk tie, while the other had on a pair of square black-framed Clark Kent glasses, the kind meant to make truly beautiful people look intellectual.

'Bye, Claire. Good luck,' Kit whispered in my ear, and then skated gracefully from the room, abandoning me.

'Please have a seat,' Sabrina Taft said, gesturing to a chair on the opposite side of the table from them with a graceful flick of her wrist. I was glad that it was her name my short-term memory had decided to hang on to, since Taft seemed to have the most seniority. Suddenly I realized with horror that I didn't know what any of them actually did at the magazine. It occurred to me that I should have memorized the name of the editor-in-chief, as well as those of the entire editorial department. I'd been so caught up in worrying about what to wear and what to say during the interview that other than flipping through the latest issue of *Retreat* on the plane ride to Chicago, I hadn't done any background research on the magazine. How could I have forgotten something so fundamental?

There was a pitcher of ice water and a glass on the table before me, and I contemplated pouring myself some in order to steady my nerves. But then I thought this might be rude, since it hadn't been offered to me, and I didn't want to commit a faux pas before the interview even began. I immediately began obsessing about how dry my mouth felt. The more I tried to ignore the tempting, icy-cold water, the more desperately I wanted it.

Sabrina Taft had placed a pair of wire-rimmed glasses on her nose and was reading over my résumé. I could see that Purple Shirt and Clark Kent each had a copy, too.

'What interests you about travel writing, Claire?' Taft asked, looking up from the paper.

This was a question I knew I'd be asked, and I put the water out of mind while I delivered my prepared answer.

'I've always loved to travel, to see new sights and

experience different cultures. It's a thrill to explore the differences not just from country to country, but even within different regions of the same country. And I'm particularly interested in the diverse aesthetics each culture has to offer – architecture, fashion, cuisine – I find it all very exciting. It's really the best job in the world,' I said, and managed to not cringe at how hypocritical I was being, considering I'd spent the past few years griping about how boring and dull the locations my job took me to were. I was aware that I sounded trite and ridiculous, but Max had assured me that this was exactly the kind of answer a place like this would want. And it seemed to be working – the trio of interviewers all seemed entranced by my answer, and were nodding along as I spoke.

'Name two of your favorite destinations you've written about,' Clark Kent interjected.

My mind went blank. This one I hadn't been prepared for. *Think, Claire, think*, I begged myself, racking my brains to think of two destinations I'd covered for *SS* that wouldn't sound hopelessly dull to these three.

'I was recently in London, which has always been a favorite city of mine. There's just so much going on there, such a fascinating blend of tradition and innovation,' I said, completely making it up as I went along. 'And, um, New Orleans is always a fun, if somewhat offbeat destination, with its unique culture and the world-class restaurants,' I finished, praying that they hadn't actually read any of my columns, particularly the one that I had slipped past the editors in Robert's absence, where I referred to New Orleans as the 'sixth ring of hell.' But what other choice did I have? Telling them that Orlando was my favorite destination? Or Williamsburg, Virginia? Somehow, I didn't think that was going to impress the Mod Squad.

To make matters worse, I have an unfortunate habit of sweating profusely when I'm nervous, and could already feel my cotton blouse beginning to dampen. I prayed that pit stains wouldn't show through my black wool jacket, and tried to relax.

Breathe in, breathe out, stay focused and calm, I instructed myself, trying to channel the tranquil and frighteningly limber woman that teaches my yoga class.

But then all hopes of keeping up a serene front collapsed when, as if in some sort of a bizarre psychology experiment, all three interviewers began posing questions to me simultaneously. They talked over one another, without pausing to give me a chance to even absorb a question – much less answer it – before having another one fired at me.

'Where do you see yourself five years from now?' Sabrina asked.

'Five years from now,' I repeated thoughtfully, hoping to buy some time before I could think of an answer. What was I supposed to say? Working here? Writing my own travel column featuring exotic international destinations? Running this magazine? No, I couldn't say that, since I had no idea what any of these three did at the magazine, and it could be tantamount to announcing I was planning on taking over one of their jobs. But then again, if I didn't sound ambitious enough, they'd think I was wishy-washy.

'If you were stranded on a desert island and could bring only three items with you, what would those three items be?' Purple Shirt interjected before I could answer Sabrina's question.

'Three items,' I stuttered. The first three things that popped into my head were a lifetime supply of tampons, a laptop with a modem connection, and my vibrator – hardly an appropriate answer . . . well, except maybe for the computer. What were three *appropriate* things, items that design-conscious people would think to bring? Expensive bath products? A pashmina traveling blanket? A personal MP3 player? But before I could answer, Sabrina was chiming in again.

'Give me an example of a time when you've acted as a leader,' Sabrina said, raising her voice and giving Purple Shirt a dirty look. Purple Shirt sighed loudly, clearly annoyed that his question was going unanswered.

I gaped at them, not sure which question to answer. And had I ever acted as a leader? There was that one time when I was in middle school, and I was put in charge of producing a Punch and Judy puppet show for our Renaissance festival, but I had a feeling that wasn't what they were getting at. And what the hell did it matter anyway if I'd ever acted as a leader? Was I interviewing for a writing job, or for a position on the Joint Chiefs of Staff?

'What would you consider your biggest weakness?' Clark Kent challenged me. Unfortunately, just as he was saying it I made eye contact with him, and at the same time the other two began bickering with one another, so I knew I was going to have to produce an answer – *any* answer – and I had to make it sound strong, confident, ambitious.

What was my biggest weakness? What kind of a question was that? It wasn't that I didn't have any weaknesses . . . but I wasn't about to trot them out – 'Well, I absolutely detest authority in every form,' or 'I'm inherently lazy,' or 'I'm completely unorganized' – in the middle of the interview. But then something popped into my mind, and before I could stop myself, I blurted out, 'I'm a workaholic.'

This caused all conversation to cease, and the threesome to stare at me bug-eyed, as if a second head had just sprouted from one of my shoulders.

'How exactly is that a weakness?' Clark Kent asked. It was clear from his tone that he knew I was bullshitting, so I needed to do some damage control.

'Well,' I began, struggling to keep my composure. 'They say that being too absorbed in your work isn't good for you. And that you should have outside interests in order to stay balanced—'

Purple Shirt cut me off. 'I don't think working hard is a weakness,' he said reproachfully, but then bailed me out by asking, 'Do you speak any foreign languages?'

'No,' I said.

'None?' he asked incredulously.

'Nope,' I said, and smiled cheerfully. My mouth was so dry, my tongue was practically sticking to the roof of my mouth. No longer concerned about propriety, I reached for the water pitcher, poured myself a glass, and glugged it down gracelessly.

'You didn't learn a language in school?' Clark Kent asked.

'Yes, I took four years of French,' I admitted.

'Oh, so you could read a newspaper in French?' Clark Kent said.

'No,' I said.

'Interview someone in French?' Purple Shirt asked.

'I only had the basics, and I've forgotten most of that. That's why I said I'm not bilingual,' I said, too exasperated not to be honest.

Clark Kent smirked, and Purple Shirt looked disapproving. Only Sabrina Taft seemed unaffected. She instead peered over her glasses and said, 'Give me three adjectives that you would use to describe yourself.'

Cynical, sarcastic, and big-thighed, I thought, and prayed for the interview to end quickly and mercifully.

After the interview was over, and I staggered into the cold, cloudy Chicago day, I felt like I was limping off a battlefield. My cotton shirt, which had been freshly ironed when I went into *Retreat*, had wilted and was sticking to my back and shoulders, and a quick check in my compact mirror confirmed my worst fears – my hair was limp, my nose was shiny, and my lipstick had partially scuffed off. The remaining caked-on traces of Clinique's Pink Chocolate on my lips made me look like I had some kind of a skin disease.

I just wasn't sure when the interview had started to go so badly, so quickly. Was it when Sabrina Taft had pursed her lips and read the words '*Cat Crazy*' off my résumé in a way that made it clear she did not find my former work experience charmingly eccentric, as I'd hoped? Or was it when Clark Kent had critically flicked his perfect, amber eyes down the length of what I'd thought was my rather inoffensive suit?

I ducked into a nearby bistro, ordered a full-fat latte and a thick slice of cheesecake – I'm an emotional eater – and once I was settled at a tiny, round wooden table, I pulled out my cell phone. I needed to call someone, preferably someone who liked me, who could reassure me that I wasn't as big of a loser as I currently felt like. But whom to call? There was only one person I wanted to talk to, one person whom I wanted to commiserate with on the nightmare I'd just been through. And that person wasn't Max, or even Maddy. It was Jack. I stared at my phone, not sure whether I should call him. I didn't know if we'd reached a point in our relationship where he'd be glad to hear from me out of the blue, and at all interested in listening to my sob story. Wasn't I supposed to be acting like a mysterious and charming enigma right now, so as to pique his interest without showing my hand?

Oh, screw it, I thought, *I've had too rough of a day to worry about my stupid dating rules*. And before I could chicken out, I hit the send button on my phone.

'Hello,' Jack answered, sounding brisk but friendly.

Just hearing his voice made my eyes start to well up with tears. I fought to hold them in, and instead croaked, 'Hi. It's me. Claire.'

'Claire,' Jack said, sounding pleased, even over the echoing cellular line. 'Aren't you supposed to be at your interview?'

'I just got out,' I said, starting to feel foolish. God, now he'd think that I rushed out to call him as soon as it was over. Which, okay, I had, but shouldn't I play it a little cool?

'And? How did it go?'

'Terrible,' I said, and then I completely embarrassed myself by bursting into tears.

'Tell me,' Jack said, and his voice was so kind and so gentle that it just made me cry harder. I wanted him to be there with me, to put his arms around me, to tell me everything would be okay. Admitting that to myself was shocking enough as it was – after all, I'd been on my own for quite some time and was perfectly capable of taking care of myself. But suddenly I knew that I didn't want that anymore. There were times, like now, when I actually wanted to be taken care of, and in return, to take care of him sometimes, too. Even more shocking was my realization that wanting this was okay. I'd always have myself to fall back on, but it would be better – it would be wonderful – to have someone to take some of that pressure off, to carry the burden with me for a change, instead of always having to do everything on my own.

'Claire? Are you there?' Jack asked.

'I'm here. I just . . .' I said, and then before I could stop myself – or even think through the implications of what I was saying – I continued. 'I just wanted to tell you that I'm coming to London to spend Christmas with you.'

'That's terrific,' Jack said, sounding elated at my impulsive decision. 'I can't wait to see you.'

'Me too,' I said, and then, feeling better than I had in days, I tucked into my cheesecake and latte while I told him about the interview from hell. Somehow, it no longer seemed as disastrous as it had before. Before I knew it, I was giggling about the way Purple Shirt had kept patting his hair, probably to make sure it was still perfectly tousled, while Sabrina Taft and Clark Kent had bickered over whose turn it was to ask me a question.

'I don't think you should go,' Max said.

We were camped out in my apartment, and I had just proven Max wrong on his theory that I was incapable of cooking by making him a half-decent Sunday brunch (well, if you ignored that the scrambled eggs were overcooked, the bacon a bit rubbery, and the pancakes were anything but light and fluffy – at least the toast was perfection). He was mostly back in my good graces, since not only had he kept his promise to treat me to dinner, he had taken Daphne and me out to Picholine for a heavenly meal. My meager salary barely keeps me in boxed macaroni and cheese, so it was a real treat. Max also spent the entire meal giving me pointers on how to talk to chichi travel magazine people, since he'd done some freelance work for *Condé Nast Traveler*, while Daphne encouraged me to hang bunches of dried lavender around my apartment, swearing that it would bring me good luck.

'And the aromatherapy will help you relax,' she promised.

Even though the interview had been a disaster, I hadn't the heart to stay angry at Max for setting me up on the date from hell, particularly after Gary called me, pleading with me not to make Max stick his tongue in Gary's ear as retribution.

'Please leave me out of it,' Gary had begged. 'Every time

I turn around, Max is standing right behind me, ready to pounce, and I can't tell if he's joking anymore.'

I took pity on them both and released Max from his task of atonement. Besides, on a purely selfish note, I needed someone to obsess with me over what to do about the whole London-for-Christmas, Jack-and-Maddy thing, and since Maddy was obviously off limits, Max would have to do. Since Daphne was spending the weekend at her mom's house in Philadelphia – when Max mentioned this, he said it in a way that suggested they hadn't parted on the best of terms, although he shrugged me off when I pressed him on it – I enticed him with the prospect of a free breakfast. Max had been a good sport and choked down most of the food I served him, and afterward we lingered over our mugs of coffee with steamed milk. We were both dressed for a lazy Sunday – I hadn't changed out of my charcoal gray cotton pajamas, and Max was outfitted in sweatpants and a Rolling Stones tour T-shirt. But as soon as I brought up my Christmas travel plans, Max had immediately shot them down.

'Why not? I thought you said not to worry about Maddy's feelings, because she'd never find out,' I said, feeling vaguely uneasy that Max wasn't agreeing with me. I mean, for God's sake, I already *knew* I shouldn't go to London. Any idiot could see that I was standing in the middle of a hole, digging myself in deeper. But the plain simple truth was that I *wanted* to go. And Max was the one morally flexible person I knew – I was sure he'd advise me to ignore my conscience and follow my bliss. He's always saying touchy-feely crap like that, which usually annoys me, but for once, I was willing to follow this line of advice. This was not the right time for him to turn into Dr Phil on me.

'I couldn't care less about her feelings. I'm worried about yours,' Max said, peering intently at me over the rim of his MoMA coffee mug.

'Why?'

'You're incapable of having a fling. You're just not wired that way. I know you're getting emotionally involved with this guy,' Max said. The sharp features of his face were serious and his voice was somber. It was a state I rarely saw him in, although his Obi-Wan Kenobi routine – the wise counselor dispensing advice – was a little undermined by the fact that his hair was sticking straight up, like a bird's ruffled feathers. He looked like a little kid who had just rolled out of bed, groggy and unkempt, and I had to stifle an impulse to smooth his cowlicks down.

'And what if I am? I thought you were always telling me I needed to loosen up, to live on the wild side. And here I am, proposing to do just that, and now you're telling me not to risk it,' I complained.

'I'm allowed to be fickle. You're my best friend, and I don't want to see you get into a bad situation,' Max said.

'I know what you're worried about, but I'm a big girl. I can take care of myself,' I said, standing up and stretching. I began to gather up the dirty dishes.

'Can you?' Max asked.

'What's that supposed to mean?' I said, exasperated. I dumped the dishes into the sink of my tiny kitchenette and returned with the last of the coffee to refill our two mugs.

'Okay, I'll tell you, but you have to promise you won't get mad,' Max began.

'I hate it when people say that. It means you're about to insult me,' I muttered.

'No, I'm not. I just want you to face facts. Because the truth is, you're just not the type to run around behind your friend's back,' Max said.

'Oh, come on,' I said, rolling my eyes. 'You don't even like Maddy.'

'No, I don't, but you do. You love her like a sister, at least that's what you've always told me. And from what you've said, this breakup has really thrown her. So when she finds out about you and Jack – and she will find out if you keep this up – she's never going to forgive you. You know it's true. You can hardly forgive yourself, for God's sake,' Max said. 'And I don't think that you're going to be able to live with the consequences.'

I fidgeted. It was true. The guilt had been weighing rather heavily on my mind, so much so that I was being plagued by yet another bout of insomnia. Even my usual cure – reading a biography until I fall asleep from sheer boredom – hadn't worked, and I now knew far more about the life of John Adams than I'd ever thought possible. I'd been dragging myself around the office looking like complete hell, yawning my way through staff meetings, and had yet to turn in my London column. It was so bad that the last few times Robert had made noises about firing me, I almost believed him.

And the thing was, no matter how much I loved hearing Jack's voice, or how well we seemed to fit together, the strange and wonderful relationship still had a taint to it. The feeling that I was doing something I shouldn't was constantly gnawing at me. It was just like the time when I cut school and had a Ferris Bueller-style day off with my friends, lying out in the sun and painting our toenails, and instead of fully kicking back and reveling in the beauty of being free for a day, I spent the entire time worrying that I was going to get caught.

'Well, when I first met Jack, when we first, um . . .' I hesitated.

'Did it,' Max prompted.

I glared at him. 'When we first went out, I didn't know that he and Maddy even knew each other. It wasn't like I set out to stab her in the back,' I said defensively.

'No. And no one could blame you for what – or should I say *who* – you did. And I don't even think it was that big of a deal for you to see him that night after you knew. It gave you a chance to say good-bye, to see the fling through to its logical conclusion. But then he came here to visit you, and you've continued to stay in contact with him, and now you're thinking about going back over there to see him. It's gone way past a fling,' Max said.

'What if I tell her now?' I asked. 'Before I leave. I'll call her, and tell her everything – well, not *everything* – but I'll tell her the basics. Fair enough?'

Max shrugged. 'I guess. But don't expect her to give you her blessing. She'll never do it,' he said.

'She might. It's been a while since they broke up. She bounces back pretty quickly from relationships, or at least she used to before Jack,' I argued.

'Maybe you're right,' Max said. But his tone of voice made it clear that he didn't think so.

And I didn't add what I was thinking, which was that even if I did work up the nerve to tell Maddy about my relationship with Jack, and even if she did ask me to end things with him, or worse, threatened to end our friendship over it, I wasn't so sure anymore that it was enough to keep me away from Jack. For right or wrong, I'd fallen for him. It scared me, and yet despite my fear, I couldn't seem to stay away from him. My favorite part of every day had become those precious moments that I got to talk to him. Snuggled up in my favorite flannel pajamas, with my down comforter wrapped around me, I'd hold the phone to my ear, listen to the warm rumble of his voice, and feel completely whole. Even though I felt like I was teetering on the edge of a cliff, flirting with falling over and breaking into a thousand bloody bits, I still couldn't stay away.

'Enough about me. What's going on with you and Daphne?'

Max feigned innocence. 'Why do you think something's going on?'

'Because you're acting sketchy every time I mention her name. And she didn't say anything about going to Philly when we had dinner the other night.'

During dinner I hadn't noticed anything amiss between Max and Daphne, but now that I thought back, they had both spent more time talking to me than they did to each other. Which wasn't at all like them.

Max shrugged. It seemed to be his stock response lately whenever I asked him about Daphne. 'It's nothing,' he insisted, in a tone that made it clear he wasn't going to divulge anything.

'Fine, don't tell me,' I said childishly. 'I pour my heart out to you, and you hold out on me.'

'I said, it's nothing,' he repeated. 'Daffy just needed a little time on her own. She's taking the train back tonight.'

I raised my eyebrows questioningly, but he just shrugged yet again, and stared moodily at his coffee.

I hoped this was just a hiccup, and not a serious problem with their relationship. I was still at the stage of needing relationship-training wheels, so a solid couple like Max and Daphne had always been an inspiration to me.

I put off calling Maddy for a few hours. First, I went to the gym, and pounded out my stress and anxiety on the treadmill for forty-five minutes, and then did a quick set of reps on the Nautilus equipment. I love my gym – it lacks the meat market scene that most have. It has the obligatory weirdo or two, standard at all gyms – the leathery-skinned woman who spends eight solid hours a day on the Stairmaster, the middle-aged guy who does some kind of strange arm-flapping routine while walking on the treadmill. But everyone pretty much keeps to him- or herself, reading magazines or listening to headphones. I've caught a few accountant-looking types checking out the buns of some lawyer-looking types, but it's usually done discreetly and with a definite lack of cheesy pickup lines. Even better, unlike most gyms, where the aerobics instructors are all perky and blonde and have names that end in 'i' – Kimmi, Lori, Jenni – the instructors at my gym are mostly male and resemble army drill instructors in both looks and demeanor, so I don't have to spend step class feeling insecure about the fact that my arms are larger than the instructor's thighs.

After I returned home and showered, I stripped the sheets off my bed and hauled my laundry downstairs to run a few loads through. Then I ducked out to the store to stock up on skim milk, cereal, and bottled water. In a last-ditch effort to put off calling Maddy, I even resorted to cleaning my apartment from top to bottom, but considering that it's only about five hundred square feet, even dusting, sweeping, and scrubbing every surface didn't take very long.

After finally running out of errands to do, I picked up the handset to my cordless phone and tapped it against my cheek, rehearsing what I'd say to Maddy and trying to anticipate what her reaction would be to 'Hi, it's me, I'm the one sleeping with your ex-boyfriend. Sorry.' Somehow, I couldn't quite picture her shrugging, tossing her glossy black sheet of hair back, and replying 'No biggie.' I was guessing it would more likely fall between tearful recriminations and shrieks of anger, and neither scenario sounded like a whole lot of fun.

When the apprehension over calling became worse than my direst predictions of how I thought the actual call would go, I finally broke down and punched Maddy's long, foreign phone number into my phone. The entire time I dialed, my hands were shaking, and my stomach had the same sickly, acidic feeling that usually follows a serious espresso binge. The phone rang, and rang, and then rang again, and for a minute the clouds parted and sunshine began leaking through at the very thought that I might have even a short reprieve from the unpleasant task of kicking in my friend's already broken heart. But then there was a click, and rather than being followed by the tinny recorded message of her answering machine, Maddy's breathless voice was there.

'Hello,' she answered.

'Hey, it's me. Didn't you get my message?' I asked.

'Hey. Yeah. Sorry. I've been meaning to call you back. I just . . . haven't had the energy to, I guess,' Maddy said, and my heart sank.

This was going to be even worse than I'd thought. She sounded terribly down, and not just with the Sunday, I-don't-want-to-go-to-work-tomorrow blues. Her sadness was more like the kind of gut-tearing dejection that likely inspired Rod Stewart when he wrote his breakup anthems. I kept hoping that she would meet someone new, or have some big triumph at work, something to make her feel better. Not only to make it easier to tell her about Jack and me, but because I knew how it feels to spend a post-breakup Sunday alternating between watching old movies on cable and weeping softly. And now, with what I had to tell her, I was going to demolish her even further. There was no doubt that she was going to hate me. Hell, I hated me for what I was about to do to her.

'What's wrong?' I asked, as if I didn't know.

'Same old same old,' she said, and then sighed. 'But I know that you're probably tired of hearing me talk about Harrison.'

'No, it's not that I don't want to hear about it. About, um, him. It's just that . . . well, I'm worried about you. I mean, the last time we talked you sounded a little unhinged. You were talking about hiring a private investigator,' I pointed out.

'I don't think it's such a crazy idea,' Maddy huffed. Then she paused, and I heard the click of a lighter and a deep inhale of breath.

'Are you smoking again?' I asked, surprised.

'No, not really. Only occasionally,' she said, and then she inhaled again. Her inhale was such a satisfied sigh that I could practically taste the wonderful earthy flavor of the tobacco, to feel my lungs expand with the relaxing cloud of smoke, and just like that, ten years of abstinence and willpower almost disappeared. I could almost smell the cigarettes, fresh out of the box, just after the foil wrapper's been ripped off.

Maddy and I had both chain-smoked our way through college – a Marlboro Light being the perfect accompaniment to a cup of coffee and gossip session – but had each given it up at about the same time we began to embrace sunscreen. In fact, Maddy had quit months before I did, and had been incredibly irritating with her superior smiles and disapproving head shakes every time I pulled out a cigarette. And now she'd started up again? After all the lectures she had given me on the evils of nicotine, after all of the badgering about how much cleaner her lungs felt since she'd quit, about how wrinkled my skin would be if I kept it up? In fact, that was what had motivated her into quitting. Maddy had given up cold turkey when she supposedly spotted a wrinkle at the edge of her mouth, although the supposedly offending patch of skin looked to me as creamily perfect as that on the rest of her face.

I, on the other hand, was able to quit only after multiple relapses and finally a six-week period spent on the patch, a time during which I became so bitchy that I was liable to fly into a rage if I thought that someone on the subway was looking at me in a vaguely critical way. Even now, just hearing the tempting sound of Maddy's self-satisfied puffs gripped me with a fierce desire to run down to the corner Korean market and snatch up as many cartons as I could carry out. And then a thought occurred to me. Sure, it might be a cliché, but there was one circumstance in which I'd known Maddy to occasionally break from her self-imposed prohibition on smoking . . .

'Did you just have sex?' I asked suspiciously.

'Why do you sound so surprised? It has been known to happen from time to time,' Maddy said.

'But . . . but . . . with whom? I mean . . . I thought you were upset about, um, Harrison,' I said, and all thoughts of smoking fled my mind, only to be replaced by a beacon of hope. If Maddy was sleeping with someone else, then surely she had to be close to getting over Jack. And if she was over him, then maybe she wouldn't mind quite so much that I'd started seeing him. She'd probably still be upset – even though I was long since over Sawyer, I didn't relish the idea of his ending up with one of my friends – but maybe it would make my news less devastating.

'I am. But that doesn't mean I can't see other men,' she said. 'Especially someone I care about.'

'No, don't get me wrong, I think it's great. The best way to get over a guy is to get out there and meet someone new, right?' I enthused.

'This isn't someone new.' Maddy exhaled smoke and sighed at the same time, which made for a long, lugubrious hiss. 'Look, I suppose I should have told you this before, but I know how you are, and I wasn't up for being judged.'

'I'm not judgmental,' I said, immediately affronted.

'Yes, you are. I love you, but you are, Claire. You know it's true. And you'll definitely judge me for this. I've, well . . . I've been seeing my boss,' she said.

'Well, I don't know if that's smart office politics, but I wouldn't exactly call it a moral dilemma,' I said, still feeling stung by the casual insult. Especially since it's judgmental to call someone judgmental. Besides, just because I can look at an issue and objectively form decisions about what is right and wrong with it, doesn't mean I'm judgmental. Does it?

'It is if he's married,' Maddy said.

My apartment suddenly seemed unbearably small. It was ridiculous, because my apartment *was* minuscule, and always had been – there are RVs that are roomier than my pad. I'd always kind of liked it that way, especially since I can vacuum the entire apartment in ninety seconds flat. But now the tiny space felt claustrophobic, and made me want to stick my head out of the window to suck in some not-so-fresh air and relieve the ringing in my ears, the pain in my chest, the shortness of breath.

I was agape at Maddy's confession. I mean that literally – upon hearing her words, my mouth actually dropped open, and I fell back against the back of my couch, stunned. I just couldn't believe it. Maddy was seeing a married man? After all of the pain that I'd gone through dealing with my own philandering father, a festering hurt that she'd been a firsthand witness to? I could now see why she hadn't told me before – she'd known exactly how I'd feel about it. Adultery was an issue that I had strong opinions on . . . and none of them good.

'Does he have children?' I managed to say, the words clogging my throat on their way out.

'Yes, he does,' Maddy said cautiously, aware that she was brushing up against a bruise.

But she was doing more than that. In fact, what she was doing was, in my opinion, the lowest of the low, indulging her own selfish, carnal impulses in a way that guarantees to hurt, and maybe even destroy, an entire family. Because that's what infidelity does. I understand that many people adopt a very French attitude toward cheating, of compart-mentalizing it away from their families, rationalizing that what the family doesn't know can't hurt them. It's really a handy strategy, as it allows adulterers to do what they like without being bothered by any of that pesky guilt. Unfortunately, it isn't so easy for the kids of cheaters to brush it aside. Once the affair comes to light – and let's face it, maybe the cheaters think they're as sneaky as James Bond, but they inevitably trip up on their egos – the feelings of confusion and betrayal and hurt can last far longer than the affair. Far longer than the marriage. As Maddy well knew, pretty much all of my relationship dysfunction could be traced to my parents' own turbulent marriage.

'Well, I can see why you didn't tell me,' I said, my voice brittle with anger.

'I knew how you'd react. I knew that you'd disapprove.'

'Yup. You're right. I think what you're doing is awful.'

She was silent for a minute. 'I know. I keep thinking that I should end it, but then I just don't. I mean, I know it's wrong, but the part of me that wants it to keep going just keeps winning. I guess someone like you wouldn't understand that,' she finally said.

'Someone like me?' I asked, my voice rising a pitch as I tried to determine whether or not this was an insult along the lines of her telling me I'm judgmental just to try to ward off criticism.

'Yeah, you know. What's right is right, what's wrong is wrong. You have a lot of moral clarity,' Maddy said.

The irony of this statement stung. Whatever moral clarity I may have once possessed had, as of late, blurred and streaked so much it now resembled an Impressionist painting. It also reminded me of why I'd called Maddy in the first place, and now was as good a time as any to spring my news on her. Not that it was my job to punish her, but let's just say I was less inclined to be protective of her feelings.

'Well, speaking of moral clarity. It's about Jack . . . I mean Harrison,' I began. I nervously clenched my free hand into a fist, and tried to remember the spiel I had rehearsed before calling her. Something about it happening without my meaning it to, not wanting to hurt her, hoping that we could move past it. Actually, it sounded like I was the one confessing to cheating. Maybe I was in a way.

'Yes, yes, I know,' Maddy sighed, and for a brief moment, my hopes soared. *She already knew! And she was still talking to me! But how had she found out? Would Jack have told her without telling me?*

But then Maddy continued. 'I was seeing Alex – that's his name, my boss I mean – while I was dating Harrison. And Harrison found out. It's the reason why we broke up.'

15

For the first year since I had started working there, I forgot to dread the *Sassy Seniors!* annual holiday party. It was normally an event I looked forward to even less than my annual Pap smear. I know everyone thinks their office Christmas party is a drag, but at most workplaces you at least get a free meal and the whole event is lubricated with plenty of cheap champagne. The staff of *Sassy Seniors!* was not so lucky.

For starters, a few years back, the powers that be – meaning Robert – decided that a big to-do was not in the company budget. So instead of treating the staff to lunch out, he decided we would celebrate the advent of the holiday season with a god-awful in-house party, complete with a potluck lunch, Secret Santa exchange, and *no* alcohol. Well, mostly no alcohol. Since my arrival at the magazine, a quart of vodka had routinely found its way into Peggy's ginger-ale-and-sherbet punch, which went a long way toward making the party feel less like a root canal, and more like a small cavity being filled without novocaine. But this year, my thoughts were so cluttered, I'd forgotten to smuggle the illicit booze into the office. It was probably just as well, as after last year's puke-in-the-Xerox-machine debacle (for once, it wasn't me), there'd been word that the punch bowl was going to be guarded by Barbara, who was more pit bull than she was woman.

Lunch was pretty much what you'd expect out of a potluck – cheese balls, a tray of crudités, casseroles made with Campbell's Cream of Mushroom soup, a limp salad, store-bought Parker House rolls, and a box of candy that was obviously a discarded early Christmas gift. I'd completely forgotten about the whole thing, of course, so at the last minute I grabbed a mostly full three-liter bottle of Diet Coke out of my refrigerator that I'd opened two days earlier, and plopped it on the potluck table, hoping no one would know it was from me. Or notice that it had gone slightly flat. I saw Peggy give the bottle the evil eye and then shoot a nasty look at me, but even knowing that I'd succeeded in irritating her didn't cheer me up as much as usual.

The thing was, I was booked on the eight o'clock flight to London that night, and I still didn't know if I was going. Okay, so my bags were packed, my mail was stopped, and my refrigerator was clear of anything that could turn rancid in my absence, so my mind was mostly made up. But as I sat there, picking at a plate of ham-and-potato gratin with a side of mashed sweet potatoes with a marshmallow topping, I still wasn't sure if I should go.

For one thing, I hadn't told Maddy about Jack and me. I'd meant to, truly I had. But what with her dual confessions of carrying on an affair with her married boss, and that she believed doing so was the reason Jack broke up with her, my original purpose in calling her had just sort of gotten lost. And I was no longer sure I even owed her an explanation. After all, if Maddy was cheating on Jack during the time they were together – not to mention cheating with a married man – then she wasn't the aggrieved party in the breakup after all. She was the bad guy.

My reason for not being sure I still wanted to go was a little less complex. If Maddy was telling the truth – and really, why wouldn't she be? – then Jack hadn't broken up with her because he realized the relationship wasn't going anywhere, as he'd claimed that first night we met on the airplane. Instead, he had ended the relationship because she'd broken his heart when she cheated on him. Which would mean that Jack had lied to me. But why? Once he knew that Maddy and I were friends, wouldn't he have expected that I'd learn the real reason behind their breakup? Something about the whole thing felt off, a funny ping on my internal sonar. But I couldn't tell if I was sensing something wrong with Jack, or if it was just my own neurosis churning things up again. After all, Maddy's adulterous admission had stirred up a lot emotions I'd preferred left in the past.

One of my least favorite childhood memories was when I was thirteen years old. My parents were having a dinner party, and by the time the plates had been cleared, the party had turned rather raucous with loud voices and guffawing laughs echoing from the dining room. Not wanting to be noticed by the boisterous adults, I'd snuck into the kitchen in search of a bowl of ice cream, when I came across my dad and Mrs Quinn, who lived three houses down from us. They were embracing, which didn't seem all that strange at first, since my parents were always greeting their friends with social hugs and kisses. But then I saw that his hand was groping under her skirt, lifting the material up, baring her left thigh, and all of a sudden I realized that they were kissing, with open mouths and closed eyes, and Mrs Quinn was making a strange, guttural throaty sound. My skin felt tight, and I began to itch all over. I fell back, returning to my bedroom, and scratched my blotchy skin until my fingernails drew blood.

'What are you eating? Don't you know that ham-and-potato dish has a cream base? And those sweet potatoes are all sugar and have about a stick of butter in them,' Olivia, the food editor, tutted, interrupting my not-so-pleasant trip down memory lane. She sat down next to me and handed me a box wrapped in red-and-green-striped paper. 'Here's your Secret Santa present! I wonder what this could be.'

I accepted the box, shaking it a little. I could hear the muffled rustle of cloth within. 'Maybe it's a sexy new nightgown. I drew Peggy this year, and I came close to getting her one of those stretch red lace ones with the faux fur trim that they sell at Fredericks of Hollywood.'

Olivia – who couldn't stand Peggy either – shrieked with laughter. 'Girl, she wouldn't know what to do with it. She'd probably think it was some kind of a Christmas decoration to hang on her door. What did you get her?'

I smiled enigmatically. 'Oh, just a little something I thought she'd enjoy,' I said.

Actually, I'd re-gifted the same tea-for-one set I'd received in the Secret Santa exchange the year before. I suspected Peggy was the one who'd originally given it to me, since she'd been unable to resist making a comment about how now that I had my own, I could stop using the office coffee cups. Just for that, I'd begun using a fresh, clean mug for every single cup of coffee.

'I bet I get another fruitcake,' Olivia sniffed. 'Every year, it's the same damn thing. I don't even eat cake, but if I did, I certainly wouldn't have fruitcake. It's a bad joke, not food.'

I shook my head ruefully. 'Why do we do this year after year? No one ever likes what they get, so why bother?'

Crappy gifts, like those given at these stupid, pointless Secret Santa exchanges, fall under the category of 'fuck-you presents.' Fuck-you presents are those that you are required to give – to co-workers, to pseudo-friends – and you want to make it clear that you (a) don't like the person, and (b) have put as little money, thought, and effort into the selection of the item as possible, while (c) immunizing yourself from any criticism by the recipient, who would appear ungrateful if she dared to complain. It's all very passive-aggressive.

'Open your present,' Olivia urged me.

I tore off the wrapping paper, opened the box, and pulled out the all-time ugliest sweatshirt I'd ever seen. It was bright red, 100 percent polyester, and had a close-up of a grinning reindeer head wrought in some sort of puffed plastic on the front. It was worse than a fuck-you present . . . this was openly hostile, I-hate-you-and-hope-you-drop-dead-right-now gifting.

Olivia wrinkled her nose. 'Well, at least it's not a fruitcake.'

'You say that as though it's a good thing,' I said darkly. 'At least a fruitcake has rum in it.'

'Oh, you opened the present I got for you!' Helen cried out. She came skipping over to the table where Olivia and I were sitting, and was wearing an almost identical sweatshirt, only hers was green and had a picture of a puffed-plastic Santa on the front. 'I know we're not supposed to tell who we gifted to, but I just knew you would love it. I thought you could take it with you to London. And look what it does.'

She grabbed the sweatshirt from me and fumbled around inside of it, and a moment later, the reindeer's antlers lit up with blinking white lights and its nose shone with a red light. Helen held it up and beamed with pride. I just stared at the offending sweatshirt, mesmerized by the lights reflecting off the shiny red polyester cloth. For the first time in my smart-ass life, I was completely speechless.

'It's very . . . festive,' I finally managed. At least I knew that the gift of the sweatshirt hadn't been meant as a declaration of war, since Helen was far too sweet for the fuck-you gifting game. But that was a cold comfort considering what came next.

'Try it on,' Helen urged me.

'Oh, no, it wouldn't match what I'm wearing,' I protested weakly, but Helen was obviously not going to let the subject go, and she cajoled and bullied me until I finally gave in and ended up pulling on the horrible thing. I immediately felt hot and stifled in the polyester – it felt like I was wearing one of those Mylar exercise suits they used to sell in the 1970s that were supposed to make you sweat off ten pounds.

'There, now don't you look Christmassy,' Helen said, beaming at me. Olivia coughed behind her hand to cover up a laugh at my expense.

I was just glad – for once – that I was working at a dorky magazine, because if I did work at a high-end travel magazine or a fashion rag, my career wouldn't have withstood the humiliation. If the hipsters at *Retreat* could see me now, they'd probably be ill at the idea that they had even considered hiring such a loser to work at their hallowed grounds of style and cool.

'So what's this about you going to London?' Olivia asked me, probably to distract me from my misery.

'I'm leaving tonight, and spending the holidays there,' I said vaguely, not wanting to get into my doubts about whether I should even go on the trip.

'I think there's definitely a man involved,' Helen said, winking at Olivia. 'I think Claire has a beau, and hasn't quite decided yet what to do with him, so she's keeping him a secret until she does.'

'No, it's nothing like that,' I lied.

I really, *really* didn't want to get into the details of my relationship with Jack with these two. First of all, even though Helen and Olivia were both dolls, they were also gossips, and anything I told them about my love life would quickly become fodder for the entire *Sassy Seniors!* staff. And besides, the whole triangle mess with Jack and Maddy was not something I wanted to talk about with anyone, knowing that I'd instantly face judgment and criticism, and I was getting quite enough of that from Max.

'Hmmm. You're quite the dark horse, aren't you? Well, I

hope it is a man. It's about time you got on with it,' Olivia said. 'You can't stay single forever, you know.'

Hmph, I thought. As though it were ever just that easy.

Okay, I was going. I'd decided, my mind was made up, and that was that. Besides, there was no way I could cancel now, it wouldn't be fair to Jack. *Jack*. Just thinking of him made me feel a little light-headed, and I knew then that I'd never actually intended not to go on the trip. I couldn't wait to see him, and I promised myself that as soon as I returned I would tell Maddy everything. I knew there was no danger of bumping into her on a London street; she was going to spend the holiday visiting her mother in Boston.

I hurried home after work (the reindeer sweatshirt safely stashed in my bag, ensuring no one would ever again see me wearing the wretched thing). I was packed and ready to go, so all I needed to do was grab my suitcase and hail a cab, and I was out of there, on my way to a nice romantic, toe-curling, sex-filled break from the real world. But by the time I got to my apartment, I was worried that I might be late for my flight. I had three hours until the estimated time of departure, but you never knew when the airport staff was going to mistake a thirtyish blondish American woman for a rabid Muslim fundamentalist who might just take down an airplane with the pair of tweezers she'd managed to sneak past security, and decide to strip-search me. So better to be early.

As I was turning my key in the lock, I was suddenly molested when a short man smelling strongly of rum ran up behind me and threw his arms around my waist. I'd learned my lesson with Jack, and didn't immediately whip out my stun gun, which was good, since this time my attacker was Max. A very drunken, lurching, red-eyed Max.

'What are you doing? Get off of me,' I said, trying to shake him loose from the bear hug he had on my waist.

'I'm so glad to see you. I'm so glad you didn't go to London,' Max slurred.

'What's wrong with you? Why are you so drunk?'

'Christmas party. Or parties. I went to three, 'cause I can, 'cause I work freelance,' Max hiccupped. 'Lemme in, I need to pee.'

I swung open my door, and he zipped past me and raced toward my bathroom. I hoped that he wouldn't be in there too long, or trip and crack his head on the sink and fall into a coma. I didn't have the time to wait for EMS to arrive and carry him out. I checked my watch and saw that I didn't even have time to change, so instead I stuffed a few magazines and the paperback novel I was reading into my work bag.

Max wandered out of the bathroom. 'Where are you going?' he cried out dramatically. 'You're not going to London, are you? You're not going to see him?'

'Your zipper's down,' I said, pointing to the gaping hole in his pants.

Max fumbled to pull it back up, but still continued with the theatrics. 'I thought we talked about this, and you agreed not to go!'

'No, I agreed I would talk to Maddy about it before I went. And I did talk to her, last night,' I said, omitting the part where I hadn't told her about Jack and me. I was guessing Max was too drunk to pick up the subtle nuances of my lie.

He stood staring at me, swaying slightly from side to side, his hair sticking up all over his head, making him look a little like Calvin from the *Calvin and Hobbes* cartoon. His normally sallow skin was flushed red, but I couldn't tell if it was from the booze or the cold air gusting around outside.

'Don't go, Claire,' he said softly.

'I have to. I have my ticket, and all the arrangements are made. Besides, I don't have any other plans for Christmas. Why are you so upset by this all of a sudden?'

'Daphne left me,' Max said starkly, and his face crumpled.

'Oh no. Oh God. I'm so sorry, sweetie,' I said. I stepped forward to hug him, and tried hard to ignore how awful he smelled as I folded him into my arms.

'It's okay, because we talked about it, and decided it would be better if we were just friends,' Max said.

'Oh. Well. Are you okay with that?'

'Yup. It's better, because I'm . . . well . . . Daphne knew, she guessed . . . so it's better,' Max babbled incoherently.

'Daphne knew what?' I asked.

Max looked at me, a strange expression on his face. 'That I love you.'

'I know, sweetie, I love you, too,' I said, speaking very slowly and kindly as though I were talking to a child on the verge of throwing a tantrum.

'No, I mean I *love* you. I'm in love with you. I don't want you to go to London, because I want you to stay here with me,' Max said. For a minute he almost sounded sober, but the effect was ruined when he suddenly belched loudly.

'Yeah, right, very funny, you've always worshipped me from afar,' I said, smiling gamely at his joke. Max always deflected his pain with humor, and this wasn't the first time he'd joked about swearing his undying love for me. He thought it was funny when we went out to eat to fall down on one knee and propose to me in front of a restaurant of applauding people (similar to his practical joke of telling the waiter it was my birthday – when it was not – so that the whole waitstaff would suddenly group at our table, clapping and singing 'Happy Birthday' to me).

'I'm not joking. I mean it. I love you,' Max said. His eyes, normally the color of Hershey's kisses when they're not so bloodshot, were dark and still. I stared back at Max. The room suddenly seemed overly warm and thick with expectation.

'Max, cut it out. That's not funny. I'm going to be late,' I said, checking my watch. I pawed through my bag to make sure I had my ticket and passport. 'I wish I could stay and talk, I really do want to hear all about you and Daphne. I promise we'll do it when I get back, 'kay?'

'I'm not joking. Christ, how many times do I have to say it? If I hadn't just downed an entire punch bowl of eggnog, I wouldn't even be saying it now. I *love* you. I've loved you for years, literally *years*. Daphne knew, she guessed. It's why we broke up. And I'm glad she left me, because you're the person I really want to be with.'

'But – I —' I stuttered incoherently.

'I know all of your stupid rules, and the one about not dating short men, but I can't help my height, and I can't help how I feel, and I – no, don't interrupt me, I want to get this out – I don't want you to go to London and see that stupid guy, I want you to stay here with me, and if you do, I swear I'll never break your heart, or do anything shitty, or cheat on you, or anything. It would be fantastic, can't you see that?' The words were falling out of him in an uncontrollable gush, and as he talked, Max stumbled toward me and grabbed my hand.

I stared at him. Surely he must be joking . . . but how could he pull it off without laughing, especially in the state he was in? I leaned forward to sniff his sweater, wondering if he'd doused himself with rum so that he'd smell drunk – Max really would go that far to perpetrate a practical joke. But his sweater smelled only of wet wool and stale cigarette smoke.

'What are you doing?' Max asked.

'Nothing,' I said. I was beginning to feel really uncomfortable.

Things didn't improve when Max suddenly keeled forward, stretched up, and kissed me directly on the lips. It was horrible. His lips were rubbery and thick, and his breath reeked of alcohol. He was holding my arm, balancing himself as he reached up at me, and his clench became unbearably tight. I started to pull away, but he just held on tighter, and then I felt his tongue, wet and pointy, probing at my mouth. It felt disgusting, like a lizard slithering against my lips.

'Stop it! Just . . . stop,' I said, turning my head away and stepping back from Max.

I didn't want this. I'd meant it when I told Jack that I thought of Max as a brother. And I'd been sure that he felt the same way about me. He and Daphne had been so great together, and despite Max's joking – or what I thought was joking – about not wanting to marry her, he'd always seemed to truly love her, to treat her with a tenderness and care that he'd certainly never shown me. So where was this confession suddenly coming from?

'Why?' Max asked, and then, to make matters just that much worse, tears began to stream down his face.

'I don't know what you want me to say,' I said, shaking my head from side to side.

'I want you to say you love me, too, or that you could love me. I want you to say you won't go to London, that you know it will never work out with that guy, but that we could have a chance. I want you to say that for the first time in your life, you're ready to actually take a chance with someone you can have a real relationship with, because that's what it would be if you and I got together. That's what I want you to say,' Max said.

'I can't say that. I'm sorry, I wish I could,' I said, meaning every word. I loved Max dearly, but I could never have romantic feelings for him, and it had nothing to do with my dating rules, or with his height. It had everything to do with chemistry and pheromones and heat and reaction, all of which I had with Jack, and none of which I had with Max. Not even a hint. The very thought of being with Max in that way felt vaguely incestuous.

Max's face contorted with – what? Rage? Hurt? I couldn't tell, but suddenly he was on his feet, barreling past me.

'Max, please, wait! Let's talk,' I called after him, but after struggling with my doorknob for a second, Max was suddenly gone. A second later, I heard his door slam shut. I just stood there, not sure what to do. Should I go after him? I knew he'd never let me in, not in the mood he was in. For all of his joking, Max wasn't one to wear his emotions on his sleeve – it was probably the reason I'd never guessed that he had feelings for me – and now that he had, and had been rebuffed, I knew he'd retreat to lick his wounds. I was the last person he'd want to talk to right now, maybe forever. And then I was gripped with a strong wave of panic . . . was this going to be the end of our friendship?

I hurried out my door and down the hall, and knocked on his apartment door. First softly, then, when he wouldn't answer, louder, banging against it until my knuckles hurt. Mrs McGory, who lives across the hall from Max's apartment, opened her door as far as the security chain would allow it, and peered out to see what the commotion was. I ignored her, and continued to knock, now with the heel of my hand, which made a loud thudding noise as it hit the wood.

'Max, please. Open the door, talk to me,' I pleaded. But my voice just echoed down the corridor, sounding like I was shouting into an empty cave. I waited and waited, listening for footsteps or some noise to indicate that Max was there, listening to me, willing to talk. Even Mrs McNosy gave up on me, muttering under her breath as she pulled her door closed. Finally, I turned away, and after fetching my suitcase and locking my door, I went down to the street to hail a cab.

16

Needless to say, I didn't get any sleep on the flight to London. Instead, I just curled up miserably in my business-class seat – the fact that Jack hadn't stuck me back in steerage would be reason enough to fall for him, if I hadn't already – resisting the urge to request one of those mini-bottles of gin and tonic every time the congenial flight attendant sashayed by.

I also wanted to ask the flight attendant how on earth she was able to work an entire shift in such ridiculously high stiletto heels. I couldn't walk one block in heels that high and narrow, so how was she able to navigate through the tiny airplane corridors, bending and kneeling and balancing trays in them, for six-plus hours? Were they like the pumps featured in that commercial where all of the women are playing basketball in high heels? And I've always wondered how *those* shoes work. Your heel is still elevated three inches over the ball of your foot – how comfortable can any shoe designer make that? These were questions I'd have liked to have answers to, but I chickened out of asking. I was afraid that the flight attendant would give me a blank, Stepford Wife look and then tell me that she never finds wearing high heels uncomfortable, and it would be just one more area of my life where I'd feel inadequate.

My mind felt like a wastepaper basket full of crumpled odds and ends, pieces of my earlier conversation with Max jumbling around with Maddy's confession about her married lover, and my trepidation over what to expect during my visit with Jack. Could Max really have meant it when he said he was in love with me? Was that possible? How could I have not known how he felt? We'd spent hours slouched against each other on the couch watching movies, eaten countless meals together, taken sunny afternoon walks in the park. I'd even fallen asleep in his bed once when we were up late talking, and we spent the entire night sleeping chastely side by side, barely touching. I'd never, not once, gotten any sort of a sexual vibe from him, never caught him looking at me in an off way or had him say anything remotely seductive to me, except when done for humorous effect. Sure, Max was touchy-feely, and had often grabbed my hand or thrown an arm around me. But that was just the way he was with everyone, even other men. I'd always considered him to be as safe and asexual as an old teddy bear, in that way you do with male friends who appear happy in their long-term relationships.

I just couldn't believe it. I'm not the kind of woman who men randomly fall in love with. Sure, I've had male friends before, but other than the occasional off-color comment about the size of my breasts, each and every one of them regarded me as one of the boys. I certainly had never entertained confessions of hidden love before. That had always been Maddy's department, along with the hundreds of other gorgeous and enigmatic women who have that certain indefinable quality that men go gaga over. I don't have that quality, and wouldn't even know how to go about acquiring it. Maybe women are born with it, or maybe it's something they learn, carefully studying those magazine articles on how to dress and make eye contact and pick out sunglasses that broadcast to the world that you are It. I am not It. I'm not even close to being It. Sure, I know some things, like what cut of pants keeps my hips from looking a mile wide, and to get my highlights retouched every three to four months, and that I look horrible with short hair. But just as I don't know how women can spend hours on their feet tottering around on spiked heels, I've never learned that Mona Lisa secret of getting men to fall madly in love with me on first sight. And even if I did have that kind of power, I would never have turned it on Max. My feelings for him were, and forever would be, entirely platonic.

Even though I had the luxury of stretching out in my business-class seat, I was soon itching to be up and off the plane. The recycled air was stale and smelled of bad breath and body odor, and my muscles ached at being immobilized for so long. About an hour before we landed, I headed to the tiny bathroom to survey the damage caused by the sleepless night spent on the plane. I brushed my hair and teeth, and touched up my makeup as best I could (I didn't dare tackle anything tricky, like mascara or eyeliner, as it would be just my luck for the plane to hit yet another patch of turbulence and cause me to lose an eye). I still looked tired and bedraggled from travel, but tired with lip gloss was better than tired without.

We finally landed – a heart-stopping endeavor that made me wonder if our pilot entertained *Top Gun* fantasies. I disembarked, and followed the signs to Customs, and joined the flood of travelers bottlenecked there. As I was jostled and bumped by grumpy passengers, I started to notice that all of the women around me were six feet tall and stunning. At first I thought I was just imagining it, but I peered right and then left, and sure enough, there was a tall, thin, gorgeous woman in every direction I looked. And, unlike me and the rest of the bedraggled travelers shuffling through Customs, these women were all made up and coiffed to look like a parade of Barbie dolls come to life.

'Ooooh, I read about this in *People*,' a middle-aged

woman behind me explained to her husband. 'They're here for a beauty pageant. Miss World or Miss Universe . . . something like that.'

Just great, I thought. Not only was I going to have to see Jack for the first time looking scruffy and grubby, but I was now going to be flanked by stick-thin leather-clad beauty contestants.

Jack was waiting for me on the other side of Customs. When I saw his tall figure first waving and then striding toward me, a wide smile on his face, I felt a rush of euphoria and grinned wildly back at him. I'd secretly hoped that distance and time would blunt the edges of my feelings for him, but apparently they did just the opposite. When he got to me, he swept me into his arms, kissed me firmly on the mouth, and then enveloped me in a bear hug.

'Hi,' I said, my voice muffled from being squeezed up against his shoulder.

'Hi,' he said, and hugged me tighter.

'I can't breathe,' I squeaked.

Jack released me, laughing, and grabbed both of my hands, holding them out to the side a little, and looking me up and down.

'You look great,' he said, gazing down at me.

Amazingly, he didn't seem to notice the parade of pageant contestants streaming by us, although I noticed quite a few of them checking Jack out. He did look quite handsome in his camel hair overcoat, his cheeks flushed to a healthy pink and his endearing smile lighting up his face. Even his unruly hair, which normally flopped over his forehead, was behaving itself for once.

'Oh, don't lie. I just got off a six-hour flight. I'm sure I look exactly like I feel,' I said.

'Nope. You look beautiful,' he said, and then kissed me again. This time his lips lingered against mine, and I savored the peppermint-flavored warmth of his mouth.

Jack had another one of his company's hired cars waiting for us. Once my luggage was loaded into the trunk, we piled into the backseat. Jack snuggled me up in his arms, so that I was leaning back against his chest, his chin resting on my head. Strangely, despite the lust that was swelling up inside of me from his close proximity, I somehow managed to fall asleep during the ride into London. When I woke up, the car was parked, and Jack was gently jostling my arm.

'Wake up, sleepyhead. We're here,' he said.

I yawned, and then shivered a little as Jack slid out of the car and I was deprived of his body heat. Between my exhaustion and the cold, my body felt stiff and unwieldy as I followed Jack out of the car, and I stretched my arms and stamped my feet trying to wake up. The driver unloaded my luggage onto the curb.

'Well, what do you think?' Jack asked. Only then did I look around and take in my surroundings.

We were standing on a little side street with two-story town houses lining either side. It was clearly a vein off of a busier street – which I could see up the block, just past a stone arch – and yet had the charming effect of appearing removed from the city. The row houses were quaint and otherworldly, and if not for the absurdly tiny cars parked in front of some of them and the faint laugh track of a television set playing in the distance, it could easily have felt like we'd gone back in time a hundred years.

'You live here?' I asked Jack, and he smiled and stepped forward to unlock a dark green door.

'They're called mews – I honestly don't know why – but whatever they once were, they've since been converted into town houses,' he said, struggling with my suitcase, yet waving me off when I offered to help. Mmm, I liked that. Because of my size, not many men rush forward to help me with my bags, apparently assuming that I can easily hoist steamer trunks up on my shoulders.

'It feels so peaceful back here. It's like we're not even in the city anymore,' I said.

'That's why I like it, too. It's small, but quiet,' Jack said, and reached an arm to usher me through the door.

I immediately felt at home. In fact, his house reminded me of my apartment, in that it was furnished to suit a lifestyle that included lots of lounging around (although Jack's idea of small was actually about a thousand square feet bigger than my place). The front living room was full of leather club chairs and comfy sofas, with ottomans sidled up all around, crowded bookshelves surrounded the walls, and the color scheme was soothing, masculine earth tones. Jack had even put up a small tabletop Christmas tree, strewn with tinsel and twinkle lights. The room was the perfect place to curl up in front of the fireplace for a day, watching movies and eating buttered popcorn. Unlike my apartment, there was a noticeable absence of clutter; Jack seemed to be far neater than I. However, when I commented on how organized he was, he just laughed.

'Far from it. The cleaning lady was here yesterday, and she makes me look good,' he said. He helped me out of my coat, and then shrugged his own off. Leaving my luggage at the foot of the stairs, he stepped forward and wrapped me into his arms.

'Hi,' I said, his nose next to mine, our eyes inches apart.

'Hi,' he said, and leaned in to kiss me again. And then, despite my prediction that I'd be too tired for such activities, we spent the next hour finding out just how comfortable his sofa really was.

Despite all my best intentions not to fall asleep again, so as to adapt to the local time more quickly, Jack and I both drifted off, still on the sofa, pretty much on top of our tangle of discarded clothes. The fire – which Jack had lit before turning his attentions to me – was still going full blaze, sparking and crackling and generally keeping us warm in our undressed state. I was amazed at how hedonistic I was around Jack. Nudity is not a good look for me, and I normally try to remain as clothed as possible at all times, especially when I'm near a man I'm interested in. As far as I'm concerned, no good can come from anyone looking at my cellulite and blemishes and how unlike Kate Moss's my butt is. And yet, I seemed perfectly content to lounge around like some sort of a brazen hussy in front of Jack, wearing nary a stitch. I glanced over at him – very much enjoying the sight of him in full-frontal glory – and then began to sort through the clothing directly underneath me.

My rustling woke Jack, who yawned and stretched, and then reached out and pulled me down against his chest, snuggling me close.

'Whatcha doing?' he asked sleepily.

'Getting dressed,' I admitted.

This caused him to stir, and open one eye. 'Why? Are you going somewhere?'

'No . . . but I was thinking of taking a shower, and making myself somewhat presentable again,' I said. 'Traveling always makes me feel gross.'

Jack nodded, and after planting a firm kiss on my forehead, he struggled up. 'First shower, then food, and then I have a surprise for you,' he said.

'Oh no, you know how I feel about surprises. The last time you surprised me, I assaulted you with my stun gun. And the time before that, you dangled me from the top of a ridiculously large Ferris wheel,' I reminded him.

'Dangled,' he snorted. 'You were as safe as houses.'

'I have never in my whole life understood what that expression means,' I said. 'Why are houses considered safer than other buildings? Don't they catch fire? Have trees fall down on them? Get swept away in tornadoes?'

'Don't worry, this won't be a tornado. Far less traumatic,' Jack said.

'Promise?'

'Promise.'

For whatever it was that he had planned, Jack had rented a car. It was silver and tiny, and when I first saw it, I thought there was no way I'd ever be able to fit into such a thing.

'Let me guess, when I open the door, fifteen clowns are going to come pouring out,' I said, looking at it doubtfully.

'It's part of the real British experience. No one here drives an SUV like you do back home,' Jack said.

'I can't even remember the last time I drove a car,' I said, and then headed for the passenger door.

'Are you going to try now?' Jack asked, watching me. 'I thought you might be too tired.'

'Absolutely too tired,' I said, stifling my umpteenth yawn. The nap had helped, but I could still use a good twelve hours of downtime.

'Then you're getting in the wrong side. Remember? Drivers sit on the right side of the car over here,' Jack said. He kissed me on the forehead, and then opened the left-hand door of the car for me. As I folded down into my seat, I immediately felt claustrophobic.

'This isn't a car, it's a tin can strapped to a roller skate,' I muttered to myself, while Jack walked back around to the driver's side of the car. I prayed that all of the other drivers on the road were also driving tuna cans, because if anything bigger than a bumper car hit us in this thing, we'd be flattened.

But once we got on the road to wherever it was we were going – Jack still wouldn't tell me, it was all part of the surprise – I immediately went to sleep again. Apparently the insomnia that plagued me at home had not followed me overseas, because every time I sat still for even a few minutes, I was out cold. Just as I was falling asleep, I had a fleeting thought about Maddy's private investigator, and wondered if she had actually hired one, and, if so, whether he was at that moment following us, but a minute later all thoughts left me as I succumbed to bone-numbing exhaustion. It wasn't until I felt the car slowing down and turning off the highway that I was roused back to consciousness. As I came to, my eyes blinking and my mouth gaping open in a yawn, I was faced with the most beautiful sight.

It was a village, bathed in the last soft light of the late afternoon and blanketed with a light layer of snow. We were driving down an actual cobblestone street, surrounded by an enchanting mix of architecture. Brick town houses were leaning up against timber-framed houses, looking like a set of crooked teeth, and all of the doors were done up in Christmas wreaths. The antiquated shop windows were full of china and picture frames, or links of sausages and sides of ham, and there was an old pub with a beaten wooden sign: *The Toad and Rabbit*. A stately and somewhat shabby church reigned over the city square. It was dusk, and the pools of light emanating from the gas-lit street lanterns were beginning to be of some use.

'Where are we?' I asked, and was a little disappointed when I saw another car pass us by, rather than a horse and carriage complete with jingle bells.

'We're in Kent, near the eastern coast. The village is called Dedham. What do you think?'

'It's absolutely breathtaking. Is this where we're staying?'

'Close, but we have a little farther to go,' Jack said, glancing over at me with a sideways smile.

I settled in, happy to gawk out the window at the old-fashioned scene, flooded with the memories of every British novel I'd ever read that was set in a similar small town. The view became even more picturesque as we left the town and headed down a bumpy country lane with brambly brush lining either side, past rolling green hills geometrically divided by hedgerows. The odd cow or sheep, undeterred by the powdery dusting of snow, ambled through the pastures. I was seized by the essential Britishness of it, and had an urge to locate a pair of green Wellies and a dog and take a brisk hike throughout the countryside before returning for a cuppa in front of the fire. In a few minutes, we were turning again, and then again, and then Jack was turning into a driveway and parking near a thicket of enormous trees that blocked the view of our destination.

'We're here,' he said, looking as excited as a small child. 'Come on, I can't wait to show you.'

We unfolded ourselves from the car, and it took me a minute of stretching so my muscles could pop back into their proper places before I followed Jack, who'd gone ahead of me down a path and out of sight. When I went after him, taking care not to fall on the slippery stone path, I gasped with delight. With an enormous grin on his face, Jack was waiting for me in front of a house – actually more of a cottage, really – and in the failing evening light, the stone façade appeared to have an almost greenish glow. The front door was smack in the middle of the house, with symmetrical windows on either side, and three above on a second floor, all flanked by black shutters, and bright lights shone from each window. A small wreath, thick with evergreen and red ribbons, hung on the door. It was a simple dwelling – nothing near the size nor scope of the rather grand yet crumbling Georgian mansion we'd passed shortly after we left the village – yet it was far more enticing.

'Whose house is this?' I asked.

'Do you like it?' Jack asked, smiling broadly.

'Yes, of course,' I breathed, sure that I had never before

and would never again see a house that was so perfect. It was appealing, warm, and welcoming, and it just drew me in, as if the house itself was eager to have me inside.

'I think so, too. That's why I bought it,' Jack said.

'You did? When did you do that?'

'Just a few weeks ago, right after I got back from New York. I'd been looking for a place for months, and then this one came on the market, so I grabbed it. I wanted it to be a surprise, that's why I didn't tell you,' Jack said. He looked quite pleased with himself.

I frowned, and questions started to flood my thoughts. Was Jack planning on permanently relocating to England? He hadn't mentioned moving back to the States, but I'd gotten the distinct impression that he was feeling displaced in his current situation. I'd assumed it meant he was homesick . . . when apparently, he was just getting the itch to get out of the city. It was a feeling I very much understood, but it was curious that Jack had never mentioned it to me before. And what did this all mean for us? If his future was here, in the English countryside, what did it mean about his intentions toward me?

Oh God, what an old-fashioned way to look at it, inquiring after his *intentions*. It sounded like something my mother would have asked a high school boyfriend, I thought, rolling my eyes.

I followed Jack up the walkway, and waited while he unlocked the black front door. Inside, the house was adorable, but nothing like Jack's streamlined, comfort-based bachelor pad in London. Here, there was a lot of chintz, and flowered china in glass-fronted cabinets, and delicate-looking chairs that I had a hard time imagining Jack being able to fit his long body into. It was much more the kind of house you'd imagine blue-haired ladies holding tea parties in, not the home of a hip, urban-dwelling businessman.

Jack must have noticed the curious expression on my face, for he laughed and said, 'I bought it fully furnished, but I'm obviously going to be making a lot of changes. I'm not really the ruffled-curtain type. In fact, if you have any ideas, you know, about what to change, I'd love to hear them.'

'Oh, I'm the last person you'd want mucking up your home decor,' I said with a laugh, thinking of my own eclectic apartment.

'I don't know about that,' Jack said, and gave me another strange look.

I suddenly became very aware of an undercurrent between us, one that I didn't fully understand. If I didn't know better, I'd have thought that Jack was suggesting we move in together, or at the very least hinting that we would in the future. This completely and totally freaked me out. It was too soon, far too soon to even be talking about it. And why the hell did he get to do this, to move too fast, to shatter the widely accepted etiquette of modern-day courtship? When a woman pushes for commitment too soon, if she were to dare suggest moving in together or shopping for an engagement ring at an early stage of the relationship, the object of her affection would bolt, his feet churning like the Roadrunner escaping Wile E. Coyote. And then anyone observing would shake her head and purse her lips, and murmur, *What did she expect would happen, acting so desperate?*

Jack was expecting something from me, some kind of a response or reaction, but I had no idea what it was that he wanted me to say. I felt off-kilter, like I was moving sideways when everything else was going forward.

'So, um, what are we going to do?' I asked, determined to change the subject.

Jack continued to look at me without speaking for a moment. But then he gave me a funny little half-smile and said, 'I'll bring our luggage in, and then I guess we should make a fire – it's freezing in here, and I don't know how well the central heating works. I brought some groceries in the car with us.'

'I'll go out and get them,' I volunteered, wanting a chance to clear my head and to get away from whatever this weird vibe was that had sprung up between us.

Was it a complete mistake for me to have come? I'd only been concerned about the betrayal inherent in what I was doing, and about the news that Jack and Maddy's breakup seemed to be more complicated than I'd initially known – something I still wanted to ask Jack about when the opportunity arose. I hadn't really thought out the part where I was spending a major holiday with a guy I hadn't been seeing for all that long, and what that meant. Suddenly I started to feel a little panicky. My shoulders tightened and I couldn't breathe deeply, instead inhaling in quick little puffs of air.

'What's wrong? Is everything all right? You must be exhausted from your flight. Why don't you sit down and rest, and I'll take care of everything,' Jack said, looking concerned. He tried to steer me toward the plump, chintz-covered sofa, but I held back, shaking my head.

'No, I'm fine. Really. Look, I'll go grab the groceries, and you go do whatever needs to be done in here, and it will all be fine,' I jabbered, and trotted out the door before he could stop me.

It was nearly dark outside, and as I skittered over the stone path toward the driveway, I noticed that the trees I'd thought were so majestic and beautiful when we pulled up now had a faintly sinister look to them. Maybe this village was an idyllic backdrop for Christmas festivities – that I couldn't deny – but what in God's name was I doing here? Did I think that Jack and I were headed toward some gooey, Barbie-and-Ken happily-ever-after? Hardly. I'd gotten over any fantasies I had about my white knight crouching down on one knee with a diamond ring in hand the night Sawyer dumped me. Okay, sure, I was just as guilty as anyone else of daydreaming about my perfect life – my magazine life – that included the handsome husband and sweet-smelling babies, alongside the stainless steel Sub-Zero and cherry dining room set. And yes, lately in these fantasies the handsome-husband character had been played by Jack. But that didn't mean that I was seriously entertaining any notion that it was really going to happen. I mean, the man had just purchased a house in the English countryside, for Christ's sake. That would be an awfully long weekend commute from Manhattan.

I popped open the trunk – as tiny as the rest of the car – and pulled out the Marks & Spencer bags resting in the back. Judging from the weight of the bags, there was easily enough food to see us through several days. Is that how long we were going to be out here, in the middle of nowhere? Days and days with nothing to do but stare at each other? It sounded . . . confining. And crowded.

'What are you doing out here?' Jack appeared from behind me, still looking concerned. 'Are you okay?'

'Yes, fine. Sorry. Just lost in my own thoughts, you know, thinking about the trees, just Christmas stuff mostly. Carols and eggnog and all of that. Anyway. Um. Did you need something?' I wondered if I sounded as crazy to him as I did to myself. From the bewildered expression on his face, I thought probably so.

'The luggage. I was going to bring it in,' Jack said. 'I think maybe you should go lie down for a little while, you seem a little out of it.'

That's a nice way of putting it, I thought, cringing to know that Jack was probably also having second thoughts about the wisdom of locking himself away in the middle of nowhere with an insane woman.

We went back in the house, and while Jack took the luggage upstairs, I hauled the store bags into the small but pleasant kitchen. He'd gotten the basics – orange juice, milk, croissants, fruit, French bread – as well as some delicious-looking prepared foods, and quite a bit of Swiss and Gruyére cheeses, and chocolate. And, happily, half a dozen bottles of wine, one of which I immediately cracked open.

I decided to take Jack's advice about lying down – maybe my panic was just a result of jet lag and general exhaustion – so I poured myself a glass of wine and took it into the den, where Jack had started a fire. I curled up on one corner of the couch, and drank my wine while I stared at the fire and took deep breaths and generally tried to keep my anxiety from spiraling out of control.

Jack came back downstairs, but instead of sitting with me by the fire, he gave me a quick kiss on the cheek and headed toward the kitchen, where he spent some time rustling around and banging cupboards. I must have dozed off yet again, because the next thing I knew, Jack was gently shaking my shoulder and as I woke up slowly, stretching and yawning like a cat, I saw that he'd brought dinner in on a tray. It looked delicious – a pot of cheese fondue, accompanied by cubes of French bread and a chilled bottle of white wine.

'Mmmm, that looks delicious,' I said, trying to figure out just how fattening it was to eat a meal that consisted of chunks of bread dipped in melted cheese. When I'd first started dating Sawyer, we'd eaten out constantly, and I'd been too busy falling in love to have any sense about what I was putting in my mouth. As a result, I gained ten pounds which I didn't lose until later, when I was pounding out my post-breakup misery on the treadmill. Not wanting to wear my fat pants again had been yet another reason for my fear of romantic entanglements.

'Merry Christmas,' Jack said, raising his glass in a toast.

'Merry Christmas,' I replied.

We ate quietly, the crackle of the fire playing nicely against the wind that had picked up while I napped, and was now howling indignantly against the windowpanes. It was a companionable silence, although I was feeling a little shy from my earlier nuttiness. I wished I could just relax and enjoy my time spent with Jack, and stop worrying about what was going on or how to sidestep being hurt. And I wondered what he was thinking about . . . it wasn't like him to be so quiet. Suddenly the silence felt oppressive, and the room overly hot.

'So, um, what's there to do around here? I mean, is there anything you have planned for us to do?' I asked, cringing at how artificial I sounded.

Jack had finished eating, and was leaning back against the couch, glass of wine in hand. He regarded me from under half-closed lids, appraising me with the same quizzical expression he'd been wearing earlier.

'What's going on?' Jack asked, nudging me gently with his foot.

'Nothing. Really. Why?'

'You're just acting a little strange, and I'm getting the feeling that you're uncomfortable here. We can drive back to London, if you'd rather stay there. I just want to spend time with you, and I don't care where we are,' he said.

He was just too damn nice. Now I felt terrible. I knew I was acting like a freak, and had been since we'd gotten to the country. Jack had gone to great trouble to deliver an idyllic English winter wonderland for Christmas, and all I'd done was gawk and shuffle around like a surly teenager being forced to spend the holidays on a family vacation away from her friends.

'No, this is perfect. There's no place I'd rather be,' I said truthfully, reaching out and taking his hand in mine. 'I think

I've just been feeling strange because of the time change.'

Jack looked relieved, and slid closer so that he could put his arm around me. 'Good. You can be so hard to read sometimes,' he said.

'You think so?' I asked.

'Absolutely. I've never met anyone like you before,' Jack said, which was enormously flattering until he continued, 'I have to work harder with you.'

'What? Really? You think so?'

He shrugged, and touched my cheek with a finger. 'Your defenses are pretty well developed,' he said.

Ouch. I knew what he was saying was true, but it didn't sound all that flattering when he put it that way. It made me feel like I was damaged somehow, one of those hardened, bitter women who end up sneering every time they see a couple holding hands and spend wedding receptions announcing there's no way the marriage will last.

'And you're used to women rolling over for you?' I asked, somewhat more pointedly than I meant to.

'See, that's just what I mean,' Jack said with a smile, although I didn't know what he meant at all.

But then Jack leaned over and kissed me. And then kissed me again. And pretty soon, my defenses came crashing down, at least for the time being.

After that first night, I was able to loosen up and relax, and the remainder of our time in Dedham was much less stressful. Christmas Day was picture perfect, complete with a fresh new dusting of snow. It was a day spent lazing around in front of a roaring fire and never-ending Christmas carols on the radio. We even navigated through the trickiest part of the holiday – the dreaded gift exchange – as easily as possible, probably because we got it out of the way first thing in the morning, while we were still lounging around in a tangle of sheets and blankets.

I had worried endlessly about what to get Jack. Deciding on a Christmas present for a new boyfriend requires the same careful planning as a chess move, with many more important considerations than any one person's individual wants or needs. The gift can't be too personal or too impersonal, it can't be too cheap or too expensive, it can't be a demand for a commitment (like a watch or cuff links), or indicate a veiled criticism (like a PDA). Once you're constrained by such criteria, there's little left on the table, other than clothing, which is hard to buy for a man you haven't known for very long. Plus, since Jack and I had for the most part conducted our relationship over the telephone, I hadn't seen much of his wardrobe. I didn't know if he already had a green sweater that exactly matched the shade of his eyes, or whether he favored conservative ties over the wild patterned kind.

I'd spent the Saturday after my return from Chicago dragging around from store to store, looking for something that would send just the right message, and was about to completely give up and buy him something horribly impersonal, like a gift certificate, when I wandered into the Coach store and saw a tray of beautiful wallets in a glass case. Twenty minutes later, I practically skipped out of the store with a bag containing a black leather double billfold wallet carefully wrapped in tissue paper. It was $108.00, and absolutely perfect in every respect – respectable price, neither overly intimate nor too businesslike, and didn't have any underlying messages.

And, that Christmas morning, when Jack tore off the green tissue paper I'd wrapped the box in, I knew I'd done well. He looked pleased, and neither over- nor under-whelmed. He admired it for a few minutes, and assured me that he did in fact need to replace his wallet, and how had I known. He then dug out a small square box professionally wrapped in silver foil and handed it to me. I ripped the paper off greedily, shook open the gold box . . . and then gasped. It was a necklace, a beautiful necklace – a delicate gold chain with seven round bezel-set diamonds – that clearly cost much more than the crappy wallet I'd gotten him. It was elegant and ladylike and maybe the nicest Christmas present I'd ever received. Certainly better than the news of my parents' imminent divorce. I gaped at it, and shook my head, while Jack smiled and looked pleased with himself.

'It's gorgeous, but it's . . .' I started to say, but then trailed off, not knowing how to complete my thought. Jack was, yet again, breaking all of the dating rules. And this one wasn't just one of my rules; everyone knows that you don't buy expensive gifts, and especially not jewelry, for someone you've just started dating. In fact, as prissy and old-fashioned a notion as it may be, I knew I shouldn't even accept it. But I didn't know how to tell him without hurting his feelings, and besides, I really, *really* wanted to keep it. Even more so after Jack helped me try it on, and I climbed out of bed to admire my newly bejeweled self in the mirror. The necklace was the perfect length – it rested right against my clavicle, and the diamonds winked and shimmered against my skin.

'It looks beautiful on you,' Jack said, and then pulled me back into bed to cuddle with him, and the moment of opportunity to protest had passed.

We spent the rest of the day taking a long walk through the snow-covered English countryside. Sadly, Jack wasn't able to unearth a pair of Wellies for me to wear, and thus complete the experience, but it was picturesque nevertheless. When we returned, we camped out in front of the fire, working our way through the pile of movies Jack had brought from London and eating the prepackaged Marks & Spencer meals. Thursday, the weather turned nasty, so we took a long drive out of town and into neighboring villages, all of which were pretty and interesting, but none of which I liked as much as Dedham. Friday we stayed closer to home, and ventured into town, looking through the ancient, crumbling church, peering in the shop windows, and stopping by the pub for a glass of disgustingly warm beer, which Jack assured me I had to drink in order to capture the true spirit of things.

'This has just been such a perfect trip. Other than the warm beer, I mean,' I sighed, as we left the pub and began the walk back to Jack's house.

'That wasn't a beer, it was a lager,' Jack said, squeezing my mittened hand in his.

'Either way, *blech*. But the pub itself was nice. Very woody and atmospheric, and everyone was so friendly,' I said.

Jack snorted. 'Yeah, well, I'm not sure they'd have given me such a warm welcome if I were on my own,' he said.

'Why? Are people upset that you bought a house here? Because you're an American?'

'No, I meant because I'm not a beautiful, sexy woman. I thought I was going to have to start beating off your admirers in there,' Jack said.

'Oh, be serious. They were just being nice, that's all. And that one guy – Bernie? – he was just an old flirt,' I said, feeling quite pleased that Jack would describe me as beautiful and sexy. Even if it was an obvious exaggeration.

'He tried to grab your ass,' Jack said.

'I think he was just a little clumsy,' I said.

Jack snorted again.

On Saturday morning, Jack and I drove back to London. In our absence, the city weather had turned bleak and gray, and the overcast sky was grimly threatening to send a downpour at the slightest provocation. I'd expected we'd spend the day – and maybe the remainder of my trip, if the forecast didn't improve – doing something indoors, like taking in a museum, or, better yet, going to a really trashy blockbuster movie, the kind with aliens and chase scenes and inane dialogue full of the punchy one-liners that play well in the trailers.

When I suggested the movie idea to Jack, naturally assuming that the lure of special effects and explosions would prove irresistible to him, I was surprised when he shook his head and said, 'I thought that we'd take a walk through the park.'

'But it's going to rain,' I protested.

'No, it'll be fine. Come on, we'll walk for a bit, and then I'll take you for afternoon tea at the Orangery,' Jack said.

'What's that?'

'A little restaurant. It's right behind Kensington Palace, where Princess Di used to live.'

I wrapped my sky blue pashmina scarf around my throat and shrugged on my fitted black wool coat, and we set off for Hyde Park on foot, winding through the South Kensington streets, past the imperious white town houses flanked by wrought iron fences. The streets were quiet and calm, until we turned onto the high street, where hordes of shoppers bustled by, weighed down with bags full of Christmas returns and post-holiday sale items. We dodged through the crowds, and a minute later we were in the park, which, except for some dog walkers marching along with upturned collars and their charges at their knees, was nearly deserted, most likely because everyone else was too smart to be out in this weather.

'How far away is this tea place?' I grumbled. The wind was so frigid, it was causing my eyes to water and my ears to turn numb.

'Are you cold?' Jack asked, looking down at me with surprise. 'I thought it would seem mild here compared to New York.'

'Mild? Not the word I would use,' I gasped, as yet another gust of wind slapped me across the face.

'We're almost there,' Jack promised.

The Orangery turned out to be well worth the frosty walk. It was a glassed-in summer house, long and sufficiently opulent for an afternoon dining locale for royals, which had apparently been its original function. When we walked in, the first thing I saw was a table groaning under the weight of one fattening pastry after another, each one looking more delicious. My willpower, already lowered by the exercise and chilly weather, was done in when I saw a toothsome chocolate layer cake. I've been on a nonstop diet for roughly seventeen years, but I have a weakness for chocolate cake.

Jack and I sat at one of the small, square, white-linen-covered tables, and ordered tea, sandwiches, and cake from a supercilious waiter, who, I presumed from his curt manner, seemed not to have a high opinion of American tourists. Just as our glasses of water (room temperature with no ice, naturally) were delivered to us, the skies suddenly opened up and began spitting down sheets of rain. Lightning crackled across the iron gray sky, and thunder boomed at regular intervals. The glass walls of the Orangery were instantly streaked and opaque from the streams of water, which turned the view of the back of Kensington Palace into nothing more than a blur.

'I guess we're stuck here for a while,' Jack said. 'Which is actually not a bad thing, because I've been wanting to talk to you about something.'

He had that determined, man-on-a-mission look on his face again, the one that made my stomach turn jellylike with fear. But I was not going to start blathering like a hapless idiot this time. Instead, I'd just keep steering the conversation back to safe ground.

'Well, if you're going to be stuck somewhere, it might as well be a place that serves chocolate cake,' I said, eyeing the plates of goodies that the waiter was delivering to our table.

But Jack didn't make a move for the cake. Instead, he ran his hands through his hair, pushing back the stubborn lock that insisted on falling back down on his forehead, and then he picked up a spare paper napkin off the table and began shredding it. I knew that I should ask him what was making him so nervous, but I couldn't bring myself to do it. So instead I said, 'I'd really like to go to the Victoria and Albert Museum while I'm here. Do you know if it's open on Sunday? Because if so, we could go tomorrow. Unless you had something else planned.'

Jack didn't answer, nor did he look up at me. Instead he finished shredding his napkin and then examined each item of cutlery lying on the table before him. I sighed. Obviously he wasn't going to let me slide by again by distracting him or changing the subject.

'Jack?' I said softly, resting my hand on his arm. 'What's wrong?'

'Wrong? Nothing's wrong,' he said, looking surprised. And then his face creased into the familiar smile that made it feel like my insides were melting, a sensation that I'd come to find unnervingly addicting.

I grinned back at him and squeezed his hand. 'You checked out on me for a minute,' I said.

'I just,' he began, and then took a deep breath. 'Don't take this the wrong way, Claire, but . . .' And then his voice trailed off, the thought not finished.

What? What was he going to say? *Don't take this the wrong way, but* . . . what? Whenever someone says 'Don't take this the wrong way,' they're inevitably going to say something that either pisses you off, hurts your feelings, or worse. So what was it? And why did he drop off that way, staring into the space over my left shoulder? I didn't want to push him to go on – certain that whatever he was going to say, I wouldn't take it the wrong way, but in exactly whatever awful way he meant it – but it wasn't quite a point in the conversation from which I could tack right and change the subject. In fact, I couldn't even bear to look at him, and instead stared at the piece of cake before me, suddenly not at all hungry. What had just minutes ago been so tempting now looked a little stale and crumbly, the frosting congealed and probably far too sweet.

'It's Maddy,' Jack said softly.

I felt like I'd been socked in the stomach. Whatever I'd thought was going to come next, whatever hideous revelation – *I don't have those kind of feelings for you, This just isn't working out, When I see you naked the theme song of the Jell-O gelatin commercials starts running through my head* – I hadn't expected this, hadn't expected the words to so neatly slice open my heart. But as much as it hurt – and, oh God, it hurt, along the lines of being subjected to a Brazilian bikini wax and assaulted with an Epilady at the same time, only worse – how could I be that surprised? Wasn't this what always happened, what always would happen when a man was given the choice of being with a goddess or a mere mortal? I was clearly some kind of a transitional person, someone that he used to salve his wounded heart after learning that the love of his life was cheating on him with her boss.

'Is this some kind of a game?' I whispered, not out of meekness, but because I was suddenly so enraged that I was afraid that if I began to use a normal tone of voice, it would come out in a high-pitched shriek that would shatter the glass windows enclosing the Orangery.

'What? What are you talking about?'

'Is. This. Some. Kind. Of. A. Game. Is that why you brought me out here? Just to get revenge, or to make yourself feel better for having been cheated on?' I demanded.

'Claire, you're not making any sense. I don't know what you're talking about. I was just trying to say . . . Maddy is *here*. She's standing over by the door. Staring at us. And from the expression on her face, I'm getting the distinct impression that you never got around to telling her about us,' Jack said.

I turned and looked at the door, and there she was – soaking wet, completely bedraggled, and yet still somehow gorgeous. Maddy looked like a movie actress who'd been doused with water for the big storm scene, and then had her hair and makeup meticulously fixed to look fresh and dewy. I looked at her, and her gaze moved from Jack to me. As our eyes locked, I saw hers widen and her face turn ashen. She stood rooted in place, her face frozen in an expression of shock and hurt. Her mouth fell open, and I could see the questions, the accusations right there, ready to tip out, and yet still she didn't move or speak.

'Maddy,' I croaked, and as I stood, the metal frame chair I'd been sitting in toppled over, landing on the marble floor with such a loud clatter that everyone in the restaurant looked over at me, first with mild curiosity, and then with keener interest as they sensed the drama unfolding between Jack, Maddy, and me. I didn't care, in fact it barely registered with me that a hush had fallen over the room and that dozens of pairs of eyes were taking us in, probably assuming that Jack was an adulterous husband, Maddy was the wronged wife, and that I was the brazen hussy elbowing my way into the marriage. All I cared about was that in all of the years I'd known Maddy, with everything that we'd been through together, I'd never seen her look so completely lost.

'Maddy,' I said again, and I could feel, rather than see, Jack stand up behind me, and seeing us together, the vision of a close and united front, probably just served to drive in the reality of our treachery even deeper. Maddy's eyes were flashing with hurt and confusion as she looked first at me and then at Jack. I wanted more than anything to go to her, to comfort her, to try to explain or apologize, and I tried to make my legs, which seemed rooted into the ground, start moving.

But Maddy didn't give me the chance. She turned and fled out into the rain, and through the streaked glass windows she became just another blurred outline as she ran down toward the gate into Hyde Park and disappeared out of sight.

'I have to go after her,' I said to Jack.

He righted my chair and motioned for me to sit down. I suddenly became aware of the hush that had fallen over the Orangery, and that everyone was staring at Jack and me, clearly delighting in the scene they'd just witnessed. I shrank down in the chair, putting a hand up to one side of my face to shield myself from their avid attention.

'Everyone's staring at us,' I hissed.

'So?' Jack shrugged. 'Let them stare. We haven't done anything wrong, Claire. It wasn't like Maddy and I were dating anymore, much less married or engaged. I can see whomever I want.'

'Yes, you're free to do that, but what about me? Maddy's my friend – or at least she *was* my friend, I have no idea how she's going to feel now. Oh no, this is terrible,' I said. Why hadn't I told Maddy everything in the beginning? Why had I let things get this far with Jack without talking to her about it? At least that way, I could have broken it to her gently, rather than having her find out this way.

'What do you want to do?' Jack asked. He put an arm around me, one hand gently stroking my back, and for some reason the gesture made my eyes water up with tears. I didn't deserve to have someone be so nice to me, and especially not someone as wonderful as Jack.

'I have to go see her,' I said. 'Right now.'

'Okay, I'll go with you,' Jack said. 'Let me just pay the check, and we'll leave now.'

'No, I have to go by myself. I think it will be easier for her, and I just . . . it's the right thing to do,' I said.

'But if I go with you, I can absorb some of her anger, keep it from being directed entirely at you,' Jack said.

I smiled at him and reached out to touch his cheek lightly. 'Thanks, I appreciate that. But I think I have this coming to me,' I said.

It was one thing to act brave about facing Maddy while I was safely tucked away in a cozy restaurant with Jack stroking my back and being supportive. It was quite another thing to be standing on her doorstep, staring up at the door and trying to work up the nerve to push the bell. I wasn't even sure if she would see me. She might just shout through the door for me to go to hell, and then what would I do? Camp out on her steps? Go back to Jack's and try to call her? And what if she wouldn't take my phone calls, what then?

Between the rain that was still pelting me, soaking through my wool coat, and the knowledge that time was not going to make this confrontation any easier, I finally took a deep breath and rapped sharply on the door. I listened for footsteps, didn't hear any, and raised my hand to knock again, when the door suddenly swung open. Maddy stood on the opposite side of the doorjamb, staring at me with a strange glow in her wide blue eyes. She looked almost malevolent, like a character in a horror movie who suddenly snaps and starts decapitating everyone with a scythe. I took a step back.

'I didn't think you'd have the nerve to show up here. But I suppose you'd better come in,' Maddy said.

Other than the creepy-eye thing, she sounded – and looked – strangely calm. It unnerved me. I was prepared to deal with her crying, or yelling at me, but not with this eerie detachment. I almost didn't want to follow her, but since she turned and walked back into her apartment, leaving the door open, I supposed I had no choice but to let myself in, closing the door behind me.

The first thing I noticed was that her apartment was shockingly messy. When I'd last been there, it had been immaculate. Now it was cluttered with empty pizza boxes, newspapers, magazines, cans of Diet Coke, overflowing ashtrays, and piles of crumpled clothing. The white slipcover on the sofa was grimy, and a fine layer of dust covered the end tables. Even the shaggy white carpet, the one that reminded me of a skinned sheepdog, looked to be in dire need of a grooming. I'd never seen Maddy live in such filth before. When we were roommates, she used to get angry at me if I left my shoes by the front door, right where I kicked them off, rather than immediately trotting them back to our shared closet.

'Let me explain,' I said weakly.

'Yes, I think you should do that,' Maddy said coldly. She flopped down on her sofa and retrieved a pack of cigarettes. She withdrew one, lit it, and inhaled deeply, before glancing over at me. 'Want one?'

'Okay,' I said. I sat down on her other couch and took the cigarette and lighter from her. Once I'd got it lit, I inhaled deeply, amazed at how even after eight years of abstinence the first puff of smoke caused my body to melt with pleasure. God, how I'd missed this – the smell, the taste, the way the cigarette felt in my hand.

'So. Talk,' Maddy said, raising her eyebrows with interest. 'Because I'm dying to know the reason why my best friend is in a foreign country with my boyfriend.'

'I thought you were in Boston,' I said stupidly. Probably not the best explanation, but I was also pretty sure that getting into an argument over just whose boyfriend Jack really was, was probably an even worse opening.

Maddy snorted. 'I was. But the private investigator I hired called me at my mom's and told me that he'd taken some snapshots of Jack with a tall, attractive blonde woman who was apparently staying with him over the holidays, so I flew back to see her for myself. You want to know something funny? When he faxed me the photo – it was of you two kissing at the airport – I even thought the woman looked a little like you. But then I said, no, that's impossible,' Maddy said, her voice dripping with anger.

'How did you know where to find us just now?' I asked quietly, wondering if this private investigator had been trailing us the entire time I'd been in England. What a creepy thought.

'I waited outside of Jack's house, and followed you to the park. And when I saw it was you there, with him – I couldn't believe my fucking eyes,' she said, spitting the words out.

'I want to explain, I just don't know how to start,' I said feebly.

'Start at the beginning, then. And, please, don't leave anything out. I think I'm entitled to know everything,' she said.

I took in a deep breath, trying to suck all of the nicotine out of the cigarette. I considered asking her for a glass of wine, but then decided against it – I'd be lucky if she didn't hit me over the head with the bottle.

'I met Jack on my flight to London back in November. We just happened to sit next to each other. And we hit it off. Then when we got here, he called me, and we arranged to see each other. At that time, I had no idea that he was the same person that you were seeing, I swear to God. Anyway, we spent time together while I was here, and it was . . .' I paused for a minute, not sure if I should finish the sentence with the word 'amazing,' as I meant to. I also didn't know how to tell her that Jack and I had become intimate so quickly, and that maybe if we hadn't, and maybe if there hadn't been such an incredible physical attraction between us, that it would have been easier to walk away once I did know. I was pretty sure that any way I put it, it was going to make her feel that much worse.

'It was . . . what? Go on, get to the part where you decided to lie to me,' she said. 'I can't wait to hear your justification for that.'

'Maddy, at that point, I still didn't know. Don't you remember, I was here for several days before you and I talked? I didn't know who he was until that afternoon when I came over here,' I said, sweeping my hand in front of me, 'and Jack showed up to pick up his things. He didn't know who I was either. It was just the most horrible coincidence, I swear.'

At this, Maddy snorted. 'Yeah, I just bet it was.'

'How could I have known who he was? I'd never met him before, or seen his picture. Hell, I didn't even know his last name, and I'd never heard you refer to him as anything but Harrison. And for some reason, I could have sworn you said that your boyfriend was British,' I protested.

'No, I never said that. Come on, I want to hear the rest, especially about how it is that you're here now,' she said. I wasn't surprised at the level of animosity in Maddy's voice, but it was disconcerting how composed she was. No tears, no histrionics, and this from a woman who cried hysterically at the end of *Pretty Woman*.

'When I left here that day, left you and Jack here, I went back to my hotel, and I thought that was it. I didn't expect that I'd ever see him again. I figured he wouldn't call me after that, and if he did, I planned to tell him that there was no way we could see each other again. But then . . .' I trailed off again.

'*But then* . . . Christ, Claire, just tell me. I've pretty much figured out that he did call you, and that you did see him again. I'm not an idiot,' she snapped.

'Yes. I saw him again. That last night before I left to go back to New York. And then once I got home he called me, and came to visit me once – I didn't know he was coming, he just showed up unannounced. And then he asked me to spend Christmas with him here in London,' I said, and stubbed out the smoldering end of my cigarette.

'And you lied to me about it,' Maddy prompted me.

'Yes. I certainly withheld the information from you that he and I were in contact,' I said carefully.

'In contact? Is that what you call having his dick inside you?' she asked, and I winced at the vulgarity, not out of my own modesty, but because it was so unlike Maddy.

'It was more than that. I know you couldn't possibly understand, because I know I did a shitty thing, both in continuing to see him and in not telling you about it, but I had . . . I *have* feelings for Jack. Strong feelings. So strong, they made me lose my head. Not that it's an excuse for what I did, but I haven't exactly been thinking clearly lately,' I finished lamely.

Maddy had also finished her cigarette, and she promptly lit another one. 'And you expect me to believe your little story? That you just happened to sit next to my boyfriend on a plane, and that the two of you fell in love, and it was all out of your control?' she asked.

'No, I'm not saying that. It was within our control, within my control, and I was so wrong to have let it happen without talking to you about it. Please believe me, I mean it when I say that, and I'm so, so sorry that I've hurt you,' I said.

'That's not what I meant. God, you are such an idiot,' Maddy said, and amazingly, she began to laugh. It wasn't her normal laugh, an effervescent and frothy sound that always reminds me of summer. This was a harsh bark, and the smile didn't reach her eyes, which were now narrowed into vengeful slits. 'You may not have known who he was, but Harrison certainly knew who you were.'

'What?' I asked, and then began shaking my head. 'No, Maddy, he didn't. I know it sounds like really long odds – astronomical odds – that we'd end up sitting next to each other on a plane, but I swear, that's what happened.'

'Claire. Don't be so stupid. He *knew* you were going to be on that flight. He called me that afternoon before he left New York, and I even made a joke that you two might end up on the same flight. He said he'd look out for you,' she said.

'But . . . how? How would he know who I was, what I looked like?' I asked.

In response, Maddy leapt to her feet and stalked into the kitchen, returning a moment later with the photograph I'd seen posted on her refrigerator. It was the one of us in Cancún, tanned and drunk, our arms wrapped around each other's shoulders, margaritas held forward in a toast . . . the same picture Jack had sworn to me that he'd never seen. I'd thought Maddy had put it up on her fridge just before my first visit to her flat, the same way newlyweds try to pull wedding gifts out of drawers and put them on display when they know the gift-giver is coming over.

'Because he saw this picture every single time he was at my apartment. He commented on it all the time, said he wanted to know the face behind the e-mails,' she said, holding the photo up for me to see. 'Did he tell you that? That I used to let him read the e-mails you sent me? He was always saying how funny you were.'

She looked down at the picture, studying it. I wondered if she, like me, was remembering that vacation. We'd gone only a few months after Maddy had lost her father, and it was on that trip that the heavy burden of grief had begun to lift, that I'd started to see glimpses of the old Maddy. But then Maddy dramatically tore the picture in two, cutting us apart, and letting our images fall to the ground.

'I guess I don't need that anymore,' she said icily.

I didn't know what to think. Was she telling the truth about Jack knowing what I looked like? Had he purposely set about meeting me on the plane? And if so, why didn't he tell me who he was? What was the point of hiding it from me? Or was Maddy just angry, and now inventing this story to make me doubt Jack? Would she do that? Although she hadn't offered a second one to me, I reached for her pack of cigarettes, extracted another, and lit it.

'I can certainly understand your anger,' I said slowly, puffing on the cigarette – my new best friend – while I tried to think of a way to make sense of everything. 'But we honestly didn't set out to hurt you. And I'm sure that even if Jack did see my picture, he didn't know it was me. My hair's different now, it's long and straight, and in that picture it was shorter and wavy.'

'You don't get it, do you? Oh, wait,' she said, and then laughed again. 'You think he's in love with you, don't you? You think that he's Prince Charming, here to sweep you off your feet. You probably felt sorry for me and my poor broken heart, while the two of you danced off into the sunset. You smug little bitch!'

I winced again. Whoever this woman was, it was not the Maddy I'd always known. She was like a brittle, hostile shell of her former self. I'd expected her to be hurt and angry, but never imagined she'd react with this vitriolic hatred.

'I didn't feel sorry for you,' I lied. 'I just felt . . . so horrible for how upset you were. And I wanted to tell you, but I didn't want to cause you any more pain. I know that was wrong of me, that it was the coward's way out, but . . .'

'I wish you had told me. Because then I could have set you straight and saved you all that worry,' Maddy said, clearly mocking me. 'Look, sweetheart. Harrison hasn't been pursuing you because he's fallen for you. I don't mean to be cruel, but you're not really his type. He goes for models, and women that are a little more . . . well, let's just say that he's a little out of your league,' she said.

This swipe, her claws fully extended, hurt. It was meant to. I knew that Maddy was angry, enraged even, but I'd never known her to be purposefully cruel. And yet, although I could rationalize that she was probably just trying to wound me by aiming a well-placed kick at my self-esteem, her words were starting to have an unpleasant note of truth to them. I knew that it was true that Jack had dated models in the past. I was a size fourteen with childbearing hips and average looks . . . why would someone who could date a Maddy, or a Katrinka, go out with me?

'Harrison found out about my relationship with Alex, my boss, right before that trip to New York. I told him the night before he left London, and he was devastated. I knew that he was thinking about breaking things off with me, but I didn't know that he was going to seek out his revenge. Think about it, Claire. I broke his heart. And then he just happens to meet my best friend on a plane and falls in love with her? Can't you hear how ridiculous that sounds?' Maddy asked, and she shook her head and stubbed out her cigarette.

My mind was reeling. I couldn't take in everything that she was saying. Was it really possible that Jack had known who I was, and pretended not to? I remembered the conversation where he'd told me he had no idea that I knew Maddy, had no idea that I was the Claire she was friends with, remembered clearly how firm he'd been, how his explanation had seemed to make so much sense. But why? Why lie to me? And why continue to pursue me after I returned to New York?

'I know you're upset, but what you're saying isn't making any sense. I know it must have been so hard for you to see us together like that – God, I can't even imagine how painful that must have been for you – but I swear, neither one of us set out to hurt you,' I said.

'Oh, really? Harrison lied to you about not knowing who you were when you met. Why are you so sure that you know what his real motives were?' she asked.

'Because if he really wanted to hurt you, he could have just told you that afternoon that we'd already slept together,' I said, more bluntly than I meant to.

Maddy looked a little shaken at that, but she covered it with another one of her cold barking laughs, and said, 'Really, Claire, fucking on the first date. That's a little desperate, even for you.'

I shook my head, refusing to rise to the bait. 'I'm sorry about everything. I truly am. And I want to do whatever it takes to put things right between us. I know you're angry now, and that you probably don't think that you can forgive me, but—'

'What did Harrison say about hiding your relationship from me?' Maddy interrupted me.

The question seemed to come from nowhere, and for a moment, I was taken aback. 'He . . . he said not to. He wanted me to tell you everything, so that we weren't sneaking around behind your back,' I said, stupidly thinking that this would convince her that his motives weren't as malicious as she seemed to think.

'He just said that once, casually, in passing?' she asked.

'No . . . no. He brought it up several times. In fact, he was pretty adamant that I not hide it from you,' I said. I had a terrible feeling that she was getting at something, but what that was I couldn't tell. It made me feel a bit like Little Red Riding Hood skipping right into the lair of the Big Bad Wolf.

'And that didn't strike you as strange? It didn't occur to you that if he really was falling in love with you, and that if he really was over me, that he'd leave it up to you how to handle our friendship?' she asked.

'I don't know what you're getting at,' I said.

'God, Claire, stop being so thick – Harrison wanted you

to tell me about your relationship because he knew that was the way he could hurt me the most. He knew how close we were, knew how much our friendship meant to me. That's how he was going to get his revenge, by using you to hurt me,' she snapped.

A sickening feeling spread through my stomach. I simply couldn't reconcile the person she was describing with the man I was falling in love with.

'If he'd told me that he'd fucked you that one time, before you knew who he was, then it wouldn't have been a betrayal. I'd have just thought he was a weasel for using you like that, and felt bad that he'd targeted you because of me. But by stringing you along, and getting you to fall for him, and then betray me, he knew that's how he'd do the most damage. In fact, I'm surprised he didn't insist on accompanying you here this afternoon in order to fully appreciate his great victory,' she continued.

'He wanted to,' I said dully. 'I told him not to.'

I couldn't process everything that she was saying, couldn't make sense of her words. Could she possibly be right? It was too horrific to contemplate . . . and yet, Jack had obviously lied to me. And he had encouraged me to tell Maddy about our relationship. And I had thought it was strange that a guy that great, that out of my league, was romancing me so hard.

'He used you. He used you to hurt me, and I have to give him his credit. It worked. The only consolation I have is that I thought I wanted that shit weasel back, and now I know him for what he is. It's just too bad you didn't recognize it sooner. You're supposed to be the smart one, right? But then, I guess it must have been quite a thrill for you to think that you were stealing a guy from me for a change, rather than the other way around,' Maddy said flatly.

I looked up at her sharply. 'What's that supposed to mean?'

Maddy sighed, and tossed her hair dramatically, her contempt for me oozing out of every pore. If I hadn't been feeling so shitty and confused, her over-the-top theatrics would have annoyed me. As it was, I was having a hard time drawing a deep breath in.

'Remember Sawyer? That loser who you cried your eyes out over every night? Oh God, Claire, don't look at me that way. I didn't sleep with him, he was hardly my type. But I can't tell you how many times he hit on me. He used to call me, said that if I went out with him he'd dump you in an instant. Of course, I told him no. *I* wouldn't do that to a friend,' she said coldly.

I shut my eyes. I hadn't thought Sawyer had the power to cause me any more pain, but there it was, the familiar throb of it lashing out at me again. Sawyer and Jack blended together on the back of my eyelids, two men turning into one, and I knew then that neither of them had truly loved me. I wasn't sure that any man ever had.

'I'm tired of talking. I want you to leave,' Maddy said.

The harsh anger had left her voice, and all that remained was a hollow exhaustion, a sadness at her discovery that the two people she had thought she loved most, outside of her family, had let her down so terribly. There was nothing I could say that would make this better, or convince her that my intention had not been to hurt her, so I just nodded, and stood up, and let myself out of her apartment.

I took a cab back to Jack's mews house.

It was still pouring out, and the rain was sheeting down the windows of the enormous black taxi. Outside, I could see Londoners hurrying along the sidewalk, black umbrellas tipped forward over their heads, somehow managing not to poke one another's eyes out with the spokes as they passed. I tried to draw in a deep breath to relax, hoping that it would keep everything from seeming so nightmarish, and found that my lungs were so tight that I could only gulp in shallow breaths of air. I didn't know what to think, how to begin figuring out what had just happened. My emotions and thoughts were so jumbled together that picking at just one could be like pulling the thread that unravels an entire sweater.

First there was Maddy. I felt like a complete and utter shit for the pain I'd caused her. I couldn't believe that our friendship truly seemed to be over, but how could I blame her for hating me? I hated myself for turning her from the sunny, sparkling woman everyone falls in love with into the caustic, foul-mouthed shrew I'd faced back at her apartment.

And if Maddy was right about Jack, then he'd lied to me and used me. How had it happened? I thought I'd inoculated myself against this kind of heartache with all of my dating rules and promises that I wouldn't again be taken in by the illusion of love. And yet somehow I *had* fallen in love with Jack, and he'd turned out to be an impostor. I'd thought he possessed all of the traits that every fourteen-year-old girl lists when asked about the qualities of her perfect guy – handsome, kind, funny, smart, dependable, attentive, romantic. But it turned out what I'd gotten instead was a vindictive, shallow asshole who had no problem using and deceiving me just to get revenge on his ex-girlfriend.

The taxi slowed to a stop, and I handed the driver a handful of crumpled bills, not even sure how much I was tipping him, before staggering out onto the sidewalk. I was almost instantly soaked, the unrelenting rain beating down like tiny pebbles against my bare head and cheeks, soaking through my already soggy wool coat. I walked up to Jack's door, unsure whether I needed to knock or just let myself in. Only a few hours earlier, before I'd learned the truth, I wouldn't have thought twice about letting myself in with the spare key Jack had lent me. But the act of letting yourself into someone's house indicated a level of intimacy I no longer had with Jack. As I deliberated what to do, getting further soaked with each passing moment, the door swung open, and there was Jack, looking down at me, his face grave.

'I called Maddy's apartment, looking for you,' he said. 'She told me you'd just left.'

'Looking for me? Or finding out how your little scheme played out?' I asked, and walked past him and into the house. I didn't wait to hear his reply, and instead stormed up the stairs to the second floor of his town house, the entire floor of which was taken up by an enormous room that doubled as his bedroom and study, to collect my luggage. Although unmistakably masculine, it was my favorite room in the house – two of the walls were lined with bookshelves, stuffed with books on every topic from history to science to the law to an impressive fiction collection, including the complete works of Robert B. Parker. When I first saw his library, it had been one more thing I'd found attractive about Jack; the only thing Sawyer ever read was the *Wall Street Journal*.

The room also contained an enormous old desk stacked with paperwork, an armoire, a short dresser, and a huge leather sleigh bed piled with pillows and a white down comforter. It was exactly the kind of bed that beckoned you to dive in and stay submerged in it for days.

Not that I'd ever spend a night there, I thought, and despite my best intentions to get out of his house before I had a complete breakdown, a knot formed in my throat.

'I'm not going to pretend I don't know what you're talking about. Maddy filled me in on her insane little theory when I called. I didn't think there was any way you'd actually believe it – it's ridiculous,' Jack said.

I turned around, and saw him standing in the doorway, his long figure leaning against the doorjamb, arms crossed in front of his chest. He was still wearing the navy blue cashmere sweater that brought out the green flecks in his eyes and tan corduroy trousers he'd had on earlier, and I could tell from his rumpled hair that he'd been running his hands through it again.

He does that when he's nervous or anxious about something, I thought, and strangely felt the urge to reach out and smooth it for him. But I didn't, remembering that his face, which only a few hours earlier had been so precious to me, was simply the mask of a very bad, very screwed-up man.

'Ridiculous? Except the part where you lied to me, of course,' I said instead, raising my chin and crossing my own arms.

I half expected Jack to deny it all. But instead, he simply said, 'Yes.'

'Yes?'

'I did lie, but it wasn't what you think,' he said, as if this were any kind of an explanation for anything.

'Not what I think?'

I was suddenly aware that I kept parroting the last thing that he said, my voice dripping with condescension and outrage, making me sound like a shoulder-pad-wearing, teased-hair diva from a bad eighties television drama.

'What I think is that you set up our "chance" meeting on the airplane, and that you lied to me about why you and Maddy broke up, and then you've continued to pursue me as part of some sort of twisted little revenge plot. That's what I think,' I continued.

Jack shook his head, looking tired and incredulous at the same time. 'Well, you're partly right . . . I did know who you were when we first met. In fact, I was originally booked on a later flight, but Maddy told me you were coming to visit her, and I saw the e-mail you sent her that contained your itinerary. It was just a coincidence that I was in New York attending a conference, and traveling back here on the same day, but I decided to take advantage of it. I switched flights, and told the ticketing agent that you and I were together so that he would assign me a seat near you. And I lied about it later when I said I didn't know who you were. But I didn't do that to hurt you, or as part of this insane story that Maddy's cooked up. I did it because I wanted to meet you, and I figured that it was going to be my only chance,' he said.

'You wanted to meet me? But that doesn't make any sense. We'd never even spoken,' I pointed out.

'We had, in a way. I know it sounds odd, but Maddy shared a bunch of your e-mails with me, and I thought you were hysterically funny . . . I couldn't stop laughing after I read that e-mail you sent her about how you toured through Disney World, trying to see the happiest place on earth through the cranky eyes of someone who had a bad back and arthritis. And when I saw your picture, saw how beautiful you are, I just couldn't let the chance of meeting you pass me by,' he said.

I snorted at the 'beautiful' comment. This ridiculous insistence that he found me just as attractive as all of the models that he'd dated in the past was the main reason I knew he was lying about the rest of it. It reminded me of the time in college when I was out at a nightclub, and some drunken frat boy had slobbered into my ear, 'Did anyone ever tell you that you look just like Elle Macpherson? You wanna come home with me?' I was no more gullible to that sort of insincere flattery now than I was then.

'And if I had told you who I was, that I was dating one of your friends, you would never have agreed to see me after that,' Jack continued.

'You're right. I wouldn't have,' I agreed. 'Which is why you had to get me into bed, get me emotionally involved with you, before I learned the truth, right? Because otherwise, I'd never have gone along with it.'

'No! God! What the hell is wrong with you, Claire? Do you really think I'd travel all the way to New York just to piss off Maddy? Or go through all of the trouble of talking you into coming out here? Why would I do that? It doesn't make any sense,' he said, flapping his hands apart with exasperation.

'It does if you were in love with her, and found out she was cheating on you,' I said quietly.

'Yes, I found out that she was sleeping with her boss. But even before that, I already knew that it wasn't going to work out between us. For one thing, I wasn't in love with her, nor did I ever tell her that I was – I don't suppose she mentioned that to you, did she? When I first met Maddy, I was at a point in my life where I didn't want to spend any more time with party girls, and she came across as smart, and goal-oriented, and successful, and nice, but I didn't fall in love with her. I tried, but I couldn't. Learning that she was sleeping around just clarified how wrong the relationship was. I didn't appreciate it, but I also wasn't so destroyed by it that I felt the need to take my revenge against her,' Jack said.

I wavered. Jack's explanation for breaking up with Maddy made some sense, but at the same time, he'd lied to me. Who was I supposed to believe? Maddy, who I'd known for years to be honest, or Jack, who I'd known for a short time, and who had spent almost that entire time lying to me? Okay, so Maddy had been more than a little harsh toward me, but who could blame her after what I'd done? And hadn't she known Jack far longer than I had, hadn't she spent more time with him? My relationship with him pretty much boiled down to three long weekends, chats on the phone, and some flirtatious e-mailing.

'None of that explains why you've been pursuing me, nor why you kept pressuring me to tell Maddy about our relationship,' I pointed out.

Jack shook his head with irritation. He strode through the room and pulled a metal magazine box off one of bookshelves and then held it out to me.

'What's that?' I asked suspiciously.

He yanked the magazines out and held them up so I could see – a dozen or so back issues of *Sassy Seniors*.

'I read everything you've ever written, even before we met,' Jack said.

I began shaking my head from side to side. 'I don't understand,' I said stupidly.

Jack put the box down on his desk and sat down heavily on his bed.

'I've been pursuing you because I've . . . because I care about you, Claire. Not that you've made it easy, equivo-cating about coming out here, and then acting all jumpy every time we start to get close. I've never dated anyone like you – you're stubborn, and difficult, and suspicious . . .' he began.

As Jack began ticking off this list of not-so-flattering traits, I raised a hand to stop him. 'Yeah, I can see why you'd be so into me,' I said sarcastically.

'I am! God, that's my entire point, and if you weren't being so deliberately thick, maybe you'd actually hear me! All I've wanted to do since even before I met you was to be with you, to spend time with you, to get to know you better. Why can't you see that? And the only reason I wanted you to tell Maddy about us was that I thought that once you did, and once everything was out in the open, that you'd relax and stop playing so hard-to-get,' Jack said. He'd raised his voice to an almost shout and was glowering at me from his vantage point on the bed.

I didn't want to hear any more. I wanted to believe him, but how could I? In my experience, all men were liars – my father, Sawyer for telling me that he loved me, and now Jack. Even Max had lied to me in a sense, since the entire time we were friends he was apparently hiding his true feelings for me. I just couldn't do it, I couldn't believe Jack, because if I did . . . if I did, it would just end up with me being hurt again, even more so than I was now.

In fact, if I was going to protect myself from him, I needed to get out of his home. Immediately. I began to pace around the room, peering under the bed, next to the armoire, behind his desk.

'What are you looking for?' Jack asked.

'My suitcase! Where's my suitcase?' I cried.

'It's right here,' Jack said, getting up and opening the enormous armoire doors. My still-unpacked, scuffed-up, emerald green bag – the hideous color chosen so that it would stand out at baggage claim – looked like an ugly stepchild nestled up next to Jack's collection of gorgeous, buttery-soft leather bags. I reached out to grab it, but Jack put up a hand.

'I'll carry it down for you. And I'll call you a cab, if that's what you want me to do. But I wish you would stay, even if it's just for a few hours, so we can talk. I'm not saying that I haven't screwed up, or that you don't have a right to be angry. But . . . I love you,' Jack said. 'Please at least hear me out.'

'Don't,' I croaked. 'Please. Don't say that.'

And then I grabbed my bag and practically ran out of his house, not looking back to see if Jack had followed me.

I went straight to the airport. I was really early – my flight didn't leave for another four days – but I was hoping that maybe I could cash my ticket in on an earlier flight. I'd ride on the wing if I had to . . . I wanted out of jolly old England and back to the relative sanity of Manhattan. I'd been hoping it would be a slow travel day, and was amazed at how crowded Heathrow turned out to be – the line at the ticket counter seemed to stretch on for a mile – and although they had a dozen people manning the counter, it took me nearly an hour to get to the front of the line.

When it was finally my turn, and I explained to the airline employee that I wanted to cash in my ticket for an earlier flight, the woman – a chilly brunette with a clipped British accent – said, 'Sorry. You can only fly standby on the same day for which your ticket was issued.' Without another word, she handed the ticket back over and looked past me at the next traveler in line, and said, 'Next!'

'No! Wait a minute, please. I need to get on a flight to New York, and today if possible. Can't I pay some kind of a changing fee?' I said.

The woman sighed with exasperation and looked me up and down. Since I'd been soaked through by the earlier rain and left to air-dry, I could only imagine how awful I probably looked – between my frizzed-out hair, streaked mascara, and rumpled clothing, I'm sure I did not impress.

'Could I see your ticket again, please,' she said, and then began typing into her terminal, her nails making exaggerated tapping sounds against the keys. Finally she said, 'No, sorry, the business-class cabin is booked on our one remaining flight out tonight.'

'Do you have anything in coach?' I asked quickly.

Another sigh. Some more tip-tapping. 'Yes, we do have a few seats . . . that will be, let's see . . . a three-hundred-dollar fee to change your ticket,' she said.

'It costs three hundred dollars to change a business-class ticket in for a coach ticket?' I asked.

The woman's thinly plucked eyebrows arched up. 'That's the standard charge, madam. If you'd rather not make the change, then . . .'

'No! Wait, here, I'll give you my credit card,' I said, fumbling through my bag for my wallet. As I slid the plastic across the counter, I said a silent prayer that the card would work. I'd been dangerously close to my limit, and although I'd mailed off a check to the credit card company before I left for London, they never seemed in all that much of a hurry to process my payment. But for the first time that day, I actually caught a break – after some more typing, and the computer spitting out a ludicrous number of printouts, and my bag being abused as it was tossed on the conveyer belt, the snippy brunette handed over a boarding pass.

'The gate is circled in red ink; boarding will begin in forty minutes. Thank you. Next!'

'No, thank *you* for all of your help,' I said sarcastically, although it seemed to be lost on her.

I wandered in the general direction of my gate, and as I did, a great exhaustion settled over me. All of the conflict and confrontation had left me feeling wrung out. I was sure that after I'd had a chance to reflect on all that had happened, my lethargy would turn to sorrow and anger and worry. But right now it seemed to be taking all of my energy just to put one foot in front of the other on the long walk to my gate.

I bought a Diet Coke from a food vendor and popped off the plastic lid to make it easier to gulp down. But just as I was lifting the cup to my mouth, something that felt roughly the size and weight of a Hummer knocked into me from behind. The cup went flying out of my hands, but not before Diet Coke poured all over me. I looked down at the dark brown stain that now covered the front of what had been a brand-new Banana Republic cream lettuce-hemmed sweater, and then looked up, trying to figure out just how it had happened. A family of four American tourists – a set of obese parents and their two piggy children – were pushing past me, their hands stretched out in front of them in order to shove aside anyone who happened to be in their path.

'Hey!' I yelled out, grabbing at the flabby arm of the father. 'Look what you just did to me, you asshole!'

One of the children, a boy who bore an uncanny resemblance to Augustus Gloop from the movie *Willy Wonka and the Chocolate Factory*, looked at the cola dripping down my front and laughed, a disgusting snorting sound. The father gave me a dirty look, and said, 'You should watch where you're going,' and then without another word continued onward, still shoving aside any unwary traveler who happened to be in front of them, while the porcine mother screeched, 'Hurry up, we're going to be late!'

I stared after them, for the first time truly understanding where the 'ugly American' stereotype came from, and then looked down again at my now-ruined sweater. I saw some schoolgirls looking at me and tittering, so I stalked off to the bathroom, in the futile hope that I could somehow rinse out the stain. Once in the ladies' room, I lost all sense of modesty and peeled off my top, rinsing it under the faucet while I stood there in my pants and sheer bra. Some of the women tutted under their breath, as if the sight of another woman in her underclothes was somehow unbearably offensive, but I just ignored them and continued to dab at the shirt with a brown paper hand towel that didn't seem to be helping much at all.

I finally realized with a sigh that the shirt was a complete loss, and I stared at it glumly. I'd made a major miscalculation – the shirt was now not only stained with the soda, it was completely soaked through, and I had absolutely nothing to wear out into the airport. I didn't even have my wool overcoat, which I'd stuffed into the outer pocket of the suitcase before checking it in. So it looked like in order to get to a gift shop, where I could purchase a touristy T-shirt to wear home on the flight, I'd either have to walk there in my bra . . . or put on my wet and now completely transparent top. Either way, I would surely be arrested for nipple overexposure.

And then I remembered . . . the light-up reindeer sweatshirt. It was still buried at the bottom of my carry-on bag where I'd stuffed it on the last day of work. It was ugly and synthetic, but at least it would keep me from being a walking peep show. I quickly pulled it on, managing to avoid my reflection in the mirror – I just didn't have the stomach for it – and tossed the balled-up ruined sweater in the trash. I checked my watch to see if I had enough time to run to a gift shop – even a cotton T-shirt emblazoned with Big Ben would be an improvement – and swore under my breath when I realized that my flight would begin boarding momentarily, and I wasn't even on the right concourse. In fact, the only way I'd make the flight at all was if I ran for it – not a pleasing thought, considering I was wearing my three-inch chunky-heeled boots, which were more hip than they were practical.

I sprinted wildly for the gate, spurred on when I heard

the final call for my flight. I made it just in time, arriving at the gate with aching feet and a red face. The polyester sweatshirt was sticking to my back, and I plucked it out, trying to let in some air. An airline employee grabbed my boarding pass and shooed me onto the plane, and a minute later I was squeezing past the flight attendants, looking for my seat, which was . . . *oh shit*. It was the very middle seat in a row of five. Things became even bleaker when I pushed forward, moving toward the back of the plane – which, past experience had taught me, was always the stinkiest place to sit due to the constant traffic in and out of the tiny back bathroom stalls – and I saw that the only empty seat on the plane, *my* seat apparently, was smack-dab in the middle of the same obnoxious family who had caused me to spill soda down my front. And there they were – the Gloop parents stuffed like sausages into their seats on one side, the two churlish kids fighting on the other side.

'Oh, please, no,' I whispered, and then in a louder, icy voice, addressed the senior Gloops. 'I need to get to my seat.'

'We just settled in,' Mr Gloop replied.

'Yeah, go around the other way,' his horrible wife added.

I stared at them, completely dumbfounded at their rudeness.

'Would you rather sit next to your children, and give me the aisle seat?' I asked.

'No!' Mrs Gloop snorted. The Mother of the Year seemed to recognize her children for the demon offspring that they were.

'We got aisle seats on purpose. If you wanted one, you should have reserved it,' Mr Gloop enlightened me.

I was overcome by a wave of rage that was grossly out of proportion to the situation. Had the security guard not confiscated my tweezers, I might have been tempted to use them to poke out the Gloops' eyes.

'Well, then, I have to get by you,' I said through gritted teeth, and barreled past them – no easy task considering their girth. As I shoved through, I accidentally stomped on Mrs Gloop's foot.

'Ow!' she screamed, as though I'd stabbed a dagger through her shriveled little heart.

'It's your own fault,' I snapped back, as I collapsed into my crowded seat, knocking the Gloop girl's elbow off our shared armrest for good measure. 'I asked you to let me by, and you refused. You know, it wouldn't kill you to be a little more decent, to have some basic manners, for Christ's sake.'

Mrs Gloop ignored me, and instead turned to her husband, whining about her toe, and how she thought it might be broken, and that they could probably bring a lawsuit against me if it was.

'It just can't get any worse,' I said out loud, shaking my head.

But it did.

At some point when we were flying over Greenland, and despite the constant jostling of my obnoxious neighbors, I had miraculously fallen asleep, the Gloop girl suddenly dug a sharp elbow into my side.

'Ouch! What the fuck?' I sputtered.

'Nice mouth. She wants to talk to you,' the girl smirked, pointing toward an annoyed flight attendant hovering in the aisle.

'What?' I asked irritably.

'There have been several complaints about the lights,' the flight attendant hissed at me.

'The lights?' I repeated, confused.

'Your shirt is lighting up the whole cabin, and people are trying to sleep or watch the movie. It's bothering everyone,' she said, pointing at my chest.

I looked down. Sure enough, at some point the lights on

my tacky reindeer sweatshirt had switched on, lighting the plane up like the Las Vegas Strip.

'Is there some way you can turn that off?' the flight attendant snapped. Why is it that the flight attendants in coach are always so cantankerous, while their business and first-class counterparts all conduct themselves as though they were charm-school graduates?

'I honestly don't know,' I sighed, staring down at the barrage of light dancing against red polyester, wondering where on earth the off button would be located on such a garment, but truly not really giving a shit. At that point, I was beyond caring about any of it – the sweatshirt, the irate flight attendant, the entire hideous Gloop family sniggering at my predicament, the fact that there was some unknown sticky substance on my right hand that hadn't been there when I drifted off. It was like I'd been sent to the ring of hell where treacherous friends are condemned to burn, and didn't really see any point in getting too worked up about the details.

And if I expected to feel better when I finally got home and walked into my apartment, I would have been sorely disappointed. Because all I felt when I got there was alone . . . actually, tired and alone (after my brief nap on the plane, the Gloop offspring spent the rest of the flight screaming at each other over who was going to play some loud, beeping hand-held computer game – it amazed me that passengers complained about my light-up sweatshirt, but no one had a problem with their fight-to-the-death wrestling match – and further sleep was out of the question). After years of suffering through a string of roommates, I considered living alone to be the ultimate luxury, even in my cramped little apartment. On the rare occasions when I felt a little lonely, I had Max right next door, who was always up for a spur-of-the-moment dinner or video rental. But now I didn't have the energy to pound on his door until he opened it, much less force him to talk through whatever it was that had happened between us before I left. What I wanted was ease and familiarity . . . in fact, I had an overwhelming and unexpected ache for family. Well, maybe not my family – the last time we'd all been together was when we were clearing what we wanted out of the house before my parents put it on the market as part of their divorce agreement – but a nice family, the kind that holds you to its bosom when times get rough, the kind you turn to in a crisis.

What happened next is hard to explain. I don't know if it was the exhaustion, or the stress, or some kind of a seismic hormonal shift, but without even thinking about it, I reached for the phone and dialed up the airline.

'Hello, I'd like to book a one-way ticket to West Palm Beach, Florida,' I heard myself say into the phone, seemingly without any power to stop myself, all the while wondering if this was what it felt like to lose your mind.

I have to admit, Florida was not the obvious place for my escape. Home to palm trees and tiki bars and topless car washes, it's a rather soulless place that smothers natural beauty with landscaping, and blots out local culture with chain restaurants, golf courses, and theme parks. And since it's home to legions of senior citizens, all of whom drive big white cars and wear Bermuda shorts with black knee-length socks, being there was hardly a vacation from my job.

Plus, my mother lives in Florida. It's not that I don't love my mother – everyone loves their mother, after all – but we weren't particularly close. We never had been, really. When I was growing up, we butted heads like territorial rams – the arguments progressed from what I would or wouldn't wear (age nine), to what friends I could hang out with (age fifteen), to what kind of life I would lead (age twenty to the present). My mother assumed I would lead a very different life – she thought I'd marry and have kids and move to the suburbs. She's never come out and said it, but I know I'm a disappointment to her.

But I didn't want to stay in the city, sitting in my apartment and staring at the phone, and I didn't have anywhere else to go. Even if I could impose on college friends I hadn't seen in years at the last minute – and during the week after Christmas – those weren't places where I could just hide out, read through a stack of books, and refuse to talk about my life in any detail. And although my mother and I don't have anything close to the perfect relationship, at least she had a strong sense of boundaries, and would more or less let me be . . . at least for a time. I doubted that she'd be able to keep herself from pointing out the deficiencies in my wardrobe, or casually suggesting that I make an appointment with a cellulite reduction specialist who for only two hundred dollars per half hour would be happy to wrap my body up in some sort of an aluminum sack. But she probably wouldn't pry too much into why I was there, which was just the kind of solitude I needed.

I flew into the West Palm Beach airport, which was just to the south of where my mother and stepfather lived, in a town called Stuart. There, they had a sprawling house in an exclusive seniors community, which boasted an eighteen-hole golf course, eight clay tennis courts, three pools, and a country club, and where ambulances made almost weekly appearances to cart one of the residents off to a local hospital.

My mother met me at the airport, looking as stylish as usual. She was as slim and petite as ever, and her sleek bob was a handsome salt-and-pepper mix. Mom was outfitted in the standard-issue uniform of all affluent Floridian women – pink Lily Pulitzer capri pants, a white sleeveless cotton sweater that showed off her toned arms, and high-heeled tan leather sandals. I took a deep breath and waved at her, all along having second thoughts about my rash decision to come here. I just knew that as I walked toward my mother she was cataloguing my faults.

But then as I reached her, my mother pushed back her enormous, round, Jackie O. sunglasses, and I saw her eyes – so similar to my own, the single physical characteristic I had inherited from her – and I was suddenly struck by how much older she looked. Not elderly, but older than I remembered her being. I guess when I think of my mother,

I always picture her as she looked in her mid-forties, the age she was when I was in the full bloom of awkward, acne-pocked adolescence, and she was lovely, willowy, and vital. Seeing her now with a fine web of wrinkles radiating from the corners of her mouth and eyes frightened me a little. I wanted to hug her, to hold her close, to somehow shield her from her own mortality.

'Hi, Mom,' I said, my voice a little shaky.

'Hi, sweetie,' she said, and opened her arms. I stepped into them, and she hugged me, and to my great surprise, my eyes watered up. After everything that I'd been through, after all of the anger and rejection and conflict that had gone on over the past few days, it was such a relief to be with someone who loved me unconditionally.

'It's so good to see you,' I said, still clutching her, like a child who doesn't want to be left behind on the first day of kindergarten.

My mother pulled back and looked at me, her eyes appraising. 'You look tired. Is something wrong?'

Now, to the casual observer, this statement probably sounds harmless enough. But this was my mother, and I knew that it was loaded with meaning. 'You look tired' was code for: your hair is too long, you're not wearing enough blush, that color washes you out, you need to put on some self-tanner, or any of the million other comments that could be made on my lack of grooming. The truth was that I knew I didn't look my best – I was sleep-deprived, overanxious, and I couldn't remember the last time I'd bothered with something simple like a manicure. But still, knowing that my mother was evaluating me, and that I was – as usual – coming up short, ticked me off.

'Nope, I'm fine,' I said, stepping out of her arms. 'I checked my suitcase, though, so I need to go to the baggage claim.'

My stepfather, Howard, was waiting by the curb with

the car, successfully rebuffing the attempts of airport security to have him circle around until his passengers were actually standing on the sidewalk, ready to load their luggage. I was surprised that airport security let him stop his car at all; lately they seem to expect anyone dropping off or picking up travelers to merely slow down to a crawl while passengers fling themselves in and out of the moving car. Howard's only a few years older than my mom (I think he just turned sixty-four, although I can never keep track), but his florid complexion – a result of overexposure to both sun and booze – made him look at least a decade older. Before retiring at the age of sixty, Howard had been a pharmaceutical salesman, the top in his field, and as a reward for his labors, he'd retired with a healthy bank account and a thick, ugly gold wristwatch which I never saw him without, and suspected he wore even in his sleep. He had a salesman's slick and charming personality, and I found myself baring my teeth in a fake smile at his many jokes as we drove back to their golf-course home. My mother stayed strangely quiet on the trip, interrupting Howard's stand-up shtick only to remind him which exit to take off the highway.

It was a relief when we finally got to their house, which, much like my mother, was elegant and serene, and seemed a million miles away from all of the problems that I'd left behind. My mom's dog, Sasha – a bichon frise whom I actually sort of liked, even if she did resemble a yappy cotton ball on legs – came twirling out, prancing and cavorting and snorting happily. She danced under my feet, and then rolled over, presenting her pink and brown mottled tummy to me for stroking.

'Hi, Sasha,' I said, and bent over to rub her.

'Don't touch the dog!' Mom and Howard screamed in unison, but it was too late. Urine squirted up in an arc, landing on the floor next to Sasha. She got up to examine the yellow puddle, and looked vaguely irritated as she sniffed it suspiciously.

'She's a submissive pee-er,' my mother explained to me, before turning her attention to Sasha. 'Mommy's very angry at you, you bad, bad girl. In fact, I don't even want to look at you. Go into the other room,' she said sharply, pointing toward the kitchen. Sasha slunk off, looking pathetic and forlorn.

'When did she start peeing like that?' I asked.

'About six months ago. Her therapist says that it's caused by anxiety,' Mom said.

'Her therapist?'

'Yes, we've been taking her to see a behaviorist. He has her on antianxiety medication that seemed to be helping for a while, but then she started this peeing thing. Anyway, Sebastian – that's her therapist, he's *fabulous* – says that it's just a matter of setting guidelines with Sasha,' Mom continued.

Upon hearing her name, Sasha came prancing back into the room, apparently already tired of her solitary confinement. Eager to get back into my mother's good graces, Sasha sat at Mom's feet, head tilted charmingly to the side, one paw raised in a silent plea for forgiveness. My mother was not at all moved. She shook her head and said, 'I'm still not speaking to you. Go back to the kitchen.'

'Mom, that's so mean! She doesn't remember what she did wrong,' I protested, taking in Sasha's sad brown watery eyes and twitching snout. 'And she looks so sorry.'

'Sorry isn't good enough,' my mother replied. 'Do you remember where the guest room is? Here, I'll show you.'

I looked back at Sasha, who had now slumped down on the ground, looking miserable, and was suddenly envious of the dog's ready access to therapy and medication.

*

For the next few days, I spent almost all of my time in my mom's screened-in pool – which she and Howard never used – sometimes paddling around slowly like a sea turtle, and the rest of the time floating about on an inflatable chaise lounge reading through my mother's collection of John D. McDonald paperbacks. McDonald's stories of beach bum Travis McGee and the assortment of women he rescued, and how they'd putter around on his Fort Lauderdale houseboat drinking Boodles gin, eating steaks, and tanning themselves to a delectably unhealthy shade of bronze, was just the escape I needed. New Year's Eve hardly registered with me. Mom and Howard invited me to a shindig at their country club, but I declined, and instead spent the night watching *Titanic* and eating cold Chinese food left over from the night before.

I knew my mom was worried about me. I'd occasionally see her peering at me from behind the French doors that connected the pool to her sunroom, and once in a while she'd venture out and ask me if I'd like to go to the mall, or to see her hairstylist, or to play a round of golf (as if I've ever stepped on a putting green in my entire life), but each time I'd shake my head and apply another layer of SPF 30 to my still-pale arms. Since my behavior was atrociously unsocial, I tried to make up for it by doing the dishes and helping to prepare the simple summer fare that they existed on year-round, although normally Mom or Howard would wave me off, and tell me not to be silly, that I was on vacation and not there to help around the house. So I let myself be gently pushed away, and I'd retreat back to my room to watch old movies on cable or return to my floating chaise.

I thought very little of Maddy and Jack and Max, and all of the messes that I left behind, which was odd for me, the chronic worrier. But it all seemed far away, almost like it had happened to someone else, and I wasn't eager to ever return to it. In fact, the day I was supposed to report back to work came and went. I called Robert's voice mail at night, long after I knew he'd left the office, and left him a cryptic message about a family emergency and needing some additional time off. I knew he wouldn't believe me, and might even fire me for it, but I simply couldn't muster up the energy to care.

After I'd been there for a few days, my mother appeared at the side of the pool one morning, the portable phone in hand.

'There's a phone call for you,' she said.

I opened one eye and looked at her. 'But no one knows I'm here,' I said.

'It's your sister. She wants to talk to you,' Mother said, holding out the phone. I paddled my float over to where she stood, and took it from her.

'Hello,' I said.

'Hi, it's me,' Alice said.

'What's up? How's everything going out there?' I asked.

'Fine. I'm still at the same firm, still dating Luke, still trying to decide whether I should stay in California or not,' she said, which was pretty much the same thing she said every time I talked to her. My sister has worked in the same job, as a designer at a graphic design firm, lived in the same apartment, and dated the same man – who was apparently panting after her with an engagement ring in one hand – for over five years, but the commitment-phobe in her kept insisting that it was all just temporary, and that she could dump it and move back to the East Coast at any time.

'Anyway,' she continued. 'Mom called me. She's worried about you, and wanted me to find out what's going on.'

I figured it was something like that. Unlike many sisters, Alice and I are not friends. There's no animosity between us, but we just don't figure all that prominently in each other's life. When our parents were married, we stayed connected through them and saw each other at college breaks and the odd family vacation. But the dissolution of our parents' marriage had meant the end to such get-togethers, and as a result Alice and I – never close as children – drifted even further apart. There were occasional phone calls, sporadic cards, the obligatory birthday or Christmas present, but nothing beyond that. We certainly didn't have the kind of relationship where I could confide in her about everything that had happened to me over the past week.

'Tell her I'm fine. I'm just . . . resting,' I said.

'She said you haven't left the house since you've been there, and that you look like you lost your best friend,' Alice said.

'That's perceptive of her,' I said.

'What?'

'Nothing. Things have just been really stressful at work,' I said.

'So who's the guy?'

'What guy?'

'The one that you're moping about,' Alice said.

'I was seeing someone, and I'm not anymore, but I'm not moping about it. It wasn't all that serious,' I lied.

'Okay, okay, I get it. You're not going to tell me, and that's fine. But maybe you should talk to Mom. She's stressed out, and was asking me if she should hide her sleeping pills from you just in case you're suicidal or something.'

'I'm not suicidal,' I said, laughing for the first time in days.

'I know, but tell her that. You know how she can overreact.'

After I got off the phone with Alice, I heard my mother talking to her in hushed tones, all the while peering out at me. I waved at her and smiled. Later that night, before she and Howard went out, I listened attentively while she told me all of the gossip from her bridge club, and that seemed to placate her temporarily. But the next day, Mom ventured out in the late afternoon, Sasha at her heels, and this time sat down at the side of the pool, dipping her bare, tan feet into the water. Her toenails had been carefully pedicured and were polished pale pink, like the inside of a seashell. With a fluttering tail, Sasha lay down behind my mother, careful to make sure she was out of the splash range of the pool.

'Oh, the water feels nice,' Mother said.

'Don't you ever go swimming?'

She shrugged. 'Sometimes, although not often. It's horrible for my hair – the chlorine makes the color brassy.'

'Then why'd you put the pool in?' I asked.

'I like to come out and look at the water. It's peaceful out here, don't you think?' she said.

I nodded. My float hit the wall on the far side of the pool, and I pushed off against the edge, propelling myself back to the center of the pool. I leaned back and looked up at the breathtaking Florida sky.

'The sky is so clear and so blue . . . it's mesmerizing. I'd probably keep getting into car accidents if I lived here, because I'd always be looking up,' I said dreamily.

'When did you get that necklace? It's beautiful,' my mom said.

I lifted my hand to touch the necklace that Jack had given me – and which I hadn't yet been able to bring myself to take off – and a stab of pain poked at my heart.

'Um, a friend gave it to me. Where's Howard? Did he go golfing again?'

'No, he's inside, watching the news, having a Scotch. I've been trying to keep him down to one a night, and otherwise have him stick to beer, but it's hard. He won't admit he has a problem,' she said.

This startled me. I'd known for a long time that Howard had a drinking problem, and a severe one at that. But I'd never heard my mother admit that he had a problem – she tended to shrug it off as boyish antics when he began singing off-key in the middle of the clubhouse, or exhaustion when he fell asleep in his armchair every night. I'd always thought that the fact that he was a genial drunk, never becoming hostile or unruly, kept her in denial.

'So what's going on, Claire?' my mother said.

'What do you mean?'

'Don't take this the wrong way, because I love having you here, but you hardly ever visit, much less fly down at the last minute. And I am your mother, after all, I can tell you're upset about something,' she said.

She'd said the same thing to me when I was eleven, and one of the girls at school had invited everyone in our group of friends to sleep over at her house, except for me. I was devastated. When I told my mother about it, her nostrils had flared with anger, and a minute later she was on the phone with the girl's mother, demanding to know why I'd been left out, and making sure that an invitation was extended to me. I could just see her doing something like that now, calling up Maddy to smooth over our falling out, or Jack to tear him to shreds for using me. Mom was elegant and chic on the outside, but underneath the salon-pampered exterior, she was a tough cookie.

'I've just been having a rough time lately. I was seeing someone, and it didn't work out, and it was kind of a big mess,' I said. Better to give half-truths than to lie outright. My mother was like a human lie-detector test when it came to Alice and me – we could never get away with anything.

'What kind of a mess?'

'It's a long story.'

My mother stretched out her legs, holding her feet out in front of her, and watched the water stream off them back into the pool. 'That's okay. I'm retired, I have time for a long story,' she said.

I don't know if I was just too tired to keep deflecting the questions, and it seemed easier to have it all out in the open, or if it was because she herself had opened up to me by admitting that her husband had a drinking problem, but I found myself telling her about meeting Jack, and then finding out that he was Maddy's ex, and continuing to see him anyway, and falling for him, and that Maddy had found out, and learning that Jack had lied to me. I told her all of it, except for the sex parts, of course, since it doesn't matter how old I get, or how cynical I appear, there are just some subjects that I can never discuss with my mother. When I was finished, she was frowning, her forehead knitted in confusion.

'I don't understand . . . why do you think that Jack was only seeing you to get back at Madeline?' she asked.

'Because he lied to me about not knowing who I was when I first met him,' I said.

'But I don't see why you're assuming that he didn't truly have feelings for you. Why would he come to see you in New York? And why ask you to spend the holidays with him in England? And didn't you say that Maddy followed you and Jack to that restaurant, and that's how she found out you were seeing him? If he truly wanted to hurt her through you, then why didn't he just tell her straight out?' my mom asked.

'Because . . . well. He encouraged me to tell Maddy about our relationship,' I said. 'He wanted me to do it.'

'Yes, but maybe he just wanted it to be all out in the open. Weren't you the one who kept putting him off, saying that you didn't want to hurt your friend?' Mother asked.

'Yeah, but come on. You've seen Maddy. She's gorgeous, and let's face it, most of the men she dates are way out of my league. I thought it was strange all along that a guy as great as Jack would be interested in me, especially since Maddy was calling him the entire time, trying to get back together with him,' I said.

'I thought you said Jack was a jerk who was perfectly capable of manipulating your feelings in order to hurt Madeline,' my mother pointed out. 'Now you're saying he's a great guy.'

'Yes, but . . . I didn't know that at the time,' I said, starting to feel a little confused. 'He seemed like a great guy. I guess he fooled us both.'

My mother just shook her head, and looked at me. 'It just amazes me. You're thirty-two years old, and you're a lovely, composed, accomplished woman, and yet you still have absolutely no self-confidence,' she said. 'You're completely incapable of looking in a mirror and truly seeing yourself.'

'What do you mean?'

'Your entire theory of how Jack used you is based on your premise – or Maddy's premise – that all rational men would immediately choose her over you. And that's ridiculous. For one thing, Maddy's an attractive girl, but compared to you, I've always thought she seemed a little washed out. She certainly doesn't have your wit or style.'

I shook my head. 'That's nice of you to say, but this has nothing to do with my level of self-confidence. I know that I'm not some sort of a great beauty, but I'm okay with that,' I said.

'Not a great beauty? Claire, you're absolutely stunning! You have beautiful hair, gorgeous eyes – my eyes, actually – perfect skin, and a figure like Liz Taylor had in her day. No, you don't look like one of those scrawny little actresses so popular today, who have no boobs and no hips, but that makes you even more of a standout,' my mother exclaimed.

I rolled my eyes. 'Thanks, but you're my mother. You have to say things like that.'

'I thought you always said I was too critical of you. Maybe I was . . . It never occurred to me that you'd end up with such poor self-esteem. Maybe this is all my fault for not telling you often enough how truly beautiful and special you are, how much you've always stood out,' she said thoughtfully.

This startled me. 'Um, well. I don't think you ever told me that before,' I ventured. I didn't want to add that the only time she'd ever bothered to comment on my appearance was to tell me what was wrong with it.

'You're probably right,' my mother sighed, kicking her feet in the water. 'I think I've always been a little intimidated by you – you're so much more ambitious than I ever was, always have been. You've always seemed to be on the brink of something . . . big. You were so smart, and pretty, and clever, and I never had any doubt that you'd make a huge splash someday. You've always just needed a little more confidence, that's all. And maybe . . . maybe what you really need to do is learn to let your defenses down.'

'They keep me from being hurt,' I said. 'Look what happened when I did let my guard down.'

'I don't think I agree with your take on things. The only thing I can see that Jack clearly did wrong was to not be up front with you in the beginning. And although he used poor judgment, I can actually see why he lied, particularly if he wanted a chance to get to know you. As for the rest of it, this idea that it was all a scheme to get revenge on Maddy, well, frankly, honey, I think it sounds a little far-fetched. If that's what he wanted, if he was that cruel and coldhearted, then why wouldn't he have admitted it when you confronted him? But instead he told you he loved you, and wanted you to stay and talk things out with him. What would be the point of saying that if it wasn't true?' Mom asked, sounding so reasonable I began to wonder if I had overreacted, and in doing so, misjudged everything.

Was Maddy's version of events completely off the wall? We'd been friends for a long time, and I'd valued her opinion in the past. Max had always insisted that Maddy was self-centered and vain . . . maybe it was just a side of her I'd never really wanted to acknowledge. Everyone has his or her faults, after all, and although a little narcissism might not be the worst thing in the world, it certainly might have colored Maddy's view of why Jack was interested in me. And if she was wrong about that, then maybe it meant that I'd judged Jack unfairly.

'But what do I do? Even if I was wrong about Jack – and maybe you're right, maybe I was – what about Maddy? I know that she said some shitty things to me, and maybe it was crappy of her to assume that Jack would never go for me . . . but God, I really hurt her. I honestly don't think she would have ever said any of those things to me, ever have been so unkind, if I hadn't been sneaking around behind her back,' I said. 'So what do I do about that? How do I make this right?'

But this time my mother, who had always in the past had the answers to these types of moral dilemmas, simply shrugged. 'Let me think about it. I'm sure we can figure something out,' she promised.

Had I known what my mother's solution would be, I would have fled the state. The next day, after I'd showered and dressed – I'd finally agreed to leave the house, my mom and I had plans for lunch and manicures – my mother knocked softly on the guest room door, and when I opened it, she was standing there, dressed in periwinkle blue capri pants and a coordinated sleeveless sweater, holding the cordless phone.

'Don't be mad,' she said, handing me the phone. And then she turned on her heel and practically ran down the hall away from me. I stared after her, and then down at the phone in my hand, and for some unknown reason, I lifted it to my ear and said, 'Hello?'

Why I did this, I don't know. Perhaps it's a lifetime of training that teaches us we should talk into a phone that's handed to us. Maybe for just a second I'd had the asinine thought that she'd somehow tracked down Maddy and Jack, talked everything out with them (the way she had done with the sleepover mom, all those years ago), and now the two of them were both on the phone, ready to tell me that all was fine, all was forgiven. Maybe I was just curious, and it simply got the better of me.

'Hello, is this Claire?' a familiar woman's voice said on the other end.

'Yes, it is,' I said, trying to place the voice. A distant relative? One of my mom's friends? Someone I should know?

'Hello, Claire, this is Dr Deirdre Blum from *Relationship Radio*. Your mother called us today because she knew you were struggling with something, and thought that you could use our help,' the woman said.

Relationship Radio . . . as in the national radio show where people called in for guidance on moral dilemmas. I'd actually heard it a few times. Dr Blum – the host and owner of the voice on the other end of the line that I'd thought sounded so familiar – was known for ripping into people when they had the temerity to call in with really stupid questions, like 'I'm thinking of having an affair with the teenage boy who cleans our pool. Should I go through with it?' or 'Is it wrong for me to go on a camping trip with the guys when my wife's nine months pregnant and set to go into labor at any time?' Some people thought she was unduly harsh – and it was true, when she really got upset, her screech could shatter glass – but to be fair, after listening to dumb questions like that day in and out, I'd probably be snappy, too.

'I'm sorry, but . . . am I . . . am I on the air right now?' I whispered.

'Yes, you are. Your mother was telling us that you've recently had a problem with a friend, and that you needed some help sorting it through,' Dr Blum said. She sounded nice, helpful even. Not at all like the shrill, shrieking harridan who'd sounded ready to reach through the phone and strangle the caller who'd insisted that getting a blow job from his coworker was not technically cheating on his wife.

I didn't know what to do. I'm a private person, and so was not keen on sharing the complexities of my love life with Dr Blum's nationwide audience. But just hanging up on her seemed rude, especially when she did seem so eager to help. I sat on my bed and took a deep breath.

'What exactly did my mother tell you?' I asked.

'She said that you began dating the ex-boyfriend of one of your friends, a relationship that she was still grieving over, but that you didn't tell the friend. And that when your friend did find out about the relationship – how exactly did she find out? Did you eventually tell her?' Dr Blum asked.

'N-No,' I faltered. 'She saw us out together.'

'Oh dear. Well, as I understand it, your friend is now quite angry with you, and understandably so, and you want to know how to make it up to her. Have you apologized?'

'Yes . . . well, I tried to, but she didn't really want to hear it. She was pretty upset when we talked,' I said.

'And do you understand why she was upset? What I mean is, you're not trying to justify your deceitful behavior, are you?'

There was a slight edge to Dr Blum's voice as she asked this question, and I had a feeling that if I did make any attempt to justify my actions, she'd rip into me.

'No, no,' I hastened to say. 'I know I screwed up. And I know she might never . . . never forgive me for what I did. But I'd like to do what I can to set things right.'

'Let me ask you this: Are you still dating this man, the one that your friend used to date?' The nice Dr Blum was back, her tone warm, inviting me to share.

'I . . . well. Not at the moment, but I'd like to continue

seeing him. It's a little complicated but . . . I . . . I care about him,' I gulped.

'Are you in love with him?' she coaxed.

'Yes,' I whispered. 'I am.'

'Well, there's only one thing you can do to set things right,' Dr Blum announced in a brisk, getting-down-to-business voice.

I perked up. Everything had seemed so hopeless, so bleak, that the very idea that there was one clear solution to the problem was encouraging. Maybe when Dr Blum was done sorting out my problems with Jack and Maddy, she'd be willing to tackle the debacle with Max, my dead-end career, and my distant relationship with my father. I could call in every day with a new issue, she'd reveal the solution to the problem, and in a few short weeks, everything in my life would be fixed. It would be like therapy, only better, faster, and free.

'What's that?' I asked eagerly.

'You have to do what you should have done in the beginning. You have to call your friend and ask her for her blessing to continue seeing this man,' Dr Blum said.

My hopes plummeted. 'But there's no way she'd give me her blessing. Especially now. She hates me,' I wailed.

'Yes, I'm sure she's angry at you. She was deceived and lied to by someone she trusted, while you were pretending to console her over her breakup—'

'I wasn't pretending. I really was trying to console her,' I interjected.

'But the *point* is,' Dr Blum continued, her tone considerably sharper. She didn't seem to appreciate being interrupted. 'You contributed to her pain by lying, and now you have to make that up to her.'

'But how will asking for her blessing make it up? And what if she says no?' I asked.

'Asking her for her permission will give your friend her

dignity back. As I wrote in my best-selling book, *Modern Women, Dumb Choices*, oftentimes when a relationship ends, the resulting pain has more to do with loss of self-worth than the actual loss of the partner. So by giving her back some control, you'll also be helping to restore her self-esteem. And you have to mean it when you ask her, or else it won't count. If she says no, then you have to respect her wishes and not see this man anymore. So call her up, apologize again, and ask her for her permission to continue seeing him,' Dr Blum pronounced.

This was a topic I wanted to explore in greater depth, but as I started to fire off another question, I realized that she had muted my voice.

'Thank you for calling, Claire. And our next caller is . . . Marie from Des Moines. Marie, you're on the air with Dr Deirdre Blum,' I heard Dr Blum say, and then the line went dead. It was actually pretty rude . . . I hadn't asked for her to butt in to my private business and dispense unsolicited advice, but now that she had, I should at least have a chance to flesh out what she was saying.

My mother appeared at the door and peered into the room at me.

'Well? What do you think?' she asked.

'I think that I'm going to kill you,' I said slowly. 'I can't believe you called a radio talk show to discuss my personal life.'

'That's not what I meant. What did you think about her advice?'

'You heard?'

My mother nodded. 'I was listening to the radio.'

I closed my eyes and shook my head, praying that no one I knew listened to talk radio in the middle of the day, and that if they did, they wouldn't be able to figure out who I was. Why had my mother given them my real name? Couldn't she have used an alias?

'I think her advice was great,' Mom continued. 'If you call and ask Madeline for her blessing for you and Jack to continue dating, I think it will go a long way to repairing the damage.'

'But it's totally futile. I doubt Maddy will even speak to me, much less give me her blessing to date Jack,' I said. 'It's completely hopeless.'

'But it's the right thing to do. And you never know, she might surprise you. You two have been friends for a long time, you've been through a lot together. Maybe she's feeling as bad about this as you are,' Mom said sagely.

'But there's Jack . . . if she says no, then I'll lose him completely,' I said.

It wasn't until I actually formed the words and heard them out loud that I realized just how terrible that would be. Ending my relationship with Jack would make breaking up with Sawyer feel more like the end of a high school crush. In fact, what the hell had I done back in London? By accusing Jack of using me in a twisted revenge plot – and I had to admit that the more time passed and the more distance I had from the situation, it did seem ridiculous – I had probably already tanked the relationship. But maybe if I called and apologized to him, and we had a chance to talk everything out, we could salvage things. Jack had told me he loved me . . . and I loved him. I didn't have a lot of experience with the whole true-love thing, but from what I'd gleaned from childhood fairy tales and *The Princess Bride*, love was supposed to conquer all. Maddy had already made it clear that she didn't want anything else to do with me, so why should I lose them both?

'It's the right thing to do,' my mother said again, her voice soft and gentle. As usual I found this maternal superpower she possessed – the ability to read my mind – a little creepy. The FBI should hire her to interrogate suspects.

And maybe because I knew she was right, I crumpled up on the bed, curled into a fetal position, and let the tears pour down my cheeks and soak into the pillow. As I cried, my breath coming in hiccuppy gulps, my chest rising and falling with a jagged irregularity, my mom sat on the edge of the bed beside me and stroked my hair.

'You'll get through this. And don't forget, things have a way of working themselves out,' Mom said. 'Besides, I know what will make you feel better.'

'What's that?' I sniffed.

'We'll go to the salon and get your highlights retouched. There's no way you're going to feel better as long as your roots are showing,' she said.

I groaned, and buried my head back in my soggy pillow.

I went along with my mom's plans for beauty salon therapy more for her sake than my own. Letting her flutter around me, directing the hairstylist and colorist and manicurist on just how to fix me up, cheered her to no end. I did draw a line at having my hair cut in the short, ultra-blonde Meg Ryan-inspired coif that middle-aged Floridian women seemed so fond of – I called it the 'Lemon Head' look – but other than that, I let her have her way. When we left the salon a few hours later, my hair was a few inches shorter, brushing against my shoulders in a blunt-edged bob, and lightened considerably with the addition of golden-blonde highlights, and all twenty digits were polished in a shiny coral (a color I personally can't stand, but it made my mother happy, and I figured that she deserved it after putting up with my Eeyore routine all week). I actually did feel a little better – never underestimate the power of beauty products, I guess.

'Do you mind if I make an overseas call from your phone?' I asked my mother when we got back to her house from the salon.

She shook her head and gave me a quick hug. 'Good luck, honey. I hope she surprises you.'

'Me too,' I sighed.

With Sasha at my heels, her nails clicking against the hard tile floor, I took the cordless phone back to the guest room. I shut the door and climbed onto the middle of the king-sized bed, followed by Sasha, who jumped up next to me, turned twice, and curled into a ball, her head resting on my pillow. Before I could lose my nerve, I punched in Maddy's phone number. It was nine o'clock London time, but I didn't expect I'd catch her at home. Unlike me, Maddy loved to spend her evenings out, taking advantage of all of the invitations to restaurant openings and gallery showings that came her way through her work connections. After a long day at work, the only thing I wanted to do was crawl into my pajamas and read trashy paperback romance novels.

'Hello.' Maddy's voice was suddenly on the other end of the line, sounding far more composed than she had the last time I'd heard her. I was so startled to reach her on the first try that my mouth went dry and I couldn't seem to form any words.

'Hello?' she repeated, and then I heard her sigh, and knew she was about to hang up.

'Wait, don't hang up. It's me,' I said. 'It's Claire.'

'Well, that just makes me want to hang up even more,' Maddy said in a clipped, businesslike tone.

The phone went dead. I hit redial and heard the phone ring four or five times. *She's screening*, I thought, trying to think of what kind of a message I could leave on her answering machine that would entice her to answer. Just as I was deliberating whether I could pull off a convincing enough British accent to pass as the social secretary for Buckingham Palace, she picked up the phone.

'Hello,' Maddy said, this time sounding more on edge, more wary.

'Please don't hang up. Just give me a minute, let me say my piece, and then you never have to talk to me again,' I said.

'And why do you think you deserve even a minute of my time?' she asked stiffly.

Ouch. I thought about invoking our longtime friendship, but had a feeling this might outrage her more than anything. 'I don't. But if you don't listen to me now, I'll just keep calling and bothering you until you do,' I said instead.

She hesitated, and was so quiet, I thought that she might have hung up on me again. But then, in a low, toneless voice, she said, 'Fine.'

Now that I had her attention, I wasn't quite sure how to begin. Should I set forth my case of why I thought that Jack and I deserved a chance together? No, she'd just react to that with hostility. Should I beg? Well, it might be a better strategy, but Dr Blum didn't say I had to surrender my dignity while giving Maddy's back.

Crap, I thought. I probably should have thought this through before I called her.

'If you don't have anything to say, I'm going to hang up the phone again,' Maddy said, interrupting my strategy session.

'No, don't do that,' I said hastily, realizing I'd just have to wing it. 'First, I wanted to let you know again how very, very sorry I am. About everything. I'm sorry I didn't tell you right in the beginning that I went out with Jack. I'm sorry that I didn't tell you that we were seeing each other as soon as I learned who he was. And I'm sorry that you found out by seeing us together instead of hearing it directly from me. But most of all, I'm sorry that I hurt you. I'd do anything to take that back.'

'I noticed that you didn't say you were sorry that you were seeing him,' Maddy said, her voice brittle.

I paused, not sure how to go on. 'Well . . . I am sorry that I dated him under these circumstances, since it meant that I had to lie to one of the most important people in my life. But,' I said, taking a deep breath, 'I'm not sorry that I met him, Maddy. I love Jack. I didn't mean for that to happen, and I'm sorry that it hurts you, but I can't help it. And he loves me, too.'

Maddy laughed. It was the same ugly, harsh bark that I'd heard on that horrible afternoon at her apartment a week earlier. God, had it been just one week? Floating around in the pool all day, every day, had eroded my sense of time.

'I already told you, Claire, Harrison doesn't love you. He loves me and he was just using you to hurt me. I know that's hard for you to hear, but it's the truth,' she said.

I'd expected to hear a repeat of Maddy's far-fetched theory – which was based entirely on the unflattering and unkind assumption that she was inherently more desirable and loveable than I was – and I had to steel myself against the surge of anger now flickering inside of me. I tried to instead focus on the giving-her-back-her-dignity thing.

'Maddy, again, I'm very sorry. I know how painful all of this must have been for you, and it kills me that I had any part in hurting you,' I said dogmatically. I figured sticking to my apology was about the safest route I had.

Maddy was quiet for a minute. 'So, you don't believe me,' she finally said. 'You think that he actually gives a shit about you.'

'Yes. I think that he does. I never thought I'd say this about anyone, but I think he might be the one. I know that must be so hard for you to hear,' I said.

'Why did you call? What is it you want me to say?' Maddy asked. Her voice was breaking a little, and I knew that she was crying. I could now understand why men hate it so much when we break down into tears in the middle of emotional conversations. It's utterly devastating and impossible to ignore.

I closed my eyes, and rubbed at my face with my free hand. This was it. This was the point where I handed over my romantic fate to her, and I really didn't want to do it. I could tell from the way she was talking to me that our friendship was history, and that she'd probably revel in the chance to hurt me as much as I'd hurt her. And as truly sorry as I was that I'd been the source of her pain, I just didn't think that giving her the power to end my relationship with Jack was really the best solution. Dr Blum had thought so, sure, but then again, I'd done a little Web research on the woman and learned that she wasn't even a real doctor. She had a Ph.D. in nutrition, for Christ's sake, and hadn't even gone to school for psychology. And so what if my mother agreed with her? Hadn't I taken a blood oath that I'd never, *ever* turn into my mother? So why take her advice on what could be one of the most important decisions of my life?

'The thing is . . . once I learned who Jack was, I should have asked for your permission before I continued seeing him. It would have been the right thing to do, and I . . . well, I screwed up. But I want to make this right, I want to make things right between us,' I said.

'I just don't think that's possible,' Maddy said. 'I don't trust you anymore. I don't think I even like you anymore. And I certainly don't want to be friends with you anymore.'

The finality with which she said this reverberated through me. I took a deep breath and forged ahead.

'I want you to know that I'm not going to continue to see Jack unless you give us your blessing,' I said, the words leaving me with a great whoosh. The phone went silent, and I thought that maybe Maddy had hung up on me again.

'Hello?' I asked tentatively.

'What?' Maddy sounded shocked. 'What did you say?'

'I mean it, Mads. I'm in love with Jack, and I think he loves me, but I'm not going to see him anymore unless you say it's all right,' I said.

'So, that's just it? You're not going to fight for him?' she asked.

'I never saw this as a competition. It was never about taking him away from you,' I said.

'How do you expect me to respond to this?' Maddy asked.

'I don't expect anything. I hope you'll give us your

blessing, and I hope that you and I can get past this, and that I can somehow make everything up to you, and we can remain friends, but . . . it's up to you,' I said.

There was another long pause, and hope began swelling inside of me. Maybe this meant she was considering it. That was a good sign, wasn't it? I'd expected her to dismiss my request – and me – with a caustic insult or two thrown in for good measure.

After a few more interminable moments of silence, Maddy finally spoke. 'I'm not going to give you my blessing, Claire. I honestly don't know why you care – it's not like your doing this is going to make things better between us. Like I said, I don't want to be friends with you anymore. And I also don't want you and Jack to be together. In fact, I hope being apart causes you two as much pain as you've caused me,' she said.

And then she hung up on me again, clicking the off button on her cordless phone with an anticlimactic beep. Technology is wonderful, but it has taken away the satisfaction of slamming a receiver down with a loud clatter when you want to not only hang up on someone, you also want to underline the force of your snub. But even so, I got the picture, and I didn't call Maddy back.

Instead, I made another call, again overseas. I wasn't as nervous about making this call as I had been about the one to Maddy. I just felt dead inside, hopeless and helpless. The finality of what I had to do was horrible, but now there was no going back. I reached up and touched my diamond necklace nervously, rolling it between my fingers, remembering how happy I'd been on the morning when Jack had given it to me.

'Hello,' Jack said.

I felt the familiar rush of warmth I always did at hearing his voice. It was like being dipped and swirled in melted chocolate.

'Hi, it's Claire,' I replied.

'Claire! God, I've been trying to get ahold of you for days, I must have left you a dozen messages! I'm so glad you finally called me back, I didn't think you were going to,' Jack said. He sounded relieved, even elated, to hear from me, which was miraculous considering how things had been left between us. Not that it made me feel any better, though – considering why I was calling him, it might have made things easier if he'd cursed and spit on the ground upon hearing my voice.

'Oh, I didn't get your messages. I haven't been home, and I haven't checked my machine. I'm in Florida, visiting my mom,' I explained. 'I came here right after I got back from London.'

'Are you having a good time?' Jack asked.

I looked at my coral-painted toenails and considered his question. 'It's been nice having the time with my mother. We've gotten closer, I think,' I said.

'I'm so glad you called. I know how angry you are, and I know that it was completely wrong for me to have lied in the beginning about not knowing who you were,' Jack began.

'I'm not angry about that anymore,' I said wistfully, wishing things were that simple. At that moment, his ploy of meeting me on the plane sounded more like an adorable story we could have one day told our future children, rather than something to break up over. 'Actually, I think it was kind of romantic, like something Cary Grant would do in one of those old screwball romantic comedies.'

'Really?' Jack asked, sounding both pleased and surprised. 'Because you were really upset when you left here . . . you were so mad, you actually believed that ridiculous story Maddy made up, about my diabolical revenge plot. You don't still believe it, do you?'

'No, I don't,' I said.

Jack let out a sigh, and when he spoke again, relief

rippled through his voice. 'I can't tell you how glad I am to hear you say that. When you left here, I . . . well, I didn't think I was ever going to see you again. I was sure that between my not coming clean about meeting you on purpose, and that garbage that Maddy told you, that I'd lost you for good.'

'I think Maddy was just so hurt and so confused that she was trying to make sense of it all,' I said.

'Her way of making sense of everything was to lash out at you and make me out to be a monster. I'm sorry she was hurt, but that's no excuse for the way she's behaved,' Jack said.

'I don't think any of us have handled this well. You lied to me, and I lied to Maddy, and she lashed out at both of us. It's all just been a mess from the beginning.'

'But . . . now everything's cleared up, right? You know the truth, and so does Maddy, and now we can just move forward.'

'There's still something you don't know,' I said, and then I paused, hoping that the sob welling inside of me would wait until I was able to get it all out. I knew I might not get through everything without tearing up, but crying hysterically wasn't going to help anything.

'What's that?' Jack asked cautiously.

'Before I called you, I called Maddy, both to apologize to her again for the deception, and . . . and to ask her blessing for you and me to continue seeing each other,' I said slowly.

'I don't understand. You did *what*?'

I was unprepared for the force of anger with which Jack spoke. I honestly hadn't known how he would react to the news that I'd put the future of our relationship together in the hands of his ex-girlfriend, whom he likely viewed as a bitter, vindictive woman bent on destroying his happiness. I'd sort of pictured it through the misty lens of a Movie of the Week – the conversation would be bittersweet, like

Romeo and Juliet exchanging vows of love while knowing that the promise of a future together would never be fulfilled (although minus the double suicide, of course). In my mind, we'd both be broken-hearted but dignified, melancholy but resigned.

'I told Maddy that you and I wouldn't continue our relationship unless she was okay with it,' I whispered.

'And what exactly was her response to this extraordinary offer?' Jack demanded.

'Um . . . she said no,' I said. 'She said she'd rather we didn't date.'

'What a shock! And I would have thought a woman who'd proven herself to be as selfish and malicious as Maddy would jump at the chance to make two people she claims to love happy,' Jack said sarcastically.

'That's not fair,' I protested. 'We hurt her.'

'How exactly did I hurt her? By breaking up with her when I realized that I wasn't in love with her? And after I found out that the entire time I was seeing her she was sleeping with her boss?'

'Okay, maybe between you and Maddy you're relatively blameless, but I certainly screwed up. If I'd been honest with her from the beginning . . .' I began.

'Then she would have insisted that we stop seeing each other then,' Jack finished.

'Yes, probably. But at least . . . at least this wouldn't have become so complicated,' I said.

'Complicated? Is that what you call this? Let me ask you a question, Claire – do you love me?' It sounded more like a demand than a question, but either way, it took me aback.

I had no idea how I should respond. After Sawyer, I'd pretty much flushed the entire idea of falling in love, and assumed that either it never really happened in real life, or at least, it would never happen to me. I was meant for more-casual flings, or if I was very lucky, one of those we-don't-have-sex-but-we're-best-friends compromise marriages.

But then Jack came along. He was everything I'd ever wanted in a man – he was headstrong and smart and funny and sexy as hell. He saw through my defenses, and still wanted to get to know me better. And when I fought the feelings I was having, he fought back, and forced me to be honest with him. So despite myself, I did love him – and in the purest, most unconditional way possible. I supposed that the least I owed him was honesty.

'Yes, I love you,' I said quietly.

He paused, and I heard him suck in his breath.

'And I love you,' Jack said softly. 'And that's all that should matter.'

'I know, in a perfect world, it would. But if we continued with this relationship, after all of the dishonesty, and all of the pain, then it would always have a taint to it. Neither one of us deserves that. And Maddy doesn't deserve that . . . she deserves to have her *dignity*,' I said, using Dr Blum's word, hoping that it would make the same sense to Jack that it had to me.

'You couldn't be more wrong. Maybe it's a little messy, and maybe we ended up hurting someone in the process, but that's not a good enough reason to throw us away,' Jack argued.

'I'm trying to do the right thing,' I said, feeling like I was reciting dialogue from an after-school television special. I knew that the fact that the conversation was breaking down into platitudes was a sign that it was time to end it and get off the phone, but I couldn't seem to bring myself to do it. It might be the last chance I had to talk to Jack, and as unpleasant as the conversation was turning, I was still savoring the connection while it lasted.

'You know, Claire, I've had it. I've spent the last two months chasing after you, trying to spend time with you to see if this relationship would fulfill its potential, and now you've finally admitted that you have feelings for me, that you love me, and then you announce that you won't continue seeing me unless you have the permission of my ex-girlfriend, a woman who has gone flying off the deep end. How do you expect me to respond to that?' Jack asked. His voice had started off with a jaw-clenched, vein-throbbing growl and escalated to a near shout that had me wincing.

'I don't expect anything . . . I was just trying to talk to you about it, tell you what I decided,' I said.

'And what gave you the right to decide this for the both of us? What kind of a game are you playing? Did you read about playing hard-to-get in one of those stupid dating books, and think that it would be some sort of a huge turn-on? Because let me tell you, I'm not going to keep chasing after you, Claire, only to have you kick me every time I catch up,' Jack said. I'd never heard him so angry – it was incongruous with the laid-back Jack with the lazy grin and crinkled-up eyes.

'I'm not playing games, and I'm not asking you to chase after me. I'm sorry about this, about everything,' I croaked. The tears, which had been threatening to erupt ever since I first heard Jack's voice on the other end of the line, began burning my eyes, and my chest felt like it had been filled with concrete.

'I'm sorry, too. But if you're serious about ending it, then this is good-bye, because I'm not going to go through this again,' he said.

I wanted more than anything to somehow reach through the phone line and grab hold of him, to pull him tightly to me and never let him go. The tears began streaming down my cheeks, the salt water burning tracks as they fell. I knew that I had – for the briefest moment – a chance to undo everything I had just said, and hold on to him. It was right there in front of me, the brass ring winking and glinting in order to get my attention, and yet I couldn't make myself grab onto it.

'I love you,' I said, wavering, my voice hoarse and jagged with tears. 'I'm sorry that it all had to end this way.'

'That's the worst part about this – it didn't have to,' Jack said sadly. 'Good-bye, Claire.'

Again, an electronic click signaled that the conversation was over, but I continued to hold the receiver up to my ear until an electronic female voice told me again and again that if I'd like to make a call, I should hang up and dial again.

After getting off the phone with Jack, I cried for the rest of the evening and through most of the night, and although I felt like I could spend another month crying, I discovered by the next morning that I had run out of tears. I'd feel my chest well up, and my throat would tighten, and my breath turn shallow and uneven, everything in place for a good, cathartic sob fest, but the tears were a no-show. It was a severe punishment; crying brought me some small relief, and to be stripped of even that seemed cruel. Still, my nightlong crying jag hadn't done wonders for my looks – I was left with splotchy skin, red eyes, and a swollen nose. My mother took one look at me and made me drink an enormous glass of ice water before fixing me a full, cholesterol-laden breakfast of freshly squeezed orange juice, scrambled eggs, crisp bacon, and a toasted bagel loaded up with cream cheese. I knew how awful I must have looked for my mother to actually be pushing food on me. Breakfast at her house normally consisted of bran flakes and skim milk – if I made a move for the full-fat cream cheese kept in the fridge for Howard, my mother would run interference, body-blocking me while she expounded on the benefits of the fat-free, carb-free, fun-free diet.

After breakfast, I jumped in the pool. Something about dunking yourself in cold water on a hot day has a remarkably restorative effect. I sliced through the water, arms swinging, legs kicking, heart pumping, and for at least a few minutes I felt weightless and free. Submerged two feet underwater and gliding along the pool like a stingray, nothing could touch me, and I reemerged feeling somewhat human.

But there's only so much healing one can accomplish overnight, even with a sympathetic mother, fattening breakfast, and refreshing swim, and by the time I took a shower, washing away the smell of chlorine with sudsy raspberry shower gel, my heart began to prick with sadness again. Then I remembered that Jack had said he'd left messages on my answering machine, and before I could stop myself, I was back in the guest room, wrapped in a fluffy blue towel, punching my phone number into the cordless phone. Once my machine picked up – I cringed when I heard my voice on the outgoing message, I sounded so stuffy and officious – I entered in my code, and a minute later, an electronic voice was telling me I had ten messages. Almost immediately, Jack's voice, rich and warm and strained with anxiety, was playing in my ear.

'Hi, Claire, it's me. Please pick up if you're there, we need to talk. Okay . . . please call me when you get in. I know you're angry, and I don't blame you, but give me a chance to explain. Okay? I'll talk to you soon, I hope.'

Jack had left six additional messages like the first one, the last recorded only an hour before I'd called him the day before. Hearing the worry in his voice, the concern for how I was doing, the anxiety at not hearing back from me . . . it took all of my strength not to pick up the phone and call him again, to take back everything I'd said the night before. I might still have a chance if I pled insanity or intoxication.

But I knew that I couldn't. I hoped that at some point the knowledge that I'd done the right thing would make me feel better, but for the time being it was cold comfort. Maybe I'd given Maddy her dignity back – and that was a big maybe – but I had nothing to show for it. Our friendship was over and I'd lost my one shot at the happily-ever-after everyone's always yammering on about.

The next two messages were from my office – one was from the day before from horrible Peggy letting me know that I was out of both sick days and vacation days, the other, left that morning, was from Robert, sounding brisk with annoyance, and asking me to call in to work immediately. I erased them both, and wondered – without really caring – whether I still had a job. I supposed it was something I needed to know eventually, but right now this whole Floridian retiree lifestyle was starting to grow on me. All that my mom, Howard, and their friends seemed to do was play golf and take turns throwing cocktail parties – it was like a never-ending college spring break (minus the wet T-shirt contests and random hook-ups). Maybe I could use my extensive knowledge of the issues facing senior citizens to worm my way into their crowd, and then pull an Anna Nicole Smith by marrying one of the older, richer men, pull a few years of wife duty (taking care to hide his supply of Viagra), and be left a wealthy widow by the time I was forty. Sure, it was a little mercenary, but at least that way I'd never again have to return to my depressing gray-walled cubicle and listen to Doris, a copy editor, drone on endlessly about her arthritic knees and fourteen cats.

But the tenth message wiped away all thoughts of gold digging. It was Kit Holiday, a message left that very morning:

'Hi, Claire, this is Kit Holiday from *Retreat* magazine. We'd love to have you come work with us, so please give me a call as soon as you can and I'll give you all of the details of our offer. I'm looking forward to hearing from you and, hopefully, to working with you.'

*

I flew back to Manhattan the next day, a Saturday. My mom seemed truly sad to see me go, and tried to talk me into staying through the weekend, but since I'd accepted the job at *Retreat* – at a significant increase in salary from what I was making at *Sassy Seniors!* – and was set to start work there on February 1, I had far too many things to do to stay away any longer. I needed to give notice at work, finish up all of the assignments I had outstanding – including taking a three-day trip to Denver that I'd managed to put off for a month – and pack up my apartment, not to mention finding a new place to live in Chicago. I was stunned that they'd hired me after that awful interview, but when I called Kit back, she'd gushed about how impressed they'd been with me. Huh.

But when I hugged my mom good-bye at the airport, and told her I'd miss her, I was being completely honest. I felt closer to her than I had in years. I'd once heard that you spend your twenties hating your parents for all of the mistakes they made raising you, and then in your thirties you start to forgive them. Maybe my mother and I had finally reached a truce, and from now on could concentrate more on getting to know each other as adults, and less on each other's faults. Still, I was ready to get back home. The new job was just what I needed – and not only because I'd been one step away from cruising for seventy-year-old men. It would be a relief to focus on something other than my personal problems.

When I gave my notice to Robert on Monday, he didn't react the way I thought he would. I'd expected him to break out the champagne and perform a Russian kicking dance on top of his desk; instead, he actually looked a little misty eyed and said that he was sorry to see me go.

'You've been spunky, but when you stopped fighting me and decided to take a little editorial advice, your writing was superb. In fact, your London article was the best you've ever turned in,' Robert said.

'Er, thanks,' I said, not sure which was more annoying – that he'd called me 'spunky' or that he continued to view the bland, colorless articles that I'd hated writing (the London piece being the worst of the lot) as my finest work.

Unlike Robert, Peggy was thrilled to learn of my imminent departure. About five minutes after I gave my notice – proof that Barbara does eavesdrop on everything that goes on in Robert's office, and then spreads the gossip as fast as her orthopedic shoes will carry her – Peggy appeared at the entrance to my cubicle, Germanic blue eyes sparkling, face flushed with excitement.

'Is it true? Are you really leaving? When?' she asked with ill-concealed delight.

'Yes. The twenty-fourth will be my last day,' I said dryly. The level of her glee was a little insulting, but at least Peggy wasn't a hypocrite. And for the next three weeks, whenever I did see her, she was almost always humming. At least I'd managed to make someone's New Year's wishes come true.

The weeks before I left for Chicago began to pick up speed, like in one of those cartoons where the passage of time is illustrated by each sheet of a page-a-day calendar ripping off faster and faster in a blustery wind. I worked long days training Enid, my replacement, and trying to finish up two features I was writing – my final travel column, focusing on Denver, and a general article on cruise deals – and when I got home at night, I packed boxes, arranged for my mail to be forwarded and services to be cut off, and generally tried to get organized for my move.

Kit Holiday had turned out to be my saving grace – she hooked me up to sublet an apartment from a professor friend of hers who was spending a year teaching at Oxford. The professor was a gruff woman with a condescending way of speaking – she used lots of large words as she spoke, and then felt it necessary to define them for me – but the rent she was charging was reasonable, and the apartment was fully furnished, so I could put my own meager assortment of furniture into storage until I found a more permanent place to live.

I tried not to think about Jack more than every five minutes or so. Sometimes I'd manage to go an entire half hour without dwelling on the lost relationship, or missing his happy-go-lucky grin, or the soapy clean way he smelled, or the way his lips felt when they lingered on mine. Other times, like on the interminably long plane ride to Denver, I could think of nothing else. I couldn't even bring myself to erase the seven messages he'd left on my answering machine, so that in my more desperate moments I could listen to his voice.

I had hoped that once Maddy thought about everything I'd said, she'd reconsider her scorched-earth policy toward our friendship. I was wrong. She didn't call, not once, nor did I try to contact her. She'd made it clear that she didn't want me to contact her, and I had to respect her wishes. If I'd thought that it would all end like an episode of *Friends*, and in the final moments of the half hour, she'd appear out of nowhere, hug me, and tell me that no matter what I'd done, our friendship was too special to let go, I would have been disappointed. And I was disappointed . . . both in myself for not being brave enough to be truthful with her earlier, but also in Maddy for not being able to forgive me.

At least my friendship with Max was still intact, if a little awkward. A few days after I'd returned from Florida, there'd been a quiet knock at my door, and I opened it to Max, wearing his Duran Duran *Seven and the Ragged Tiger* tour T-shirt and looking sheepish.

'You interested in Chinese take-out and *Terminator 2*? I promise I won't try to stick my tongue down your throat,' he said, and after that, things more or less returned to normal between us.

I thought Max and I should talk things out and wanted to make sure that he was okay, but since I couldn't think of a way to bring up what had happened without embarrassing him, I let it go. I didn't even feel comfortable asking him about his split with Daphne (since the catalyst for the breakup was – according to Max – his feelings for me). Every once in a while, Max would make a joke about the Jekyll-and-Hyde effect rum had on him, but I always just laughed it off, as I knew he wanted me to.

On that first night we hung out together over Chinese takeout, I filled him in on everything that had happened during my trips to London and Florida. For Max's benefit, I was careful to play down how heartbroken I was over Jack, but I didn't leave anything major out.

'So what do you think? Do you agree with Dr Blum and my mom?' I asked him.

Max shrugged. 'I think you did the right thing for you. You know I never liked Maddy – and I like her even less now. I can't believe she was so harsh to you,' he began.

'She was angry and lashing out,' I interjected.

'Yeah, but it was still shitty of her to talk to you like that, and it was even shittier for her not to accept your multiple apologies. I think she's gone way overboard on the scorned-woman act. If that's the kind of person she is, then maybe you're better off without her,' Max continued.

'Maybe,' I said, unconvinced. Lately, I'd been missing Maddy more than ever. Girlfriends are a necessity for nursing you through a broken heart.

'But like I told you before you left, I don't think you're the kind of person who could have continued to have a relationship with someone, knowing how much it would hurt a close friend, whether or not the friend deserved your loyalty in the first place. So, for your sake, you did the right thing. I don't know if you gave Maddy back her dignity, but at least you acted in a way that preserved your own,' Max continued wisely.

Normally at this point he'd have hugged me, but the awkwardness around our last physical contact still hung between us, so instead we exchanged shy smiles and watched Arnold Schwarzenegger blow things up.

On my last day of work, the weather gurus were predicting that a foot of snow was going to be dumped on New York, which would almost certainly mean that the entire city would shut down while we dug out of the mess. For the first time in my tenure at *Sassy Seniors!* I was hoping we wouldn't have a snow day. Ever since the Jack/Maddy debacle – or The Incident, as I'd come to think of it – I'd been feeling much like Han Solo must have after he was lowered into the carbon freeze (and the very fact that I was making an analogy between my pathetic love life and a *Star Wars* movie was a sure sign that Max had made me sit through that stupid movie an unhealthy number of times). But the idea that I was going to be free of *Sassy Seniors!* – free of Robert, free of Peggy, free of traveling to crushingly dull locations on a shoestring budget – allowed a little bit of optimism to leak into my frozen heart. So the last thing I wanted was to wait at least another day, if not more, before I could clean out my desk, bid my co-workers farewell, and never have to set foot in the dank, depressing office again. And things finally seemed to be turning my way when the storm that had been on a direct course for New York suddenly veered south at the last minute, sparing us completely.

I was also glad to be getting rid of Enid, the homely reticent forty-something woman who would be taking over my job after I left (she had already brought in a poster of a fuzzy kitten clutching to a tree limb for dear life with the caption 'Hang in There!' written across the bottom, which she meant to tack up on the cubicle wall once I deserted it, doubtlessly planning to hang it up next to her favorite *Cathy* cartoon strip). I'd spent the last week training her, and she gave me the creeps. Enid tended to stare at me with glazed-over eyes and a gaping mouth while I talked to her, and even when I said something that prompted a response, she'd continue to stare for a few beats before she responded. I had no idea if she was so incredibly bored by my tutelage that she'd mastered the ability to sleep with her eyes open, or if she just completely lacked all social skills and had no idea how to interact with normal people, or if she'd maybe fallen so head over heels in love with me that she was struck dumb in my presence (although she was so asexual, I tended to doubt the latter). I also didn't know where Robert had found her – although Enid claimed to have prior copy-writing experience, I had to keep explaining to her that she couldn't put phrases inside a set of quotation marks unless she was directly quoting someone.

'You don't put your own descriptions, your own thoughts, in quotation marks just for emphasis,' I reminded her again on my last morning, while looking over a practice column I had assigned her to write on New York.

'But I'm quoting myself,' Enid insisted, while breathing heavily through her mouth.

I sighed, and rubbed my eyes, and tried to remind myself that in a few short hours neither Enid nor the travel column would be my responsibility anymore. Besides, I had no doubt that Robert would love her work – her column on visiting Manhattan made the city sound about as appealing as the dust bowl from *The Grapes of Wrath*. And I could already tell that Peggy adored Enid; despite my many attempts to indoctrinate Enid in the art of annoying Peggy – sequestering her favorite coffee cup, liberal personal use of office supplies, making creative claims on the expense account report – Enid had brought in her own coffee cup on the very first day (emblazoned with the bold statement 'I ♥ My Tabby'), which she washed out dutifully every afternoon. And every time Peggy goose-stepped down the corridor, Enid would find some excuse to rush out and fawn over her. Peggy was in heaven – not only was I close to being gone, I was being replaced by someone she could turn into her own personal toady.

'You know, your voice sounds sort of familiar. Have you ever called into *Relationship Radio*?' Enid asked.

'No,' I said firmly.

'I just love Dr Blum. I listen to her every day, and a few weeks ago there was a woman who called in who sounded a lot like you,' Enid continued. 'She'd done something really horrible, like sleeping with her best friend's husband . . .'

Great. Now, not only was I notorious, but she wasn't even getting the story right.

'Well, that certainly wasn't me,' I said crisply, and then escaped to the bathroom before Enid could push the subject any further.

I'd been thinking about sneaking out after lunch – what were they going to do if I did leave early, fire me? – but Olivia and Helen blocked my escape and ushered me into the staff room, where they had a little farewell gathering, complete with a cake, waiting for me. I was so touched, I even felt a little guilty over my ongoing boycott of the office birthday parties. I thanked everyone, and told them all I would miss working with them (a complete lie, of course, but what else was I going to say?), and shook Robert's hand and told him I appreciated the opportunity to write for the magazine, which I realized was true as I said it, even if I had hated almost every assignment he'd sent me on. Maybe it wasn't a glamorous job or one that I'd particularly enjoyed, but it had turned out to be a stepping stone to a better position, and for that I was grateful. And then, flying on the sugar rush of yellow cake and soda, I finally skipped out of the office, a free woman at last.

It finally snowed the next morning, but since I had planned to spend the day indoors packing anyway, I didn't care. As long as the airport would be open in a week, so I wouldn't miss my flight to Chicago, a monsoon could fall on the city in the meantime. I was just in the midst of wrapping framed photographs in sheets of bubble wrap when the phone rang. I assumed it was Max again; we had plans for pizza and a movie that evening, and he'd stopped at the video store en route to the photo shoot he had scheduled for that day. He'd already called from his cell phone three times to pretend to ask for my input on a movie selection (amazingly, whenever Max was the one to pick up the video, whatever movie I suggested we watch was *always* checked out, leaving him free to pick up one of his selections).

'I just don't believe that they're out of *Sleepless in Seattle*, *The Princess Diaries*, and *Hope Floats*,' I said into the phone, not bothering with a hello.

'Hello? Claire?'

It wasn't Max after all . . . it was a woman. And not just any woman. It was Maddy.

'**M**addy?' I asked, even though I knew exactly who belonged to the silvery voice on the other end of the line. I'd only logged about ten thousand hours on the phone with her over the years, so there was no mistaking her for someone calling up to sell me car insurance or student loan consolidation packages.

'Yeah,' she said softly, and then paused. 'Is this a bad time? It sounds like you were expecting someone else.'

'Yes . . . I mean, yes I thought you were Max calling, but no it's not a bad time,' I said quickly.

I sat down on my couch, and was surprised at how nervous I felt talking to someone who I'd once been so close to that she'd felt perfectly comfortable asking me to inspect her bikini wax to confirm that it was symmetrical.

'I tried you at your office first, but they said you weren't working there anymore. When did you leave?' Maddy asked.

'My last day was yesterday. I'm moving to Chicago in a week, and starting a job there with *Retreat*, the travel magazine,' I said.

'Really? That's great! I love that magazine,' Maddy said, and sounded so warm and effusive, I was beginning to wonder if she'd suffered a head injury that had caused her to suffer short-term amnesia, and had blocked out everything that had happened between us nearly a month ago. This Maddy was friendly and sweet, and about a million miles away from the snarling, furious Maddy I'd parted on such bad terms with. In fact, if I remembered correctly, the last thing she had said to me was something about wishing plague and pestilence upon me. Okay, maybe not exactly, but close.

'Yeah, I'm pretty excited about it . . . but, um, I'm a little surprised to hear from you,' I said cautiously.

In response, there was dead silence on the other end of the line.

'Are you still there?' I asked.

'I'm here. I just . . . this is hard for me,' Maddy said, her voice small and hurt. 'I'm still angry at you.'

'I know. You have every right to be,' I said. 'I'm so sorry about everything.'

'Wait, that's not why I called. I mean, I know you're sorry, but I'm not trying to rub your nose in it, I just . . . I just wanted to do the right thing,' she said.

I had no idea what she was talking about, so I just said, 'Okay,' drawing the word out into two long, questioning syllables.

'The thing is . . . I'm still angry at you for lying to me, but I understand why you did it, or at least I think I do. I was acting pretty nutty there for a while, after breaking up with Harrison I mean, and I think that maybe you just didn't tell me what was going on because you didn't want to hurt me any further,' she continued.

'Of course I didn't,' I exclaimed.

'But that's not really an excuse for your getting together with him. That was a pretty shitty thing to do,' she said.

'Yes, it was,' I agreed, still not sure where we were going with all of this.

'But you're not a shitty person. I know that, I know you. Once I stopped being quite so mad at you, I started to think that there must be a reason you were acting so out of character. And I figured there were only two possible reasons – either you resented me, hated me even, over all of those years we were friends,' Maddy began.

'I never hated or resented you,' I cried out. 'I'll admit, it's hard not to be a little jealous sometimes of, well, of how ridiculously beautiful you are, and how you have that magic ability to make all men fall madly in love with you on sight. They actually knock me into garbage cans in order to get to you.'

'You know, I don't know why you think that. That I'm prettier than you, I mean. I've always been jealous of *your* looks,' Maddy said. 'You're incredibly sexy and curvy, and yet sophisticated at the same time. I've always felt like a little girl in comparison to you.'

'Oh, please,' I said sarcastically. It was like Julia Roberts saying she wished she looked like Drew Carey.

'It's true! I don't have any breasts to speak of, and I'm so short I get carded every time I try to buy a bottle of wine in the U.S. I always wished I had that fifties movie-star glamour thing you have going on,' Maddy insisted.

'Maddy, you don't have a single physical flaw on your entire body, that's how perfect looking you are. And I've seen men follow you home from the grocery store with their tongues lolling out,' I pointed out.

'But that's not because of how I look. I mean, haven't you ever known a woman who wasn't really all that hot but got a lot of attention? Oh, like Bridget McCormick, remember her from freshman year dorm? She wasn't very pretty at all – she had that awful curly hair, and her face was sort of flat and squashed in – but every guy at school thought she was the hottest thing. Remember?' Maddy asked.

'Yeah, I remember her. Didn't she get asked to every single frat formal one year? It was some kind of a school record. But you're right, I never thought she was very pretty. I just assumed that she was one of those women who men think are attractive but women don't, the same way that a lot of guys don't think Gwyneth Paltrow is anything special, but most women I know would cut off an arm to look like her,' I said.

'Bridget knew how to play the game. The whole trick to getting and keeping male interest is by being rude to them. You throw them a smile, maybe even flirt a little, but then you make it clear that you have no interest in them whatsoever. If you come across as too eager to get to know them, there's no challenge, and that's what guys live for,' Maddy said.

'But I've been off dating, off men, for years, and my disinterest hasn't caused men to flock to me,' I pointed out.

'That's because you really weren't interested in meeting any of them! You don't do the flirting thing at all, but just put out strong vibes that you want to be left alone. Men want a challenge, but they want a challenge they can win,' Maddy said.

Now that she'd described her technique to me, I remembered all of the times that I had seen her hot/cold routine – she'd smile, expose her neck, coquettishly touch a man's sleeve, only to then lose all interest in her target, leaving him a confused, panting, hormonal mess. I just hadn't realized that she'd been employing an actual method, as opposed to the kind of instinct that I thought came naturally to everyone but me. But if Maddy was right – and having seen her results, I suspected she was – then it meant that the Great Secret of the It Girls had finally been revealed to me. I was finally in possession of the power to drive men mad with lust for me . . . that is, if I could figure out how to stop sending out signals that I wanted to be left alone. Or if I even wanted to.

This reminded me of what Jack had said about having to work harder with me, and how my defenses kept going up, even while I was growing more and more smitten with him.

But even if I did need to work at lowering those defenses and letting people in – and clearly, there were benefits to doing this, as I'd tried it with my mother and our relationship was better now than it had been since the day I hit puberty – I still didn't think that I wanted to play Maddy's game. I didn't want to attract a man whose interest was piqued only when he thought he couldn't have me. It was funny to think back to when I first met Jack, that I'd thought he might be a Chaser. I couldn't have been more wrong about him. He wasn't at all interested in games, and just wanted a relationship without all of the bullshit. I felt a tug of regret in my stomach, and closed my eyes for a minute.

'What was the other reason?' I asked quietly.

'What?' Maddy asked.

'You said that you could only think of two reasons why I'd go out with Jack behind your back. Either I resented you – which I don't – or . . .' My voice trailed off as I waited for her response.

'Or you were really in love with him,' Maddy said. Her words were tinged with sadness.

'Yes,' I said. 'I was in love with him.'

'Past tense?' Maddy asked.

'No . . . I do still love Jack, but I told him that unless you said it was all right, we couldn't see each other again. And I meant it, I haven't talked to him in almost a month,' I said.

'But that's why I was calling. I am angry at you, Claire, and it's going to take a while for that to go away, but I love you. You've been my best friend for what – fourteen years? – and I can't imagine going through the next fourteen years without you. And I'm truly sorry for all of the ugly things I said to you, you know, about Harrison only dating you to hurt me. I know that's not true, I know him better than that. And I definitely know how great you are. He'd be lucky to have you. So what do you think?' Maddy asked, and I heard her draw in a deep, shaky breath. 'Do you think we could try being friends again?'

'Of course! You don't have to ask,' I said. My throat constricted, and my eyes began to water with tears. 'And I'm so sorry for everything. I promise you, I'll make all of this up to you somehow,' I sniffed.

'Well, I know a good start,' Maddy said. 'I think you should call Harrison . . . Jack . . . and tell him what you told me – that you love him and you want to get back together with him.'

'Do you mean it? We would have your blessing?' I asked, my voice catching in my throat.

'I'm not your father giving away your hand in marriage,' Maddy snorted, and then laughed, and I could tell then that everything would be all right between us. 'But yeah, I mean it. I want you to. And you and I, we're okay, or at least we will be.'

'But . . . but . . . the last time I talked to Jack, and told him that we couldn't see each other anymore, he told me that there were no second chances,' I cried. 'He told me that if we said good-bye, that was it.'

'All you can do is try. Be honest, tell him how you feel, and put the ball in his court,' Maddy said.

'I thought you just said that the key with men is to lead them on and then ignore them,' I said.

'God, no. That's only if you want to attract a crowd of them. Once you've found the right one, the last thing you want to do is play games. This is real life, Claire, not a Jackie Collins novel,' Maddy said sensibly.

And then Maddy and I had a nice long chat, just like old times, catching up on everything that had happened over the past month that we'd been estranged. She'd dumped her boss, and reported that so far the breakup wasn't affecting her job. She worried that it was only a matter of time before it would, so she'd sent out a few résumés to test the waters, but she was up in the air about whether she should stay in London or return home to the States. She'd also decided to try staying single for a while, which was a surprise coming from the woman who was never without a boyfriend.

'I really went off the deep end after Harrison and I broke up, and the way I reacted kind of freaked me out. It makes me think that maybe I should try spending some time on my own, and figure out what I really want,' Maddy said.

'And I'm just the opposite. I've been alone for too long, and I'm tired of it,' I said, knowing that this admission was a big step for me.

'Call him,' Maddy advised again. 'Get off the phone with me now and call him.'

'He might not even want to talk to me. I don't think I'm his favorite person right about now,' I pointed out.

'Call him anyway,' Maddy repeated. 'I'll talk to you later.'

'Wait, don't hang up!' I cried, but she was gone.

I knew that if I didn't act immediately on Maddy's directive, if I thought about it too much, I'd chicken out. So before I could talk myself out of it, I called Jack at his office. His secretary answered the phone and informed me that Mr Harrison was in the middle of a meeting and couldn't be interrupted. I considered telling her it was an emergency, but I could tell from the steely tone of her middle-aged voice (there was no mistaking this one for a miniskirt-wearing sex kitten; I was guessing she more likely fell in the support-hose-and-sensible-heel category) that she wouldn't buy it.

'It's very important that I talk to him, today if possible. Is there a good time for me to call back?' I asked politely, after giving her my name and telephone number.

'I'll give him the message that you called,' the gatekeeper said, neither promising that he'd return my phone call nor giving away when he'd be available.

I thanked her and hung up the phone, and tried to distract myself from waiting for the phone to ring by wrapping every cheap, plain Ikea plate I owned in two layers of bubble wrap. When he hadn't called back by two p.m. – which made it seven p.m. in London – I tried him at work again, only to hear a recorded message that the office was closed. I hoped that Jack just hadn't gotten my message – and tried not to think about the alternative, that he had and decided to blow me off – and called him at his town house. The phone rang four times before an answering machine clicked on, and Jack's slow, warm voice was telling me to leave a message after the tone.

'Hi, it's me . . . Claire, I mean. There's something I need to tell you, to, um, talk to you about, and it's important. *Really* important. Please call me as soon as you can, tonight if possible. Thanks,' I finished rather lamely before hanging up. I'd thought about adding on an 'I've missed you,' or even an 'I love you,' but then had a flash of fear that there might be a new girlfriend on the scene – who in my worst nightmares would end up being lithe and beautiful and intelligent, maybe the British über-model Sophie Dahl – and that they would be listening to the message while entwined around each other.

'Who was that, darling?' she'd ask with a posh British accent.

'No one important,' he'd reply, hitting the delete button to erase my message, before dragging her over to the couch – our couch – to make love to her in front of the fire. The thought made me sick to my stomach.

The hours dragged by, and the phone did keep ringing – each time causing my heart to jump into my throat – but it was only telemarketers, or once Max saying he was running late. I tried Jack again at five p.m., and then at six p.m., each time hanging up without leaving a message when the machine picked up, and feeling more and more disheartened with each passing hour. By the time Max showed up with our pizza and movie – a compromise, *Turner and Hooch* – it was after midnight in London, and I was starting to give up hope. During the time when Jack and I were phone dating, he was never out this late. The only explanation I could think of was that there *was* a new girlfriend on the scene . . . and he was staying over at her apartment.

'What's wrong?' Max asked, wiping the tears out of his eyes and pausing the movie at the point where Hooch was chewing up Tom Hanks' police car. 'We're watching the funniest movie of all time, and you're not laughing at all.'

'I'm just a little distracted,' I sighed.

'What's up?' Max asked.

I hesitated. Things had normalized between Max and me, mainly because we were both pretending that his drunken declaration of love and poorly received kiss had never happened. He knew that things hadn't worked out between Jack and me, and he'd been warm and understanding when I told him about it, but I didn't know how he'd receive the news that Maddy had given us the nod to get back together . . . or that I'd been calling Jack all afternoon without any success.

'I'm guessing from your silence, and from the fact that you've been staring more at the phone than you have at the movie, that it has something to do with a certain British guy. Am I right?' Max asked. 'And I know, I know, he's not really British, that was a joke.'

I nodded, biting my lip. 'Maddy called me today, and she and I patched things up. She also told me that . . . um, well, that I have her blessing to pursue things with Jack. I tried calling him earlier, but haven't heard back from him yet. I'm sorry, I was going to tell you earlier, but . . .' I said, my voice trailing off.

Max nodded. 'So what are you going to do?' he asked carefully.

'I'm going to tell Jack what Maddy said, and see if we still have a chance together,' I said. I paused for a moment, before adding, 'What do you think?'

Max smiled ruefully and pulled my ponytail. 'I hope that this guy is smart enough to call you back,' he said. 'Because if he doesn't, I will personally kick his limey ass for you.'

I laughed. 'Promise?'

'Promise.'

'Well, that's good to know,' I said. I hesitated for a minute, and then asked, 'Have you heard from Daphne?'

Max shook his head. 'I called her a few weeks ago, and apologized for being such an ass about everything – hell, I *groveled* – but she didn't want to hear it.'

'And that's it? You just called once?' I asked.

'God, no, that was just the first time. I called her so often, I'm surprised she didn't slap me with a restraining order. For a while she screened all of my calls, but then two weeks ago she finally picked up. Now we talk at least once a day, although she still says she just wants to be friends. She told me she's dating some guy she met through PETA,' Max said gloomily. 'I'm not even a vegetarian. I don't have a chance in hell of getting her back.'

I punched him lightly on the arm. 'Of course you do. Daphne adores you. She's just hurt right now, but she'll come around.'

'And what if she doesn't, what then? And you're not even going to be here to help me. I can't believe you're moving to Chicago,' he said.

'I know, it feels strange,' I agreed. 'But we'll talk lots.'

'It won't be the same,' Max said simply. And I knew he was right. It wouldn't.

Max left at eleven, and I curled up on the couch, phone in hand, hoping that Jack had just gotten in too late the night before and was planning to call me before he left for work in the morning. I closed my eyes for just a minute, and when I next opened them the sun was streaming through the windows and filling my tiny apartment with light. I looked over at my wall clock and saw it was nine a.m. I stretched and tried to sit up, although sleeping in a semireclined position all night had wrenched my neck. I rubbed at it, and tried to remember how I'd come to be spending the night on my couch instead of in my nice, comfy bed.

Then I remembered. *Jack*. I grabbed for my answering machine, hoping that I'd somehow slept through his return call and that he'd left a message for me. But a mocking red zero just stared back at me. There were no messages.

I flipped on the coffeepot, and while it brewed, I stood under a hot shower, letting the water run against my sore neck while I kneaded it, trying to get the muscle spasms to unclench. By the time I was rinsing conditioner out of my hair, I was finally starting to feel human. Once out of the shower, I wrapped myself in my enormous, carnation-pink terry cloth robe, brushed the snarls out of my wet hair, and returned to the kitchenette for the freshly brewed coffee. I retrieved a frozen bagel from the freezer, toasted it, and ate my breakfast while perched on my kitchen counter, the way I used to when I was a teenager.

What was I going to do now? Should I assume from his silence that Jack was not interested? I'd left him two messages, after all, and it was unlikely that matters would have conspired so that he didn't get either one. Even if his secretary forgot to tell him I called – which was unlikely, the woman sounded like a paragon of brutal efficiency – it was doubtful that some sort of a freak electric storm in London would have caused his answering machine to short out and erase the message I left there. But I couldn't give up now. It went along with my new policy of lowering my defenses; yes, the result might be that I ended up getting kicked in the teeth, but that was a risk I was going to have to take.

I hopped down from my kitchen counter and searched through the pile of throw cushions on my couch until I located the phone. I carefully dialed Jack's office number, and hoped that he would pick up his own extension, as he had in the past.

'Jack Harrison's office.'

Crap. It was the secretary again, sounding like her girdle was cinched about an inch too tight.

'Hi, this is Claire Spencer calling for Mr Harrison,' I said, feeling ridiculous for being so formal.

'I'm afraid Mr Harrison is traveling on business and will be out of the office for several days. Would you care to leave a message?' the secretary asked.

At hearing this, my sagging spirits perked back up. Jack was out of town – so that was why he hadn't answered his phone last night! And that was why he hadn't returned my messages! I knew that he wouldn't just blow me off that way, it was so unlike him.

Feeling like I still had a chance, I forged ahead. 'I don't know if you remember me, but I called yesterday,' I began.

'Yes, I gave Mr Harrison your telephone message,' she said.

'Oh . . . you did. Because he didn't call me back,' I said, deflating again. I was also starting to feel like a complete fool. The secretary's disapproving tone was making me feel like a stalker.

'I'm certain he was otherwise engaged. He left London this morning,' the secretary said. I could tell that she was a nanosecond away from hanging up on me, so I jumped in quickly, eager to pump her for as much information as possible.

'He left this morning? So he was in London all day yesterday? Are you sure?' I asked.

'Quite certain. I personally arranged for the car service. But I will tell him that you called again. Good-bye,' the secretary said quickly, and hung up before I could ask another question.

So that was it. Jack had gotten my messages, and he hadn't called me back. The silence wasn't hard to read . . . he'd meant it when he said that there were no second chances. Knowing him as I did, I was surprised that he wouldn't even hear me out, but then again, he'd just dealt with an ex-girlfriend going a little wacko on him, so maybe he had a new policy of good-bye really meaning good-bye.

And the really crappy thing about it was that there was nothing I could do. If he wouldn't pick up the phone when I called – last night, if he wasn't out with Sophie Dahl, he must have been screening my calls, and at this point I didn't know which scenario was worse – then I couldn't tell him that Maddy had stepped aside, and he and I were free to see each other, or that being estranged from him was so painful that sometimes I'd found it hard to breathe, or that I was willing to let down my defenses, ready to lower the bridge over the alligator-infested moat and invite him into my fortress. I was in New York, he was in London, so it was hardly as though I could stand outside his house, tossing pebbles at his window and calling for him until he either agreed to speak to me or called the police. I managed a wry smile at the image of my chasing Jack down, banging on his windows and screaming his name, like Dustin Hoffman breaking up the wedding at the end of *The Graduate*, as if that would ever happen. It was all so ridiculous.

Or was it? A random idea blew across my mind, like a cloud puffing lazily over a summer sky, the kind of thought that should have drifted away never to be considered again, had I not reached out and grabbed onto it out of sheer desperation. It was a completely implausible scheme . . . and yet, it might be the only chance I had to win back the man I loved. If I couldn't get Jack to talk to me over the phone, then I needed to confront him face-to-face, to knock on his door or even throw rocks at his window until he agreed to talk to me. I needed to go to London.

I looked around my apartment, taking in the two dozen cardboard boxes already packed full of my personal belongings. In five days, the movers were coming to put my furniture in storage, the shippers were picking up my boxes, and I had a one-way plane ticket to Chicago to start my new life. How on earth was I going to fit in an overseas trip in the middle of all of that? What if I didn't get back in time? Jack's secretary had said that he was out of town on business – what if he was away longer than a few days? What if I got all the way out there, and I ended up having to wait for a week or even longer before I even got to see him? What if I did manage to corner him, and he still refused to talk to me? Or what if I waited outside his town house, and when he finally returned he had some giggling, twig-thin blonde on his arm? It was a crazy idea to even consider doing such a thing, to set myself up for hurt and ridicule while at the same time risking all of the plans I'd made for my future in Chicago . . . wasn't it? Of course it was.

A half an hour later I was booked on a British Airlines flight to London, leaving in a scant few hours – and at a fare so large it was doubtful I'd ever be able to afford to eat again. I was so frantic, I couldn't figure out what to bring with me, so I just threw every halfway decent item of clothing I owned, clean and dirty, into a suitcase, not stopping to question whether I would really need my red tankini or black linen sundress for a January trip to London. Max – who answered my frantic phone call and promised to meet the movers and shippers for me if I wasn't back in time to do it myself – appeared in the middle of this packing mania, and watched me for a few minutes with a mix of concern and admiration while I tore open box after box, emptying out the contents onto the floor while I searched for the various items I needed for this last-minute trip.

'Do you think I'm crazy?' I asked him suddenly, stopping my wild search for my missing passport.

Max shook his head, and gave me a big hug, like the kind he used to give me before things became awkward between us. 'I think you're brave,' he whispered in my ear. Then he looked past me, into the box I'd been ransacking. 'There's your passport, right there on top of that pile of Pottery Barn catalogues. Wait . . . you packed your old Pottery Barn catalogues? Claire, this one is from four years ago.'

'Oh, my passport!' I crowed. 'Thank you, thank you, thank you! Now, where the hell did I put my toiletry bag?'

'I'm getting out of here before I'm buried in the rubble. Have a good trip, and call me to let me know what happens, okay? It's the least I deserve, since I know I'm going to get stuck repacking this mess,' Max said, before disappearing and leaving me alone.

When I'd finally squashed in everything I could possibly need for any situation that could arise, from a long hospitalization to a sudden detour to the Bahamas, I zipped my suitcase shut and heaved it up. If I could get out of my apartment and catch a taxi in the next five minutes, then I should be able to make my flight. I didn't want to think what would happen if I missed it; I didn't have any room on my Visa card to purchase another ticket.

I pulled the suitcase down the four flights of stairs out of my building, the weight of the upright wheeled bag threatening to crush me with every step, and then, out of breath and completely frantic with anxiety, I raced out of my building, spotting a cab with its light on pulling away from the curb.

'Wait! Taxi!' I screamed, running down the stone steps that led up to my building, dragging my suitcase behind me, trying to flag down the cab before it drove away. But at that moment, in what could only be described as a cosmic turn of fate – or my comeuppance for having bought a cheap-ass suitcase at a discount store for twenty dollars – the main zipper on the bag broke, causing the overstuffed bag to split open. My personal belongings exploded onto the dirty, icy sidewalk like candy spilling out of a piñata.

'No!' I wailed, looking first at the damaged suitcase and then at the taxi that was speeding off down the street.

I leaned over the hemorrhaging bag, futilely picking at the zipper to see if it could be repaired with a few safety pins or some duct tape. My heart sank when I saw that it could not. This suitcase would not be flying to London today, and neither would I. It was over. I'd lost. There was simply no way I could track down another, better suitcase, repack, and make it to the airport in time to make my flight. And the ridiculously expensive plane ticket I'd purchased? It was, of course, of the nonrefundable, nonchangeable, don't-miss-your-flight-or-you're-fucked variety.

It can't end this way, I thought miserably. In the movies, the plucky heroine would make the flight and get the guy just by cutely wrinkling her nose at him. She would not end up defeated and alone, and with every last pair of underwear she owned spread around on a grungy New York sidewalk. Shivering miserably, I knelt in front of my bag, shoving clothes back into it and trying to figure out how the hell I was going to carry this thing back up to my apartment. There was no way I could leave it out here on the sidewalk unattended while I went upstairs to fetch a garbage bag to put everything in; if I did, by the time I came back down, the neighborhood's assortment of vagrants and drifters would have helped themselves to the contents, and would each be decked out in my beach sarong or silk Victoria's Secret underwear.

What in the hell am I going to do now? I wondered desolately, tears of frustration pricking at my eyes. But then I steeled myself, and shook my head.

No, I thought. This is *not* how it's going to end. I'll just have to leave my stupid suitcase here and go without it. So what if it means losing all of my clothes? It's just stuff, easily replaceable.

I began to rummage through my things, trying to pull out enough clean underwear for my trip, along with my favorite flannel pajamas and two prized TSE cashmere sweaters I couldn't bear to lose, to stuff into my carry-on bag.

But then, before I had the chance to stand back up, I sensed that someone had appeared behind me. A familiar and amused voice said, 'I'll help you with your bag if you promise not to shock me again with your stun gun.'

24

I twisted around and gaped up, wondering if I'd actually had some kind of an emotional breakdown caused by the extreme distress I'd been under since Christmas – the suitcase explosion being the proverbial last straw – and as a result was now delusional. Because I could swear that standing in front of me was Jack, looking handsome, if a little rumpled and travel-worn, in faded Levi's and a navy blue pea coat. It looked like Jack, and sounded like him, and he was so close to me that if I reached out, I thought I might even be able to touch one denim-covered knee. But it couldn't possibly *be* Jack . . . could it? My hallucination suddenly knelt down beside me, inspecting my damaged suitcase.

'I think it might be a total loss,' he said, pulling at the zipper. 'Do you have another suitcase you can use?'

'No, um, this is my only one,' I replied, still staring at him.

'Well, we'll just have to go track down another one for you. Where are you off to this time?' he asked.

My hallucination was still examining my bag and not looking directly at me. It gave me a chance to drink him in totally, from his disheveled hair to his crooked nose to his wonderful broad shoulders and long, rangy legs. I inhaled, and my senses were filled with the clean, soapy aroma that was unmistakably Jack, and suddenly I knew that it was really him. While I was willing to believe that my eyes could play tricks on me, I was sure that my olfactory senses weren't so easily fooled.

'London. I was coming . . . going . . . to find you,' I stuttered. 'What are you doing here?'

This time Jack did look at me, and as I gazed into his green-flecked eyes, I immediately knew that everything would be okay. It was the same expression I'd woken up to on Christmas morning, the same naked honesty I'd seen when he told me he loved me. These were not the eyes of a man who had fallen into the waiting arms of Sophie Dahl, or Jenny the travel agent.

'I came to find you,' he said simply. He rested a tentative hand on my shoulder, and I grinned at him. But before I could throw myself into his arms, Jack stood up and then reached down and pulled me to my feet. 'Rather than having this conversation sitting on the sidewalk, why don't we go up to your apartment.'

'What are we going to do about the suitcase?' I asked, looking at it doubtfully. 'Do you want to stay here for a minute, while I run upstairs and get a bag or something to dump the clothes in?'

'No, I'll just lift it as is,' Jack said, and after we stuffed everything back into the suitcase, he heaved the bag up, grunting at the effort. 'What's in here?' he gasped, staggering up the front stairs of my building.

'Oh, just about everything I own,' I said, laughing, and held the door open for him.

We went upstairs, moving very slowly, and by the time we got to my apartment, Jack looked ready to pass out. He dropped the suitcase just inside my door, kicked it rather maliciously, and then collapsed on the couch, his face red and his breath so short it sounded like he'd just run a marathon. I hurried to get him a glass of water before joining him on the couch.

'I think I liked it better when you greeted me by shocking me with your stun gun,' Jack said. He glanced around my apartment, taking in the boxes. Some of them were still neatly packed and taped up; the others, the ones I had ransacked, were torn open, some lying on their sides, others upside down, all of the contents scattered across the floor. 'Were you robbed?'

'No, no. I'm in the process of moving,' I said, smiling.

I'd been unable to wipe the grin off of my face, even as I watched Jack struggle up the stairs with my bag, refusing my offers to help. Still, I felt a little shy around him, and since he hadn't made a move to kiss me or pull me back into his arms, I hung back and waited for his cue.

'I got the job at *Retreat*, in Chicago,' I explained. 'But never mind about that, tell me, why are you here?'

'Chicago,' Jack repeated, and he frowned.

'What?'

'You're moving in the wrong direction,' he said.

I wriggled with frustration. My move to Chicago was the last thing I wanted to talk about.

'Come on, tell me what you're doing here. I mean, this is either an incredible coincidence, your showing up here just as I was going to look for you, or . . .' I said, my voice trailing off in a question mark.

'Okay, let me just catch my breath, and I'll tell you everything. And then I want you to tell me about this move,' he said, shrugging out of his coat and then reaching for his glass of water. After he took a few gulps, and his color faded back to its normal rosy hue, he began to talk.

'Ever since we last spoke, I've been trying to get Maddy to see me. I knew that you meant what you said, and that as long as she forbade our seeing each other, you wouldn't. You're so stubborn, I knew there was no chance you'd bend, so I had to get her to change her mind,' Jack explained.

'But I thought . . . I mean, when we talked, you said . . .

you said that you weren't going to chase after me anymore,' I said hesitatingly, almost worried that if he was suddenly reminded of this oath, he would slap his hand against his forehead, say 'Now I remember,' and walk back out of my life.

'I know, but I was angry and stupid. I thought that maybe you were playing games with me, although Maddy assured me that when it comes to relationships, you really are that closed off and defensive,' he said, smiling to soften his words and let me know that he was joking. Sort of.

'So you did talk to Maddy,' I said, wondering why in the hell she hadn't mentioned that to me on the phone yesterday.

'Yup. She finally agreed to have dinner with me, just a few days ago. I was a little nervous about seeing her, after how wiggy she went – did you know that she'd hired a private detective to follow me?'

I hesitated, but figured there'd been quite enough half-truths flying around, and so nodded. 'She'd talked about it, but I really didn't think she'd go through with it,' I explained.

Jack shook his head incredulously. 'Hell hath no fury,' he muttered, and took another gulp of water. 'And when it came down to it, she was the one who cheated on me, not the other way around. But that doesn't matter, and it's not why I wanted to talk to her. I had to convince her to forgive you, to make her see how much we cared about each other, and how wrong it was for her to keep us apart.'

I stared at him. 'You told her all of that? But . . . I'm surprised she'd even listen to it, after how angry she was.'

Jack shrugged. 'I can be very charming and persuasive when need be,' he said, smiling. 'And I let her call me every nasty thing she could think of first, which helped her to blow off some steam.'

'And so what happened?'

'Once she ran out of insults, she finally quieted down and started listening to what I had to say. And she began to slowly come around to acknowledging that our relationship wasn't quite as she had remembered it. I don't think we were ever that happy together, or even capable of making the other one happy. It's probably why she started seeing her boss,' he said.

'Wow. So you guys are okay, then?' I asked.

'Well, after everything that's happened, I doubt that we'll do the Jerry and Elaine thing and stay best buds, but I think that we basically parted as friends. Especially since she said that she wanted to patch things up with you . . . and that she wouldn't stand in our way if we still wanted to see each other. But I'm guessing you already know that part,' Jack said.

I nodded. 'She called me yesterday and told me the same thing. Not about having dinner with you – she left that part out – but the rest of it,' I said.

'I wanted to surprise you by coming out here, so I asked her not to mention our talk,' Jack said, smiling mischievously. 'But I guess it wasn't the best plan, since if your suitcase hadn't burst open, I might have completely missed you. It must have been fate.'

'Hmmm. Fate. Maybe so,' I said.

And then he pulled me toward him and kissed me hard on the mouth. Nothing had changed – it had the same toe-curling, dipped-in-chocolate sensation as before. Wanting to lose myself in him, I kissed him back eagerly, more than ready to push aside all of the concerns and anxieties that had been percolating in my mind over the past month.

'Wait,' Jack said, leaning back and breaking off our kiss. 'If you were coming to London, then that means you were going to chase after me for a change.'

'Yup. I guess I was. That's progress, right?'

'The very best kind,' Jack murmured, and he leaned in

for another kiss, and this time, nothing interrupted our reunion.

A little while later, when we were comfortably snuggled up together in my bed – one of the few places in my apartment that wasn't covered with cardboard boxes – and I was lying perpendicular to Jack, my head resting on his bare stomach, while he lazily stroked my hair, I asked, 'So this means we're back together, right?'

'After everything I've been through in the past month? It better,' he said sleepily.

'I just wanted to make sure,' I said happily. 'Besides, the last month hasn't been all that easy for me either, you know.'

'Good,' he said.

'Good?'

'Well, I don't want to be the only one who was pining away,' Jack said, tousling my hair.

'Mmmm, pining, that's a nice word. Hey, know what?' I murmured, starting to feel my eyes grow heavy as his head massage lulled me to sleep.

'What?'

'I haven't taken off my necklace since you gave it to me, not once,' I said.

'Really?'

'Yup. How's that for devotion?' I mumbled. 'Love you.'

I didn't hear what he said in response, because a moment later I'd drifted off to sleep. Despite the fact that I was stark naked, with every non-modelish flaw hanging out there for Jack to see, and despite that I'd bared myself with the most intimate of declarations, I was completely at ease, all of my defenses discarded to one side. Now *that* was progress. Maybe there was hope for me after all.

'I think you're going to have to get over your obsession with ice,' Jack said, laughing at me as I emptied the ice cube tray into my glass before filling it with water.

'No way. You can take the girl out of the U.S., but you can't deprive her of her creature comforts,' I replied, happily rattling the ice cubes around in my glass.

'Getting used to room-temperature beverages is only the beginning. Now that you're an official resident of London, you're going to have to get used to all sorts of things. For instance, don't refer to your trousers as "pants," because here that means "underwear." And you don't ask where the bathroom is, ask for the loo,' Jack said.

'Trousers and loos. Gotcha,' I said. 'But I'm still not giving up my ice.'

The doorbell rang. 'I'll get it,' I said, hopping off of the sleek stainless steel stool that nestled up against the black-granite-counter-topped island in Jack's – or should I say *our* – kitchen. Granted, it had only been a few days since I'd moved to London from Chicago and begun cohabitating with Jack, but I still felt like I was on one of my frequent long-weekend visits. It was going to be hard to get used to the idea of living full-time with my boyfriend, although the fact that he had such a fabulous town house and idyllic, newly redecorated country house certainly made it a lot easier. I'd spent the last year subletting what turned out to be a pit of an apartment from Kit's anthropologist professor friend, who had an unhealthy obsession with unframed posters, sisal carpeting, and papa-san chairs acquired from Pier One. She shared the same crunchy-granola taste that Robert, my old editor from *Sassy Seniors!*, loved, and that was about as far away from my beloved Pottery Barn yuppie porn as you could get. Jack's house – I mean, *our* house – was a salve for my wounded aesthetic.

'Oh my God, I can't believe you're actually here,' Maddy shrieked as she blew into the front hall. She hugged me and then thrust forward her left hand to show off the enormous sparkly bauble residing on her ring finger.

'Look, look, look,' she said, waving her hand in front of me.

'So you're still going to go through with it?' I asked jokingly.

She snorted. 'You'd better believe it. You should see my dress. It's Vera Wang,' she bragged shamelessly.

Maddy had not only bounced back after her breakup with Jack, but she'd gone through a period of intense self-examination, even going to therapy for a while. Both her mother and I had encouraged her to see someone after she lost her dad, but she'd resisted, and as a result, she had a lot of repressed baggage to work through. After all of this introspection, one of her conclusions was that by always needing to have a boyfriend, even if it meant being in a shallow relationship or with someone who, like Jack, was inherently unsuited to her, she'd lost a lot of opportunities for personal growth. To make up for it, she decided to call a moratorium on all dating, and swore up and down that she wasn't going to have another boyfriend until she'd spent some time finding herself. Two weeks later, she met Colin Wentworth, the acerbic and brilliant British conservative columnist. They fell madly in love with each other, and were engaged a few months later. Normally, I'd have been alarmed at the rapid pace of events, but after seeing Maddy and Colin together, and how much they adored each other, I began to think that maybe she'd actually gotten it right for once.

'Besides,' Maddy continued, her voice dropping to a whisper, 'if we don't get married soon, the dress will have to be let out to make room for the bump.'

She rubbed her stomach in a self-satisfied way, and I stared at her for a minute while what she said processed. The bump . . . her stomach . . .

'Ohmigod, you're pregnant!' I screeched, and hugged her again.

'Shh, shh,' Maddy said. 'It's supposed to still be a secret.'

'It won't be for long. Pretty soon you'll be as big and round as a pumpkin,' I said, laughing. 'But how do you feel about it? I thought that you didn't want to do the minivan, suburban-mom thing.'

'A little freaked out at first. But it all feels . . . right. And Colin is thrilled, of course. Besides, there's a whole industry of chic, high-end baby products out there catering to hip, urban moms. I've been having a ball shopping for everything, and I've barely scratched the surface,' she said gleefully.

'Am I supposed to pretend that I haven't overheard everything you two have been saying, or can I offer the new mommy congratulations?' Jack asked, appearing in the hallway behind us. Maddy laughed, and he hugged her and kissed her cheek, which I was glad to see. For a long time, the two of them had been uncomfortable when they were together, and normally when I was in London on one of my frequent trips, I'd have to spend time with each of them separately. But in the past few months, and especially since Maddy had met Colin, Maddy and Jack had begun to ease up around each other. We'd even double-dated a few times.

'This calls for champagne,' Jack said, leading the way back to the kitchen.

'Or milk for one of us,' I reminded him.

'Yes, but please put it in a wineglass, so I can at least pretend,' Maddy requested.

Once we were settled in the kitchen, and had toasted the new mother and bride, Maddy filled us in on the latest wedding plans. The afternoon ceremony was only a few weeks away, and was going to be followed by a glam reception at the Ritz. I was to be her sole attendant, and she promised me that I'd love the dress.

'I thought about dressing you in pink ruffles, because when else am I going to have the opportunity to torture you with bridesmaid fashion, but I couldn't bring myself to do it. The pictures would have looked too awful,' she said, grinning.

'So what does it look like?' I asked.

'It's a simple navy blue sheath that will just glide right over your curves. Oh, and it has a plunging neckline. It's going to look *amazing* on you,' Maddy promised.

'Mmmm, plunging neckline. I like the sound of that,' Jack said.

'All right, enough wedding talk. Tell me, how're you settling in? What did *Retreat* say about you going freelance?' Maddy asked.

'They weren't thrilled, especially since I'd only been there for a year,' I admitted. 'But they did say they would throw some work my way. And Jack says he has some contacts here that he can put me in touch with. You play squash with someone at *Hello*, right?' I asked, and Jack nodded.

'And I know a few people, too . . . I know one of the editors at *Living, Etc.* and I think also someone at British *InStyle*,' Maddy said. 'I'll check on Monday, and see if I can set up some lunches for you, 'kay?'

'Great,' I said happily.

Strangely enough, I hadn't yet gotten flippy about my decision to go freelance, and the lack of security that it meant. Considering that I'd packed up my entire life and moved to a foreign country in order to be with the man that I adored, when only eighteen months ago the very idea that I would ever fall in love seemed as remote as my winning the New York lottery, the change in my career path seemed less dramatic. Sure, I loved my job at *Retreat* – but trading it in for this new life with Jack hadn't been a hard decision to make. I felt like I was on a wild ride, and for once in my life, instead of bracing myself for the impact of the inevitable crash, I was just enjoying it. After all, life changed, people changed. Maddy was a prime example. I don't think even she could have expected that she was so close to meeting and marrying the love of her life, and now impending mommyhood to boot.

Later, after Maddy had left to tackle some last-minute wedding preparations, Jack and I lounged around, listening to a Diana Krall CD and trying to decide what we wanted to do about dinner and whether we felt like actually getting up and going out.

Jack nudged me, and asked, 'So what do you think about Maddy's news?'

'The pregnancy, you mean? I was surprised that it happened so soon, but not shocked that she's so happy. I always figured she'd be a great mom. Besides, I doubt she'll leave her party days behind her. She'll probably just find a group of glamorous moms and get herself on the A-list for all of the happening kiddy parties,' I said, and snuggled up against him. My hunger hadn't become intense enough to motivate me into getting up, especially when Jack's broad chest made such a comfy resting place.

'I'm just glad that the two of you are okay, and that there weren't any lasting hurt feelings,' Jack said. He wrapped his arms around me and rested his chin on the top of my head.

'Well, it took a while, but everything seems back to normal now. And everything got a lot better when she met Colin,' I said.

'Yeah, I noticed. Short engagement, though,' Jack said.

'True, but that's Maddy for you. She's a free spirit. And honestly, I know that such a brief courtship would spell problems for most people, but I think those two are going to make it. They're just so perfect together. I've never seen her so happy,' I said, tilting my head back so I could look up at him.

'First Max, now Maddy. All of your friends are getting married,' Jack commented.

'Mmmm,' I agreed. Max had finally won Daphne back, as I knew he would, and they were engaged about five minutes later. Jack and I had attended their wedding in Manhattan in June.

Jack just smiled enigmatically, and got the same strange reflective expression that used to freak me out. Now I just reached over and touched his cheek, and asked, 'What are you thinking about?' I'd come a long way.

'Nothing. So what did you decide you wanted to do about dinner?' Jack replied, and although I knew that there was something brewing behind those crinkly, half-moon eyes, I also knew that it was pointless to push it. When he got his mind set, Jack was intractable, and he wouldn't tell me whatever it was until he was ready.

The morning of Maddy's wedding, London was hit by a storm. Icy torrential rains and heavy winds threatened to soak the guests as they poured into the glamorous Ritz, the women holding on to their hats and the men brushing rain off their jackets. Despite the weather, the bride remained ebullient throughout the ceremony and practically shimmered at the reception. I'd worried that her recent bouts of morning sickness would keep her from fully enjoying her wedding, but to the contrary, I'd never seen Maddy shine brighter as she flitted around, showing off her Vera Wang to its best advantage and kissing everyone in sight.

After I'd had my picture taken so many times that I was half-blind from the flash, I hunted for Jack. He was in the main ballroom, chatting with one of Colin's four brothers, all of whom looked identical to one another, and to Colin.

'Which one was that?' I whispered as Jack grabbed my hand and led me out to the dance floor. The band was playing a jazzy rendition of 'It Had to Be You.'

'Michael, I think. Is Michael the one who's in finance? Because that's what he said he did for a living,' Jack said.

'I don't know, I can't keep them straight. Remind me to ask Maddy if Colin was a quintuplet,' I said, and then laughed as Jack swirled me around and dipped me.

'Your dress, by the way, is as incredible as promised,' Jack said, leering at my breasts.

'There will be none of that at the reception,' I mock-chided him, but was pleased that he'd noticed. My cocktail dress was as gorgeous and un-bridesmaid-like as possible. It was a sleeveless midnight-blue satin knee-length sheath, with a plunging neckline highlighted with sequins.

Jack pulled me closer so that we were dancing with my head resting on his shoulder. I may have been wrong about a lot of my dating rules, but this just proved I was right about the not-dating-shorter-men thing. After all, no woman wants to dance with her partner's head nestled in her cleavage, her head propped up on top of his.

It was only after Maddy and Colin were seen off amidst a swirl of tossed confetti and well-wishing that the reception began to wind down. Just before they left, Maddy had been in tears, not because she was regretting her new marriage, but because she wasn't ready to take off her wedding gown.

I'd gone with her up to her suite to help her change, but once there, she refused to let me unbutton the fifty satin-covered buttons that cascaded down her back.

'Then don't change, just keep it on,' I said.

'We're flying to Greece! I can't wear it on the plane,' Maddy sniffed.

'Why not? Sure, maybe it would be difficult to use the bathroom on board, but if you can hold it in, it would be totally worth it. Aren't you the one who's always saying you have to suffer to be beautiful?' I teased her, and finally talked her into trading in the sumptuous white dress for a to-die-for deep pink Prada shift with a matching jacket that she'd selected as her going-away outfit.

I didn't find Jack again until after the crowd sending the newlyweds off had cleared out. As I walked toward him, I was carrying the three calla lilies tied together with a simple cream bow that Maddy had carried in her ceremony.

'You caught the bouquet?' Jack asked.

'No, Maddy said that she wasn't going to put the single women through the humiliation of fighting over it, so she just handed it to me,' I said, and tipped my head back so that Jack could kiss me on the lips.

'Maybe she's trying to tell you something,' Jack said, and I just shrugged. I may have been able to, for the most part, set aside my dating rules, but good sense suggested that discussing bouquet tosses and future engagements was not the best topic to bring up with my new live-in boyfriend.

He called for our car, and it was only once we settled in, and the car began to navigate the London traffic, that I realized we weren't going home.

'Where are we going? This isn't the way to your – I mean our – place,' I said.

'Another surprise,' Jack said.

'I thought we'd talked about this surprise thing you're so fond of,' I grumbled.

'Have I led you astray yet? Don't you think it's time you started to trust me?' Jack asked, squeezing my hand.

'I do trust you. I just —' I began.

Jack interrupted me before I could finish. 'I know, I know, you hate surprises.'

The driver took us through Westminster and then pulled over to one side of Westminster Bridge. I was struck by how ethereal London's government district looked at nighttime. Parliament and Big Ben glittered against the night sky, casting ghostly images onto the Thames River. And other than passing traffic, the entire area looked deserted, which just added to its supernatural charm. It was hard to believe that I actually lived here, I thought, as goose pimples spread over the backs of my arms.

'Why are we stopping?' I asked.

'Come on, I'll show you,' Jack said, getting out of the car and then holding out his hand for me.

Shaking my head with confusion, I tried to figure out where he was leading me, and it wasn't until we'd descended a familiar flight of stairs that I realized we were walking toward the same terrifyingly enormous Ferris wheel Jack had made me ride on our first date, all those many months ago.

'The Eye! Is this the surprise?' I asked.

'It's part of it,' Jack said.

'But we already did this one, don't you remember? Hey, just how many girls have you brought up here, anyway?' I asked, suddenly suspicious.

'Only the ones that I later coax into moving overseas and into my house with me,' Jack replied.

'You didn't have to coax me.'

'I asked ten times before you said yes,' Jack said.

'Yes, but I said I'd think about it the first time you asked,' I said. 'But really, we've already done this. If you want to keep springing these surprises on me, don't you think you should come up with new ones? Repeating the same ones over and over sort of takes the thrill out of it.'

'The last time we rode the Eye, we did it during the day. It's a whole different sight at night,' Jack said.

'You don't really plan on going up in this thing, do you? How do you even know if it's open?'

'I have a feeling we're just in time for the last ride of the night,' Jack said.

Jack kept a firm hand on my back as we approached the Ferris wheel, correctly presuming that I was doing my best to find a way out of this. I'd already survived the ride once, so why tempt fate with a second trip? With some relief I noticed that although the Eye was lit up and rotating, there were no passengers, and as we got closer, the only person in sight was a uniformed guard.

'It's closed,' I said triumphantly.

Jack ignored me, and instead addressed the guard, holding out his hand to the man in greeting. 'Barney?'

'Mr Harrison? Right this way, sir,' said the guard, walking up the incline toward the loading dock. Jack placed a hand on my back and gestured for me to follow Barney.

'They know you by name? Just how often do you come here?' I whispered.

Jack just smiled, and with a sigh of frustration I traced Barney's steps.

'Mind your step, miss,' Barney said, and stood at the open door of one of the pods as we entered it.

The wheel turned slowly, and our pod began to ascend. Just like the first time we rode the giant Eye, Jack came up behind me and gathered me in his arms, leaning me back against him. This time, though, he began to nuzzle my neck and ran his hands down my bare arms, as the pod continued its upward climb.

'You're not planning on having sex up here, are you? Because it's absolutely out of the question. This thing still scares me to death, as you well know. And see that camera up there?' I said, nodding toward a prominent camera mounted at the top right-hand corner of the pod. 'The security guards will be able to see everything we do.'

Jack laughed. 'Don't worry, I didn't bring you up here in order to have my way with you. Although now that you mention it, it is a tempting thought . . .'

'So, why did you bring me up here?' I asked. The pod was nearly at the top of the giant circle, and the entire city of London was laid out before us, lit up as far as the eye could see. It was truly a spectacular sight; I could even see Tower Bridge twinkling in the distance.

Jack spun me around to face him, and as he looked down at me, there was an unmistakable mix of tenderness and nervousness in his face. 'I love you,' he said, and just as with every time he had uttered those words to me before, my breath caught in my chest.

'I love you, too,' I said, touching first his cheek and then the tip of his crooked nose. I particularly loved his nose. Jack was a handsome man, and I was completely attracted to the whole rangy, muscular package, but this imperfection was especially endearing.

Suddenly he smiled roguishly and dropped to one knee. I was so stunned, all I could do was stare at him, while I desperately tried to prevent myself from making a smart-ass comment that would ruin it . . . because suddenly I knew what was going on. It was the white-knight moment I didn't think I'd ever experience, and certainly not in such a romantic, over-the-top way. Jack fished in his inside jacket pocket for a minute and then pulled out what had to be the most gorgeous ring I'd ever seen. It was a single, perfect, sparkling square diamond, flanked on either side by a round sapphire. Jack grabbed my left hand and slipped the ring onto my finger. It felt cool and heavy and absolutely fabulous, and when I looked down at it, it winked up at me, assuring me that it was just as beautiful as it had looked in his hand.

'Claire Spencer, will you do me the great honor of marrying me?' Jack asked. And although he was smiling, I could tell that he was afraid of what I might say.

I wanted to tell him not to worry, and that as scary as it was handing my heart over to him, I knew for once that I'd given it to someone who would protect it with his life. And I wanted to tell him that the time I'd spent with him had turned me into a different person, someone who resembled the old Claire, but was a bit less cynical and a lot more open to the possibility that I didn't have all the answers to everything after all. At the very least, I wanted to tell him that he needn't be frightened of what I'd say, because I'd rather toss myself off this terrifyingly large wheel than do anything that would hurt him. But I was so nervous, and so overcome with emotion, that I couldn't think of how to say these things, or any of the other thoughts rattling around inside of my head, eager to get out if only they had a more eloquent person to say them.

So instead I simply took his hand, and said:

'I'd love to.'